Astride a Pink Horse

ASTRIDE A
PINK HORSE

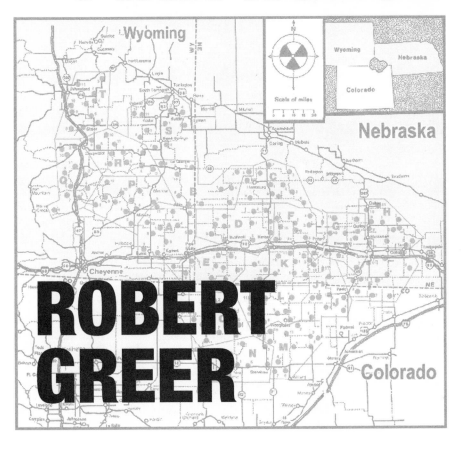

ROBERT
GREER

North Atlantic Books
Berkeley, California

Published by
North Atlantic Books
P.O. Box 12327
Berkeley, California 94712

Back cover © istockphoto.com/Royer
Cover and book design by Brad Greene

Cover art adapted from *Nuclear Heartland: A Guide to the One Thousand Missile Silos of the United States,* edited by Samuel H. Day and published by Progressive Foundation, 1988.

Printed in the United States of America

Astride a Pink Horse is sponsored by the Society for the Study of Native Arts and Sciences, a nonprofit educational corporation whose goals are to develop an educational and cross-cultural perspective linking various scientific, social, and artistic fields; to nurture a holistic view of arts, sciences, humanities, and healing; and to publish and distribute literature on the relationship of mind, body, and nature.

North Atlantic Books' publications are available through most bookstores. For further information, visit our website at www.northatlanticbooks.com or call 800-733-3000.

Library of Congress Cataloging-in-Publication Data

Greer, Robert O.
  Astride a pink horse / Robert Greer.
      p. cm.
  Summary: "This gripping thriller about deceit, revenge, and broken government promises starts with a veteran's murder and takes us back to the horrors of World War II and the dawn of the atomic age"—Provided by publisher.
  ISBN 978-1-58394-369-4
  1. World War, 1939-1945—United States—Fiction. I. Title.
  PS3557.R3997A93 2012
  813'.54—dc23

                                                                    2011037893

1 2 3 4 5 6 7 8 9 SHERIDAN 17 16 15 14 13 12

For My Angel,
PHYLLIS

Acknowledgments

I would like to offer my appreciation to Francis Newman for his valuable insights into radiation physics and to Jane and Norb Olind for providing me with important information about the Laramie River Station power plant near Wheatland, Wyoming.

To my longtime editor, Emily Boyd, and to Kathleen Deckler, as always, thanks for your support, patience, and willingness to help.

To Kathleen Woodley, my secretary for more than a quarter century, I can only say, "What would I do without you?"

Finally, to Connie Oehring and Adrienne Armstrong, I offer my deepest thanks for bringing their keen editorial skills to the manuscript.

Author's Note

The characters, events, and places that are depicted in *Astride a Pink Horse* are spawned from the author's imagination. Certain Denver and Western locales are used fictitiously, and any resemblance between the novel's fictional inhabitants and actual persons living or dead is purely coincidental.

"I Am Death—The Destroyer of Worlds"
Bhagavad Gita

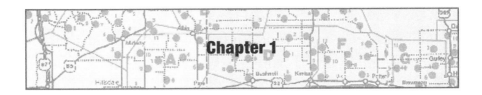

If Lyle Sudderman had been paying attention to his surroundings instead of twisting his grease-stained U.S. Postal Service letter carrier's cap nervously from side to side on his head and muttering obscenities to himself, he might have realized sooner that the brown lump lying between a knot of sagebrush and a small boulder just inside a sagging cyclone fence fifty yards away wasn't a dead steer or a mule deer that had somehow nosed its way onto the fenced-off patch of government land. Despite his current state of fluster, Sudderman, a longtime poacher, decided that the high cost of store-bought meat required at least a quick peek.

It occurred to him that the mysterious lump lying amid several industrial-looking steel-and-concrete structures could also be a human body. He swallowed hard, eased his postal truck onto the highway shoulder, and stared at the mile-square fenced-off parcel of Wyoming heartland just off Grayrocks Road, six miles northeast of the small farming and ranching community of Wheatland.

It was windless and a sweltering 98 degrees. He was a little ahead of schedule, it was almost time for lunch, and he needed to think for a moment. He stared at the lump in the field once again and realized that it hadn't moved in all the time he'd been watching it. Thinking, *God forbid I should get accused of letting my freaking engine idle and use one extra ounce of precious*

U.S. government gas, he killed the truck's engine and jammed his bulky key ring with its fifteen keys, a penlight, and a Moose Lodge medallion into a pants pocket. He sat back in his seat, glanced across the highway at the Laramie River Station power plant with its sixty-story-high smokestacks, smiled, and muttered, "Been here before."

Over a quarter century as a faithful government servant, and what was he about to get as a reward for his loyalty? A fucking cut in pay. Come October, the Postal Service planned to eliminate a day of mail delivery from his route, and that meant a smaller paycheck. This time around, his twenty-six-year membership in the National Association of Letter Carriers wouldn't help, nor would his ass-kissing and glad-handing. Word had come down from the postmaster general himself, and Lyle knew he wouldn't be able to avoid being part of the cuts. Perhaps he shouldn't have been so quick to buy the twenty acres he'd purchased in the Laramie Mountains the previous winter.

Turning his attention back to the mysterious lump, Lyle stepped out of his truck after making certain that the warning flashers were on and headed across the thirty-acre patch of swampy river-bottom grass.

A two-mile-long stretch of finger canyons marked the northern edge of the river bottom. Rolling, treeless, tobacco-brown hills, seared by the August heat, rose above the canyons. Thinking that for some reason the mosquitoes seemed to be less pesky than usual, Lyle worked his way toward the fence that marked the northern boundary of the government parcel. When he was a few yards from the fence, a swirling wind tunneled its way from the river bottom through willows and cottonwoods until every tree and shrub seemed to quiver.

Lyle glanced over his shoulder toward the power plant before jogging the rest of the way to the fence and scaling it, as he had many times with friends during his boyhood.

Inside the compound, he found himself staring at what was mostly vacant land—land that in his youth, he and his friends had laughingly dubbed "ground zero." He glanced around at the half-dozen "No Trespassing" signs wired to the fence until his eyes found a single rusted metal sign that defined with certainty where he was. The sign simply read, "T-11."

Making his way past a three-foot-high flat concrete structure that had always reminded him of a home-plate-shaped foundation for a home, he paused for a moment to glance around at the compound's seven telephone poles. Once during his teens, he and several friends, on a dare, had climbed every telephone pole inside the boundaries of Tango-11, laughing and challenging one another as the power-plant smokestacks across the highway belched clouds of orange smoke and steam. Even then, they knew what the government had at one time housed behind the cyclone fences.

Lyle looked at the concrete pad and rail spur that had once been the heart of T-11, then swallowed hard before walking to within a few feet of what had brought him there. Suddenly he was laughing, fidgeting with his cap, and stamping his feet as he realized that what he was looking down on was neither a dead man, a steer, nor an antelope but simply a knotted-up, buckskin-colored blanket with a mass of tumbleweeds trapped inside. The Wyoming wind had blown the ratty old bedcover against a tire-sized piece of concrete.

Shaking his head and wondering how he could have mistaken a blanket and a bunch of tumbleweeds for any kind of animal, he mumbled, "Shit," tugged at the bill of his cap, and turned to leave. He'd retrieved his keys from his pocket when it occurred to him that, though his poaching venture had come to nothing, there nonetheless was something oddly out of place in Tango-11. It took him a while to zero in on it, although he realized later it should have been obvious to him the second his feet had landed inside the fence. As the azure sky seemed to swallow the entire abandoned Tango-11 nuclear-missile site, he could see that, less than thirty paces from where he stood, the hatch cover over the personnel-access tube, a twenty-four-inch-diameter shaft that rose from deep in the ground to poke its head three feet in the air, was propped partially open. The adjacent fifty-by-fifty-foot concrete slab that covered the site's more important nuclear-missile payload bore looked undisturbed.

Lyle removed his cap and scratched his head in dismay. Never once during his dozens of teenage late-night visits to Tango-11 had he seen that hatch cover raised.

With his heart racing and his left eye twitching, the forty-four-year-old postal worker strolled cautiously toward the charred-looking hatch cover. He'd once heard from a friend in the air force that a hatch cover like the one he was staring at weighed all of 2,700 pounds, and he knew from his mostly forgotten high school Wyoming history studies that the mobile concrete-and-steel slab that covered the missile silo itself weighed at least a hundred tons. Knowing full well that something that weighed over a ton couldn't have popped open on its own, he suppressed the urge to shout, in some strange homage to his youth, *Buddy, Clint,*

4

Sammy, Will, come have a look! When he was a couple of feet away from the hatch cover, he could see that a rusted metal hook, the kind commonly attached to the heavy-duty chains that local ranchers and farmers used to pull their tractors and backhoes out of swampy pastures, was keeping the hatch cover open. He whispered, "Damn," as his eyes followed a chain that was attached to the hook down into the darkness of the access tube.

He had no idea how deep the access tube sank into the sandy Wyoming soil, but with a belly-up-to-the-bar, can-you-top-this tale now swirling through his head, he knew he was going to have a look down its throat.

Taking his penlight and keys from his pocket, he leaned against the hatch cover and tried to shine the light down into the access tube, but he couldn't see much beyond the V-shaped opening. Laying his keys and penlight aside, he tried without success to shift the cover until, winded and sweating, he decided he'd need a lever of some sort. When he spotted a five-foot-long tree limb, he ran to get it, returned, and jammed one end of the limb beneath the hatch cover, wedging it into place. With the concrete lip of the access tube serving as his fulcrum, he plopped all 245 of his portly pounds down on the far end of the tree limb and crossed his fingers.

The hatch cover rose with a squeaky, resistant groan until it was almost perpendicular to the sky, then stopped with a single loud click. Rivulets of sweat trickled down the back of Lyle's neck as, smiling and flushed with success, he tossed the tree limb aside and scooped up his keys and penlight. Standing just inches from the hook, he leaned over the open access tube and aimed the penlight's beam directly down into the earthy-smelling bore.

At first he couldn't see anything, but as his eyes accommodated to the darkness and he followed the chain down from the hook, he was able to make out two dark, flat objects about fifteen feet below him. The objects, which reminded him of the wooden paddles he'd played paddleball with as a boy, were pressed tightly against the tube's curved steel wall. For several seconds he stared down at the oddly shaped objects, recognizing finally that they were touching one another. When he realized that they were much narrower than his boyhood paddles and that each one appeared to be attached to something long and stick-like that extended perpendicularly away from it and deeper into the access tube, he muttered, "Damn."

It was only when he poked his head, an arm, and the penlight deeper into the access tube that he realized that the chain next to him wasn't looped around paddles at all, or even around a couple of bizarre pieces of military hardware left over from the Cold War, but instead around two human ankles, and that the two flat objects he'd been staring at so intently were the soles of two human feet.

A rush of adrenaline shot through him, and the suffocating mucus of fear plugged his nostrils as he gawked at the unmistakable curvature of a man's buttocks. Thinking that he was staring at a kind of naked bungee jumper who'd decided to dive headfirst into an abandoned nuclear-missile access hole, he let out a guttural, primordial wail that belched up from the depths of his being and echoed off the access tube's walls as he sprang back from the hatch cover and bolted for his truck.

When pressed later by the Platte County sheriff, and then by the Warren Air Force Base Office of Special Investigations major who'd quickly arrived from Cheyenne to interrogate him about why he'd entered the Tango-11 site and what he'd found, Lyle Sudderman found it difficult to remember the exact sequence of events from his midday odyssey. He remembered rescaling the Tango-11 fence after finding the dead man, and he recalled tripping his way across undulating river-bottom pastureland to dial 911 from the cell phone in his truck. He remembered the hatch cover and the tree limb he'd used to open it, and of course he remembered the chain. But what he remembered most, he told his interrogators, was the strange, haunting, ghostly vision of a schoolyard full of children playing paddleball in the hot summer sun.

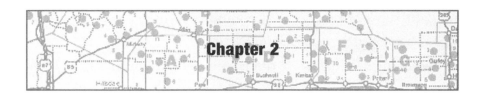
"Damn it, Cozy! I need you to get your laid-back Caribbean cruise of an ass in gear and up there to Wheatland right now. And I want the whole story—lock, stock, barrel, and bullets, if there're any involved." Frederick Dames frowned in frustration, moved the phone receiver from his right ear to his left, and muttered, "Friends!"

Elgin Coseia, known to his friends simply as "Cozy," a nickname the man fuming on the other end of the line had given him during their baseball-playing days at Southeastern Oklahoma State University, adjusted his lean, six-foot-four-inch frame against the cushions of his living room couch, tugged on the drawstring of his faded basketball warm-ups, and took a deep breath. "I'm headed that way, Freddy. I told you that an hour ago."

"Headed that way, my ass." Freddy ran a hand through his thick auburn hair, hair that made his head look too large for his stocky, five-foot-nine-inch fireplug of a body, and shook his head.

"I needed to tie up some loose ends before I left."

"Yeah," said Freddy with a smirk, suspecting that Cozy's loose ends more than likely involved some long-legged woman or, even better, a nap. "Time you got your Dominican butt moving, Elgin. I can get other people to play your position. I mean it, Elgin. Call me when you've got a handle on our Wyoming story. Do you hear me?" Freddy's normally ruddy complexion turned a deep shade of red as his temporal muscles twitched.

Aware that Freddy's use of back-to-back *Elgin*s meant his best friend was absolutely and thoroughly pissed, Cozy said, "Got it."

"Good, because the next time we talk, I expect to be looking at a story on the Net," said Freddy, slamming down the receiver and wondering how he and Elgin Delonero Coseia continued to remain best friends. But best friends they were, odd-couple buddies since their freshman college year, when Freddy had first saddled Cozy with his nickname. Freddy had come up with the name not as a contraction of "Coseia," as most people thought, but rather in recognition of Cozy's uncanny, stealth-like ability to get himself into position from the shortstop hole and take a second-base pickoff throw from a pitcher to tag a surprised base runner out. *The man's as cozy as cotton* had been the way Freddy had initially characterized Cozy's slide-step move-in behind the runner. After that, the nickname just stuck.

Before his four-year college baseball career was over, Cozy would be credited with the highest number of pitcher-to-shortstop second-base pickoffs ever recorded in NCAA Division II baseball history. Three of them had come during the 2000 Division II college baseball championship series.

Twelve years had passed since Southeastern Oklahoma State had won the Division II college baseball title, and in that time all the adulation, hoopla, and promises of millions had also disappeared. It had all been lost for Cozy in a single improbable few seconds just months after his and Freddy's college graduation. For more than a decade now, a lackadaisical and often morose Cozy

Coseia, his baseball dreams lost to him forever, had been trying to recapture who and what he'd been.

Sitting on the couch, he stared across the narrow, sparsely furnished room toward a photograph that hung slightly crooked on the wall facing him. The antique mahogany school desk where he wrote most of his news stories for Freddy Dames's web-based Digital Registry News hugged the wall beneath the photo.

"Regional news for the digital age," Cozy said, rising from the couch as he muttered Freddy's trademark business slogan. Easing his weight onto his emaciated, badly scarred left leg, he continued to stare at the glossy black-and-white photograph of him and his title-winning teammates. The photograph showed Freddy and half the team piling on top of Cozy moments after he had hit a title-clinching, game-winning, two-run triple.

Shaking his head as if the gesture might erase the heartache of the past eleven years, he limped over to the photo, straightened it, eyed it wistfully, and continued out his front door to head for Wyoming.

Wyoming Platte County sheriff Art Bosack, a onetime pro-rodeo saddle bronco rider who occasionally still rode his horse out on criminal investigations, arrived to begin his investigation into what would become known as "the Tango-11 murder" not on a horse but in a hail-damaged Ford pickup badly in need of new tires.

His deputy, Wally Sykes, a recent criminal justice graduate of a small college in Great Falls, Montana, was so wide-eyed when the county coroner and Bosack pulled the body of a rail-thin, six-foot-two-inch black man from the access tube that he hardly heard the crunch of sagebrush and the swish of grass that told him someone was approaching the hastily taped-off crime scene.

Seasoned and crime-scene-savvy, the coroner, who with Bosack was kneeling over the dead man, looked past the sheriff toward the crunching sound to see someone dressed in air force fatigues approaching. Nudging the sheriff, he said, "Looks like the wild-blue-yonder boys you've been expecting are here, Art."

Bosack barely looked up from examining the deepest of five stab wounds in the murder victim's back. Puzzled by the pattern of the wounds and the superficial nature of all but three of them, he ran a latex-gloved index finger from wound to wound, connecting them in the shape of an imaginary pentagon.

"Strange. Real strange." He grunted, looked up at Sykes, and said, "Wanna go meet our flyboy?"

The greenhorn deputy glanced across the Tango-11 compound toward a Jeep Cherokee that was parked fifty yards away on the highway shoulder. Recognizing suddenly that the person approaching them was a woman, he simply stared. Their visitor was still fifteen feet away when the sheriff stood, eyed the gold oak leaves on the woman's shoulder epaulets, flashed her a friendly smile, and said, "How do, Major? Heard we had an OSI officer from Warren headed our way." He stripped off a glove and offered her his right hand.

The tall, lithe special investigations officer, who had been dispatched from Cheyenne's Warren Air Force Base seventy-five miles south, returned the smile as she walked up to the body. "Took me a little bit longer to get here than I expected. A tractor-trailer rig was jackknifed on the interstate," she said, scrutinizing the partially tarp-covered body lying at her feet. "Sheriff Bosack, I take it?" She extended an arm above the dead man's head and shook the sheriff's hand.

"Yep," said Bosack, trying to recall whether he'd ever met a female OSI officer and knowing for certain he'd never met an African American female one. "The man standing to your left is my deputy, Wally Sykes, and the one still kneelin' there, lookin' like he's prayin' for rain, is our Platte County coroner, Dr. Sam Reed." The way Bosack said the word *doctor*, as if it were the equal of a military rank, seemed to be the only thing that caused the woman to announce her name.

"I'm Bernadette Cameron." There was a self-assured directness in her tone. She extended a hand to the coroner, realized he was still fully gloved, and pulled the hand back.

"Got gloves in your size if you wanna get down and dirty here with us, Major," the sheriff said.

"Think I'll wait," said Bernadette. "Just fill me in on what you've got."

"Sure," said Bosack, thinking that with a little more makeup, civilian clothes, a tad longer hair, and a set of earrings, the cinnamon-skinned, green-eyed major would be a knockout. "One of our rural-route mail carriers found him about four hours ago, danglin' from a chain by his ankles inside that missile-silo personnel-access tube over there." Bosack pointed toward the raised hatch. "He was naked as a jaybird when we found him. I'm guessin' somebody with explosives know-how blew the hatch cover. Before our mail carrier lifted it usin' a tree limb, I mean."

"Or somebodies," said Bernadette. "And just so you're aware, that hatch cover would have been easy enough to raise without an explosive charge if you had the entry code."

"Don't think anybody had that," said Bosack, eyeing the charred hatch cover. "Wanna have a look?"

"In a minute," Bernadette said, looking down at the body. "African American," she said, pausing.

"Yeah," said Bosack.

"How long do you think he'd been hanging inside?"

Bosack glanced at the coroner. "Whatta you think, Sam?"

"Hard to tell," the coroner said, rising to his feet. "I'd say from the amount of body decomposition, the number of insect and rodent bites, and the lack of skin elasticity that he'd been hanging there for a couple of weeks at least."

"Not much smell," said Bernadette, kneeling next to the body and sniffing.

"What smell there was is still down there in your tube, Major, and there's really not much of that. Over time the smell of death dissipates," said Reed.

"Any identifying marks?"

"Just a couple of tattoos," said the coroner.

"Where?"

The coroner hesitated before responding, "On his penis. You can have a look if you'd like." He teased back the bottom edge of the heavy-gauge black plastic covering the dead man.

Bernadette took her first good look at the body. The man's skin, on the grayish side of black, looked corrugated and picked at. It sagged, mostly along the arms and neck, and skin ulcers covered the man's chest. His penis, missing most of its circumcised head, was peppered with dried-up erosions that looked like insect bites. Even so, the letters "ICBM," stenciled in red, white, blue, and red again, could be made out running along the top of the shaft.

Watching the major's eyes narrow thoughtfully, the coroner said, "There's another tattoo on the underside." He carefully lifted the blackened nub of a sex organ with a gloved index finger. "Can you see it?"

"Yes," said Bernadette, recognizing the insignia of Warren Air Force Base's 90th Missile Group. "Strange, and a little ritualistic."

"Looks like somebody used a dull knife or maybe even a pair of scissors to do the job. Pretty ragged edges," said the sheriff, shaking his head. "That insignia seals the deal though, don't you think, Major? He's gotta be one of your boys outta Warren."

"We'll have to see," said Bernadette, glancing around the Tango-11 compound and looking for where the killer might have broken through the fence to gain enough access to drag a body inside.

Realizing what she was looking for, the sheriff nodded to the east. "Whoever killed him cut a hole big enough to drive a truck through in your eastern boundary fence over there. Didn't see much evidence of drag marks over to here, but like Dr. Reed said, the body's been here for a while. No question, though, he probably wasn't killed here."

"Missile-site security is sort of a top priority for us," said Bernadette, glancing down at the body once again. "So we'll be looking real hard at how someone did what they did here."

"I know the division of labor, Major. Been there and done this kinda thing before. The murder's mine. The security breach is yours. So let's get back to what's mine for a second. We found the head of the dead man's penis wadded up in a piece of paper that had been jammed into his mouth. I'm guessin' the killer was lookin' to not only make a point but shut him up. Wanna show her, Sam?"

Dr. Reed leaned over, picked up a baggie from a spot of bare earth near the victim's arm, opened the bag, took out the dried-up penis head and a crinkled piece of paper, and held them up for Bernadette to look at. "I think the killer probably used the paper to stop the bleeding and sop up some of the blood," said Reed.

"Reasonable," Bernadette said, staring at the paper. "Looks like it's got some lines drawn on it."

"My take, too," said Bosack. "I'll have it analyzed, and I'll let you know what we find out."

The sound of a vehicle pulling off the highway and coming to a stop on the shoulder cut the conversation short. Looking back toward the highway, the sheriff announced, "Dually." A satellite-receiver-style antenna poked from the bed of a white truck with dual rear tires. The truck's nose was pointed toward them.

"Colorado plates," said Deputy Sykes. "Recognize the rig, Sheriff?"

"Nope."

"Who'd be coming out here right now besides law enforcement?" asked Bernadette.

Smiling knowingly and eyeing Bernadette's Jeep, the sheriff asked, "Have you got a police scanner in that vehicle of yours, Major?"

"No."

"Well, you should."

"And the reason for that would be?"

"So you can keep up with the press," the sheriff said with a wink. "I'm willin' to bet six months' pay that dually we're starin' at belongs to a journalist."

Bernadette watched in silence as the driver slipped out of the pickup.

"Yep," said the sheriff. "The antenna. The Colorado tags. Pretty much says it all. We've got us an outta-state newshound lookin' for a story."

By the time Cozy Coseia worked his way from the highway shoulder, through sagebrush and timothy hay up to his knees, and to the open north gate of Tango-11, Wally Sykes was waiting for him.

"Afraid this area is off-limits to visitors today," Sykes said authoritatively.

Slightly winded and limping, Cozy reached into the right-hand pocket of his jeans for his press credential. As he did, Sykes's left hand moved casually to the butt of his .44.

Quickly closing the gap between Cozy and Sykes and thinking that his new deputy was going to need a little schooling on when it was appropriate to reach for one's service weapon, Sheriff Bosack, who with Major Cameron had been examining the charred "A-Plug" hatch cover, called out to Cozy, "What can I help you with, bud?"

Surveying the Tango-11 compound slowly and holding up his press credential for the sheriff to see, Cozy said, "Heard you've had some trouble out here today."

Without answering, the sheriff examined the press credential, then looked Cozy up and down. He had no doubt that the gangly visitor in aviator sunglasses had been watching their every move through binoculars for a good ten minutes before coming to join them, and Bosack didn't particularly like being scrutinized from a distance.

Ignoring the sheriff's silence and still taking in every inch of the compound, Cozy nodded toward where the coroner and Bernadette Cameron were kneeling. "Looks like you've got yourself a dead man on your hands," he said, taking special note of the air force officer's presence.

Realizing that from where he stood, Cozy couldn't tell whether the body was that of a man or a woman and thinking, *Good ploy,* the sheriff said, "We're attendin' to official police business here, Mr. Coseia. The press will get a briefing later." He glanced toward Cozy's truck. "See you're outta Colorado."

"Denver. But like they say, bad news travels fast," Cozy said, thinking that Freddy Dames's southern Wyoming "information scouts," a trio of nosy, aging Vietnam vets whom Cozy had always considered no more than overpaid police scanner eavesdroppers, had finally earned their keep.

Still staring at the press credential, the sheriff said, "Digital Registry News. Hmm. Web-based outfit, I take it."

"Yep. Regional news for the Rockies."

"Great slogan," the sheriff said sarcastically. "But I think you'd better move on. I'll have Deputy Sykes here walk you back to your vehicle."

Cozy removed his sunglasses and tried to stare the deputy down.

When the sheriff said with authority, "Please show Mr. Coseia back to his truck, Wally," Sykes broke into a broad, eager-to-please grin. Waving Cozy ahead of him, he said, "Think you better move it, Coseia."

Watching the two men turn and head for the truck, the sheriff found himself wondering whether the curly-headed, hazel-eyed reporter with nut-brown skin was American Indian, Cuban, or perhaps maybe even Colombian. Whatever his heritage, he seemed to the sheriff to have the instincts of not simply a reporter but a lawman, and that bothered him. In the time they'd talked, he'd watched Coseia size up the compound, the dead man, the coroner, and Major Cameron. There was something else about Coseia that bothered the sheriff. Something small but troubling. He'd never liked sparring with a man with whiskey-colored eyes.

There was one thing Coseia hadn't been able to hide, however: his very noticeable limp. As he made his way back to his truck, the limp became even more pronounced.

As the sheriff watched Cozy slip into his dually, he had the sense that Elgin Coseia was a man for whom hiding things was important—his eyes, that limp, and other things, more than likely. With his attention still focused on Coseia, the sheriff hardly heard Major Cameron walk up beside him.

"Who was our visitor?" she asked, holding a pair of aviator sunglasses that she hadn't been wearing on her arrival in one hand.

"A reporter," Bosack said, turning to face her. "And you can be jack-sure he's just the first of 'em."

"He seemed to stare at Dr. Reed and me from behind those sunglasses for quite a long time. Think we'll see him again?"

"Absolutely," said the sheriff, watching Cozy's truck move slowly along the highway shoulder and knowing as he watched the dually's retreat that the man behind the wheel was no doubt staring through sunglasses directly back at them.

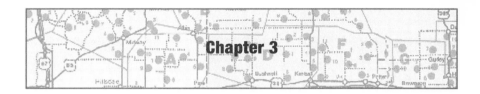

Chapter 3

She could hear Rikia down in the basement making his strange guttural airplane sounds as he piloted an imaginary World War II Japanese fighter in a dogfight over the Sea of Japan. It always upset her when her forty-eight-year-old cousin cloistered himself in the basement to play mindless toy airplane games for hours on end. But Kimiko Takata knew better than to interrupt him. Any intrusion ran the risk of sending him deeper into his fantasy world, a world filled with samurai warriors, long-dead and mostly forgotten Japanese fighter pilots, and above all honor. A world he could sometimes remain immersed in for days.

If left undisturbed, he would come up for air in thirty or forty minutes. She knew his routine. After all, Rikia Takata was a man of rigid routine. And when he came upstairs, they'd have plenty of time to talk about the news flash she'd just watched crawl across the bottom of her television screen. Time to discuss the unwelcome intrusion that had sent her rushing to her medicine cabinet for Pepto-Bismol and two aspirin.

Unaware of Kimiko's distress, Rikia remained at the imaginary controls of a Mitsubishi A-6M, known commonly as a Japanese Zero. He was sequestered in a musty cellar in a quaint Queen Anne cottage in Laramie, Wyoming, engaging the American enemy in another air battle. Rikia's lengthy groans and high-pitched nasal whines rose from the cellar as he clutched a U.S. F4U Corsair model airplane in his right hand and an A-6M in his left.

Shigeo Fukumoto, Japan's most famous World War II ace, was piloting the A-6M, and a less skilled American pilot, as always, was behind the controls of the Corsair. A low-pitched groan rose from the pit of Rikia's stomach, becoming louder and louder as he swirled the planes around in a circle above his head, then swung them up and down through the air. Inch by inch and second by second, the A-6M closed in on the Corsair's tail as the *rat-a-tat-tat* of machine-gun fire reverberated from Rikia's tongue. Suddenly the machine-gun fire stopped as the Corsair, hit and out of control, spiraled toward the top of a nearby Ping-Pong table, emitting flames and smoke from its tail, and disappeared into the choppy waters of the Sea of Japan. Smiling, Rikia whispered, "Justice."

Skimming the tabletop to make certain of his kill, the ghost of Shigeo Fukumoto then nosed his A-6M skyward to disappear in an imaginary curtain of clouds.

Erupting in a near-sexual climactic sigh, Rikia set the two model airplanes down on the Ping-Pong table, stepped to his left, and recorded another chalk mark and Fukumoto kill on a blackboard he'd mounted as a teenager on the basement wall. He'd recorded thousands of kills since then, but his kill number for the year stood at fifty-three.

Emotionally drained, he moved the two model airplanes he'd been playing with to their respective Japanese and American ends of the Ping-Pong table to join planes from other Allied and Axis nations.

A very nervous-sounding Kimiko opened the basement door and called out, "Rikia, come up here, please, and now! It's important!"

Rikia frowned, stomped to the foot of the stairs, and yelled up to the woman who'd pretty much raised him, "Can't it wait?"

Staring down at her slightly built, unshaven cousin, Kimiko said, "No, Rikia. It can't!"

Shaking his head and muttering, "Damn!" Rikia started up the stairs. "This had better be important," he announced, fighting to enunciate properly through his tongue-tied speech impediment.

Kimiko flashed him a steely-eyed look and said, "It is." She grabbed him firmly by the arm when he reached the first-floor landing and walked him into the kitchen. "Have a look," the surprisingly strong, 105-pound, seventy-six-year-old Kimiko said, waving at the television screen with her free hand.

Rikia slipped out of her grasp and turned to face the blonde, Cheyenne-based newscaster seated behind a desk that seemed to swallow her.

Kimiko slapped the top of the TV and said, "Listen!"

With a look of concern plastered on her face, the newscaster said theatrically, "Neither air force officials nor the Platte County sheriff are saying much about the man that a postal worker found hanging by his ankles inside a missile-silo personnel-access tube at the abandoned Tango-11 missile site near Wheatland. Nor are authorities saying how long the murdered man may have been there. Channel 4 has confirmed that the body is that of retired Air Force Master Sergeant Thurmond Giles, a decorated African American nuclear-missile maintenance technician. A joint air force–sheriff's office briefing and news conference has been scheduled for seven o'clock this evening in Wheatland. As always, Channel 4 News will be there to keep you abreast of the story."

"Sometimes bad things happen to people," Rikia said, smiling.

"And sooner or later the authorities will want to talk to us, Rikia. We both know that."

"So we talk to them." "Them" came out closer to "tem," but Kimiko was used to the garbled sounds of Rikia's speech.

"Yes, we will. Just be prepared."

"I'm always prepared." Rikia stepped over to his tiny, gray-haired cousin and draped a supportive arm over the shoulders of a woman who'd survived Wyoming's infamous Heart Mountain Relocation Center for Japanese Americans during World War II. Smiling as he stared down at the dozens of tiny moles dotting her forehead, he said reassuringly, "I have to be. Look who taught me."

Aware that his office conference room wouldn't be large enough to accommodate all the media types, voyeurs, gossipmongers, and just plain nosy folks who'd show up, Sheriff Bosack had scheduled his seven p.m. news briefing at a courtroom in the Platte County courthouse.

The courtroom, which lacked a balcony, otherwise resembled the room made famous during the Scopes monkey trial, right down to its massive support columns, echoey wood-plank floors, and dank mustiness.

His stomach groaning, the sheriff started up the courthouse steps a little before seven. In the eight hours since Thurmond Giles's body had been discovered at the Tango-11 site, Sheriff Bosack, who'd skipped breakfast so that he and Sam Reed could get in a few minutes of North Platte River fly fishing that had never materialized, hadn't had a bite to eat. Thinking with each new step, *This too shall pass,* he'd barely reached the top when Freddy Dames startled him by slipping out from behind a twenty-foot-tall concrete pillar. "What do you think, Sheriff? Have you got a hate crime on your hands, or do you think we're looking at some kind of *Back to the Future* killing linked to the antinuclear movement?"

Freddy was the final straw in the sheriff's hunger-panged, media-sniping, military-accommodating, politician-pleasing day. With barely a second of hesitation, he shoved Freddy backward into a surprised Cozy Coseia. Recognizing Cozy, the sheriff shook his head, muttered, "I should've known," and continued into the courthouse.

"Told you to wait," Cozy said, brushing himself off. Freddy's ambush hadn't paid off, but others like it had in the past, and Cozy knew that his stocky, chestnut-haired, risk-taking best friend wouldn't change his MO anytime soon.

"Wait, my ass!" Freddy adjusted his sport coat. "We've got the story of the decade staring us in the face, man. Might as well take a shot at priming the pump. Let's get inside."

Freddy pushed his way through a set of double doors and headed down a hallway toward the courtroom with Cozy at his heels, to find standing room only in the courtroom. They carved out a space for themselves between a Denver-based freelance news photographer whom Freddy knew and a group of four ponytailed spectators. The ponytails, two men and two women, appeared to Cozy to be in their early fifties and looked as if they'd been shot from some 1970s antinuclear-demonstration cannon. When one of the women appeared to wave, Cozy cocked a suspicious eyebrow at Freddy, then scanned the rest of the room. A half-dozen agitated-looking teenagers, all of them black, occupied a front courtroom bench. A balding, overweight man sitting at the end of the bench seemed to be in charge of them.

Prosecuting and defense attorneys' tables sat to the right and left of a lectern at the front of the courtroom. As many cameras and lights and microphones as Cozy had ever seen at a news conference streamed or beamed down on the lectern and tables. Behind the tables in a TV-equipment-free buffer zone, the sheriff stood talking to a tall, fit-looking air force officer with shiny silver colonel's eagles on his shoulder epaulets. The only other person Cozy recognized among four other people standing behind the tables was the air force major he had seen at Tango-11.

No longer dressed in fatigues, the major now wore air force dress blues. Her skirt was figure-flattering, and she looked provocatively striking in a military-advertising-poster kind of way. As she turned toward him, Cozy noticed pilot wings pinned just above the edge of the welt pocket of her uniform and found himself wondering why on earth a pilot would be assigned to an OSI unit.

When Bernadette Cameron caught him staring at her, she averted her eyes, took a seat, and began talking to the man seated next to her. Turning to Freddy, Cozy was about to point her out, but for some reason he decided, momentarily at least, to keep the major to himself.

Watching Freddy nod, then smile at the four ponytails surrounding them, Cozy had the sense that Freddy was doing everything he could to communicate silently with them. He was about to ask Freddy if he knew them when Sheriff Bosack stepped up to the battery of microphones, thumped the center mike, and said, "Glad to see everyone here tonight."

As Freddy mouthed, *Sure,* the sheriff was off and running. Indicating to the assemblage that after his remarks and those of Colonel Joel DeWitt from Warren Air Force Base there would be a short Q and A, the sheriff detailed the day's events. For most of the people in the room, his dry summation was no more than a rehash of what they already knew. Confirming that the murdered man found at Tango-11 was retired Master Sergeant Thurmond Giles, whose identity had been conclusively proven via a dental records review, and that a joint Platte County Sheriff's Office and U.S. Air Force Office of Special Investigations inquiry was under way, Bosack ended his surprisingly brief remarks by thanking the air force, Colonel DeWitt, and the people of Warren Air Force Base in Cheyenne, home of the 90th Missile Wing, for their assistance. Then he sat down.

The word *blowhard* coursed through Cozy's mind within seconds of Colonel Joel DeWitt stepping up to the microphone to paternalistically announce, "Ladies and gentlemen, let me assure you first and foremost that today's break in and breach of security at the decommissioned Tango-11 site in no way represents a risk to our nation's security."

With an *I'm in charge* look plastered on his face, DeWitt then delivered several minutes of uninformative platitudes, thanking seemingly every elected and law enforcement official in the state of Wyoming, from the beaming Deputy Sykes, who stood just a few feet from Cozy, to the governor. When Freddy nudged

Cozy and whispered, "You've got to be kidding," Cozy, who was busy watching Major Cameron's attempt to keep from rolling her eyes, ignored him. Shrugging, Freddy slipped a small spiral-bound notebook out of the inside pocket of his sport coat and began jotting notes.

Cozy was startled. He couldn't remember his techno-savvy best friend taking handwritten notes about anything since college, aside from the occasional summation of his stock market trades for the week or the quarterly earnings for the Silver Streak Oil Corporation, which his father owned.

Surprised that Freddy seemed to be taking the briefing so seriously, Cozy shrugged and turned his attention back to Colonel DeWitt, who was busy recounting the supportive phone call he'd received earlier that day from Wyoming's governor. Only when the colonel mentioned that the air force's investigation into the Tango-11 break-in would be in the capable hands of Major Bernadette Cameron did Cozy's ears perk up.

"Major Cameron, also from Warren OSI, is well schooled in handling situations such as this," DeWitt announced. The words had barely left his mouth when the two ponytailed men standing next to Cozy rushed the podium, yelling, "No more nukes! No more nukes!" Their two women companions immediately dropped to the floor, took handcuffs from their purses, and handcuffed themselves to one of the claw-footed legs of the nearest bench just as the teenagers in the front row began shouting, "Racist dogs!" in sync with "No more nukes!"

Freddy Dames dropped to one knee, slipped a handheld tape recorder out of his sport coat pocket, and shoved it into the faces of the two female protesters, who continued to scream, "No more nukes!"

Cozy moved out of the way of Deputy Sykes's delayed bull rush to the podium. Surprised by Freddy's uncanny readiness, Cozy looked toward the front of the room to see Major Cameron drop one portly, lunging male protester like a rock with a knee to the groin. The sheriff had the second man down on the floor, with both arms behind his back and handcuffed, before most people in the courtroom had a chance to do much more than ooh or aah in amazement.

With digital cameras clicking everywhere and television cameras rolling, Cozy watched the ponytailed, redheaded man whom the major had taken out roll around on the floor, groaning in agony, as chants of "No more nukes!" and "Racist dogs!" continued to echo through the courtroom. Staring around at what seemed to him to have been a very well-orchestrated eruption, Cozy caught Freddy smiling, tape recorder in hand, asking questions of spectators while his photographer friend from Denver snapped photo after photo. Noting the photographer's steadiness in the midst of the chaos, he realized suddenly that Freddy was in fact directing the photographer's every move. Much of what he was witnessing could only have been planned in advance. Cozy lowered his head, shook it in disbelief, and mumbled, "No, Freddy; you didn't."

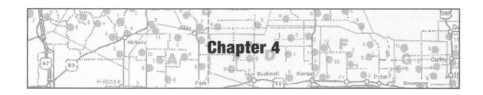

Chapter 4

An hour after Sheriff Bosack's tumultuous press conference, Cozy and Freddy Dames sat eating burgers and fries at the Wheatland Inn just off I-25. A passing late-evening thunderstorm laced with golf-ball-sized hail had put on a twenty-minute light show before slowly moving off to the east, leaving behind drizzle, minor flooding, and a few distant claps of thunder.

As Freddy toyed with his burger, Cozy shook his head disgustedly, upset that Freddy had admitted to using the sheriff's press conference to manufacture news.

"You didn't tweak anything, Freddy," Cozy chastised. "You turned that press conference into the lead story on the nightly news. Damn it, you're regressing, slipping back to your old ways. Stealing bases against the sign, trying to make something happen on the field when you shouldn't, swinging for the fences when it's three and oh and you've been told to take a ball."

"It helped earn us a national championship, didn't it?"

Cozy glanced down at his left leg, keenly aware of the dark turn the conversation could take if he continued to argue his point. "So you dredged up four over-the-hill, tie-dyed hippies to crash a press conference just so you'd have a story?"

"They weren't hippies, and I didn't dredge them up. I simply knew they'd be there."

"What?"

"I said I knew they'd be there. While you were up here in Wheatland stumbling around, doing things by the book, and waiting for the Tango-11 story to unfold, I took what you told me on the phone right after you first called to tell me about the dead man, and I did a little Twittering. Someone out there in cyberspace must've been sitting at a computer screen when I did because within minutes of my post about the body in the missile silo, I had tweets from a couple of professed antinukers saying the murder victim might be one of theirs."

"Shit, Freddy, the body wasn't in the silo; it was in the silo's personnel-access tube. And how the hell do you know those tweets you got didn't come from the damn murderer? Don't you care anything about facts?"

"Parts is parts." Freddy forced a smile.

"Unbelievable," Cozy countered. "How could you write any kind of a story that was halfway factual between the time I called you after leaving the murder scene and when you met me here in Wheatland at five o'clock? Hell, you were highballin' it up I-25 for most of that time."

"Technology, my man, technology. Something you'd better start taking to heart, or you're gonna earn yourself a ticket right out of the world of investigative reporting. An iPhone and a laptop slice through time, my friend, and like it or not, they're necessary tools of our trade these days. How else do you think I could have been on top of a story like this so fast? I suggest you spend a little more time learning how to use them and a little less time worrying about facts."

"Like I should've spent more time learning how to ride a motorcycle?" Cozy said, frowning.

Aware that for the sake of their friendship, the conversation needed to end right then, Freddy rose from his chair with a grunt, slipped his wallet out of his back pocket, fished out a fifty-dollar bill, and tossed it onto the table. "Come on, man, let's go."

Cozy glanced at the grease-stained check for $14.38 and stood. Freddy was a few steps from the restaurant's front door by the time Cozy had enough feeling in his left leg to start that way. Moving slowly toward the door, with pins and needles shooting through his calf, Cozy brushed past their waitress.

Spotting the fifty on the tabletop, the waitress called after him, "I'll bring you your change, sir."

"Keep it," Cozy said, responding the way he knew Freddy would've.

"Are you sure, mister? It's a fifty," the puzzled waitress asked.

Uttering words he never would have used except in anger, Cozy said, "I know, but the guy who left it has money to burn."

"He must be some kind of millionaire."

"Times a hundred." Cozy continued walking, leaving the startled waitress shaking her head and wondering who on earth the man who'd left the fifty was.

The two best friends hardly said a word to one another during the short drive back to their motel. As Cozy pulled his dually into the space next to Freddy's Bentley, Freddy broke the silence. "Those antinuke protesters are the key to our murder, Cozy. I know it."

Not the least bit surprised by Freddy's cocksureness but reluctant to challenge him and start a conversation that might end like the last one, Cozy asked, "What makes you so sure?"

"Because one of those tweets I mentioned came from someone who said I should be talking to a woman named Sarah Goldbeck. Whoever it was pumped Goldbeck up like she was the Second Coming. Said if I wanted to find out who killed that sergeant, I needed to be at that press conference."

"Second coming of what? Those worn-out protesters of yours looked like some over-the-hill gang to me, especially the redheaded guy, the one that lady air force major drop-kicked in the nuts."

"Hell, they're a bunch of fricking pacifists, Cozy. What would you expect? What I'm getting at is that, pacifists or not, somebody among the four who were there at the briefing, or some tweeter out there in their extended antinuke family, is linked to that Tango-11 security breach and murder. And we need to nail them." Cozy shrugged and shook his head. "Cop talk—and risky, Freddy." It wouldn't be the first time Freddy Dames had lined up to play cops and robbers. The previous summer he and Cozy had brought the hammer down on a Mexico-based car-chop ring that had ended in a 110-miles-per-hour car chase on I-70. A chase that had earned them each a ten-thousand-dollar fine, four months of community service, and a warning from a disgruntled judge that they never again become involved in vigilante activities.

"So what's the game plan?" Cozy asked, suspecting that Freddy was already three steps down the road toward doing precisely what that judge had warned him against.

Looking pleased, Freddy said, "We wait for our four protesters to post bond, which I'm guessing will be sometime tomorrow morning, and go have a talk with them. There's no way they'll be charged with any more than disorderly conduct, or maybe interfering with an official police proceeding. I'm guessing they'll all be home tie-dying shirts and smoking doobies by noon. And maybe one of them will turn out to be my Twitter friend."

"What about that redhead who charged the major? No way in hell he'll be able to sidestep an assault charge."

"Maybe not, but if he ends up in jail, we'll still have three people to talk to. Who knows, one of the women might end up being Sarah Goldbeck. Bottom line is, it's worth sticking around this burg to see what happens."

"Okay. I'm game."

"Que sera, sera." Freddy patted Cozy reassuringly on the shoulder before moving to get out of the dually.

"Que sera," said Cozy, repeating two of the three code words he and Freddy had begun exchanging before taking the baseball diamond during their freshman year at Southeastern Oklahoma State. The words would ultimately turn into part of a baseball-tossing warm-up routine and good-luck chant, played out to the sounds of the 1950s chart hit "Whatever Will Be, Will Be" at college baseball stadiums across the West during their senior-year championship run. Suddenly Freddy was humming the tune, nudging Cozy and urging him to do the same. By the time they reached the motel's front door, they were harmonizing perfectly.

"Let's say we're back up and at it by eight," Freddy said as they walked across the motel lobby.

"Works for me." Thinking, *Que sera, sera,* Cozy watched Freddy hurriedly take off down a hallway for his room before he limped in the opposite direction toward his.

Cozy had as fitful a night of rest as he'd suffered through in years, and as he sat on the edge of his bed, happy to see the morning sunlight, rubbing the feeling into his left leg, and staring out the window, he had the sense that he'd been on an all-night treadmill.

Just before three a.m., he'd sat straight up in bed to the sound of a semi's air brakes being set just outside his window. Unable to get back to sleep, he'd paced the room for a while, read a brochure highlighting Wheatland's quiet, friendly, country-living lifestyle, and puzzled over whether the Giles murder might have been racially motivated before plopping back down on the bed to stare at the ceiling for another half hour. He'd finally drifted off to sleep a little before four only to have the dream that had chased him for years thread its way through to his subconscious.

The dream always started out the same, with him walking into a Harley-Davidson showroom and asking the only salesman there, a man dressed totally in black save for a pair of spit-shined white baseball spikes, if he could take a motorcycle for a test ride.

The salesman's emphatic *No!* always sent him storming out of the showroom to jump on a brand-new red Harley and speed off, and the dream always ended with him barreling helmetless on the motorcycle down California's coastal Highway 1 to ultimately be swallowed by a foggy mist. Never, in any of his thousands of dreams, had he emerged from that fog.

Still rubbing his leg and staring at the wedge of sunlight knifing its way between the room's partially opened drapes, Cozy sighed and ran his other hand through his always unruly mop of coal-black hair. Realizing that he was badly in need of a haircut, he waited for the circulation in his leg to catch up with his scalp massage.

Missing most of the calf and without a fibula, Cozy's left leg had been bone-grafted twice. With a third of the girth it had had during his baseball-playing days, the leg was now functional but quick to give out. A frown crossed his face as he thought about the fact that just about everything below his left knee had come from a cadaver. He stared at the leg's puckered skin for a couple of seconds before finally rising from the edge of the bed and limping across the room to the shower.

A shave and a chin nick later, as warm water streamed over his shoulders and down the middle of his back, he found himself wondering how Freddy had slept and whether or not Freddy, a baseball natural who'd turned down the big leagues and the son of a wealthy, reclusive Oklahoma oil tycoon, ever had bad dreams.

Forty-five minutes later, Cozy sat bleary-eyed across the table from Freddy in a drafty restaurant a short drive up the street from their motel. As he listened to Freddy talk with his mouth full, he found himself wondering how on earth someone with Freddy's silver-spoon upbringing could have developed such bad table manners.

Freddy, who'd mockingly taken to calling the four antinuke protesters from the previous evening "the Gang of Four," took a sip of coffee and, in response to Cozy's question about how they should proceed with their investigation, said, "So we'll double-team our Gang of Four."

"Or three if Mr. Redhead ends up behind bars."

Freddy laughed. "I'm still thinking that OSI major somehow mistook the man's jewels for a soccer ball. Makes you wonder whether all the military's female special investigation types are stone-cold ass-kickers like her."

"You've got me, but I can tell you this—she hasn't always been OSI. She was sporting pilot wings on her uniform."

"Damn, my man. Sounds to me like you were looking pretty close. And they call me a womanizer." Freddy forced back a chuckle. "Well, since the major seems to have caught your eye, I'm thinking you should be the one to drive down to Cheyenne and talk to her. See if she'll give us anything newsworthy. And while you're at it, take a look into the racial hate-crime angle. I'll stick around here and try to finesse what I can out of our Gang of Four and Sheriff Bosack."

Cozy looked perplexed. "You don't think any of those warmed-over peaceniks from last night are going to implicate themselves in a murder, do you?"

"Who's to say? Maybe their brains are a little on the overdone side after all their years of protesting. I can tell you this, though. The person I got that anonymous tweet about yesterday, Sarah Goldbeck, was one of the two women protesters last night. And believe me, she's the thread to our story. She was the one standing to my immediate right just before she chained herself to that bench. Pulled her photo off the internet."

"The mousy-looking woman sporting '60s-style wire-rims? That sad, lost-looking wretch orchestrated last night's fiasco?"

"I'm not sure whether she orchestrated it, but she got the disruptive ball rolling, didn't she? Let's say we quit guessing about all the whys and wherefores and who'll talk and who won't for the moment and head over to Sheriff Bosack's office to find out how far along the law is with our Gang of Four's arraignment." Freddy glanced at his watch. "Eight forty-five. My guess is not a whole lot moves around this burg before nine, so I'm thinking we've got ourselves a little time before our gang's free and we can start with the questions."

"Your call," said Cozy.

"You're damn sure agreeable this morning. You must've slept like a baby. Better than I did, I'm betting. Damn I-25 truck noise kept me up half the night."

Cozy smiled and winked at his friend. "It's a natural Caribbean siesta kind of thing, mon," he said, deciding to keep his restless nightmare of a night to himself.

"Must be genetic for damn sure, since your lanky butt grew up in Pueblo, Colorado." Freddy stood and eased his way from behind the table.

Cozy nodded as he thought briefly about the blue-collar southern Colorado steel town he'd grown up in after moving to the U.S. from the Dominican Republic at the age of six to be raised by his maternal grandmother, dead two years now. Iron-willed but loving, Andrea Delaney had come to the States with her husband, an American sailor she'd met while he'd been on leave in Bermuda and she'd been on vacation there. They'd ended up in Colorado when he'd left the navy to take a better-paying job as a steel worker in Pueblo, only to die in a mill accident a couple of years later.

"Must be," Cozy said, tossing a twenty onto the table, rising, and thinking as they left that, unlike the extravagance of Freddy's fifty the previous night, there'd be just enough change left to make a decent tip.

A few minutes later, with Cozy standing at his side ready to restrain him, Freddy Dames stood in the waiting room outside Sheriff Bosack's office, fuming. "What the shit do you mean they left for Cheyenne!" he said to Wally Sykes.

"I told you, the judge arraigned them a little after eight this morning. We don't like to let our problems fester around here." Tiny droplets of spittle accompanied the deputy's response. "The arraignees paid their disorderly conduct fines, or arranged to have them paid, and an air force van shuttled all four of them down to Warren Air Force Base a little over twenty minutes ago."

Freddy eyed Cozy, then Sykes, and finally the wall in front of him as if he were looking for something or somebody to blame. "So where the hell's the sheriff?"

"He won't be here till around ten." Freddy took two steps backward and plopped down on a narrow bench that hugged a wall in the windowless room. "I'll wait."

"Suit yourself," said Sykes, stepping back from what had been a nearly toe-to-toe stance with Freddy.

Two of a kind, Cozy thought, shaking his head.

Adjusting himself on the bench and looking as if he were prepared for a long siege, Freddy looked up at Cozy. "I want you to get on down to Warren and start digging. I'll deal with the lunkheads here in Wheatland." He glanced back at Sykes. "What a fuck-up!"

"Watch your language, Dames, or you'll do your waiting outside." Sykes eased his left hand toward the butt of his gun. Thinking, *Uh-oh,* Cozy stepped over to Freddy, grasped him firmly by the right arm, and walked him through the front door and out onto the sidewalk. "You need to stand out here for a while and calm the hell down, Freddy."

Upset by Cozy's intervention, Freddy said, "And you need to head down the road to Cheyenne, Elgin."

"Stay out here or go back to the motel, but don't take your stupid-acting ass back into that office until the sheriff arrives. Do you hear me, Freddy?"

After several seconds of silence, Freddy leaned back against the whitewashed clapboard building and said to the only person in the world besides his father who could get away with calling him stupid, "I'll try."

Satisfied that Freddy would do as he'd asked, Cozy turned to leave. "I'll call you from Warren," he said, heading for his truck.

As he limped toward the dually, he suddenly realized that he was leaving Freddy without any means of transportation. "How'll you get back to the motel?" he asked, turning back to Freddy.

"Walk."

"That'll work," Cozy said, thinking that after Freddy talked to Sheriff Bosack, a two-mile cooling-off walk might be just what the doctor called for.

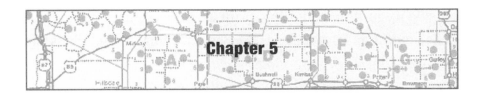
Cozy's job generally required him to pack around a laptop, cell phone, and voice-activated recorder. But unlike Freddy, who always traveled with half-a-dozen new age electronic devices, Cozy, old school to the core and suspicious of gadgets, preferred a spiral-bound notebook and a fountain pen. He'd been ordered by Freddy six months earlier to get an iPhone, but he'd ignored the request.

When he made a nine thirty a.m. call to Bernadette Cameron, told her who he was, and asked if he could drop by for an interview later that morning, he was surprised that his temperamental, call-dropping cell phone operated perfectly for once. Bernadette was professional and polite, suggesting that eleven thirty would work for a meeting.

He offered a quick "See you then," hung up, and turned back to his laptop to do some background checking on the nation's ballistic missile history, the country's current nuclear strength, and Major Bernadette Cameron. Ten minutes later he knew that the statuesque, green-eyed major had been a UCLA tennis star, an *Essence* magazine cover girl, and a swimsuit model during college, but he'd found little about her military career except that she'd been an air force officer for nine years.

A half hour later he found himself self-consciously glancing into the dually's side mirror to check on the state of his hair after gassing up in Wheatland for the drive to Cheyenne. Now, as he pulled onto F. E. Warren Air Force Base, he found himself thinking, *A kickboxing black supermodel—damn!*

Warren, the largest military installation in Wyoming, occupies a vast, flat, former hay meadow just west of I-25 and sits directly across the highway from the stadium and rodeo grounds used for the historic Cheyenne Frontier Days.

Although he'd spent twenty-six of his thirty-two years in Colorado and considered himself a Westerner through and through, Cozy found the contrast between the three alabaster-white, non-payload-bearing nuclear missiles that sat just outside the base's fence and the folksy "Daddy of 'em All" rodeo grounds just across the interstate a little strange. Thinking, *Only in America,* he pulled his truck to a stop at the guard gate, rolled down his window, flashed his press credential at the MP airman manning the booth, and said, "I'm here to see Major Bernadette Cameron. She's OSI." Uncertain why he'd added the OSI except that it sounded like a more reasonable descriptor than "swimsuit model," he waited for an okay to proceed.

When the boyish-looking MP asked, "Is the major expecting you?" instead of waving him on, Cozy said, "Yes."

The guard stepped back into his booth, checked a computer screen, and returned with a driver's-license-sized plastic base pass and a small black-and-white map of the base. "The major's office is in Building 246, sir." He handed Cozy the pass and pointed to a spot near the bottom left-hand corner of the map. "Just follow the road you're on, take a left at the second stop sign, and take that road until it dead-ends. Building 246 will be the last building on your right."

"Is everything on base so easy to access?" Cozy asked, unable to curb his reporter's instincts.

The MP, who'd obviously been asked the question before, responded with a smile. "We're air force–friendly here at Warren, sir." He snapped off a salute, pivoted, and returned to the guard booth.

Thinking that air force–friendly or not, any American military installation whose primary mission involved the handling, deployment, and activation of nuclear weapons must of necessity be armed to the teeth, Cozy pulled away from the guard gate and continued down Randall Avenue, scanning the roadsides for the high-tech deterrents and armaments he knew had to be there even though they couldn't be seen.

Building 246 turned out to be a nondescript two-story redbrick structure that sat by itself in what was still a hay meadow. A cluster of twenty-foot-tall piñon trees rose from the native Wyoming buffalo grass surrounding the building, and a small blue sign with white lettering near the front steps read simply, "Building 246." Four slightly off-kilter cement steps led up to the heavy-looking metal entry door.

Cozy parked on the street, got out of the dually, and walked up the steps through the front door into a short stub of an entryway. The entry led to a hallway that ran north and south. A sign that was too busy for its size, with arrows pointing in every direction, was tacked to the hallway wall. Spotting "AFOSI 805" near the middle of the sign and a stubby arrow below it that pointed left, Cozy shrugged and headed in that direction.

Halfway down the hallway he passed a woman dressed in civilian clothes. The woman offered him a brief inquisitive look, and they both continued walking. Major Cameron's office, the last at the end of the hall, had a substantial-looking oak door with a tarnished brass nameplate at eye level that read, "Bernadette Cameron, Major, USAF."

Cozy knocked several times before Bernadette swung the door partially open and asked, "Can I help you?"

"Hope I'm not interrupting. I'm Elgin Coseia," he said, realizing that up close, Major Cameron's dark brown hair was much curlier than it had looked from a distance. A thin, barely visible three-inch-long line of what he suspected were acne scars ran along the right angle of her jaw almost to her chin. Her skin was youthful-looking, on the dark side of café-au-lait, and as he stared at her in the dull light, it was easy to see that she was indeed striking enough to have been a model.

Avoiding his stare, she said, "No, no. Just swamped with paperwork. Come on in, Mr. Coseia." She swung the door back, extended her right hand, and offered Cozy a firm handshake. "Bernadette Cameron. Pleased to meet you."

Cozy slipped his hand out of hers to step into an orderly but confining fourteen-by-fourteen-foot room furnished with a desk and chair, a single straight-backed teakwood visitor's chair with a matching side table, a credenza, and an institutional-looking four-drawer lateral file cabinet that hugged the back wall. An expensively framed black-and-white photograph of the Eiffel Tower hung above the file cabinet, and a photograph of a smiling, flight-suited, slightly younger-looking Captain Bernadette Cameron, clasping a fighter pilot's helmet to her side and with a jet fighter in the background, sat on top of the cabinet. Next to that was a photo of a man in air force dress blues. A brigadier general's star was visible on each of the man's shoulder epaulets, and although he looked pleasant enough and was smiling, Cozy had the sense that behind the smile was someone who could be unforgiving.

Bernadette took a seat behind her desk and motioned for Cozy to pull the guest chair up to the desk. Pointing to the photo of her on the file cabinet and scooting his chair forward, Cozy asked, "You're a fighter pilot, too?"

"I used to be." There was clear regret in Bernadette's tone.

"So what kind of plane are you standing next to in the photo?"

"An A-10 Warthog. They're designed for close air support."

"Ugly-sounding name."

"As they say, beauty's in the eye of the beholder." Bernadette sat forward in her chair and forced a smile. "But we're not here to talk about my flying days, Mr. Coseia."

Sensing that he'd touched a raw nerve, Cozy said, "You're right. We're here to discuss a murder investigation."

"I'm sorry to disappoint you if that's why you're here, but the investigation into the murder that occurred at Tango-11 isn't part of my assignment. That investigation's the purview of civilian authorities. My office is purely and simply involved in addressing the security breach."

Thinking that the major's response sounded rehearsed, Cozy said, "Okay. So you're investigating a security breach and not a murder. Either way, I'd sure like to know why the air force was so quick to whisk those four antinuke protesters from last night out of Wheatland and down here to Warren."

"For questioning."

"Seems to me that Sheriff Bosack would've been the one to have first crack at them."

"There's no special order to the investigative process, Mr. Coseia. The sheriff needed to talk to the protesters, and so did we."

"Yeah. But from what I've heard, he got all of twenty minutes, while you folks down here at Warren got a lot more." Realizing suddenly that Bernadette Cameron's eyes were the same deep shade of green as his late grandmother's, Cozy found himself staring at her once again. "So where have you stashed the protesters, and when do we in the press get a crack at them?" he asked.

"They aren't stashed. They're simply being interviewed. They'll be off this base and on their way home by early afternoon, I can assure you."

"I see," said Cozy, still hoping to make contact with Sarah Goldbeck before day's end. "Is Sarah Goldbeck their ringmaster?"

"I'm afraid I can't provide you with any more specifics about the protesters, Mr. Coseia."

"Fair enough," Cozy said, not wanting to remain stuck in one gear. "Let's move on to the dead man, Thurmond Giles. Retired master sergeant, veteran of the Cold War and America's silo wars, and African American. Any chance we could have a hate crime on our hands, Major?"

"Anything's possible, Mr. Coseia."

"You're sounding less and less forthcoming, Major."

"I'm only stating fact."

"So you are," Cozy said, trying his best not to sound exasperated. "Can you tell me if there were any serious blemishes on Sergeant Giles's military record?"

"I can tell you that Sergeant Giles was discharged honorably after twenty years of service."

"Major, please. You're sounding like a windup doll. We both know that I can dig up what's in Sergeant Giles's service record. I just want to know whether or not Giles butted his head up against any air force rules during that twenty years."

"What I can tell you is that Sergeant Giles was a skilled technician and that his fitness reports indicate that he was always one of his missile detachment's best."

"Glowing reference," Cozy said, sarcastically. "Mind telling me what his job assignment was?"

Bernadette hesitated briefly before responding, "For most of his air force career, Sergeant Giles was assigned to missile maintenance squadrons."

"So his job was servicing nukes."

"If that's the terminology you prefer, yes."

"Did he have any special technical expertise?"

"The sergeant's specialty was missile-warhead maintenance."

"Hmm. So in effect, the late Sergeant Giles was what you might call an atomic-bomb maintenance expert?"

"Nuclear-missile warheads are not atomic bombs, Mr. Coseia."

"Nope, but a rose by any other name," Cozy said, shaking his head. "So let me see if I can't sort this all out. We've got a high-level security breach at a mothballed missile-silo site and a murdered man on our hands. And as it turns out, the dead man isn't just your friendly neighborhood air-conditioning and refrigerator repairman but your local atom-bomb maintenance jockey."

"Your sarcasm is not very funny, Mr. Coseia."

"Perhaps not. So what about the racial angle? Anything there?"

"It will be looked into thoroughly. We've already been in contact with the local NAACP."

"I see," Cozy said, sitting back in his chair. "Has the air force had any past problems at Tango-11?"

"None."

"What about problems at other deactivated missile-silo sites?"

"Nothing more than what you'd expect. Minor vandalism, rare instances of trespassing; that's about it. People around this part of the country know what abandoned missile-silo sites look like, and they generally stay away from them."

"Well, they didn't this time."

"And we'll ultimately find out why. Now, is there anything else I can help you with?"

"Not that I can think of at the moment," said Cozy, sensing that he was about to be shown the door. "But I'm sure that sooner or later something'll pop up. I'd appreciate having your business card if you don't mind."

"Not at all." Bernadette slipped a business card from a holder on her desk and handed it to him. "Hope I've been helpful," she said, standing and extending her right hand across the desk to the still seated Cozy.

Recognizing as he rose and Bernadette broke their handshake that in heels the statuesque major stood nearly as tall as he, Cozy asked, "Why'd you stop flying?"

Bernadette's answer came slowly. "I developed severe hay fever."

"Hay fever? The air force grounded you for that?"

"Fighter pilots can't have hay fever, Mr. Coseia. It's a nonnegotiable rule."

"Been there with the rules game a time or two myself, Major. Sorry."

The sincerity in the casually dressed, ruggedly handsome reporter's tone caused Bernadette to glance self-consciously around her office as if she were in search of an answer to a problem she hadn't been able to solve.

"Thanks for the info, Major," Cozy said, heading for the door.

"You're welcome." Watching Cozy limp across the room, she asked, "Catch a cramp?"

"Nope. Just my own special kind of hay fever," he said, leaving Bernadette standing behind her desk looking puzzled by the strange answer.

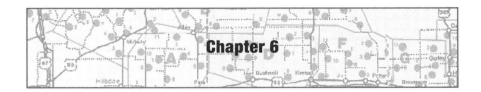

Chapter 6

During the twenty minutes that he'd been talking with Sheriff Bosack in the sheriff's spartan office, Freddy Dames hadn't been able to get one ounce of information that he considered to be worth writing about.

He had a potential blockbuster of a news story, the first salvo of which he'd been able to serve up on the web ahead of every regional news outlet in the Rockies and the Southwest. But he couldn't keep the story coming if he couldn't continue to prime the pump, and it looked as if the man he'd initially pegged as a country bumpkin, a man he now knew had once been a professional rodeo star, wasn't the rube he'd believed him to be.

The frustrated look on Freddy's face told Bosack that he was leading for the moment in what he unfortunately expected to be an ongoing race. Glancing up at the school clock on the wall behind Freddy, he said, "We've been sittin' here talkin' since close to noon, Mr. Dames, and to tell you the truth, I'm winded." Bosack rose from the leather captain's chair his staff had given him for his birthday the previous year, stepped from behind his desk, and walked over to the only window in the room to adjust the blinds.

Hoping to drag something newsworthy out of Bosack, Freddy said, "So throw me a bone, Sheriff, and I'll skedaddle."

"I've told you as much as I'm gonna, sir. You were there last night for all the shenanigans, and you're holdin' my official press release in your hands. I'm thinkin' that should about do it."

"Yeah," Freddy said, slapping the rolled-up press release down into his palm. "Who, what, when, and where, but what my readers want to know, Sheriff Bosack, is why. Why was Sergeant Giles murdered? It remains the most important of the five Ws of journalism, you know."

"Can't answer that for you, I'm afraid."

Freddy shrugged. "So what's the NAACP saying? Do they think the Giles killing was racially motivated?"

Deciding to finally toss Freddy his bone in the hope that it might get him to leave, the sheriff said, "It's sure soundin' like they do. I had the president of the local chapter down in Cheyenne, a preacher named Wilson Jackson, puffin' at me like a lovesick toad, right there where you're sittin', first thing this mornin'. Made me late deliverin' my prisoner up north to Douglas, damn it. Maybe Jackson's the one you should be talking to instead of me. Why so late in gettin' to the hate-crime issue, Mr. Dames?"

"Because nukes are a bigger story, Sheriff."

"But there aren't any nuclear weapons involved here."

"As far as you know."

Wagging an index finger at Freddy, Bosack said, "You wouldn't put somethin' out there on the World Wide Web that's not true just to garner headlines, would you, Mr. Dames?"

"Nope. I wouldn't. But I'm not so certain about my competitors. It's a get-there-first-or-be-squeezed-out-of-existence world we live in these days, Sheriff."

"Well, do me a favor and try and keep all of your news-business backstabbin' down south there in Denver, where it won't taint my little burg up here." The sheriff made a final adjustment to the blinds. "I'm thinkin' we're pretty much done for now, Mr. Dames. If I get anything worth reportin' back to you, I'll let you know."

"I won't hold my breath," Freddy said. "Got a final question for you. It's about the number of stab wounds the murder victim sustained. I understand that there were five."

"And where'd the bird come from told you that?" Bosack said, clearly surprised.

"Can't reveal my sources, Sheriff. That would be unprofessional."

"Well, professional or not, looks like I'm gonna have to put a muzzle on Doc Reed," the sheriff said, still fishing for Freddy's source.

Freddy flashed the sheriff the blankest of stares, unwilling to tell him that he'd hijacked the information about the stab wounds from someone other than Dr. Reed. "So I'm guessing we can call it a day," Freddy said, rising from his chair, shaking the sheriff's hand, and heading briskly for the door. As he pulled the door open, he called back over his shoulder, "You've got my card."

"Right there on my desk." The sheriff nodded toward the desktop.

"Good." Freddy closed the office door silently behind him, thinking as he did that Bosack might well blow a gasket if he ever found out how Freddy had learned that retired air force sergeant Thurmond Giles had died from blood loss and the irreversible shock caused by the five stab wounds in his back.

Muttering, "Money talks and bullshit walks," Freddy found

himself thanking Wally Sykes and humming a favorite Motown tune as, grinning from ear to ear, he headed across the sheriff's office parking lot, ready for the two-mile walk back to his motel and car. For a young newlywed like Sykes, with his first child on the way and in his first real job, two thousand dollars represented a lot of money. So confirming the number of stab wounds that a murder victim had sustained to a reporter, when in fact word was already out that the victim had been stabbed to death, wasn't much of an ethical breach as far as Sykes was concerned. In fact, what did it matter when from what Doc Reed had told the young deputy, three of the five stab wounds would have been fatal? And in the end, what did two thousand dollars really matter to Freddy? It was no more than what he paid his gardener each month to keep his lawn healthy and mowed and his shrubs trimmed.

Even after a thirty-year absence, Sarah Goldbeck had no trouble finding Kimiko Takata's russet Queen Anne cottage with its recently painted white trim and robin's-egg-blue gutters. The cottage on Fourth Street in downtown Laramie was a place where Sarah had spent countless hours in her late teens. But she hadn't been inside the house since her mother, a University of Nebraska physicist, and Kimiko, both prominent late '70s and early '80s antinuclear activists, had planned one of their final missile-silo protests in the living room. Dead for more than twelve years now, her mother had once been editor of the *Bulletin of the Atomic Scientists,* a member of the peace activist group NukeWatch, and a close friend of many of America's leading antinuclear activists, including the leading activist of that period, Philip Berrigan.

Sarah had been in her early teens during most of her and her mother's visits to the cottage on Fourth Street. Old enough and well schooled enough to appreciate and understand what Kimiko and her mother were involved in.

She had marched beside the two of them back then. Walked and chanted "No more nukes" with them and scores of other antinuclear activists, including her now common-law husband, Buford, who was currently resting at their Hawk Springs, Wyoming, home, nursing his pride and testicular injuries following their morning grilling by OSI officers at Warren.

It was hard for her to believe that thirty years earlier, Kimiko's house had been the staging place for demonstrations that would for years wave the antinuke flag and goad air force personnel, FBI agents, and the police. A place where Kimiko and Sarah's mother had planned how to vandalize nuclear-missile sites and where she'd learned to antagonize silo guards without being arrested and to chain herself to the entry gates of sites across the Rocky Mountain West.

Then, in a flash, it was all over. The notoriety, the glamour, the purpose. First came two strategic arms limitation treaties, SALT I in 1972 and then SALT II in 1979, followed by the INF treaty of 1988 and the current international strategic arms reduction treaty. All of these pacts bargained away America's intercontinental ballistic missile strength while at the same time marginalizing the antinuclear movement.

It didn't matter that developments in missile guidance technology now made long-range nuclear missiles all but obsolete, or that in the more than forty years since their introduction nature's very own forces—water, erosion, and corrosion—had rendered the missile silos beneath the American heartland virtually useless. What mattered to her now was the fact that most of the people she'd grown up idealizing, even worshipping, were dead, and their cause and many of the reasons for it had come and gone.

She'd therefore been surprised and certainly curious when, six months earlier, Rikia Takata, two years her junior and a boy she'd played with as a child in the house on Fourth Street, had called her and suggested that they meet and talk about a new battery of antinuclear strategies.

Since then she'd met half-a-dozen times with Rikia and his now reclusive cousin, Kimiko, but never at the cottage on Fourth Street. They'd discussed ways to try once again to put the antinuclear movement on American front pages and back in the public eye.

Their meetings, however, had usually turned out to be unproductive and almost always consisted of Rikia sitting and reading or staring off into space while Kimiko, a World War II–era Japanese internment camp survivor, reminisced about bygone nuclear protest days or pined over the loss of relatives at Hiroshima.

Now, as Sarah continued up the sidewalk toward the front door of the house on Fourth Street, realizing as she reached the porch that it had settled so that it now sloped badly to the east, she thought about the recent events at Tango-11 and why she was really there. She found herself regretting the fact that just six months earlier she'd become a part of an antinuclear revival party that she never should have joined.

She'd called ahead from Hawk Springs to let Kimiko know she was on her way to Laramie to talk about things they dared not discuss on the phone. As she stood on the porch steps, head turned, looking back into the sunshine and over Kimiko's immaculately manicured front lawn, she had the sense that she had stepped back in time.

The feeling of nostalgia passed quickly, and she found herself thinking about a man whom she, Kimiko, and Rikia had all once known: Thurmond Giles. A man they now needed to talk about openly and frankly. There could be no reminiscing about the past, and she'd make certain that today there'd be no staring off into space by Rikia, no retelling of sixty-five-year-old Japanese history by Kimiko, and no discussion of the old protest days by herself. Someone they'd all detested had been murdered, and ultimately they'd all likely be suspects. Everyone would speak his or her mind this time around. This time nothing could be left unsaid.

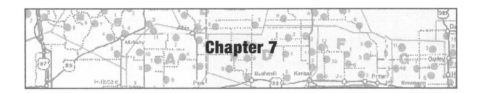

Chapter 7

Staring at Freddy Dames in disbelief as he strained to be heard over the engine rumble of the half-dozen idling eighteen-wheelers surrounding his pickup, Cozy practically yelled across the seat, "Freddy, you what?"

"You heard me," Freddy shot back, watching Cozy check out the pump prices at Cheyenne's Flying J truck stop. "I paid the little snot of a deputy for the information about the stab wounds. Now we know one thing for sure. Giles could have died from any one of at least three stab wounds in the back. According to Sykes, the other two were too superficial to have killed him." Freddy shifted his weight forward in the seat and glanced through the windshield at the darkening sky. "Looks like we'll be heading into rain on the drive home. Hope we don't catch any hail," he said, looking out toward his Bentley, which sat a couple of gas pumps away, already fueled.

"Damn it, Freddy! Would you stay on point?"

"I will if you'll try and remember this: no harm, no foul. We've got a news story that could earn us a Pulitzer, man."

"Or time behind bars."

"There you go again, turning all negative on me. For once would you try thinking a little more positive?"

"Yeah, positive," Cozy said, thinking, *You passed on a major league baseball career when you had all the tools to be a star, and instead you cruised around the world for half a decade drinking champagne and screwing anything in a skirt. And now, after buying some two-bit, web-based news outlet that peddles information that's barely a cut above gossip, you're looking for the big score.*

Not wanting to press the issue, Freddy said, "So here's the agenda. I want you to head over to Hawk Springs, talk to the Goldbeck woman, and get her and her swollen-balled husband's take on the Giles murder. In the meantime, I'll post a story or two back in Denver."

"Are you sure Hawk Springs is where they live?"

"Yes. I had Lillian dig up the dirt on them, and you know what that means. The information's rock-solid. Lillian turned over a few other rocks, too. Turns out Goldbeck's mother was a prominent University of Nebraska physicist and a mover and shaker in the antinuke movement during the late '70s and early '80s. Seems Sarah went underground between the time the movement faded and when her mother died. For most of the past twenty-five years she's been living in Hawk Springs, earning a pretty good living as a potter."

"Guess if Lillian's the one who dug up the info, it's golden," Cozy said, aware that Lillian Griffith, Freddy's rat terrier of an executive administrative assistant whom Freddy paid $200,000 a year, rarely made mistakes.

Eyeing the nearly pitch-black sky, Freddy said, "I better get started for Denver. By the way, you haven't told me what you got out of that sexy kickboxing major this morning." Freddy cupped his testicles and smiled. "I'm thinking she could put a love hurt on you till you screamed. Wouldn't want to piss her off, though."

"Not much, but I did find out that Sergeant Giles was a nuclear-warhead maintenance expert and that Major Cameron, that's her name, has had a few calls from the local NAACP about the murder being a hate crime."

"Funny, I got the same thing from Sheriff Bosack. He said that some black preacher out of Cheyenne had been doggin' him, saying the murder had to be a hate crime, too."

"The hate-crime issue sure wasn't at the top of Major Cameron's list of reasons for the murder," said Cozy.

"What was, then?"

"Nukes. Them and somebody out there looking for a little revenge."

"Insightful lady. My top take, too," said Freddy.

"Pretty *Twilight Zone* crazy, if you ask me."

Freddy cracked a sly smile. "Yeah. Just crazy enough to keep the Digital Registry News name on people's lips and out there on the airwaves for months. I've already posted one story. I'll make sure that what I post next hypes a possible racial motive for the killing and also profiles sad little Sarah Goldbeck all grown up. By the way, I got the name of that preacher who's been pestering Major Cameron and Sheriff Bosack. Wilson Jackson. A man with two last names." Freddy shook his head. "Never have liked dealing with anybody with two last names. Always means there's an overactive ego involved somewhere."

Smiling at Freddy's assessment, Cozy said, "I'm less worried about egos than I am about screwing with the air force and the government."

"Do you know anybody who better deserves a screwing?" Freddy asked with a chuckle, just as several large raindrops splattered against the truck's windshield. "Hey, I'm outta here." He swung his door open, ready to sprint for his car. "Need your story on Goldbeck by tonight, and make it a good one. We need the pub," Freddy called back over his shoulder.

Watching Freddy try his best to outrun raindrops and thinking back to their years on the baseball diamond, Cozy smiled and whispered, "Slide, Freddy, slide."

Bernadette Cameron's office was rich with the scent of freshly cut alfalfa. She'd learned to dread the sweet, pollen-rich smell that always filled the room right after a heavy rain and announced that her hay fever would quickly kick into high gear for at least the next couple of days.

She was busy poring over papers, missile-silo site maps, charts, and military personnel records. Maps now covered most of her desktop. Maps with hundreds of red dots that pinpointed the locations of deactivated air force missile silos across Montana, North and South Dakota, Nebraska, Wyoming, Colorado, and Missouri.

For close to two hours she'd been trying to come up with a connection between the Tango-11 break-in, the Giles murder, and the hundreds of air force flight squadrons and flight wings that had once overseen a thousand land-based missile sites and just over 2,300 nuclear warheads during the height of the Cold War. She hadn't found a connection, but she knew a lot more about

Thurmond Giles than she'd known hours earlier. She knew, for instance, that Giles had served most of his twenty years in the air force as a member, at one time or another, of the 564th Minuteman Missile Squadron at Malmstrom Air Force Base in Great Falls, Montana; the 66th Strategic Missile Squadron at Ellsworth Air Force Base in Rapid City, South Dakota; the 321st Strategic Missile Wing at Grand Forks Air Force Base in North Dakota; and finally her own 90th Missile Wing at Warren. She'd also discovered that Giles had at least one very large blemish on an otherwise distinguished air force career. While stationed in Rapid City, he'd run afoul of regs forbidding fraternizing between enlisted men and officers. That indiscretion had involved a liaison with a female lieutenant, and it had cost him a pay cut, a reduction in rank, and a transfer.

The lieutenant, who at the time had been married to a civilian air force contractor, had been a nuclear-warhead electronics expert. Details concerning the affair had been hard to piece together, but Bernadette had been able to uncover the fact that Lieutenant Annette Colbain and her husband, Howard, were white, that the punishment meted out to Giles and Colbain had been pretty much equal, and that Lieutenant Colbain had received a career-busting flag-officer-level reprimand, a transfer to Whiteman Air Force Base in Missouri, and a pay cut. Six months later her marriage had ended in divorce.

Bernadette hadn't yet been able to determine what had happened to Annette Colbain's husband or how he'd reacted to his wife's affair, but she did know that Annette Colbain had left the service after a three-year tour of duty and that Sergeant Giles's otherwise distinguished, much-decorated military career had drifted laterally and then downhill after the incident. Reasoning that Howard Colbain might have had at least two reasons for wanting to kill Giles, jealousy and revenge, she sat back from her desk and decided to take a break. As she sneezed and walked over to the only window to check on the rain, she had the sense that the answers to the Thurmond Giles murder and the Tango-11 security breach wouldn't come easily or quickly.

Thunder, wind noise, and the sound of BB-sized pellets of hail hitting her window gave the rolling High Plains thunderstorm a sense of raw power. Aware that hail damage, power outages, and flooding were part of life in southeastern Wyoming, she'd begun to wonder whether the storm might not have flooded the engine compartment of her ground-hugging Austin-Healey when a light tapping on her office door broke her concentration. She'd barely uttered, "Come in," when Colonel Joel DeWitt pushed open the door and walked in. Eyeing the maps and piles of paperwork on her desk before looking her up and down from head to toe as if he were hoping to find some flaw in her appearance, he said, "Working hard, I see."

"I've been trying to come up with a motive for the Giles murder," Bernadette said, turning to face her up-bucking superior. DeWitt, now a desk jockey like her, constantly boasted about his three-month stint as an Iraq War A-10 pilot. In addition to being a braggart, DeWitt was also a man who constantly played air force politics and had a reputation for crushing the careers of subordinates. Suppressing a sigh, Bernadette walked back to her desk and took a seat.

"Seems pretty simple to me," said DeWitt, who remained standing. "Our former crackerjack warhead maintenance sergeant paid the price for rubbing someone the wrong way."

"Perhaps. But if so, why the missile-silo theatrics? Why not just dump his body in a dark alley somewhere and be done with it?"

"Beats me."

"Well, it sure has me puzzled," said Bernadette. "There has to be a reason that Giles ended up at Tango-11."

"I'm thinking the reason is more than likely linked to those antinuke protesters from last night. Maybe they wanted to let people know that they're still around. So they decided to hang the good sergeant upside down from his ankles at a silo site to get the publicity ball rolling once again."

Bernadette shook her head. "I'm not buying it. They had their hour in the sun. And why the genital mutilation?"

"That I can't answer," DeWitt said with a shrug. "But I know this. Those antinuclear folks have been linked to killings before. What about that Echo-9 fiasco over in Bismarck several years back? You're a little too young to remember that, though."

"I've read about it. But that was different. A truck on its way back to town to pick up more protesters skidded on ice and plowed into those airmen at Echo-9."

"Factually, you're correct, Major, but those airmen wouldn't have died if the protesters hadn't been there. So, in my book, any way you slice it, a bunch of antinuke wackos triggered those boys' deaths."

"And if our protesters from last night turn out not to have been involved in the events at Tango-11? What then?"

"Then I'd pursue the hate-crime angle. I've had NAACP types calling and traipsing through my office all day, spearheaded by a local-yokel preacher named Wilson Jackson. What a bag of wind."

Thinking, *Takes one to know one,* and recalling her own phone conversation with Reverend Jackson, Bernadette nodded understandingly. "Have you had a look at Sergeant Giles's UIF papers?"

"Of course."

"He had some problems, sir."

"He had *one* problem, Major, and it cost him a loss in rank and a transfer," DeWitt said, sounding defensive.

"What eventually happened to Lieutenant Colbain and her husband?" Bernadette asked, suspecting from the colonel's reaction that he more than likely had insight into the Annette Colbain–Thurmond Giles story that she didn't.

"My understanding is that Lieutenant Colbain left the service when her tour was up. I had Sergeant Milliken do some extra digging into what happened to her and her husband in the long run. Turns out the husband still does civilian contracting for the air force. Milliken couldn't get a solid lead on the lieutenant."

"What does the husband do?"

"The same thing he did before his wife started two-timing him. Heavy-equipment transport. Hauling around pipe and dozers and Cats—things like that."

"So he's still got a link to the kind of equipment and the kind of materials used in the construction and repair of missile silos. Interesting."

"Very."

"Sounds like Mr. Colbain is someone I should talk to."

"I'd start with Sergeant Milliken, then. If anyone can get the lowdown on Colbain and his unfaithful, under-the-radar ex-wife, that man can."

"I'll do that," Bernadette said.

"By the way, has the coroner's report come in on Giles, and have you been able to find out what he did for a living after he left the air force?"

"All I've been able to find out so far is that he went to work for an electronics firm in Seattle after he retired. And there's no official coroner's report yet. But I do have verbal confirmation that three of the five stab wounds in Giles's back were serious enough to have killed him, and that wadded-up piece of paper they found stuffed in his mouth along with the head of his penis was probably used to shut him up and to absorb blood. There weren't any fingerprints on the paper, but Sheriff Bosack said it's probably a piece torn from a map of Wyoming's missile-silo sites. He's faxing me a photocopy of it."

"Sounds like the killer needed a map to get to Tango-11. Now, that's strange," DeWitt said, stroking his chin thoughtfully. "You'll need to look into the issue more thoroughly, Major. There's one other thing you need to keep in mind. Our job here is to handle the security-breach issue, not to investigate a murder."

"I know that, sir. That's why I'm going to take a closer look at that protest leader from last night."

"The Goldbeck woman. Why? You already talked to her and her minions. What more is there to learn?"

"I did, but that was here on our turf, where I'd expect her to have her guard up. I've been thinking that a follow-up interview at her home in Hawk Springs might yield better results."

"There's nothing much out there but sagebrush and gophers, you know."

"And the pottery shop she runs," said Bernadette. "Goldbeck mentioned the shop during the interrogation this morning. She's pretty proud of it. I've checked out her website, which looks, by the way, as if it could've been designed by the animation folks at DreamWorks. Her pottery sells for thousands."

"Sounds like she's making enough money to finance a few protests."

"Or a murder. I'll know more after talking to her this evening."

Looking at Bernadette as if she somehow posed a threat, DeWitt said, "Good. Get what you can out of her, but remember, don't have the air force take any lumps. We've already had enough unnecessary publicity with this Tango-11 thing to carry us through the year. Preachers, protesters, media types, and of course that smear piece on the web."

"What smear piece?"

"A trash piece by some web-based outfit out of Denver calling themselves Digital Registry News. Surprised you haven't seen it. They obviously had a reporter at Sheriff Bosack's press conference last night. The story was written by the Digital Registry News publisher himself, some flake named Frederick Dames." Watching a flash of recognition spread across Bernadette's face, DeWitt asked, "Know him?"

"No, but I think I've met his wingman. A tall, curly-headed, athletic-looking guy named Elgin Coseia. He dropped by my office earlier today. Pumped me for information for a good half hour. What was the story on the web about?"

"What's with any news story these days? Mudslinging and hype. I suggest you have a look at the piece and judge for yourself, Major. Especially since you're mentioned in it."

"I'll do that. Right now, in fact." Unnerved, Bernadette spun around in her chair and turned on the computer on the credenza behind her.

"Just remember, as far as this Tango-11 investigation goes, no news is good news for the both of us, Major."

"I'll keep that in mind," Bernadette said, upset with herself for having talked to Cozy Coseia.

"Here's a final piece of advice," said DeWitt, turning to leave. "You need to work on masking your feelings a tad better. I'd say from the look on your face that if that Coseia fellow were here right now, you'd take his head off."

"I'll work on the problem," Bernadette said, knowing she'd be fighting an uphill battle. Hiding her feelings had never been her style, nor had biting her tongue. Her grandfather, a Tuskegee airman, hadn't been able to do either when he'd once told Eleanor Roosevelt, when she'd visited Tuskegee at FDR's request, that Negroes could fly airplanes as well as, if not better than, any white man. And her outspoken father, an air force fighter pilot during Vietnam who should have been one of only three American aces from that war but who was never credited, had always had the same problem.

Kimiko Takata's house looked smaller, more confining, and much darker inside than Sarah Goldbeck remembered. The only thing that seemed the same after such a long absence was the smell of ginger that filled the living room where she, Kimiko, and Rikia now sat.

Kimiko had greeted her at the front door with a polite bend from the waist before ushering her into a living room filled with lithographs of Japanese country scenes, expensive Japanese pottery, and Oriental rugs. The room's furniture, as delicate as that in a dollhouse, was exactly as Sarah remembered. Thinking that someone who'd spent a year and a half living in barracks in an internment camp should want more light, Sarah kept her thoughts to herself, taking a seat only after she'd been offered one and smiling at Rikia Takata, who'd given her a limp-wristed handshake before quickly taking a seat in a chair next to the room's small bay window and immediately starting to clean his fingernails with a small screwdriver.

Looking embarrassed, Kimiko said, "It's great to have Sarah come to visit after such a long time, isn't it, Rikia?"

Slightly built, fragile-looking, and severely tongue-tied for most of his formative years—so severely tongue-tied, in fact, that even after corrective surgery as a teenager he still had a noticeable speech impediment—Rikia, who'd always looked oddly out of place to Sarah with his buzz cut, classic Asian features, and oblong face, simply nodded.

Before seating herself, Kimiko rolled a tea cart with cups, a large pot of steeping tea, a bowl of cubed sugar, and a dozen or so raspberry-filled jelly pastries into the living room from the kitchen.

As Sarah studied Kimiko's face, she realized that the woman who'd once been her mother's best friend looked every bit of her seventy-six years. Her once thick, coal-black hair was now thin and gray. Her eyes were cloudy, and she'd lost a few pounds over the years.

Ignoring Sarah's stare, Kimiko quickly filled three cups with tea and, without asking Rikia or Sarah if they cared for any, offered the cups to them, sat back, and adjusted herself in her seat. Plopping two cubes of sugar into her tea, she asked, "How did things go during your interrogation at Warren this morning?"

"Fine," said Sarah, still upset that neither Kimiko nor Rikia had felt it necessary to take part in the Wheatland courthouse protest that Kimiko had helped organize. "Fine in spite of Buford's injury, that is. Some overzealous air force officer, a woman, no less, kicked him in his privates during the protest. I was so angry about being hauled down to Warren from Wheatland and interrogated like a common criminal that I forgot to mention Buford's injury when I called you earlier."

"Is Buford all right?" Kimiko asked.

"He's sore, but he is okay."

"A woman," Rikia said, indignantly, straining to correctly enunciate his words. "Leave it to the U.S. military to turn a ballerina into a brute."

"You're right there," said Sarah.

Sensing a need to move quickly past Rikia's upset, Kimiko said, "I didn't think there'd be as much television coverage as there has been about the protest. Especially since all we were really hoping for was to take advantage of the events at Tango-11 and enlighten people."

"Well, we ignited a bonfire," said Rikia, beaming.

"I'm not sure we did," said Sarah. "But what's selling is a

murder, not our message. But for what it's worth, we did have a dozen TV crews at the protest last night. Some from as far away as Denver and Salt Lake City."

Rikia rubbed his hands together excitedly and shouted, "Good! Good! Good!" An authoritative glance from Kimiko silenced him.

"So where do we go from here?" Sarah asked, watching the rebuked-looking Rikia take a long sip of tea.

"I'm not sure that we go anywhere," said Kimiko. "We've made our point. At least for the moment."

"But there are hundreds of other missile-silo sites out there," said Rikia, looking disappointed.

"But none I'd wager with a dead man dangling on the grounds," said Sarah.

Rikia sat forward in his chair, prepared to offer a response, but the stern, intimidating, and unwavering look on Kimiko's face told him that the best thing he could do right then was to remain silent. Looking pleased when he did, Kimiko smiled and offered Sarah more tea.

Sarah watched the steaming tea flow into her cup. Nodding a thank-you to Kimiko, she took a sip of the lemony tea and relaxed back in her seat to think about where the three of them were headed from there.

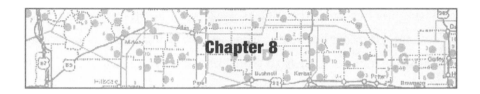

Chapter 8

Muscular and clean-shaven from the crown of his head to the tips of his toes, Silas Breen was a slow-thinking, freckle-faced, six-foot-nine-inch, twenty-four-year-old giant of a black man with a strong resemblance to Howdy Doody. A Gulliver among Lilliputians, he had once been a high school basketball star, clumsy but powerful enough to overwhelm his prep school counterparts for four years and earn himself a college athletic scholarship to Kansas State. But after a year of college ball, his coaches could see that smaller, quicker, and more thoughtful players would forever run circles around the chubby-cheeked Breen.

With his scholarship gone and his academic skills weak, Breen dropped out of college after the first semester of his sophomore year to bump his way around the West for a couple of years, making stops in Santa Fe, Denver, Rapid City, and Bozeman before finding his niche.

Eleven months earlier he'd bought a used twenty-six-foot U-Haul Super Mover truck at auction; put a set of illegally recapped tires on it; reconditioned the radiator, transmission, and rear end; painted the truck shamrock green except for its white cab and cargo-bay roof, in honor of his beloved Fighting Irish of Notre Dame; stenciled "Breen's Moving & Storage Company" on the side panels; and gone into the moving and hauling business.

Using his brawn and contacts that his father had from twenty-five years as an army supply sergeant, he'd made enough money since starting his business to think about hiring someone to help him, and maybe after that to buy a second truck.

But those were matters he planned to look into after he finished his current job, a long-haul trip that would earn him big dollars. He wasn't sure why he'd ended up landing the plum of hauling old hospital equipment from Ottawa, Ontario, to Amarillo, Texas, especially since he was being paid 20 percent over scale, but he was happy he had.

There were a few oddball things about the gig besides the fact that it had materialized out of the blue, the most glaring one being the fact that he didn't know for certain who'd hired him. But when it came to the sort of money he was getting, Silas didn't much care.

What he did know about the person who'd hired him was that only their first communication had been by phone. Every contact since then had been by fax, including the one telling him he'd been hired. He'd been paid half down for his services: $3,100 in cash that had arrived at his apartment in Buffalo, New York, in a padded, heavily taped ten-by-thirteen-inch manila envelope one day before he was to start the job. The envelope had borne a Las Vegas postmark and no return address. The only other things he knew for certain were that the name F. MANTEW always appeared in capital letters on his correspondent's faxes and that F. Mantew wanted his shipment delivered within three days.

When he'd picked up his load three hours earlier from a warehouse in Ottawa, most of the seven-ton shipment had been crated. He hadn't paid serious attention to his primary cargo, twenty heavily banded eight-by-four-by-four-foot crates, other than to marvel at their stoutness, and since he wasn't about to look his gift horse in the mouth, he'd attributed that stoutness to OSHA shipping regs.

The combination of his cash down payment and F. Mantew's secrecy had, nonetheless, put him in an inquisitive mood, and he'd made certain that the twenty crates matched up exactly with what was printed on his shipping documents and bill of lading. He'd also decided to take a more thorough look at his cargo when he stopped for the night in South Bend, Indiana, to pay homage to the Notre Dame campus and the Fighting Irish.

Now on the outskirts of Syracuse and cruising along comfortably at sixty-five after a forgettable trip down I-81 from Ottawa, Silas had a feeling that although he wasn't necessarily headed for trouble, he might be headed for a surprise. Trying his best to convince himself that concern about his shipment was unwarranted and that he had three full days ahead of him to ride his current wave, he slipped a Muddy Waters disc into his grease-stained dashboard CD player and began humming along to the old blues master's four-minute-long lost-love lament. Reminding himself that he, not F. Mantew, was in the driver's seat for now, he hummed a little louder.

He had half the money due him in his pocket, and, more importantly, he was in possession of F. Mantew's goods. Leaning down and feeling beneath his seat for the crowbar that had once belonged to his grandfather, he forced a smile. He'd never liked surprises, even as a child. So if any surprises were in store, he might as well be ready with a surprise of his own. And if Granddad's crowbar wasn't enough to handle that surprise, the .32 in his glove compartment certainly was. His reluctant smile turned into a grin as he sat back up to focus on the road. The grin became broader as he hummed along with Muddy and fantasized about what would be his first trip ever to Notre Dame.

Bernadette left Cheyenne for Hawk Springs, Wyoming, an hour and a half ahead of Cozy's departure for the same windswept community. She'd stopped outside the tiny community of LaGrange to have a look at two decommissioned missile sites, Bravo-10 and Bravo-11, a little before four p.m., hoping to see for herself just how secure the sites were. She also hoped to ferret out any possible link between those two sites and the murder that had occurred at Tango-11. A rainstorm had followed her most of the way from Cheyenne, petering out just before LaGrange and leaving behind a massive arching rainbow.

After rummaging around the abandoned Bravo-10 and -11 sites for fifteen minutes each, looking for linkages and clues to the Giles murder, she decided that, aside from the lingering post-thunderstorm wind howl and the half rainbow that remained, there was little to suggest that she wasn't traipsing around some barren moonscape in search of nonexistent clues.

She had received one piece of additional information about Thurmond Giles before leaving Warren that she thought might ultimately prove helpful. The information had come by way of the pesky, persistent, never-take-no-for-an-answer Sergeant Milliken, who'd told her that Giles had been an interservice league basketball star for at least five of his twenty years in the air force and that he'd had friends in high places who'd used his hardwood skills to wave the air force flag. She planned to follow up on that information once she returned to Warren. Now, with her clothes sticking to her, her hair curling up from the humidity, and not one shred of helpful information gleaned from Bravo-10 or -11, she slipped back into the comfort of her air-conditioned air force–blue Jeep and headed for Hawk Springs. As she gained speed, she thought that although it was unlikely, it was entirely possible that Sergeant Giles's death and the security breach at Tango-11 had nothing to do with Giles's ethnicity, with nuclear missiles, or with revenge, and she wondered what she might be overlooking.

The trail of dust rising from behind Bernadette's Jeep caused Buford Kane to get up from his chair on the front porch of the log home he'd built almost single-handedly and mutter, "Who the hell?"

As he stood clutching the ice pack that had been resting in his lap, he spotted the air force emblem on the Jeep's door, shouted, "Damn it!" and slammed the ice pack to the porch floor. Mumbling, "Shit," he stroked his ratty-looking beard; stared down the winding gravel road leading uphill to his house; and hobbled, testicles throbbing, into the house to return with a Remington 12-gauge, pump-action shotgun. He aimed the gun squarely at the nose of the approaching Jeep, following it with the barrel as it snaked its way toward him. Less than a minute later, Bernadette stopped the Jeep twenty yards from Buford's front porch, slipped out of the vehicle, and walked cautiously toward him, stopping at the foot of the porch steps.

Recognizing her, with his shotgun still aimed at the Jeep, he thought about the pain and humiliation she'd caused him. "Can't you read, lady? There're no-trespassin' signs tacked to every damn fence on this place. And just for the record, just so I don't say somethin' politically incorrect, mind tellin' me if you're one of them don't-ask, don't-tell lesbians the military seems intent on recruitin' these days?" Buford snickered for a second before the look on his face turned deadly serious. "Why in the hell are you here, Major?"

Sounding and looking unintimidated, Bernadette said, "I'm hoping you might help me a little more with my Tango-11 investigation by answering a few follow-up questions. I'd like to get more information on any other antinuclear people who might not have been with you last night, and I'd appreciate what you can tell me about Reverend Wilson Jackson. I'd also like it if you'd set that shotgun you're holding aside. I'll only take a few minutes of your time, and Ms. Goldbeck's, of course. Is she home?"

"No, she ain't. As for me, I'll give you your frickin' few minutes." Aiming his shotgun at the nose of the Jeep, he squeezed off two rounds. Moments later, lime-green antifreeze started dripping onto the ground. "Think you're gonna need a tow," Buford said, grinning.

"You're using very poor judgment, Mr. Kane," Bernadette said, unflinching.

"You're the one using poor judgment, lady. Let me share a little somethin' with you. Twenty-five years ago, before I hooked up with Sarah, I was a biker. And not just any old kinda biker, either. You ever heard of the Outlaws?"

Bernadette nodded, aware from years of living in the Golden

State that the California-based Outlaws had once battled the Hells Angels for American biker-gang supremacy.

Still grinning, Buford said, "Bet you thought that since my old lady's a pacifist, I'm one, too. Well, I ain't, sweetie, and her bein' antinuclear sure as hell don't translate into me bein' antigun."

Eyeing the porch steps and suspecting that in three to four quick strides she could be on top of him, Bernadette said, "Why don't you put the shotgun down, Mr. Kane."

"And if I don't? What then? You got the balls to disarm me?"

"I won't be leaving until we talk, sir."

Looking suddenly less sure of himself, Buford took a long, deep breath. "Okay, then. You can stand there in the sun and sweat because we won't be talkin' about nothin' anytime soon."

"Then we can both sweat," Bernadette said, smiling and relaxing into a parade-rest stance.

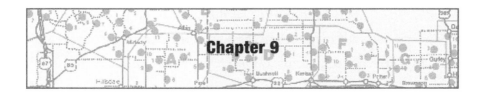

Chapter 9

A rusty no-trespassing sign swung lazily from the top wire of the fence that represented the western boundary of Buford Kane's thirty acres. Staring at the sign, Cozy briefly stopped the dually before continuing across a cattle guard that marked the property entry. A hundred or so yards later he stopped again and slipped his binoculars out of the glove compartment to take a better look at the house at the end of the winding gravel lane. When he spotted the frustrated-looking man Bernadette Cameron had taken out of commission the previous evening holding a shotgun on her, he whispered, "Oh, shit!"

Slipping a baseball bat from beneath his front seat, he stepped out of the truck and took off in a sprint through knee-high timothy grass toward the house. Halfway there his left leg began to throb. Forced to jog, he suddenly found himself thinking, *Pick off.* He slowed to a walk and finally slipped out of the tall grass and behind a line of cottonwoods that bordered a dry creek bed just west of the house. With the cottonwoods obstructing any view that the man with the shotgun might have of him, he worked his way toward the house. Realizing that he wasn't simply sweating but huffing and puffing, he told himself he'd be spending a little more time in the gym.

Stepping from behind the last of the cottonwoods, he headed for the porch in a half crouch. His leg had started to tingle, a sure sign that any second it might give out on him. Wondering why he hadn't simply driven up to the house, he reminded himself that if he had, the shotgun-toting man might have opened fire on the major. As he duck-walked his way along the length of the house's three-foot-high cinder-block foundation toward the front porch, he thought, *Hope the major's as quick on her feet as she was last night.* Huddled safely below the top of the foundation, he glanced up toward the porch's safety railing, took a deep breath, popped his head just above the porch floor, and slipped his bat between two railing support struts. Leveraging the bat firmly against one of the two-by-two struts with enough force to pop it with a loud crack, he yelled, "Pick off!" and dove for the ground, leaving the bat behind on the porch.

The shotgun blast that followed took out two more support struts. Then Cozy heard a thud, followed by the telltale gasping sound of someone who had had the wind knocked out of him.

He rose to his knees to see Bernadette, up on the porch, standing over the shotgun-wielding man's outstretched body. She was holding Cozy's baseball bat, the fat end of which she'd shoved into Buford Kane's belly, in her right hand and watching Kane roll around on the porch clutching his midsection and sucking air. The intense look on Bernadette's face shouted anything but *air force–friendly.*

Staring at the bat and then at Bernadette, knowing full well what it was like to have the business end of a thirty-five-ounce piece of hickory jammed into your stomach, Cozy said, "Looks like you're two for two with your friend there."

Nudging the shotgun out of Buford Kane's reach with the toe of her shoe and tossing the bat aside, Bernadette said, "And I hope that ends it." It was only when she knelt to check on Kane's breathing that Cozy realized her hands were trembling.

Sarah Goldbeck arrived ten minutes later to find Buford strapped to a straight-backed chair on the porch and Cozy and Bernadette sitting in rocking chairs on either side of him. Buford's forearms were free, and he was awkwardly sipping water, but with Cozy's belt tightly looped around the subdued-looking redheaded ex-biker's torso, Buford was still having trouble breathing.

In response to Sarah's "What on earth!" as she bounded up the porch steps, Buford wheezed, "I'm not sayin' nothin' till the sheriff gets here."

Glancing at the shotgun lying beside Cozy's rocker, then at the damaged porch railing, Sarah looked disappointedly at Buford and said, "Well, somebody better explain what happened—and right now!"

Bernadette's description of what had occurred was punctuated by wheezes and intermittent apologetic looks from Buford. Bernadette also introduced Cozy as a reporter from Digital Registry News who was there to do a follow-up on the Tango-11 break-in.

Teary-eyed and doing her best to come to grips with what she'd just been told, Sarah looked pleadingly at Bernadette. "Please don't file charges, Major Cameron; please. Buford's been in trouble with the law before. Serious trouble. I didn't mention that to you this morning down at Warren. I figured if I did, it would surely buy us more trouble. He was a biker before we met, and he's got a criminal record. Please don't call the sheriff. If you do, his past will catch up with him, and I'll lose him for sure. He's been such a decent man for so many years."

The graying, stringy-haired, owl-eyed woman's pleas reminded Bernadette of those she'd once heard uttered by her own mother, a woman who'd spent most of her married life trying to get her hard-drinking husband, whom she dearly loved, to stop drinking.

"I'm not here to press charges against your husband, Ms. Goldbeck," Bernadette said. "As I told you this morning, my responsibility is to investigate the Tango-11 security breach. I can't, however, speak for Mr. Coseia."

"I'm just here to report the news," Cozy said, surprising everyone.

Looking relieved and nodding excitedly at her common-law husband, Sarah said, "We can help you with both those things, can't we, Buford?"

Buford aimed a reluctant "Yes" in the direction of the approaching twilight.

"Good," said Bernadette, as she tried to gauge exactly how upset Colonel DeWitt was going to be at having an air force vehicle disabled by a shotgun blast, not to mention the minor issue of Cozy being on the scene. Locking eyes with Sarah, she said, "Now that we're all on the same page, what more can you tell me about those protesting friends of yours from last night? Something you may have forgotten to mention when we talked this morning, perhaps? Anything about the real size of your group?"

"Nothing more. And that's the truth," Sarah said adamantly. "Most of those other people who were yelling and chanting were simply high school or college kids out for a night of excitement. Wilson Jackson, that preacher I told you about this morning, paid them twenty dollars each to come to the press conference and disrupt it." Looking over at Buford, who was still wheezing, she said, "Can't you unstrap him from that chair?"

"If he agrees to sit still and be cooperative."

"He will." Sarah shot the deflated-looking former biker a look that said, *Sit still, and don't you dare move a muscle.*

"Might as well unstrap him," Bernadette said to Cozy.

Rubbing the circulation back into his arms, the burly redhead let out a grunt of relief and said to Sarah, "Why don't you tell the major about Kimiko not showin' up last night?"

"Why drag her into this?"

"Because she and that ivory-towered nutcase of a nephew of hers said they were comin', and they didn't. Left you holdin' the bag, as usual. I never have understood the connection between the three of you anyway."

When Cozy pulled a stubby pencil and a small spiral-bound notebook out of his back pocket and began writing, Buford said, "That's K-i-m-i-k-o. It's Japanese. And her nephew, the nerd's name is Rikia. Their last name's Takata."

"So who exactly are they, and why would either of them have had any reason to break into Tango-11 or kill Sergeant Giles?" asked Bernadette as Cozy hastily took notes.

"They're friends of ours, and they wouldn't have had a reason," Sarah snapped.

Bernadette entered both names into the BlackBerry she'd slipped out of her pocket without offering a response.

Sounding eager to finger-point, Buford said, "They live in Laramie. Rikia's an egghead math professor with a card or two missing from the deck, over at the University of Wyoming, and just so you know, they're both first-tier nuke haters, even more so than Sarah." Looking Sarah's way, he said, "The cat's out of the bag. Might as well give 'em the whole nine yards."

"I'm afraid Buford's always been a little uncomfortable with Kimiko and Rikia," Sarah said. "I can assure you, they're both very decent people. And for the record, Kimiko's not Rikia's aunt. They're actually second cousins. As for her hatred of nuclear weapons, she has every reason to hate them. Her father was at Hiroshima when we A-bombed the place. He'd sent Kimiko from Japan to live with relatives in San Francisco less than a month before the war began. She might have actually fared better in Japan because within six months of her arrival here, our hypocritical government rounded up Kimiko and her American-born relatives, packed them off to Wyoming, and imprisoned them at Heart Mountain. That place was nothing more than America's own Rocky Mountain version of Auschwitz, as far as I'm concerned." Sarah shook her head in disgust.

Vaguely aware that the Heart Mountain Relocation Center east of Yellowstone had been a World War II–era internment camp for Japanese Americans, Cozy looked quizzically at Bernadette. Realizing from the look on her face that she knew the place as well, he continued taking notes as Bernadette entered "Heart Mountain survivor" next to Kimiko Takata's name in her BlackBerry.

"That place is a permanent black eye on this country, just like nuclear weapons are," Sarah said, her voice rising.

Tugging at Sarah's shirtsleeve and hoping to stop her before she launched into one of her antinuclear tirades, Buford said, "None of us were even born then, Sarah."

"Doesn't matter. God never intended for us to be beasts."

"There was a war goin' on, Sarah."

"Let's not start down that road, Buford, please."

"Yes, let's not," Bernadette said. "Do you have phone numbers and addresses for the Takatas?"

When Sarah didn't immediately answer, Buford said, "Yes."

"I'd appreciate having them."

"I have that information inside the house," Sarah said, heading for the front door.

"I'll go in with you," Bernadette said, rising from her chair, intent on making certain that the common-law wife of the man who'd earlier tried to shoot her wasn't going for another weapon.

Bernadette glanced back at Cozy before stepping through the front door and nodded toward the shotgun lying next to his chair. As the door closed behind Bernadette, Cozy picked up the shotgun and activated the pump action. A live shell ejected and thumped down onto the porch deck. "Always seems to be one left in the chamber with these pumps," Cozy said, looking at Buford.

"Always does," Buford said, grinning and staring out toward the orange glow of sunset.

Carlos Alvarez, the OSI officer whom Joel DeWitt had assigned to keep tabs on Bernadette, was having trouble hearing the colonel on his cell phone. "We've got a bad connection, Colonel. I can hardly hear you. Just a sec." Alvarez moved the phone to his opposite ear.

"How about now?" DeWitt asked impatiently.

"Better," said Alvarez.

"Want to finish bringing me up to speed now, Captain?"

Alvarez, who'd had his binoculars trained on Sarah Goldbeck's front porch for the last fifteen minutes, said, "Major Cameron just went inside the house with the Goldbeck woman. Kane's still outside on the porch with the guy who's been taking notes."

"Describe your note-taker for me."

"Tall, six-two or six-three, and sort of Hispanic- or Indian-looking. He's got curly black hair and an oval-shaped face, he's clean-shaven, and I'd say he's got a bum leg."

"He's one of those reporters from last night, no question. Name's Coseia. Anything else?"

"Not much, except that it's one real strange situation here. When I first drew a good clean bead on the front porch through my binocs, that reporter was unstrapping the big redheaded guy we interrogated at Warren this morning from a chair."

"Sounds like old Buford Kane must've been a bad boy. I'll be sure and ask Major Cameron what the old motorcycle rider did to deserve such treatment once she's back here."

"It won't be long, sir. She's out of the house now and back out on the porch, and it looks like she and that reporter are leaving together. Yep. They're headed down the porch steps." Following a lengthy silence, he said, "The major's getting into a truck with him. She's leaving her vehicle here, sir."

"Odd that she'd leave her vehicle there. Tail them."

"Yes, sir," said Alvarez, who'd been unsuccessfully trying to bed the statuesque African American major since the day she'd arrived at Warren.

"And Alvarez, I said tail them, not jump on her tail, if you get my drift."

"Sir, I'm afraid . . ."

"Can it, Captain. Just stay off their radar. I don't want Bernadette to know I've got somebody following her around. We'll compare notes once you're back here at Warren."

"Yes, sir," said Alvarez, snapping his cell phone closed. As the dually headed slowly back down the winding gravel lane toward him, he cranked his engine, made a U-turn, and moved slowly down the lane to keep from kicking up any telltale dust. Two miles up the highway, he pulled off at the entryway to a ranch and swung in behind the dually after it passed him. Envious of the man behind the wheel of the truck because the driver was going to have a full hour alone with Bernadette Cameron, Alvarez settled in glum-faced for the drive back to Cheyenne.

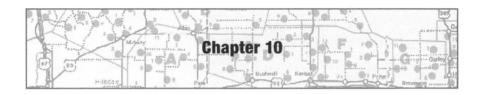

Chapter 10

Cozy had just set the cruise control on the dually (a fifty-thousand-dollar gift Freddy Dames had given him for breaking a story about a four-state Bureau of Land Management cattle-grazing rights scam involving nepotism and old-fashioned good-old-boy favoritism) at seventy when Bernadette, pushing up her fatigues shirtsleeves, said, "I didn't thank you properly back there for saving my bacon or for offering me a ride home. Thanks."

"You're welcome, but I think you would've been quite capable of saving your own bacon, Major."

That issue settled, Bernadette relaxed back in her seat, extended her legs, which were nearly as long as Cozy's, and said, "Quite a combo, Ms. Goldbeck and Mr. Kane, don't you think? Peacenik and beatnik, or dove and hawk, perhaps."

"Like they say, when it comes to love and war, you never know," Cozy said, dimming his lights for an oncoming semi. "Hawks generally do a lot more killing than doves do, though. You'd have to wonder if an old biker like Kane might not be capable of killing someone."

"Food for thought. But you'd have to come up with a reason for that killing, and in this case a reason for dumping a body at a former nuclear-missile site. Could be that Ms. Goldbeck, Mr. Kane, and Sergeant Giles have a past. A confrontation that occurred at Tango-11 during the '70s or '80s, perhaps."

"Are you speculating, or do you have facts?" Cozy asked, smiling.

Bernadette returned the smile. "There you go, Mr. Coseia, sounding like a reporter and spoiling my supposition. It was just a thought."

"It's a terrible cross to bear, this thing we call the truth. And by the way, I prefer 'Cozy' to 'Mr. Coseia.' Only the IRS and folks I owe money to call me that."

"Then Cozy it is. And just so we're even, I'm partial to Bernadette. Now that we're on a first-name basis, mind telling me how Digital Registry News scooped the major networks, CNN, and the newspaper big boys on both coasts with your Tango-11 story?"

"That's easy. My boss, Freddy Dames. Only one thing in the world drives him—winning."

"I see. So how'd you get wind of the Giles murder so fast, being that you were 175 miles away in Denver?"

"Simple. We work the territory. Regional news, it's our beat. Casper to Albuquerque—Salt Lake City to Kansas City. Our job is to get there first."

"That's certainly lots of territory, but you really didn't answer my question."

Thinking, *Savvy sista,* Cozy said, "Guess I didn't. Let's just say that even in this age of computers, we have folks out there who are paid to listen in on police scanners. Old-fashioned but effective."

"Whatever works for you, I guess. So where will you be heading next with your headlines?"

"I'm thinking my next stop should probably be the Takatas.

Did you see the sparks that started flying when Buford Kane mentioned them?"

"Would've been hard to miss. The question of the hour, however, is how would either of the Takatas have crossed paths with Sergeant Giles?"

"As part of the antinuclear movement back in the '70s and '80s; how else?"

Bernadette smiled. "Easy to speculate. Harder to prove. Remember, now, we're only interested in the facts here."

"Touché," said Cozy, watching Bernadette ease up in her seat and glance into her sideview mirror. She stared silently into the mirror for the next mile before turning to Cozy to ask, "Would you slow this rig down a bit? But don't hit your brakes, okay?"

"Sure." Cozy turned off the cruise control and let the truck coast momentarily. "Mind telling me what's up?"

"I think we've got somebody on our tail. Somebody in an air force–issue Jeep like the one Buford Kane plugged. They're easy to spot even in the dark when that's the vehicle you look at all day. I want to see if the gap between us closes as we slow down."

Cozy glanced in his mirror at the set of headlights behind them. "Still there."

"Yeah, I see. And the gap between us is pretty much the same."

"Any idea who it might be?"

"Someone my immediate superior has following me around."

"Take it your boss doesn't trust you."

"He doesn't trust anybody. But I can handle him."

"No evasive maneuvers necessary, then?"

"No, just keep driving."

Certain from what he'd seen of her that Bernadette Cameron could take care of herself, Cozy asked, "So how long have you been in the air force?"

"Pretty much all my life. My father was an air force fighter pilot. His father was a Tuskegee airman—99th fighter squadron."

"Man! You're talking one iron-willed pair of color-barrier-busting brothers there."

"They were," Bernadette said proudly. "But my granddad always claimed that they were a lot more badassed than barrier-busting."

"So what's your dad do now?"

"He's retired."

"Pretty proud of you, I guess."

"Yes, but a little disappointed that I'm no longer flying A-10s." The somberness in Bernadette's voice let Cozy know he'd broached a subject that he should have avoided. Returning to the business at hand, he asked, "So besides the Takatas, the shotgun-toting Mr. Kane, and Sarah Goldbeck, do you have any more murder suspects on your list?"

"You're starting to sound like a reporter again, Cozy. I'm afraid my investigation can't be quite the open book you're looking for. So far you've ended up being in all the right places at all the right times with this Tango-11 thing. But I'm afraid your information pipeline's about to end."

"You're cutting me off," Cozy said, sticking out his lower lip in a mock pout.

"Have to," said Bernadette, seeing the lights of Cheyenne twinkle in the distance.

"Tell me you'll still take my phone calls," Cozy said with a wink.

Unsmiling, Bernadette said, "I'll take them, of course."

"Glad to hear that." Cozy slowed down to just under sixty and glanced in his rearview mirror. "He's still there. Maybe we should just stop and confront him."

"He's my problem, Cozy, okay?"

"Your deal, Major. Sorry for pressing."

"Thanks. Now, mind if I ask you a question?"

"Go for it."

"It's a little personal."

"As personal as mine have been?"

"More so, I'm afraid. It's about that limp you tend to hide so well. It's not service related, is it?"

"Nope," said Cozy, wondering when Bernadette had first spotted his limp. "A present from a motorcycle accident. That's why I drive trucks. Lessens the chance of me ever becoming pavement bait again."

"Sorry I pried."

"No problem. Things happen." He eased the dually off the interstate onto Randall Avenue and past the three Minuteman missiles flanking the guard gate. When he stopped, Bernadette leaned over, said, "Hi, Skip," to the guard at the gate, flashed him her ID, returned the guard's salute, and said to Cozy, "Let's head this chariot of yours to my office."

"Funny what a ruckus mama bear, papa bear, and baby bear back there can cause," Cozy said, pointing back toward the three missiles, which stepped down in size from east to west.

"I'm afraid they're not storybook characters to be loved."

"I understand their purpose. I'm just wondering if they might not have cousins out there somewhere in the world who are linked to our murder?"

Ignoring the question, Bernadette glanced out the rear window. "No more Captain Alvarez."

"Guess he got cold feet," Cozy said, happy to be able to attach a name to the person who'd been following them.

"I wish. He's just using a different entrance. My car's parked out in front of my office, by the way."

"So how will you explain your missing Jeep?"

"With reams of paperwork. No worries, though. I've got motor-pool friends who'll help me out." She flashed Cozy a know-ing smile. "The air force still has brothers around who revere the Tuskegee airmen."

"And their granddaughters, no doubt," said Cozy.

The impish smile on Bernadette's face told Cozy that she obvi-ously knew when to be spit-and-polish and when to work the system.

Pointing at the only vehicle parked in front of her building, Bernadette said, "There's my car."

"Nice," Cozy said, admiring the Austin-Healey roadster that was lit up by his headlights.

"It was my father's. He used to race it. It's a '67 3000 MK III—totally restored. When he gave it to me after the air force grounded me, he claimed it would give me a chance to still be able to fly by the seat of my pants."

"Has it?"

"Some. But I'm neither the pilot nor the driver my dad is."

Cozy flipped the cab lights on and flashed the green-eyed major an encouraging smile. "I bet you are."

Recognizing a refreshing earnestness in Cozy's tone, an earnestness that she'd found lacking in the competitive and all-too-often jealous air force jet jockeys she'd rubbed shoulders with for years, Bernadette said, "I'd hate to take that test."

"You'd pass," Cozy said, watching her get out of the truck. "Like the bigwig politicians and Madison Avenue types say, let's keep the communication lines open, okay?"

Looking concerned, Bernadette asked, "You don't write stories that smear the military like your boss, do you? I've read a piece by him and it wasn't very flattering."

"Haven't yet."

"Then we'll keep the lines open. Good-night." As Bernadette slipped into her car, she had the feeling that she'd just returned from the absolute strangest of dates. As she pulled the sleek-looking roadster away from the curb and fell in behind the dually, she had no way of knowing that Cozy was thinking the very same thing.

Cozy's two cell-phone calls to Freddy Dames, placed as Cozy headed south down I-25 for Denver, went to voice mail, remaining unanswered until just after ten thirty, when a noticeably tired-sounding Freddy finally called back.

"What's up?" Freddy asked, talking over a high-pitched whine in the background.

"Not much. Other than the fact that I just spent an evening with that dropkicking air force major from the protest last night."

"Miss Black, Beautiful, and Buxom," Freddy said with a snicker.

"Yeah. But I'm thinking after tonight you'd best add 'brainy' and 'badassed' to that list. So what about you?"

"I'm in Denver at Centennial Airport, about to head *Sugar* down to Phoenix for a business meeting tomorrow morning. From there I'm headed to Albuquerque to talk to a guy named Howard Colbain. He's the former husband of an air force lieutenant who had an affair with Sergeant Giles."

Aware now that the whine in the background was coming from Freddy's twin-engine Gulfstream, a plane Freddy affectionately called *Sugar,* Cozy asked, "How'd you get the lowdown on the ex-wife and on this guy Colbain's whereabouts so fast?"

Quoting their *No excuses, sir,* former college baseball coach, Freddy said, "Ours is not to reason why, Cozy boy. Ours is but to do or die. But since you asked, I got the info from a place that you, my yellow-tablet-writing friend, would probably never have looked. The internet."

"Maybe not," Cozy said smugly, "but my Converse All Star ways have managed to help me dredge up four suspects in the Giles murder to your one."

"So, who are they?" Freddy asked, chagrined at having apparently been outdone.

"For starters, I've got a World War II–era Japanese internment camp survivor—and her cousin. They're a couple of nuke-protesting buddies of Sarah Goldbeck's who for some reason didn't find it necessary to show up last night for that press conference and protest in Wheatland. There's Goldbeck herself, of course, and Goldbeck's *Easy Rider* '60s throwback of a common-law husband, Buford Kane, who, by the way, got himself involved in an O.K. Corral–style standoff with Major Cameron earlier this evening."

"Didn't he get enough of her at that press conference?"

"Seems like he didn't. This time he leveled a shotgun on her—and lost," Cozy said, failing to mention his role in the incident.

"Did she shoot him?"

"Nope. Just kicked his ass again."

"Tough lady."

"On top of being bases-loaded fine."

"If I didn't know better, Elgin Coseia, I'd say you sound smitten."

"Come on, Freddy. Lighten up."

"Okay. Just promise me you won't start sending the major any sweetie-pie candygrams. Hold on. I've gotta tell the tower something." Sounding disgusted, Freddy was back on the line twenty seconds later. "You want anything done right these days, you've got to do it yourself, damn it. You still there, Cozy?"

"Yeah."

"So what about your two Japanese suspects? They got names?"

"Takata. Kimiko and Rikia Takata."

Freddy slipped a pen out of his shirt pocket and jotted the names on a notepad. "Wish I'd had their names before I posted the story I just wrote. Adding those two to the mix would've made the piece a whole lot juicier. But what the hell. The way this Tango-11 thing is unfolding, you and I'll be writing stories for months. So what did you get Major Cameron to give up for the cause besides pheromones, my man?"

Recalling his pledge to Bernadette not to smear the air force and wondering what Freddy had written, Cozy said, "Not a lot. I do know that her boss is having her tailed by some kiss-ass captain, though."

"Umm," Freddy said as the second of his two cell phones began ringing. "Wait a sec. Got another call I need to take." Returning quickly to his conversation with Cozy, he asked, "Where are you on the interstate?"

"Coming up on the Dacono exit."

"Afraid I'm going to have to turn you around and head you back to Wyoming."

"What?"

"I need you to head back north, Cozy. That call I just took was from Lillian. I tagged a request for additional information about the Tango-11 murder to the end of that story I posted. Told our readers we were looking for anything out there that might shed light on the killing and that we were willing to pay for it. Lillian says she's already had more than a dozen responses. Most of 'em pure horseshit, of course, but she said a couple sounded legit. One of them came from some guy who lives up near Buffalo, Wyoming. Needs to be checked out."

"And I'm guessing that I get the pleasure?"

"You do unless you want to fly *Sugar* down to Albuquerque. The man who called Lillian didn't give his name. Just told her he knew someone, a rancher neighbor of his, who hated the air force and anybody associated with it. Now, get this, and I'm quoting the guy who called: 'Especially missile-squadron types.'"

"So who's the missile-squadron-hating neighbor, and what's his story?"

"You're going to have to call Lillian for the details. All I know is that she was told his name's Grant Rivers and he runs a cattle ranch outside of Buffalo."

"Damn, Freddy. That's four hours north of Cheyenne."

"I know," Freddy said, suppressing a chuckle. "So you get the chance to head back north from Denver in the morning, and maybe even the opportunity to have coffee and doughnuts with Major Cameron. Gotta go. You know how this bird of mine guzzles jet fuel. I'll talk to you tomorrow."

"When do you get back from Albuquerque?"

"Tomorrow night, late. I'll need you back from Buffalo by then because I may also need you to check on that black preacher, Wilson Jackson. And just so you know, I ripped the air force a new one in the first piece I wrote. Go online and have a look. See you tomorrow night."

"But—" was all Cozy could get out before Freddy was gone. Upset at having to drive all the way to Buffalo and then maybe back to Cheyenne to talk to some preacher before he could head home to Denver, he muttered, "Shit," and slapped his dashboard with an open palm. Thinking that a four thirty a.m. start from Denver would probably be necessary for the long trip he was staring at, he floored his accelerator and didn't let up until he was doing a hundred and five.

Silas Breen reached the outskirts of South Bend a little before midnight. Beaming like a starry-eyed teenager with a crush and with a MapQuest printout of the Notre Dame campus lying open on the seat next to him, he headed straight for campus.

A flat tire had slowed him down outside Toledo, and he'd only been back on the road for half an hour when a hailstorm that had lasted a good twenty minutes had put him even further behind schedule. Nothing, however, was going to stop him from visiting the college he'd once dreamed of attending.

By the time he reached the campus, he was shaking, and when he finally made it to his number-one destination—not the famous Notre Dame football stadium or the basketball arena but rather the symbol of the school recognized worldwide, the administration building's golden dome—he was teary-eyed. For several minutes he simply stood beside his truck, motionless in the street, mesmerized by the strategically lit dome with its statue of Mary, the mother of God, on top. He would have stood there in awe for much longer if the Big Ben chime of his cell phone hadn't broken the trance.

The person on the other end of the line, responding to Silas's absentminded "Silas," was cryptic and abrupt. "Bravo 3 here. Reached your base yet?"

"I'm in South Bend now," Silas said. Suddenly clearheaded, he wondered why F. Mantew insisted on communicating with some kind of half-baked military code when he wasn't doing it by fax.

"And you're out tomorrow, yes?"

"By tomorrow afternoon, after I've toured the campus. Just like we agreed," Silas said, thinking that Mantew's response sounded somehow rehearsed.

"Don't linger. Bravo 3 out."

"Bravo 3, my ass," Silas mumbled after closing his cell phone. He'd been raised on army bases—spent most of his life on them, in fact—and he'd had to listen to the same kind of nonsensical gibberish from his father for most of that time. "Bravo, my ass!" he yelled. Thinking that the slow-talking, insistent Mantew had sounded as if he was in an echo chamber, Silas slipped back into his truck. He'd savor the whole enchilada that was Notre Dame tomorrow, he told himself, cranking the engine. Experience all there was to experience. Staring out the open window of his truck and up at the statue of Mary one last time, he crossed himself, smiled, and slowly drove off.

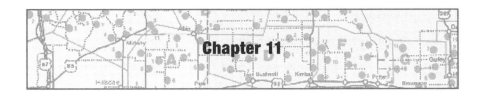

Chapter 11

Laramie's tree-lined University of Wyoming campus had always held a special rustic, turn-of-the-twentieth-century charm for Bernadette. It was an idyllic, old-school charm that as much as announced to traffic speeding by on Interstate 80, *No need to stop and drop your tainted bicoastal baggage here.*

Before being grounded, she'd done recruiting for the air force there, and she'd always found it especially rewarding when some young co-ed, enchanted by the possibility that she, too, might have the chance to become a fighter pilot, made the initial step toward becoming one.

Her visit to campus this time, however, was solely to talk with Dr. Rikia Takata, who according to the math department's website was not only the holder of the department's lone endowed professorship but also one of the nation's leading theoretical mathematicians and an expert on using mathematics as a tool in the fight against terrorism. She'd also scheduled a meeting with Dr. Takata's department chairman, who'd sounded eager to speak with her when she'd called earlier that morning until she'd mentioned that she was spearheading the investigation into the Tango-11 break-in.

She'd skipped breakfast, and she was feeling a little queasy when she slipped into a metered parking space in front of the building that housed the mathematics department. Deciding to let her stomach settle a bit, she picked up the paper on the seat next to her and reread a profile of Professor Rikia Takata that she'd downloaded off the university's website: "With Dr. Rikia Takata leading the way, researchers at the University of Wyoming are formulating powerful new algorithms designed to facilitate quick and thorough searches of massive amounts of data. These searches may well allow investigators to penetrate the well-disguised rules that govern the behavior of terrorists.

"Among many other tools, Dr. Takata and his research team assemble and access data from billions of cell-phone calls, email messages, web-surfing records, credit-card receipts, and train and airline manifests in order to, in a very real sense, enter the minds of terrorists. Takata, a 2010 recipient of a MacArthur Genius Grant, further seeks to develop formulas that will define in mathematical terms precisely what the optimal arrangement of secret terrorist cells might look like and to eventually construct methodologies for destroying such cells."

Thinking, *Why not just give the man a cape and tights and stamp a great big* S *on his chest?* Bernadette set the glowing profile aside, stepped out of her vehicle, and headed for her nine o'clock meeting with the mathematical version of America's next caped crusader.

Ross Hall, the native Wyoming sandstone building she was headed for, looked boxy and institutional. Once inside, however, she found the building to be airy and inviting. The hallways bustled with students headed for nine o'clock classes, and as she wove her way between them, she found herself thinking back to her own college days at UCLA. Nothing she'd seen so far looked like a gymnasium, which was what Dr. Takata had told her his office looked like during their phone conversation the previous evening, but thus far she'd seen only students, hallways, and doors.

As she brushed past several smiling students, all of whom looked pleasantly surprised by her uniform, she understood very well that she was rubbing shoulders with the sons and daughters of farmers and ranchers, outfitters, seed sellers, ditch riders, and county linemen, not the children of privilege she'd known at UCLA.

Rikia Takata's office door, two feet taller than any other door in line with it, had six-inch-tall brass numerals screwed into it at eye level announcing to anyone within eyeshot that they'd reached Room 118. A nameplate below the room number sporting similar-sized letters read, "Rikia Takata, PhD." An expensive-looking antique door knocker to the right of the nameplate gave the door a look of tenured-professor permanence. When a chubby-cheeked blonde girl who looked to Bernadette to be no more than seventeen or eighteen pulled the door open and called back, "See ya, Dr. T.," Bernadette scooted around her and into the room to see a small-boned Asian man waving good-bye to the girl. Beckoning Bernadette inside with the opposite hand, he looked her up and down and deadpanned, "Major Cameron, I presume? I'm Dr. Takata. Come in."

Trying her best to disregard his obvious speech impediment, Bernadette extended her right hand, clasped Rikia Takata's loosely in hers, pumped his arm once, then followed him down a narrow stub of hallway that quickly opened onto a thirty-foot-square room.

Enjoying the surprised look on Bernadette's face, Rikia said, "Welcome to my gymnasium, Major."

"Thank you," she said, suspecting that the open, airy room with its twelve-foot-high ceilings and polished hardwood floor was courtesy of MacArthur Genius Grant money. The maple-wood floors and high ceiling did give the space the feel of a gymnasium, and the life-sized painting of a basketball backboard, hoop, and net on the west wall, done in brown-and-gold University of Wyoming school colors, served to emphasize the point.

Rikia smiled as Bernadette's gaze drifted from that wall down to the half-dozen computers lined up like little soldiers on three picnic-style tables that ran along another wall. An antique rolltop desk, dwarfed by the space and stacked high with papers, occupied the very center of the room. A high-backed leather captain's chair sat just to the right of the desk. Lining the wall opposite the picnic tables were eight identical ten-foot-tall mahogany bookcases, all overflowing with books.

"So what do you think of my gym?" Rikia asked finally.

"Impressive," Bernadette said, half expecting Takata's response to be *Of course*. But instead he walked over to a corner of the room, retrieved a basketball from the floor, and tossed it to her.

"Have a shot at the basket."

Looking puzzled, Bernadette said, "I don't think . . ."

"Go ahead. You won't hurt anything, and if you do, what the heck—it's only state property." He smiled, flashing a set of misaligned teeth. Bernadette shrugged and aimed a shot at the painting on the wall. The ball hit the backboard a few inches above the rim and ricocheted toward a computer keyboard. Before it could make contact, Rikia sprang across the room, grabbed the ball, set it on the floor, and placed one foot on top of it. "So how can I help you, Major Cameron?"

"As I mentioned during our phone conversation last night, I'm hoping you can help me resolve a security breach that occurred at a decommissioned military installation known as Tango-11 near Wheatland."

Rikia skillfully kicked the basketball into the corner it had come from. "Your problem has been all over the news, Major. I'm afraid that solving murders is outside my skill set, however."

"I wouldn't expect that it would be in your field, Dr. Takata, but my understanding is that you and your cousin, Kimiko, have long-term ties to the antinuclear movement, and I'm looking into the possibility that the break-in and trespass at Tango-11 might have involved antinuclear activists. In fact, Sarah Goldbeck, whom I've spoken with at length, has told me that she was surprised that you and your cousin didn't show up for a protest that occurred at the Wheatland Courthouse the other night." Smiling wryly, Bernadette said, "She was expecting you."

"Seems you know a lot about me that's secondhand, Major. As for that protest you mentioned, my cousin and I were busy."

"I see. Is there any chance that either of you might've known the man who was found murdered at the Tango-11 site, Thurmond Giles? He was a retired, heavily decorated air force sergeant."

"I've heard the name, of course; it's been all over the news. And as I understand it, your victim was African American. But no, I didn't know him, nor did my cousin. And I don't particularly like your inference, Major. Your question suggests that my cousin and

I could be suspects." Rikia's eyes widened in mock surprise, and he thumped his forehead. "Oh, I almost forgot. We're Japanese, and in America that would of course make the two of us permanent suspects."

"I don't think there's any need to—"

"You're right, Major. You didn't think. You barge into my gym, take a shot at my basket, and then try to link me to a break-in and murder at some military installation. You're nothing more than a female version of Orwell's Big Brother. Now, would you please leave my gymnasium?" In his anger, Rikia had to struggle even harder than usual to enunciate.

"I'm sorry I offended you, Dr. Takata."

"And I'm sorry you're dressed in that terrorist uniform. Now, leave." With both arms outstretched, he waved Bernadette toward the door.

"For the record, I'm wearing a United States Air Force uniform, sir."

"Terrorist, U.S. military—one and the same," Rikia said, his arms still waving.

"We'll talk again, Dr. Takata," Bernadette said, straining to control her anger.

Ignoring her, Rikia sprinted to the door, slammed it shut behind her, and called out from behind it, "One and the same!"

Dr. Art Dagoni's mathematics departmental chair suite occupied the second floor of Ross Hall at the opposite end of the building from Rikia Takata's first-floor "gymnasium." The suite had neither the trappings of a private-sector corporate office nor the airiness of Takata's large room. Shaded by a string of stately, fifty-year-old Colorado blue spruces, the pedestrian-looking space, even with its secretarial outer office, was several steps down the academic ladder from Rikia Takata's accommodations in terms of size and visual appeal.

When she'd made the appointment to talk to Dagoni and explained why she wanted to speak with him, the trepidation in his voice had all but screamed, *Not Rikia again!* Now, as she sat in the cramped outer office staring at the closed door to Dagoni's office, Bernadette had the sense that she might be in for her second confrontation of the morning.

The door swung open less than five minutes into her wait to reveal a thick, meaty, gregarious-looking man of medium height. Glancing toward his secretary with eyes that seemed much too small for his head, then back at Bernadette, he said, "Major, please come in." They shook hands, moved into his office, and took seats across from one another. A small octagonal table, littered with books and academic journals, sat between them.

Small talk, with Dagoni leading the way, took up the first few minutes of their conversation. Where Bernadette was from, how long she had been in the air force, and whether she liked what she did quickly segued into a summary of the high points of Dagoni's seventeen-year tenure as mathematics department chairman.

When Bernadette finally asked, "So, how's it been working with Rikia Takata?" the smiling Dagoni, sounding rehearsed, said, "He's a MacArthur Genius Grant recipient, you know."

"Yes. I also know that he's the second cousin of a Heart Mountain internment camp survivor. That he's been at the university for fourteen years; that he's regarded by his colleagues as standoffish, eccentric, and a little paranoid; and that his research centers on ways to fight terrorism."

"You've done your homework," Dagoni said with surprise. "But if I may correct you, Dr. Takata's research actually involves the development of algorithms designed to calculate and access mathematical equivalencies. Terrorism is simply the subject of that application. More simply put, Major, what Dr. Takata is actually investigating is how the various pieces and fragments of any one thing come together to form the whole."

"I see," Bernadette said, nodding. "Is he a hard man to work with?"

Dagoni smiled. "Aren't we all at times?"

Thinking, *Second sidestep,* Bernadette asked, "Do you know his cousin Kimiko? She was at one time a very prominent antinuclear activist, I understand."

"Yes, I do. And she's quite a pleasant person, considering what she's been through."

"No hard feelings about her internment camp experience at Heart Mountain?"

"I'm afraid you'd have to ask her that yourself. My impression has always been that Rikia is more resentful of our government's internment of Japanese Americans during the war than she is. He's actually quite vocal about it, and it's the one thing that I'd say has rubbed his colleagues a little raw over the years. This is Wyoming, after all, and it's not the kind of place where you continually want to criticize America. Now, may I ask you a question?"

"Certainly."

"You don't actually believe that Rikia or Kimiko is in any way tied to that missile-silo murder near Wheatland, do you?"

"Investigating murders isn't part of my job, Professor. My assignment is to investigate a break-in and the security breach that occurred on U.S. Air Force property."

"If that's the case, as Rikia himself might say, you don't want to overlook anything, big or small."

"I certainly don't. Let me ask you this: Do you think Dr. Takata might have considered breaking into a secure government facility in order to promote that equivalency research of his and prove a point?"

"No!"

Surprised by Dagoni's supportive and adamant reply, Bernadette said, "What's Dr. Takata got on his academic plate right now?"

"I'm not sure of everything that he's involved in at the moment. I do know he's scheduled to give a major equivalence theory paper at the Western States Mathematical Society meeting this week in El Paso. You might ask him about his research schedule when you speak with him."

"We've talked, and we struck a bit of a sour note. My uniform seemed to upset him."

"Dr. Takata's antimilitary. Always has been."

"Just another piece of the puzzle," Bernadette said, smiling. "Sooner or later we'll get to the whole." She slipped a business card out of her pocket and handed it to Dagoni. "By the way, how does Dr. Takata handle giving research papers with that speech problem of his?"

"That's what research fellows are for," Dagoni said insightfully.

"So they give his talks for him?"

"Happens all the time."

Nodding, Bernadette said, "Call me if any more puzzle pieces turn up, won't you?"

"I certainly will."

Bernadette stood to leave, and Dagoni stood to shake her hand. "I couldn't help but notice your pilot wings. I fly myself," he said proudly. "I didn't know they assigned pilots to OSI."

"They don't." Bernadette turned and headed for the door, leaving Dagoni looking surprised as he struggled with yet another puzzle.

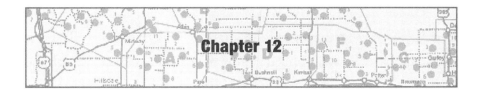

Chapter 12

Cozy's early-morning start from Denver put him at the base of the eastern slope of the Big Horn Mountains and within fifteen miles of Buffalo, Wyoming, by eleven a.m. More than a century earlier the quiet ranching community had been home to Wyoming's fabled Johnson County wars, a series of shootouts, skirmishes, and killings that had erupted in 1892 during a dispute between large and small ranchers over cattle grazing rights. Although the wars had long since ended, squabbles over grazing and water rights still arose in the valley on occasion.

After getting home to Denver late the previous evening, Cozy had called Grant Rivers, the man Lillian Griffith had told him an anonymous caller to Digital Registry News had complained about, swearing that Rivers was tied to the Tango-11 murder. The half-asleep-sounding Rivers had grudgingly agreed to meet Cozy at his Four Creeks Ranch the next day at noon—but, he emphasized, only if he could give his side of the story on why Carl Ledbetter, the man Rivers claimed to be Digital Registry's anonymous source, had tried to link him to a murder.

As Cozy gazed from his truck at red-rock foothills and a river valley of endless green, he had the feeling that he was driving through some lost nineteenth-century fantasy world. The frontage road he turned onto from I-25 was precisely where Grant Rivers had said it would be, and a mile and a half later the county road that Rivers had told him to take a left on was there as well. As he headed down the washboard road toward Four Creeks Ranch, he had the sense that the raspy-voiced Rivers, who'd sounded when they talked as if he'd either smoked for far too long or had major throat surgery, might turn out to be some kind of High Plains reincarnation of the Marlboro Man.

Four miles later, still awed by the scenery, he crossed a cattle guard and drove beneath the massive log entryway to Four Creeks Ranch. A black, hand-forged, three-foot-tall "Lazy M" brand hung from the entryway crossbeam, swinging back and forth in the breeze. Just beyond the entry the ranch opened up into a secluded valley rimmed by steep red-rock walls and massive outcroppings. Tens of thousands of acres of heavily treed national forest rose in the distance from the valley floor. Whispering, "Damn," and drinking in the unspoiled beauty, Cozy continued driving.

Rivers, who'd sounded like a man who wanted exoneration and also like someone who had nothing to hide, had said he'd be cutting hay by the time Cozy arrived. "Just look for a big old John Deere 4640 and a swather and you'll have found me" had been his parting instructions. When Cozy spotted the tractor and a hay swather stopped midway down a fence that bounded the northern edge of a six-hundred-acre alfalfa field, a field that he could see also had a landing strip, he headed straight for them. As he got closer and realized that a man was standing inside one of the tractor's six-foot-tall tire rims, he was pretty sure he'd found Grant Rivers.

Uncertain how he'd be received, since Rivers had deadpanned

during the previous evening's conversation that he didn't much like reporters, Cozy mulled over an interview strategy. Pulling the dually to a stop, he realized that the man had stepped from the tire rim and was now down on one knee, fidgeting with the tire's valve stem. When the man looked up and waved for Cozy to join him, Cozy slipped out of his truck; walked several yards to the fence that separated them; and, careful not to drag his bad leg, vaulted the fence scissor-style.

It was easy to see that the ruddy-complected man wrestling with the valve stem was frustrated. Pudgy and sixtyish, with thick, bushy eyebrows and pockmarked skin, the man wore a grease-stained engineer's cap. Cozy suspected that at one time he had been all sinew and muscle, but that day had come and gone. Thrusting a meaty hand at Cozy as he walked up, the man announced in a voice that sounded as if it were being filtered through an echo chamber being bombarded by hail, "Grant Rivers."

"Elgin Coseia," Cozy said, shaking Rivers's hand.

"Well, if you ain't, I'm guessin' you're his twin since you're drivin' a dually with Colorado plates, just like you said you'd be." Rivers smiled, showing a set of downhill-sloping dentures.

Glancing down at the tire that Rivers had been struggling with, Cozy said, "Looks low."

"Yep. It's got a slow leak." Rivers dusted off his hands and squared up to Cozy in the noonday sun. "Been tryin' to decide whether to repair it or shoot it. But since I know you ain't up here to ogle the Big Horns like most visitors, or to listen to my tractor woes, I'm thinkin' we should handle your issues straight off so's I can get back to mine."

"Works for me," Cozy said, glancing across the field to where another big John Deere sat idling. A man wearing a cowboy hat and smoking a cigar occupied the cab. Looking back at Rivers, he said, "Like I mentioned last night, I'm looking into that murder that happened outside Wheatland a couple of days back."

"No need to pussyfoot around the issue, son. I know all about what happened at Tango-11. Believe it or not, we get the news up here, too." Rivers adjusted his cap backward, then forward again on his head.

"Any chance you knew the dead man, Thurmond Giles?"

"Don't think I knew him, but you never know. Back years ago I thought I knew my neighbor up the road. The one who sicced you on me in the first place, fuckin' Carl Ledbetter. That damn water-stealin' bastard's been lookin' for a way to slipstream my water rights away from me for years. Maybe the SOB thinks that by gettin' people to thinkin' I killed somebody, he'll get my water. But he won't, and he ain't. Now, to answer your question, me and your dead man could've crossed paths back in the late '70s and early '80s when all them antinuclear protests were takin' place out this way. But I couldn't swear to it." Rivers suddenly looked perturbed. "Got myself hung up in the middle of that protest mess back then, though Lord knows I tried my best not to. Had protesters show up at a missile silo that was right on my doorstep, and more than a few times, I might add. Even took a few shots at the bastards before the air force finally sent some of their boys out to shoo 'em off."

"Giles was an African American, if that helps jog your memory."

"Wouldn't've make no difference to me if he was a Martian. I don't really recall knowin' the man." Rivers dusted off his hands as if to say, *Next question*. The quizzical look on Cozy's face triggered a brief Rivers laugh. "Guess I should explain a few things to you, son. Things that go back to the '80s and them antinuke protests I just mentioned—by the way, what's your political persuasion? You right-leanin' or left?"

"I'd say I'm pretty much middle of the road."

"Well, I ain't. I'm hard-line libertarian, and proud of it. Ain't always been that way. But I am now, and I'm guessin' that it's my political leanin's as much as him covetin' my water rights that put me on old Ledbetter-down-the-road's enemies list. Anyway, here's the deal. Your snitch, and that's what the hell Ledbetter is, is more than likely hopin' that he can get information about me that goes back some twenty-five years to come out. Stuff that goes back to when I used to ranch in Nebraska over near Kearney in the sandhills."

Rivers looked eastward and frowned. "Back then the government wanted a slice of the sixty thousand acres I owned to build themselves a couple of missile sites like the one they found your dead man at. And originally, at least, not very much of a slice. Just over eighty acres is what they started out sayin' they wanted." Rivers, who'd started to sound like an overworked foghorn, looked a little embarrassed and cleared his throat. "Me bein' patriotic and all, I sold 'em the land. Next thing I know the government's got my water rights and my BLM grazin' rights tied up in court. And the bastards didn't stop there. They went right after my forest service grazin' permits." His face seared with anger, Rivers said, "What the turds really wanted wasn't just a single spot for their missiles, not at all. They wanted land for a dozen of their damn missile-silo sites and my goddamn water rights to boot.

"It took me over four years, a hell of a lot of lawyerin', and most of the money I had in the world to wrestle them sons of bitches to the ground. But I did. Got my water rights adjudicated proper, and every one of my BLM and forest service grazin' permits solidified. The only downside to the deal was that the SOBs got to keep my original eighty acres and their two fuckin' missile silos. Knowin' that even with the courts findin' in my favor, they might come back, I sold out lock, stock, and barrel to an oil-drillin' company with pockets a whole lot deeper than mine and moved my ranchin' operation from Nebraska to here. But not, unfortunately, before I got to enjoy a couple of hell-filled years of havin' a bunch of damn antinuke protesters camped out on my damn doorstep at them two missile silos the air force built."

"I'm thinking you made the right choice with your move. Beautiful country you've got here," Cozy said.

"Forty thousand acres of paradise, to be sure," Rivers said proudly. "Not as big as my Nebraska spread, but it's a lot more peaceful, there's not a damn missile silo in sight, and there aren't any air force MPs, high-tech nuke jockeys, or stringy-haired hippies traipsin' across my land!" Looking pleased, he went on, "So to net it all out, it's entirely possible that your dead man could've been out there at my place in Nebraska. Maybe he even manned a silo back on the land the government snookered me out of durin' them protest years, but like I said earlier, if he was there, I damn sure didn't know him. Got any kind of better description on him besides the fact that he was black?"

"Not too much more, really. He was six-one or -two, skinny, and when they found him he had five stab wounds in his back, and the head of his penis and a wad of paper had been stuffed in his mouth."

"Sounds like somebody was lookin' for revenge. But I ain't the guy," Rivers said dismissively.

"Do the names Sarah Goldbeck or Buford Kane ring a bell?"

Rivers glanced skyward thoughtfully before responding. "Can't say that they do. Who are they?"

"A couple of longtime antinuclear folks. What about Kimiko or Rikia Takata? Know them?"

"Nope." Rivers's response was immediate and emphatic, so much so that Cozy found himself wondering why. Thinking that he'd need to dig a little deeper into the life and times of Mr. Grant Rivers, he said, "Any other gripes or insights you'd like to share with me?"

"Just one." Rivers's face turned almost salmon pink. "You might as well know about it because you're a reporter, and we all know that what reporters do for a living is dig up dirt. Anyway, those air force jack-offs, the ones the government sent out to my ranch in Nebraska to deal with them protesters? The brass who hold themselves up as bein' so God-fearin', country-lovin', and high and mighty? Well, they're all a bunch of lyin' bastards."

"Why so?"

"Because they kicked my boy outta that blessed U.S. Air Force Academy of theirs down in Colorado Springs, that's why. Claimed he was caught cheatin'." Rivers glanced toward his landing strip. "And that's after I spent years teachin' the boy to fly. Fuckin' liars. Cost me a bundle in attorneys' fees to fight that battle, too."

"Did you win?"

"Nope. But the whole deal let me know once and for all to never get involved with anything that has to do with the goddamn government. Best thing is, my boy, Logan, found out what kinda bastards they are as well."

"So what's Logan do now?"

"Helps me run this place. It's a better deal for the both of us." Rivers looked across the field to where the other tractor was now slowly pulling a brush chopper along a heavily weeded fence line. When the driver leaned out of the cab and waved their way, Cozy asked, "Logan?"

"You bet," Rivers said proudly. "We done here for the day?"

Thinking that the opinionated, right-leaning old rancher had been quite cooperative, maybe even a little too much so, Cozy said, "Yes."

"Good. 'Cause I need to get back to that tractor tire and my hayin'."

"I may need to talk to you again, and maybe to your son as well."

"I'm always here for the askin'. As for Logan, he ain't. He's part owner of a farm implements store down in Cheyenne. Spends a good deal of his time down there. He flies up here to help me when he can."

Glancing across the field toward the tractor and recognizing that he was outnumbered, Cozy decided that right then wasn't the time to go toe to toe with Rivers and son. He instead slipped his wallet out of a back pocket, teased out a business card, and handed it to Rivers. "Call me if something comes up related to the Giles murder that you may have forgotten to mention."

"Nothin' comes up much out here, friend, except alfalfa and the wind." Rivers slipped the card into his shirt pocket. "Gonna mention me in what you're plannin' to write?"

"Probably."

"Well, be sure and get the name right. It's Rivers with an *s.*"

"I'll make certain I do. And it's Logan with an *L,* I presume."

"I'd appreciate it if you'd leave my boy outta this," Rivers said, clearly annoyed.

"I'm afraid I can't."

With the vein that ran along his left temple suddenly pulsating, and without so much as a parting word, Rivers turned and took two giant steps toward his tractor. In a couple of seconds and with the agility of a gymnast, the sixty-one-year-old cattle rancher was up in the cab. A plume of black smoke rose skyward as he cranked the engine and took off across the alfalfa field toward the second tractor, the slow leak in his tire seemingly now of little concern to him.

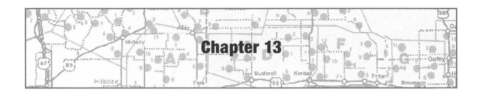

Chapter 13

Silas Breen had been to his mountaintop. He'd walked the Notre Dame campus, seen the golden dome, tiptoed onto the grass of the hallowed Notre Dame football field, and admired the mural of Touchdown Jesus. His sightseeing journey, however, had put him a little behind schedule with his delivery, and just before two p.m. he decided it might be best to call the Amarillo, Texas, number he'd been given to check in with F. Mantew in case of an emergency.

The squeaky-voiced woman who answered, "Amarillo Secretarial Temps," told him that no one named Mantew was at that number but that she had received a fax from an F. Mantew instructing her to tell a Mr. Breen if he called that the final destination for delivery of his goods was now Lubbock rather than Amarillo. She didn't mention that she'd been promised two hundred dollars in cash to go beyond her normal job duties, which entailed simply receiving a fax and holding it for the recipient, not passing along messages.

"Where'd the fax come from?" Silas asked, upset that he would now have to drive 120 miles beyond his original destination. Sitting in the cab of his truck in the parking lot of the motel where he'd spent the night, with his lower lip poked out in protest, his legs stretched out on the front seat, and his cell phone pressed firmly to one ear, he waited for an answer.

"I'm not certain, but the area code's a Mexico one."

"Mexico?"

"That's right, sir."

"And you're sure the fax is from someone named F. Mantew?"

"That's the name on the document, sir."

"Okay," Silas said with a sigh. "Can I get your name?"

"It's Doris."

"And the name of your company again?"

"Amarillo Secretarial Temporary Office Services."

"So where am I supposed to go in Lubbock?"

Thinking that she was earning every cent of her potential two-hundred-dollar bonus, Doris said, "The fax says your delivery destination is 181 East Clarkson, sir."

"And there's nothing else with the fax? No other instructions? No explanation as to why the change in cities?"

"No."

After a lengthy, jaw-clenched pause, Silas said, "Thanks," hung up, and set his cell phone aside. He stepped down from the cab onto the recently tarred, nearly empty parking lot of the Motel 6 where he'd slept so well. Looking around and listening to the rumble of traffic speeding by on nearby I-90, he walked to the back of his truck, unlocked the padlocked rear cargo door, and shoved the door up with a grunt.

He stared into the semidarkness for a few seconds to let his eyes adjust, then unclipped a flashlight from a mount just inside the door, snapped the beam on, and shone it into the cargo hold. Every one of the twenty crates he'd left Ottawa with was there, tied down and undisturbed, exactly as they'd been when he left.

Looking puzzled, he climbed up into the cargo bay, walked between the crates, and counted each one. The identical wooden crates were stacked in twos, atop one another, upright-freezer-style. A three-foot-wide, cargo-free center aisle separated the two rows of ten crates each. Two toolboxes, the kind designed to straddle a pickup bed, sat on either side of the cargo door. Fighting the urge to uncrate one of the boxes or look inside the padlocked toolboxes, Silas looked baffled. He poked, prodded, and sniffed his way around a half-dozen eight-by-four-by-four-foot crates for the next several minutes, deciding finally that the crates looked no different from the hundreds of other crates he'd hauled hither and yon since starting his moving business. The wood was cheap but sturdy, and the crates had been professionally assembled. There was no smell coming from them, no bugs escaping from or crawling around on them, no leaking chemicals, and, most importantly, no hazardous-cargo markings, the very last thing he'd double-checked for before signing the shipment manifest in Ottawa. Even so, there was something strange, even a little foreboding, about his cargo.

Mystified and wondering if he'd been snookered into hauling unmarked chemical waste, stolen goods, or maybe even drugs, Silas backed his way out of the truck, reclamped his flashlight in place, closed the cargo door, and made a mental note to call Ottawa later in the day to see if he couldn't get a better line on what he might be hauling besides "hospital equipment."

As he padlocked the cargo door, he glanced nervously around the parking lot. He saw half-a-dozen randomly spaced cars, a single pickup, and two idling tractor-trailer rigs. As he walked back to his cab, he realized that his hands were shaking. He decided that during one of his next road breaks, he'd call his father, Otis, in Kansas City, and discuss the whole strange situation with him.

For too long, racing off to Heart Mountain had been Kimiko Takata's answer to far too many things. Dropping everything to drive four hundred miles from Laramie across Wyoming to a place that had caused her so much pain had always seemed ludicrous to Rikia, but he'd known from the moment the news about the murder at Tango-11 first aired that a trip to Heart Mountain was imminent. Kimiko referred to her trips to what remained of the World War II–era relocation camp as "pilgrimages." She claimed these pilgrimages helped to cleanse her soul.

She'd lived at Heart Mountain for two months in 1943 and all of 1944, and Rikia had come to understand that Kimiko's soul had been permanently tarnished during her fourteen-month internment in that dusty, treeless, high-desert world.

He couldn't help but think that if he'd kept his meeting with Major Cameron to himself instead of running home at noon to tell Kimiko about it, he might not have ended up losing what would amount to two half-days of work. He'd still be polishing up the paper his grad student would deliver for him in El Paso, and he wouldn't be packing up his ten-year-old Volvo station wagon for a trip to a place he detested. It hadn't helped that Sarah Goldbeck had called Kimiko early that morning to tell her about Major Cameron's visit to Hawk Springs, infusing Kimiko with a sense of purpose that had made her all the more eager to make the seven-hour trip to Heart Mountain.

Now, as he tossed his sleeping bag into the back of the station wagon, Rikia found himself hoping that Kimiko might for once at least decide to stay at a motel in either Powell or Cody instead of trespassing onto an off-limits section of what was now Heart Mountain Memorial Park to spend the night camping illegally.

It was hard for him to understand why, at seventy-six and with worsening arthritis and what he suspected was creeping dementia, Kimiko continued to make her pilgrimages. But she did, always returning to Laramie seemingly reenergized. If he'd been in her shoes, he would have long ago burned every square acre of the god-awful former internment camp, but Heart Mountain was Kimiko's cross to bear, not his. It had also been her own choice several years earlier to accept a twenty-thousand-dollar reparation handout designed by the U.S. government to wash away the sins of Heart Mountain and hopefully gain the silence of the internment camp survivors. He saw Kimiko's choice to take the money as a form of dishonorable acquiescence, something he never would have been party to.

When Kimiko called to him from the back porch, "Are you finished packing the car, Rikia?" he muttered a disconsolate "Yes," stuffed a pair of hiking boots in next to his sleeping bag, and shut the Volvo's tailgate.

"Did you remember to pack plenty of water?" she asked, headed down their Russian-olive-tree-lined driveway toward him.

"Yes," he said, his response barely audible.

"And you brought along your grandfather's diary, of course?"

"It's on the front seat."

Kimiko's eyes lit up. "Good. It would be a tragedy to forget that."

"Yes, I know. We'd be forced to turn around and come back," Rikia grunted.

Frowning and eyeing him sternly, Kimiko said, "I'll have none of your insolence, Rikia."

Knowing that Kimiko could never again lock him in the basement, a linen closet, or the pantry and feed him only rice and water for days or beat him with a razor strap, as she'd done when he'd crossed her as a child, Rikia nonetheless took her warnings seriously, aware that she might instead choose not to speak to him for weeks.

His childhood disobedience, driven by the taunts he constantly had to endure at school because of his speech problem, had been addressed with punishment, but Kimiko had not sought medical attention for the real problem until he was in his teens. By then he'd already suffered through periods of depression after having been forced to come live with her following the death of his parents in a mid-1970s San Francisco car crash. The crash had occurred only a year after his father had come with his wife and son from Japan to teach physics at San Francisco State University. Frail, retiring, and tongue-tied, Rikia hadn't as yet adjusted to his new Bay Area environment before he'd had to move to a strange, desolate place called Wyoming.

"I'll just get a couple of sodas from the refrigerator in the garage and we can leave," Kimiko said, still peeved by Rikia's remark about the diary. As he watched her walk into the garage, he had the sense that she would have loved nothing more right then than to step back forty years in time and flail his bare behind with a handful of thorny Russian-olive branches.

"I'll read to you from the diary once we're under way," she called out from inside the garage. "After your visit from that military police major, I think we're both in need of hearing your grandfather's words."

Thinking that Major Bernadette Cameron represented far more of a problem than the military police, Rikia nodded to himself. He'd urged Kimiko time and again over the years to cut her ties with Sarah Goldbeck and dim-witted Buford Kane, but she never had. And now—although Major Cameron had never actually said so—because of Kimiko's uncommon sense of loyalty or her creeping senility, they'd both become suspects in a murder.

Kimiko reappeared from the garage holding two soda cans in her misshapen, arthritic hands. "Let's go, Rikia." There was an urgency in her tone that had Rikia quickly slipping behind the wheel of the station wagon. Suspecting that he had at least sixty miles and a good hour of driving ahead of him before Kimiko began reading from his grandfather's diary, he felt a temporary sense of relief. A feeling that quickly disappeared as he backed the station wagon out of the driveway and thought about the fact that his hour-long respite would be followed by a six-hour sermon.

After returning to her office from Laramie, Bernadette had spent a half hour completing her preliminary report on the security breach at Tango-11 for Colonel DeWitt, detailing near the end what had happened at Sarah Goldbeck's the previous evening. Just before lunch, she'd spent a few minutes scrutinizing aerial, satellite, and topographic maps of half of the nearly three hundred deactivated missile-silo sites in Wyoming, Colorado, and Nebraska and trying to find any link between those sites and the Tango-11 site. She'd also spent several minutes studying the flattened-out photocopy of the wadded-up piece of paper from Sergeant Giles's mouth that Sheriff Bosack had faxed to her. Certain that the piece of paper had been torn from a Wyoming missile-silo site map, and that the single locator dot near the center represented Tango-11, she'd wearily gotten up from her desk at twelve thirty and gone to lunch.

Now, at a little past two thirty, she was busy trying to track down what Thurmond Giles had done for a living and where after leaving the air force sixteen years earlier. It had been relatively easy to track the movements of someone who'd been one of the air force's most qualified and decorated senior enlisted electronics and nuclear-warhead maintenance technicians, especially since Giles possessed the kind of technical expertise the civilian world coveted.

She'd made a couple of phone calls to air force retirees who'd known Giles, both of whom had told her that after leaving the service, Giles had taken a job with Gromere Electronics and Engineering, a Seattle-based weapons guidance system firm with a long history of hiring military retirees with high-grade electronics skills.

Contacting Gromere hadn't been difficult, but getting through to someone who'd known Giles was proving to be much harder. After suffering through a series of phone transfers and finally being connected to someone who had known the man, she found herself explaining for the third time who she was and that she was investigating a security breach and break-in at a government facility where there'd also been a murder. After assuring that third person, a supervisor in the human resources department named Elaine Richardson, that her call involved possible national security issues and that, under the circumstances, the call wasn't an invasion of the deceased sergeant's privacy, she quickly learned that Giles had left Gromere four years earlier.

Speaking haltingly and obviously upset, Elaine Richardson said, "And you say they found Thurmond stabbed and hanging by his ankles inside some missile silo out in the middle of nowhere?"

"He was actually found inside the personnel-access tube adjacent to the missile silo itself."

"Figures."

"Why's that?"

"Because Thurmond was the kind of person who could rub people the wrong way. His superiors, his coworkers, and jealous men especially. He had a habit of choosing women who should have been clearly off-limits to him. Women who'd already been picked by someone, if you know what I mean."

"Yes, I do."

"That's what got him headed down the road and out of here at Gromere. Fooling around with the wrong woman."

Sensing that the somber-sounding Elaine might have wanted to add, *Instead of me,* Bernadette asked, "And it got him fired?"

"It sure did. It also got him pretty much blackballed from ever being employed in the weapons guidance system world again. We're a small, close-knit community, Major. Everybody knows everybody, East Coast to West. In a community that small, you don't pull on Superman's cape."

"And Giles did?"

"Yes. He yanked the president of Gromere's chain by fooling around with his daughter."

"And the president is?"

"I know where you're headed, Major, and I can assure you it's down the wrong road. The president at the time was Roman Haverton, and he's dead."

"And the daughter?"

"Cicily Haverton. Dead as well. She died in a skiing accident a couple of years back. Out your way, in fact, in Jackson Hole."

"Sounds like you keep up."

"Like I said, we're a close-knit industry."

"No reason for revenge on the part of either of the Havertons, then?"

"Nor their heirs. There aren't any. Cicily was an only child."

"I see. So where did Sergeant Giles go after leaving Gromere?"

"To Canada."

"Quite a leap."

"It's not really much of one from Washington, and with all of his years in the air force, Thurmond had connections there."

Bernadette jotted a note to herself to double-check on any of Thurmond Giles's military connections that she might have missed. "Who'd he go to work for in Canada?"

"A company named Applied Nuclear Theratronics of Canada Ltd."

"Guidance systems again?"

"No. They make radiation therapy equipment—machines for treating cancer patients."

"Quite a switch from nuclear weapons guidance systems."

"Not really. In either instance you're dealing with a product that's got a nuclear payload at the end."

"Interesting way of looking at it," Bernadette said, continuing to jot notes.

"It comes from years of looking at what some people might refer to as the right and wrong ends of the nuclear industry. Pretty much the same missile-warhead guidance systems we manufacture here at Gromere, with a few adjustments, of course, can be programmed to control the movement of uranium rods in a nuclear power plant. As Mr. Haverton was fond of saying, it's a stupid rabbit that has but one hole."

"Makes sense. So how long did you keep up with Sergeant Giles after he left Gromere?"

"Until about six months ago, actually. That's when he stopped answering my emails and phone calls."

"Was he living in Canada?"

"Yes. In Ottawa."

"Do you have an address for him?"

"Somewhere I do."

"Four years is a long time to keep up with a former coworker, don't you think?"

"He was a friend, and a very interesting man," Elaine said defensively.

"I'm sure he was. When you find his address, would you please email it to me?" Bernadette recited her email address.

"Certainly."

"Is there anything else about Sergeant Giles that you can pass along?"

"No." Elaine took a breath, obviously trying to maintain her composure. "What a horrible way for a person to die. To be stabbed and then hung upside down like some side of beef. I hope you find whoever did it."

"Actually, that's the job of the Platte County sheriff's office back here in Wyoming. My investigation's centered on break-in and security-breach issues."

"You mean the air force doesn't really care what happened to Thurmond?"

"Of course we do. But the separate responsibilities of civil law enforcement and the air force are pretty clear-cut in cases like this."

"You don't think someone out there roped Thurmond into trying to peddle nuclear secrets, do you?"

"In a case like this, nothing can be discounted."

"Thurmond's murder could've been racially motivated, you know."

"We're aware of that."

"Well, I hope to God there's no espionage involved, but to be honest with you, I wouldn't dismiss it. If anyone out there knew the inner workings of an atomic warhead—how to wire, repair, activate, or transport one—it would have been Thurmond. Maybe someone killed him to gain that knowledge."

"Maybe," Bernadette said, gauging from the somberness in Elaine's voice that the other woman had probably known Thurmond Giles more intimately than she cared to admit.

"So, do you think Thurmond might have been peddling government secrets?"

"I'm afraid I can't say."

"You're sounding very evasive, Major."

"Let's just say that at the moment, I'm unwilling to speculate."

"'Speculate,' 'evasive'—when you come right down to it, they're just a couple of words. Thurmond, on the other hand, was a living, breathing human being. Please tell me you'll find his killer, Major Cameron."

"I'll do my best," Bernadette said, suspecting that any reexplanation of her limited role in investigating what had happened at Tango-11 would fall on deaf ears.

"Thank you. Thank you so much."

"I'll be in touch."

"Okay," Elaine said, clearly fighting back tears as she hung up.

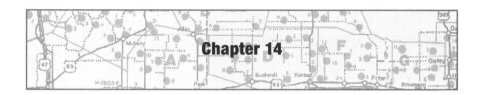
The displeased look on Joel DeWitt's face told Bernadette that she'd made a wrong turn somewhere in her Tango-11 investigation. Moments earlier, without knocking, DeWitt had walked briskly into her office; pulled a chair up to her desk; and in an authoritative, superior-to-subordinate tone said, "I don't appreciate being blindsided, Major. You above all people should know that."

"Sir, I didn't—"

"Let me finish, Major. This morning I had to drive up to Douglas, and you know how much I hate that pig-ugly, two-hour drive. On my way back I stopped in Wheatland and talked to Sheriff Bosack about where he was with our Tango-11 problem. The sheriff was fuming. Seems someone, and we both know who, ran an internet story, masquerading as news, suggesting that the investigation into the security breach and murder at Tango-11 might very well be beyond the ability of the local sheriff and the Office of Special Investigations here at Warren." DeWitt slipped a piece of paper out of a trouser pocket. "Let me quote: 'The small-town sheriff, known to often ride his horse out on investigations, and local air force OSI brass from Warren Air Force Base in Cheyenne, very likely don't have the necessary experience or the skill to determine what happened at Tango-11, or why.'"

As Bernadette leaned forward to respond, the sour-faced colonel waved her off. "And there's more. While I was there with the sheriff, some buffoon from homeland security showed up, and that, I need not tell you, Major Cameron, presents a rather serious problem. All we need is a bunch of those loose-lipped incompetents sniffing around. After Bosack got rid of him, the sheriff informed me that he'd spoken with Sarah Goldbeck earlier in the morning and learned that you and some reporter from the same outfit that ran that ambush story on the web had an altercation with Goldbeck and her husband last evening. Were you planning to fill me in, Major?"

Suspecting that by now Colonel DeWitt had already had a full report from Captain Alvarez detailing everything that Alvarez had seen at Sarah Goldbeck's, and that Sheriff Bosack's reputed anger was merely water to prime DeWitt's own aggravation, Bernadette said, "Sir, I emailed you a preliminary report about what happened last night in Hawk Springs a little earlier."

"Are you inferring that I should've read your report by now, Major?"

"No, sir," said Bernadette, knowing that when DeWitt did read her full report he'd probably heat up from a simmer to a boil.

"Good. The byline on that smear job of an internet piece says Frederick Dames, by the way. Digital Registry News again! I want them out of our hair. Am I clear, Major Cameron?"

"Yes, sir."

"Now that that's settled, I need to remind you of something else you seem to be forgetting. Our first priority here at Warren remains the Tango-11 break-in and security breach. Let Sheriff Bosack worry about who killed Sergeant Giles. It could be that the killer was simply out to settle a score, and Tango-11 was nothing more than a stage prop. One to be talked up on the nightly news, and effectively stroke the killer's ego."

"Perhaps," said Bernadette. "But Sergeant Giles's air force career had warts, Colonel. Ugly ones. His service record's full of them. From what I've been able to dig up so far, the sergeant was quite a womanizer. I'm amazed that he lasted in the air force as long as he did, even if he was one of the most seasoned and skilled missile-warhead maintenance techs in the business. I've had more than a half-dozen verbal confirmations of that expertise. I hate to say it, but it's possible that he decided to sell his skill and knowledge to someone. Someone he ended up getting crossways with, and that person killed him."

"I'd prefer another motive, Major. A much cleaner one for us. We absolutely don't want anything that smells like espionage on our plate. Let's hope Giles's womanizing did him in."

"We can only trace the problem to its source, Colonel."

"You're right on the money there, Major, and your job is to button our Tango-11 problem up and make it go away. I can't overemphasize the fact that situations like this have been known to derail careers."

Thinking, *Mine, Colonel, or yours?* Bernadette asked, "Has any more surfaced concerning the possible hate-crime angle in all of this?"

"Nothing solid. But I'm thinking that, unfortunately, something's bound to bubble up sooner or later. Wilson Jackson, that black activist preacher in town, has left me a half-dozen messages since yesterday. For the time being, I'm letting him simmer."

"He might go to the media."

"Let him. Civilian hate crimes and murders are unfortunately outside our jurisdiction," DeWitt said, smiling.

Not at all surprised at DeWitt's willingness to turn a blind eye to the hate-crime angle, Bernadette asked, "Is there something specific you'd like me to pursue, sir?"

"Yes. Read the latest internet piece by that guy Dames; stay away from reporters like his shag boy, Coseia; and consider the possibility that the trigger for this whole Tango-11 fiasco might have been someone's desire to seek revenge on a used-car salesman of a womanizer."

"And if that wasn't the trigger, sir?"

"It needs to be, Major!" DeWitt rose from his chair, looking as peeved as when he'd first arrived, and took a couple of long, powerful strides toward the door before pausing to add, "And remember, Major, no more talking to reporters." Frowning, he snatched the door open, stepped through it, and slammed the door behind him.

Upset over what he considered exorbitant Albuquerque airport landing fees, Freddy Dames thumped the uncooperative GPS unit in the Mustang convertible he'd just rented at the airport with an open palm and, zipping along at twenty miles per hour over the speed limit, sped toward the offices of the Colbain Transport and Equipment Corporation.

The Colbain corporate offices, twelve miles from the airport, turned out to consist of a five-acre patch of fenced land and a flat-roofed, corrugated-metal building with peeling paint. The land and building sat along an abandoned-looking stretch of poorly maintained New Mexico highway. A sign that read, "Do Not Litter, $500 Fine," was posted a few yards from a cluster of empty motor-oil cans, fast-food trash, and weeds at the property's entrance.

The fences consisted of rusted barbed wire, oil-rigger sucker pipe, a few wooden support posts, and the occasional four-foot-high concrete abutment. Overall, the place had the look of a junkyard rather than a successful heavy-equipment and transport company.

As he pulled into a parking lot on the west side of the flat-roofed building, Freddy counted more than a dozen pieces of heavy equipment sitting in a separate, smaller fenced-off area behind the building. It was high-dollar equipment that included a couple of front-end loaders, at least three long-haul flatbed trailers, two new-looking dump trucks, three bulldozers, and a half-track. Recognizing that he was looking at inventory that could move a small mountain and always appreciative of the entrepreneur, Freddy thought, *Nice.*

Still admiring the inventory, he parked the Mustang, got out, and suddenly found himself thinking about his college summers, spent wildcatting for oil with his geologist father, Cozy, and an uncle in Texas hill country. Aware that Colbain's junkyard-looking acreage and his dilapidated crazy quilt of fences helped to camouflage what was there as much as to protect it, Freddy whispered, "Slick."

When someone stepped up to the car, seemingly out of nowhere, to ask, "Help you, bud?" Freddy turned to find a six-foot-seven-inch, 275-pound blockhead of a man with a stringy goatee and misty-looking blue eyes staring at him.

"I'm looking for Howard Colbain."

"Inside." The man pointed to the building, never taking his eyes off Freddy until he had walked through the front door.

Inside, Freddy found a jovial-looking man with a noticeable paunch and a scar that ran diagonally across most of his fore-head standing in the center of what looked more like a doctor's waiting room than a corporate office. The poorly lit, crescent-shaped room, which smelled of gasoline, greasy shop rags, and cigar smoke, was furnished with seven cheap-looking maple chairs that all hugged an arching back wall. Two dust-covered tables bookended the chairs, and half-a-dozen World War II–vintage pinup calendars hung on the walls.

Waving Freddy into the room, the man, outfitted in jeans and a coffee-stained white T-shirt, asked, "Mr. Dames?"

When Freddy said, "Yes," the man bolted toward him, firmly gripped Freddy's extended hand, and said, "Howard Colbain."

Thinking that Colbain's long, skinny arms, pencil-thin neck, and protruding belly gave him a veritable Michelin-Man look, Freddy wiggled his hand out of the other man's grasp and said, "Pleasure."

"Been expecting you. Grab yourself a seat."

Freddy tried to find a chair that wasn't covered in dust but couldn't. Dusting off a chair with the edge of one hand, he finally took a seat.

"Believe it or not, this building used to be a chiropractor's office," Colbain said, smiling and taking a seat next to him. "I bought it because of the acreage out back." That said, Colbain's smile melted away. "So, now that you know my life story, Mr.

Dames, what's the real reason you're here? It can't simply be to talk about Thurmond Giles. We could have done that on the phone. And just so you know from the start where I stand when it comes to the good sergeant, I hope the devil has the bastard's soul roasting on a spit."

"Straightforward enough," said Freddy. "The answer to your question about my visit's pretty straightforward, too. Face-to-face beats phone-to-phone any day. You don't mind being taped, do you?" Freddy asked. Without waiting for an answer, he slipped a cigarette-pack-sized digital recorder out of his shirt pocket and turned it on.

"Not at all," said Colbain. "And since we're being candid here, I'll tell you right off, I didn't kill the bastard. Should've years ago, but I didn't. The slimy black bastard stole the only thing that ever mattered to me in this world—aside from this business of mine, of course." Colbain drew a long, reflective breath. "He took my wife from me, Mr. Dames. Stole her from right under my nose. But what could she have possibly known about filthy black devils like him? She was just an Iowa farm girl who had the mistaken notion that we're all cut from the same cloth. Before she went off to college, I don't think she'd ever seen more than a half-dozen black people in her life. And she'd sure never met a silver-tongued devil like Giles. He charmed her right out of her pants while I was busy trying to build this business. Voodooed her in his own special way. Poor Annette; she never had a chance."

"I see," Freddy said sympathetically. "Where's your wife now?"

Colbain's eyes widened with surprise. "Figured you'd know about Annette. She killed herself. Shot herself in the head with a

.38 long-barrel after our marriage deep-sixed, her military career tanked, and she finally figured out that her lover boy had gotten the goody out of her and was moving on."

"How long after your marriage broke up did she commit suicide?"

"Three years, almost to the day. Poor thing; she suffered for a long time," Colbain said, shaking his head. "The last time I saw her she was nothing more than a hunched-over stick figure with saggy skin and a face full of spider veins."

"The two of you never considered reconciliation?"

"Not on my part. You only get one chance in this life to do me wrong."

"So what did Giles do for that three years before Annette killed herself?"

"Moved on to a couple other duty stations, where it's my understanding he tried to do the same wife-stealing thing. But the air force was on to him by then, and when he tried to put the moves on another woman—a captain this time—at a base up in Montana, the air force sent him packing. Not before they covered the whole thing up and buried it in reams of paperwork, mind you. After all, they needed his expertise. But they busted him down two ranks, stuck him out at a base in the Mojave Desert, and pulled him off missile maintenance duty, the one thing in the world that I know mattered to the lecherous bastard. And that's where he stayed for the last couple of years of his career, pretty much a nobody supply sergeant handing out belt buckles and uniforms to new recruits until he retired."

"You seem to know an awful lot about Sergeant Giles," Freddy said, checking his tape recorder and relaxing back in his seat.

"I should. I kept tabs on that fucking scumbag for years until I realized that what I was doing was causing me more harm than him."

"Sounds to me like you took one heck of a long-term psychological hit."

"I did, and a financial one, too. I kept a private eye glued to Giles's ass for years. That's how I found out about his shenanigans at that base in Montana."

"Effective but costly," said Freddy. "Do you have any documents or records to support your claim about his problems in Montana?"

"Not really," Colbain said sheepishly. "The brass in charge of the base were busy looking out for their careers. They deep-sixed the paperwork documenting his transgressions. You've got to remember, this all happened over twenty-five years ago. Back before that sexual harassment stuff had any real traction."

"So when did you stop keeping tabs on Giles?"

"Seven years or so back. After I finally figured out that he'd probably never get what should've been coming to him." Colbain broke into a broad, toothy grin. "Turns out I was wrong, though, doesn't it?"

"You mean you had Giles tracked for fifteen years?"

"Closer to sixteen. But like I told you, for a couple of those years the air force had him passing out uniforms in some no-man's-land in the California desert. There wasn't much need for me to track his scaly black ass then. I can tell you this, though. Giles was one angry man for the whole time the air force had his butt boiling out there in the desert. He even sued them—brought in a civilian lawyer to plead his case. Claimed his technical skills were being eroded and that he was being discriminated against. But in the end, he lost." Colbain burst out laughing. "Mr. Big Shot Missile Maintenance Man got his ass kicked by the government."

"How big a wig in the warhead maintenance game do you think Giles was? From what I've been able to gather, he was just another member of the team."

"Another member, my ass. Like I said, things in the military can get whitewashed. Giles was as big as you can get in the air force for a noncom. Annette told me so herself. And he supposedly had an ego to go along with his rep. A rep that in the end, as they say, turned out to be gone with the wind."

"And you had nothing to do with the break-in at the missile-silo site where his body was found, or with his murder?"

Colbain paused and thoughtfully stroked his chin. "You're suddenly sounding like a cop, Mr. Dames. But the answer to your question is no, I didn't."

Unable to tell from Colbain's placid look or body language whether he might be lying, Freddy said, "Nope, I'm just a newsman. But sooner or later the cops, air force OSI, and probably even the FBI will show up on your doorstep, Mr. Colbain. I'm just the leading edge of that wave."

"I know the drill. I've already had calls from some air force OSI major in Wyoming and a man named Bosack who claims to be the Platte County, Wyoming, sheriff. Haven't returned 'em, though," Colbain said, snickering. "And since I didn't kill Giles, I don't really much care who calls, or for that matter what jerk from what government agency drops in. Now, here's a question for you: Why's the Giles murder such a big story in your world?"

"Because, Mr. Colbain, we're dealing with two extremely large elephants in the room: murder and national security."

"As far as national security goes, I wouldn't have put it past Giles to sell out anyone, including his country," said Colbain. "And as for the murder angle, like I've said, I couldn't be happier."

"I wouldn't boast too much about my feelings to the cops if I were you," Freddy said, feeling that Colbain was suddenly sounding a little too smug. "It just might get you arrested.

"Last question," Freddy added quickly as his recorder began to beep, indicating that its battery charge was low. "What happened to Giles after he left the service?"

"I'm not sure. Like I said, I'd quit spending money on having the bastard tailed by then. Last I heard from my PI, he was headed from Seattle for a job in Canada. But I know someone who can probably tell you a lot more about what he did after the air force than me. An ex-army sergeant named Otis Breen. Giles played interservice league basketball both with and against him, and I know for a fact that they were pretty close. I'll get his phone number for you. It's in my office." Colbain got up quickly from his seat.

"Thanks. How well did you know Sergeant Breen?" asked Freddy, standing and rubbing the back of his right leg, happy to be out of his uncomfortable chair.

"Never met the man. That PI I had shadowing Giles for all those years dug up the connection. Knowing anything and everything about Giles was therapy for me back then. The kind of therapy that probably kept me from killing him."

Freddy's recorder stopped, its battery dead. Smiling, Colbain said, "Make sure, whatever you write, that the essence of my anger shines through, Mr. Dames. Now, let's head into my office, and I'll get Otis Breen's phone number for you."

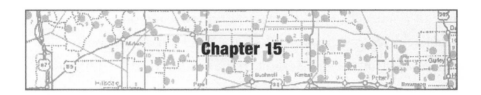

Chapter 15

Decidedly nervous, Bernadette dialed Cozy's cell-phone number. Although she'd been ordered not to talk to him, she found herself drawn to the man who'd saved her butt in Hawk Springs. Perhaps it was because, unlike the Captain Alvarezes of the world, Cozy hadn't seemed eager to either get in her pants or use her as fodder for his own career advancement. In fact, he'd seemed quite capable of taking or leaving her, and, although she was hesitant to admit it, that intrigued her.

She wasn't pleased, however, with what Freddy Dames had said about OSI or the air force in his two internet stories, and that was another important reason to talk to Cozy.

When Cozy hadn't answered after six rings, she sighed, glanced across her office at the photo of her father, and found herself wondering how someone as knee-jerk as "Jackknife" Cameron would have gone about handling a tough problem like Tango-11. Thinking, *With guns a blazing,* she smiled and continued to listen to the ringing, hoping Cozy would pick up.

When Cozy finally answered, "Coseia here," she sat straight up in her chair.

"This is Bernadette."

"Great to hear from you, Bernadette." Cozy set the king-sized bag of potato chips he'd nearly devoured aside on the seat of his truck, cleared his throat, and set the truck on cruise control.

"Guess I should get straight to the point. I read Freddy Dames's latest story, and it isn't very flattering to the air force. You assured me that your stories wouldn't take that tack."

"Mine won't. But Freddy has a tendency to put a negative spin on things."

"I'd say it's more of a tendency to color things yellow in a journalistic-smear sense—yellow enough, unfortunately, for Colonel DeWitt to have set his sights on him. DeWitt may be preening and up-bucking, but he's also very cagey, and he can be vicious. He'll end up with two, maybe even three, stars on his shoulders before his career's end, and people like him don't get that far in the military without a little duplicity in their hearts and a battery of important people behind them. Trust me, DeWitt'll have someone on your boss's tail, and maybe even yours, by the end of the day. FBI, homeland security, perhaps even someone from air force OSI who owes him a favor—but he'll have somebody."

"Freddy can take care of himself."

"And you?"

"I can hold my own."

"I hope so. Just consider what I've just said to be a heads-up, and don't be surprised at being hauled off to some warehouse to have a talk with somebody from the FBI."

"I won't."

Deciding not to rush into telling Cozy about her meeting with Rikia Takata, Bernadette said, "So how about a little tit for tat? What have you got for me that's new?"

"Only this. My boss's executive secretary stumbled onto a lead late last night that sent me running up to Buffalo today before dawn to talk to a rancher named Grant Rivers. Turns out Rivers doesn't have much of a fondness for either our government or the air force. After the air force put two missile-silo sites on his Nebraska land back in the late '80s, he claims the government did its best to steal his water rights and land. To pour salt on the wound, his son later got booted out of the air force academy on a cheating charge."

"Reasons enough to carry a grudge, but how's Rivers tie in to the Giles murder? Did he even admit to knowing Giles?"

"He told me he didn't. He also denied knowing Sarah Goldbeck or Buford Kane. But he did admit to being in the middle of a couple of skirmishes that took place between nuclear-arms protesters and air force security personnel back in the '80s on that property that was once his. No question, he needs to remain someone of interest."

"Agreed. Dig anything else up?"

"No. But I've got something pending. Freddy wants me to check out that Cheyenne preacher, Wilson Jackson."

"Thankfully, for the time being, the good reverend seems to be Colonel DeWitt's cross to bear."

"Glad to hear that DeWitt will be getting his hands a little dirty with something, too. Do you have anything else for me?"

Bernadette's response came hesitantly. She didn't like it that she and Cozy seemed to be trading rather than sharing information, and she didn't relish the fact that she was disobeying a direct order by talking to him. "I've found out a lot more about what Sergeant

Giles did after he left the air force," she said finally. "But I'd prefer talking to you about that in person."

"Afraid your phone's bugged?"

"You never know."

"Fine. I'm on I-25 and headed back your way from Grant Rivers's ranch right now."

"Is ten this evening too late?"

"Works for me. I'm going to grab a bite to eat, then take my time getting back to Cheyenne."

"Where do you want to meet?"

"The Cheyenne airport. And I'll pick you up."

"That's an odd place to meet."

"Not if your conference room's the main cabin of a Gulfstream. Freddy Dames called me a little bit ago. He talked to a guy named Howard Colbain today. Colbain's a potential suspect. Freddy's going to fly into Cheyenne from Albuquerque a little later this evening and he wants me to meet him at the airport so we can compare notes. Three heads might well be better than two. You still game?"

"Yes," said Bernadette, feeling a bit guilty about never having mentioned Colbain to Cozy.

"Fine. I'll call you when I'm a half hour out of Cheyenne, and you can tell me then where to pick you up."

"Your boss owns his own jet?"

Cozy chuckled. "A Gulfstream 150 with the cabin configured so that Freddy has space for his motorcycle, a pull-down bed, and a full bar. Sort of puts the two of you on common ground, don't you think?"

"Not really," said Bernadette, still upset over Freddy's critical internet piece. "Besides," she said proudly, "I flew government-owned fighters, not corporate toys."

Aware that Freddy had plunked down $18 million for *Sugar,* Cozy said, "I'm willing to bet that Freddy's accountants have Uncle Sam somehow paying for his toy, too. I'll call you later, okay?"

"Okay," said Bernadette, wondering as she hung up how two men who were obviously as decidedly different from one another as Cozy and Freddy Dames could be friends.

For Rikia Takata, the trip from Laramie to Heart Mountain had been predictable and boring, and now, as his aging station wagon bumped across an eroded sagebrush flat toward the gathering twilight and onto Heart Mountain property, he knew he wouldn't enjoy the next twelve hours.

Shifting her weight in the Volvo's front seat, Kimiko, who'd driven during the second leg of the trip, stared out at the russet-colored sky. "It's time to read the passage," she said softly. "And in English, please, Rikia."

Knowing that the English translation of what his grandfather had written sixty-seven years earlier always seemed to fill Kimiko with a deeper anger than the same passage in its original Japanese, Rikia looked out on the orange-and-purple glow of the sunset. Aware that Kimiko would continue her ritualistic Heart Mountain agenda no matter what until sunrise the next morning, he opened his grandfather's leather-bound diary and began reading aloud from it: "'I was working as a news photographer outside the city of Hiroshima's water plant when I heard a loud explosion and almost instantly felt a searing rush of heat. My first thought was that a nearby army base's gas tanks had exploded, but sadly the thought soon disappeared. I knew in my heart what the flash of light that I had seen to the north represented because for more than two months Japanese newspapers, including my own, had been printing stories warning everyone that a new type of bomb would soon be used by the Americans on the Japanese people. The stories claimed that the bomb had the capability of wiping out an entire city. However, even as a newsperson, I had no reason to believe that the stories were any more than propaganda published by fainthearted men like the editor of the *Nippon Times*.

"'But as I stood there in the suffocating heat, panting like a dog, realizing that the hair on my arms had disappeared as I'd listened to the rumbling explosion of thunder from another world, I knew the special bomb that the newspapers had spoken of had been dropped on our city.

"'Out of reflex, I suspect, I decided that what I needed to do was take pictures of what was occurring, so I headed in the direction the explosion had come from. When I reached a collapsed army warehouse that had been flattened like a cardboard box, I stopped to watch a white column of smoke that soon turned to pink rise in the sky. Eventually the top of the column began to swell until after twenty minutes or so the entire ungodly-looking thing had the appearance of a saucer on a stick. I took picture after picture of the strange-looking column with the saucer on top, never knowing whether or not the pictures would come out.

"'After another ten minutes or so, rain began to fall, rain that was at first dirty brown and then smoky black. The rain seemed to release a kind of poisonous gel that stuck like glue to my skin. Shivering in disbelief, I put my camera away and headed toward the city. I walked for nearly an hour, making my way into and through clouds of dust. I walked along the edge of a foggy yellow drizzle that hugged the river. I walked for a good twenty minutes without seeing anyone until, out of nowhere and directly in my path, I saw a cavalry horse standing alone in front of a clump of leafless trees that had been scorched to their roots. The horse was salmon pink. The blast from the bomb had seared off all its hide. As the pitiful-looking beast approached me, faltering with each step, I realized that it was carrying a rider who was charred almost black from head to toe. I watched for a few moments as animal and rider, unaware of my presence, veered to my left and walked toward the river to disappear into the yellow haze. Thoughts of my wife and children, coworkers and countrymen, worked their way through my head, but it was the image of the charbroiled rider astride a pink horse that stayed with me the rest of the day.'"

Rikia stopped reading and looked at Kimiko, who'd pulled the station wagon to a stop. He knew that she expected him to read for the next five pages, on to a point where his grandfather borrowed a bicycle from a local doctor only to realize as the doctor handed the bike over to him that the doctor's fingers had been fused to the handlebars. But he didn't. Perhaps it was because everything around him seemed so suddenly peaceful. Or maybe it was because, for a change, Kimiko wasn't urging him to read on. Whatever had sparked the change in her ritual was known to her alone. A minute or so later, when she moved to get out of the station wagon, he knew that she was back on track. Once she was out of the vehicle, he knew she would perch herself on the three-legged stool she'd brought and stare trance-like toward Heart Mountain Butte, and remain there mumbling to herself, sometimes in Japanese, sometimes in English, until he'd set up their campsite.

He'd often wondered why Kimiko insisted that their visits to Heart Mountain remain such a raw, primitive experience. Why after so many years couldn't they at least bring modern camping equipment or, even better, stay in a motel? He'd asked her once when he was a college student, after two hellish rainstorm-filled days at Heart Mountain, why they had to endure such god-awful conditions. She'd simply replied, "Because it tests our courage, our commitment, and our sanity. Things you'll surely need in abundance one day, Rikia." He'd never forgotten that comment even though their trips to the remote, 740-acre patch of nowhere named after nearby Heart Mountain Butte now numbered in the sixties, and the internment center's military-style barracks and ancillary buildings, which had once sat a mere sixty miles east of Yellowstone National Park, had either been sold to local residents or allowed to decay.

It wasn't until 2007 that 124 acres of the internment camp became a national historic landmark. Somehow Kimiko had learned that the barrack she had lived in had been on a fifty-acre parcel carved from the original Heart Mountain acreage and purchased by the Heart Mountain Wyoming Foundation in the late 1990s. On one of their trips to Heart Mountain, she'd even been able to pinpoint the barrack's exact location, pointing out a rusting water spigot and a granite building foundation corner in which she'd once carved her initials. Now, whenever they made a trip to Heart

Mountain, she made a point of turning over a spadeful of dirt at that site. Burying the past, Kimiko called it.

Rikia had just finished preparing their campsite when Kimiko finally rose from her stool and turned her gaze away from Heart Mountain. Knowing better than to engage her while she was still so focused, he remained silent and watched her walk away from the mountain into what had become darkness.

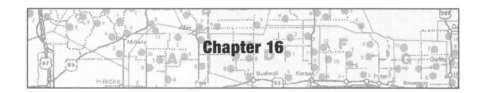

Chapter 16

Following Cozy's introduction moments earlier, Bernadette and Freddy Dames had circled one another like determined heavyweights, Bernadette looking incensed and Freddy not at all apologetic. Deciding to save her grievances until later, however, Bernadette had tempered her upset and now sat at the controls of Freddy's Gulfstream 150, surveying the cockpit and thinking that for $18 million the plane should have had more legroom.

The flight deck was clearly more posh, user-friendly, and inviting than the utilitarian, space capsule–like, black-on-black, instrument-filled cockpit of an A-10, a space she would've given anything to be cramped inside right then. But it was a flight deck, and it was the first time she'd set foot in an aircraft cockpit for over a year. All but salivating, she found herself excitedly fiddling with every switch, button, and toggle in sight as Cozy looked on, smiling.

By the time Freddy, who was standing behind her in a half crouch, had finished his spiel about the aircraft and Cozy had brought both of them up to speed on his visit with Grant Rivers, Bernadette's hands were moist with a strange, lost-opportunity kind of anticipation. Gazing wistfully out the cockpit window, she found herself eager to take *Sugar* for a ride.

"So what do you think of my *Sugar*?" Freddy asked Bernadette as Cozy, tired of crouching, headed for the main cabin.

Bernadette turned and realized that Cozy had stopped to stare at a motorcycle that was secured to the cabin's rear bulkhead by four leather straps. She said, "I like. But the motorcycle's a little bit on the overkill side of speed, don't you think?"

"I like to enjoy speed wherever I am."

Bernadette watched Cozy continue to stare at the motorcycle as if it were something venomous. "I'm not sure Cozy feels the same," she said, watching a look of guilt spread across Freddy's face. She knew she'd touched a nerve when Freddy stood, nearly bumping his head on the ceiling, and said, "I think it's time we get to the business at hand."

Moments later, as they sat around a small, marble-topped table in the main cabin, Freddy, still looking uncomfortable, said, "So here we are. Three peas in a pod. Who wants to start?"

"I think we should thank Bernadette for meeting with us first," Cozy said. "She's taking a heck of a risk, especially since she's been ordered not to talk to us."

"By some pinhead?" Freddy shot back.

"Can we stay away from any name-calling, Mr. Dames?" Bernadette said, looking to Cozy for support.

"Ease up, damn it, Freddy, okay?" Cozy's authoritative response to his boss surprised Bernadette. Thinking, *Secure brother,* she tried not to smile.

"Yeah, yeah, sorry, and like I told you earlier, Major, I prefer Freddy. Why don't we start with what I dug up on Howard Colbain since Cozy's already given us a thumbnail on the right-leaning Mr. Rivers."

"So, how did Colbain strike you?" Cozy asked.

"Much like Rivers, he's angry. Turns out Sergeant Giles destroyed his marriage and, in his eyes, at least, drove his former wife to commit suicide."

Bernadette looked startled. "Suicide?"

"Yep. Shot herself in the head with a .38 a couple of years after ending her affair with Giles."

"So Colbain had a reason for wanting to kill the good sergeant," said Cozy.

"Absolutely. And I'd say Colbain's got enough resentment and pent-up anger trapped inside him to have done it. Not quite the same level of anger as Grant Rivers's, though. I'd say Colbain is a high simmer, and Rivers is more of a full boil. Even so, I don't think either of them could've muscled Giles into that missile-access tube on their own. Colbain has a big blockhead of a yardman who could have helped out."

"And Rivers could have had help from that tractor-driving son of his that Cozy mentioned," said Bernadette.

"And both men know their way around heavy equipment," Freddy added. "They probably have the mechanical and explosives know-how to blow an access-tube hatch cover." He looked at Bernadette for confirmation.

"True on all counts," Bernadette said. "But like those tricky old college exam questions we've all sweated through like to ask, is what we've dug up on the two of them, although perhaps true, unrelated to the Giles murder?"

"Good point," said Cozy. "Why drop Giles's body off at Tango-11 after you've stabbed him to death somewhere else if you're Colbain or Rivers? You'd only risk incriminating yourself, it seems to me."

"Maybe Rivers was simply out to thumb his nose at the air force one last time. And maybe Colbain's one of those catch-me-if-you-can types," said Freddy. "I can tell you this about Colbain: he's a bulldog. He had a PI tracking Giles for sixteen years, and that's one hell of a long time to stew. Right now I'd put him at the top of my list of suspects."

"What about you?" Bernadette asked Cozy.

"No reason to scratch either man off."

Suddenly sounding almost competitive, Freddy said, "Here's another Colbain nugget. Turns out that all those years he had Giles tailed paid some dividends in the end. His PI found out just before Colbain cut the money spigot off that Giles was leaving Seattle and a job he'd had for years for one in Canada. Do either of you have any information about that?"

"No," Cozy said, looking at Bernadette.

When she hesitated, Cozy said, "You're in up to your eyeballs now, Bernadette. Might as well lay everything you've found on the table."

"I could get court-martialed."

"And the pope could renounce his religion. Come on, Major, we're dealing with a murder here," said Freddy.

"Actually, we could be dealing with issues that are far more serious than that. I found out that after Sergeant Giles left the air force, he went to work for a weapons guidance system firm in Seattle and from there, like Colbain's PI confirmed, Giles moved to Canada to work for a company that makes radiation therapy equipment."

"And the connection between what he did in the air force and what he did for those companies in Seattle and Canada is?" asked Freddy.

"The connection, I'm afraid, is nuclear."

"Any chance Giles could have gotten himself involved in selling nuclear secrets?" Cozy asked.

"Perhaps," Bernadette said, nodding. "He had immense practical and technical knowledge about nuclear warheads and their maintenance. And there's no question that after the air force stuck him out in the California desert, effectively ending his career, his ego was bruised. I've read through his personnel file."

"More like crushed, according to Colbain," Freddy said.

"What better way to exact a little revenge on the people who did the crushing than to peddle a little inside dope about the workings of the American nuclear-missile arsenal to someone out there who might be interested?" said Bernadette.

"What could he have told them?" Freddy asked.

"Lots," Cozy said quickly. "Like how the pieces of a nuclear warhead fit together, maybe, or insight on how the things are wired. Maybe he could even have told somebody how to trigger one."

Bernadette shook her head. "All of those would be a stretch."

"Okay," said Cozy. "So, back to my earlier question. Why kill Giles, move his body to an abandoned missile site, since according to Sheriff Bosack he clearly wasn't killed at Tango-11, and string him up naked for the world to eventually see if you're involved in secretly buying U.S. military secrets?"

"I don't know, frankly," said Bernadette. "Maybe we should ask a psychologist."

"Or somebody like Howard Colbain or Grant Rivers," said Freddy.

"Which means we've come full circle, and we'll need to dig a whole lot deeper to figure out what the real murder motive was," said Bernadette.

"So, we'll do that," said Freddy. "For the time being, why don't we move on to the Takatas; Sarah Goldbeck; and sweet, lovable ol' Buford Kane. How do you think the four of them fit into all this?"

"I'm not sure," said Bernadette. "Other than we know for sure that Goldbeck and Kimiko Takata spent years trying to put the brakes on all things nuclear."

"So maybe by killing Giles in the manner they did, they get their antinuclear message resurrected," said Freddy.

"Maybe. But just like Rivers, Goldbeck, Kane, and the Takatas claim they've never heard of Giles."

Freddy shook his head in disbelief. "Strange that nobody who's a suspect, except Colbain, has ever heard of the murdered man. Damnedest thing."

"Well, somebody out there knew him," said Cozy. "You talked to Rikia Takata, Bernadette. What's your take on him?"

"Calling the man 'excitable' would be an understatement, and like Colbain and Rivers, he's angry."

"About what?" asked Freddy.

"About the internment of Japanese Americans here in Wyoming during World War II, for one thing, and about not getting his scientific due, for another."

Cozy looked puzzled. "But it was his cousin Kimiko who was interned, not him, right?"

"Right. And who knows, she may be even angrier than he is. We'll just have to find out."

"I like your use of the word *we*, Major," Freddy said, smiling. "It's almost as if you've been recruited to the dark side."

Bernadette's unsmiling silence caused Freddy to quickly ask, "Is there anybody else who might have known or interacted with Giles that we're leaving out?"

"There's that preacher here in Cheyenne, Wilson Jackson, but thankfully, he's Colonel DeWitt's cross to bear, not mine. He could have known Giles. DeWitt's been avoiding him like the plague, by the way."

"Well, knock me over with a feather," said Freddy. "Someone who might have actually known the murdered man. Why's DeWitt dodging the good reverend?"

"Because he doesn't want what at this stage is a simple break-in and security-breach investigation to turn into a hate-crime investigation. If it does, there'll be lawyers and FBI types crawling all over Warren, looking in every sock drawer. That's never a good spot for anyone who's looking to make general to be in."

"I warned you earlier that we'd likely need to talk to Reverend Jackson," Freddy said to Cozy. "You up for staying in Cheyenne another night and talking to him tomorrow morning? I would, but I've gotta be back in Denver for a seven a.m. meeting."

Shrugging, Cozy said, "Yeah."

"Great. I'll have what we've discussed here tonight knitted into a story by first thing in the morning. How about 'Nobody Knows Thurmond' as the header?" Freddy said, chuckling.

"It's pretty much accurate," said Cozy.

"More accurate than your first two stories," Bernadette said, frowning. "No more hammering the air force, Freddy, okay?

Because if you do, I'll become very uncooperative. I'll also make sure someone hammers back."

"Message received, Major."

"And I'd be real careful with my finger-pointing in the future if I were you," said Bernadette. "The FBI doesn't care whose sock drawers they ransack."

"I've had FBI types on my doorstep before. CIA types, too," Freddy said. "Handled 'em both."

"And us OSI types? Have you dealt with us before?"

"No, I haven't, but I'll be sure to give you a heads-up on the experience after I've worked with one for a while," Freddy said with a wink. "For now, is there any other serious digging we need to do?"

"We should probably look a little more closely at those Seattle and Canadian leads that have turned up," said Cozy.

"And I'll keep trying to connect with an army friend of Giles's," said Freddy. "A guy named Otis Breen who Giles played interservice league basketball with. Howard Colbain gave me his name. I haven't been able to catch up with him by phone yet."

"Guess at this stage, any lead's worth working," said Bernadette. "Why don't you give Cozy and me this guy Breen's contact info, too?" Sounding exhausted, she asked Freddy, "Mind if I take another look at the cockpit?"

"Be my guest." As she rose and headed for the cockpit, Freddy whispered to Cozy, "Guess it's hard to take the hunt out of the dog."

"Guess so," Cozy said, watching Bernadette disappear into the cockpit.

A couple of minutes later, Cozy stepped into the cockpit to find

Bernadette staring out into the darkness. Handing her Otis Breen's phone number, he said, "Ready to run you home."

When she turned to face him, he couldn't help but notice a look on her face that he knew all too well. It was the hurt-child look of someone who's lost an opportunity to fulfill a dream.

"She just left with that same reporter who was at Hawk Springs," Carlos Alvarez announced as he sat in the dark in his Jeep just outside a Cheyenne airport security fence, night-vision goggles in hand, talking nervously on his cell phone to Colonel DeWitt.

"And the other man with them? What happened to him?" Colonel DeWitt asked.

"He's still in the plane."

"Has to be Dames, Coseia's boss," said DeWitt. "He's a pilot. I've checked. How long were they inside?"

"From the time Major Cameron and Coseia arrived until a couple of minutes ago. Forty minutes or thereabouts."

"Well, well, well. The flypaper gets stickier. Stay with Coseia and Cameron."

"Yes, sir. They're getting into Coseia's truck. My guess is, he's taking her home."

"Question is, to whose home? His or hers?"

Sounding and looking deflated, Alvarez said, "Good question."

"I'm going to need a lot of help on this one, Captain. Especially if things start to go south and I have to lean on Major Cameron. Her father's a retired one-star, you know. And not without influence. He's the son of a Tuskegee airman, no less. Gotta watch how hard you lean when you're dealing with that kind of history."

"I understand, sir."

"Good that you do. Thanks to Major Cameron, this whole Tango-11 fiasco is likely to end up with the two of us sitting at some murder trial in a civilian courtroom. Think you can handle the pressure if it comes to that?"

"Absolutely."

"Good again. Call back and debrief me when you're done with your surveillance for the night."

"Yes, sir." Alvarez closed his cell phone and laid it on the seat beside him. He'd had the sense from the way Bernadette had avoided him at work that she might have spotted him as he'd trailed her from Hawk Springs. He'd make certain this time, however, to stay far enough behind the reporter's dually to remain undetected. Disappointed, he thought that if Colonel DeWitt did pull Bernadette off the Tango-11 investigation and he ended up as her replacement, he'd lose any chance of bagging the woman whom nearly everyone in the missile detachment called "Brown Sugar" behind her back. He hoped it wouldn't come to that, but his ambition, like Colonel DeWitt's, trumped a roll in the hay any day.

For Silas Breen, it had been one dog of a day. After he'd left South Bend on an emotional high, things had gone downhill fast. First, he'd had trouble with his truck—minor trouble, but trouble nonetheless. The time required to repair another blown tire and replace an uncooperative radiator thermostat had put him further behind, and, combined with the hours he'd spent at Notre Dame, he now found himself close to twelve hours behind his delivery schedule. Add in the extra mileage he'd have to log traveling to Lubbock instead of Amarillo, and he expected to arrive fourteen to fifteen hours late.

He could try to make up the time by running all night, like old-time over-the-road truckers used to do, but if he did, the *Star Wars*–looking mileage, time, and distance computer sitting just inches from his right hand, a tool that had replaced outdated handwritten truckers' logs, could be his undoing. Especially if he were unlucky enough to have some eager port-of-entry flunky at a weigh station demand a point-to-point time, distance, and mileage printout. If he got caught cheating the system that way, he'd likely receive the kind of hefty fine that would wipe out a good portion of the trip's profit. Shaking his head, muttering, "Shit," and speeding down I-55 past a sign that read, "St. Louis—46," he expected that it would be one in the morning before his head hit any pillow.

He'd talked to only three people since leaving South Bend: the young girl who'd taken his McDonald's order just south of Chicago, the toothless old man at a gas station who'd illegally plugged his flat tire instead of breaking it down and patching it properly, and the Mexican who could barely speak English who'd fixed his radiator problem. More importantly, though, he hadn't talked to F. Mantew all day. He'd finally decided that that was a good thing. If Mantew didn't care about him being on time with his delivery, why the hell should he?

Holding up an arm to ward off the headlight glare from an oncoming semi whose driver had failed to dim his lights, he muttered, "Jerk," slowed his rig, and retrieved a peanut-butter-and-jelly sandwich from the open cooler on the seat next to him. When a second truck rolled by, its lights on high beam as well, he countered by flashing high beams of his own and yelling, "Asshole!" before angrily chomping into his sandwich and mumbling with his mouth full, "Fuck Mantew."

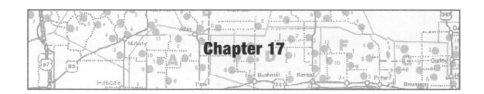

Chapter 17

Kimiko Takata refused to leave Heart Mountain until she'd watched the sunrise, so while Rikia sat in the backseat of the station wagon with the vehicle's interior lights on and a flashlight in one hand, working out math calculations and putting the final polish on his paper for El Paso, Kimiko sat outside, her eyes fixed on the sun.

"Do you know how many lives were destroyed here?" she asked Rikia, breaking a fifteen-minute silence.

Repeating the number he'd heard her quote since his childhood, he said, "Thousands."

"Thousands out of the 10,767 who were imprisoned here, to be exact."

Rikia wanted to shout back, *But there aren't any people here now, Kimiko. No more internment camp, no more barracks, no more barbed wire, and no more guards. Just a bleak, dusty sagebrush plain.* He knew better, however, than to challenge Kimiko when she was in one of her increasingly frequent retrospective moods. Those moods sometimes transitioned into long, blank, empty stares, and any attempt to question her would only serve to spike what he'd come to realize was creeping dementia.

Adjusting herself on her stool, Kimiko swept her right arm in a slow arc from west to east. "Barbed-wire fences surrounded this dreadful place for as far as you could see. Guard towers equipped with high-beam searchlights surrounded the compound, and although the American government has always claimed that the guards were unarmed, they weren't."

Remaining silent, Rikia continued with his equations.

"The barracks were no more than tar-paper shacks." Kimiko slammed an arthritic fist into her palm. "Barbaric! There's no other word for it." Pointing toward Heart Mountain Butte, she talked in a whisper as the sun peeked from behind a thin layer of clouds. "We only had a single stove for heat and one light fixture in the center of the room, and we sometimes slept ten to a room."

Rikia barely looked up. He'd heard Kimiko's Heart Mountain stories scores of times before. He knew all there was to know about the tragedy of her flight from Japan before the war. She had been sent by her father to America to live with relatives so she'd be out of harm's way when the American invasion of Japan that he had long been predicting came. The invasion never came, however, only Hiroshima and Nagasaki and the bomb. Shaking his head and completing an equation that now took up the better part of three pages, Rikia jotted, $21H + 21H \pm X + Energy$ and smiled as Kimiko continued.

"I'd only been in America for nine months when they stuck me in this awful place. Are you listening to me, Rikia?"

"Yes, and I know. It was a terrible time back then, and unfortunately for us Japanese, it hasn't changed." Rikia had his own reasons for hating the people he was now forced to call his countrymen—people who had killed his relatives and in all likelihood, as far as he was concerned, planted the seeds for Kimiko's dementia. Even now, in spite of his reputation as one of America's most stellar mathematicians, his colleagues, educated people who should have known better, whispered and joked about his speech impediment and his Goodwill-bought clothes. Those things, however, amounted to no more than pinpricks to him. What infuriated Rikia most about living in a country he'd never had a choice about coming to was that, in spite of his lofty academic credentials and international reputation, his life's work remained scoffed at, labeled by most of his American colleagues as no more than pseudoscience.

Over the years, their skepticism and lack of support had caused his National Institutes of Health and National Science Foundation proposals to be denied and had delayed groundbreaking publications. If it weren't for the backing of a few highly regarded Japanese and European mathematicians, he had every reason to believe that by now his work would have largely been dismissed.

When Kimiko announced loudly, "Sun's almost up," he ignored her and began putting his papers away. Unwilling to listen to any more of her Heart Mountain stories and sounding frustrated, he said, "You've seen your sunrise, Kimiko. I think we should go."

Kimiko's response, "Yes. I think we should," surprised him. She added, "Now, when the authorities come to question me about Tango-11, I will have the resolve to stand up to them. I only needed a dose of Heart Mountain medicine to bolster my courage."

Rikia simply answered, "Good."

Twenty minutes later they were back on the highway, headed home for Laramie. Kimiko's dull, accusatory monotone echoed in Rikia's ear as she read from her father's Hiroshima diary:

"'Suffocating clouds of dust swirled around me. Thick, stifling, blackish clouds filled with everything from the tiniest of dust particles to sheets of human skin. I could see that houses had collapsed or been blasted totally apart all around me. In every direction, twenty-foot-tall telephone poles continued to ignite and explode like towering pine trees caught in some horrific forest fire.

"'People meandered past me as I walked along the road. The anguished looks on their frequently skinless faces begged for explanation. As I headed along the river once again to watch a group of catatonic-looking survivors place sliced cucumbers on the soon-to-be-fatal burns of their neighbors, my thoughts drifted back to the charbroiled man astride his pink horse.'"

The early-morning reception Bernadette got when she called Otis Breen at his home in Kansas City was cold and clearly on the suspicious side. Breen, who admitted to having known Thurmond Giles and to have played interservice league basketball with and against him, remained evasive until she announced, stretching the truth, that she was the lead air force OSI officer in charge of investigating Sergeant Giles's murder.

Sounding stunned, Otis Breen asked, "What did you say your name was again?"

"Major Bernadette Cameron."

"And you work out of?"

"Warren Air Force Base in Cheyenne."

"Wyoming. Understand the wind blows a tad bit out that way. So, how did Thurmond buy it?"

"A rural-route mail carrier found him dangling by his ankles from a chain inside the personnel-access tube to a Minuteman missile silo. He had five stab wounds in his back."

"Can't say I'm surprised," Otis said after a brief silence.

"In addition to the stab wounds, the head of his penis had been cut off, wadded up in a piece of paper, and stuffed in his mouth."

"That figures, too. Thurmond wasn't very picky when it came to findin' somewhere to stick his member. I wouldn't put it past a jealous girlfriend or some jealous husband to do him in."

Thinking suddenly about Elaine Richardson, Bernadette said, "Food for thought."

"So, how'd you get my name?"

"By way of a man named Howard Colbain. Turns out a couple of decades back, Sergeant Giles had an affair with Colbain's wife. Any chance you know Colbain?"

Breen took a long, deep breath before answering, "Nope. But I may have known the wife. A chunky little white girl outta Iowa. I'm thinkin' her last name was Colbain, at least, and that she was a second lieutenant."

"Right on both counts," said Bernadette, who'd been able to gather several official air force photos of the late Annette Colbain.

"Then yeah, I knew her, and I'm pretty sure she ended up killin' herself. Thurmond mentioned that to me once."

"She did."

"Means she couldn't have killed Thurmond, then."

"No. But from what you're confirming about Sergeant Giles, there may have been more jealous husbands or spurned women out there. Can you think of any other reasons why someone might've wanted to kill him?"

"Yeah, money. That and the brother's over-the-top ego. They both tended to keep him in hot water."

"Can you give me a for-instance?"

"Sure. Back in the early 1980s we had a pretty high-flyin' interservice all-star basketball team. One that would've matched up pretty well with some NBA squads. I was twenty-five at the time. Could've jumped outta the gym back then," Breen said proudly. "Thurmond was a year or so older. We ended up playin' just about everywhere on the planet for a couple of years. Here in the U.S., Asia, Europe, you name it—real easy duty. Anyway, somewhere along the line Thurmond got it in his head that we should set up a wagerin' system that would allow folks to bet on our games. Nothin' involvin' point-shaving or shenanigans like that. Just good old-fashioned illegal bookmaking on the side. Thurmond worked out a system that eventually had him and a couple of other guys on the team makin' serious money. A grand or so a game, it came out later."

"And you weren't involved?"

"I ain't that stupid. We were in the military, remember? No need riskin' time in the brig over a game meant to be played by children. Anyway, like always, Thurmond ended up with his tit in the wringer. And just like always, he skirted the problem because of his connections. A couple of high-muckety-muck generals who I was later told were in on the bettin' scam with him got him off with just a hand slap."

"And nothing of consequence ever came of it?"

"Not a damn thing but a bunch of military gossip. Thurmond was charmed like that. The only time I ever saw the spell broken was when the air force ended up sending him off to some Mojave Desert no-man's-land of a base in California as punishment for his over-the-top workplace womanizing. It was a shame, really, especially for somebody with Thurmond's talent. I expect you already know that that squirrelly lookin' SOB was one of the top warhead maintenance men and troubleshooters in the business. It was common knowledge even among us army types that if the air force had a problem with a nuke back then, anything from a wiring problem to missile transport issues to a loose-fittin' bolt, they called Thurmond."

"And he'd fix it?"

"Absolutely, and because of those skills, unlike most senior enlisted guys, he spent a hell of a lot of his time winin' and dinin' with the brass. A habit that along with his womanizin' cost him in the end. But it's always that way when someone higher up the food chain is lookin' to take the glory, right, Major?"

Ignoring the bait, Bernadette said, "And did someone higher up the chain end up with what should have been Sergeant Giles's glory?"

"You got that straight. Wouldn't have, though, except for Thurmond's big mouth. Told me so himself. Turns out that when those disarmament treaties with the Russkies started taking shape in the late '80s and the air force was told to downsize its nuclear arsenal, Thurmond's the one who got the assignment to straw-boss the crews who were deactivatin' those puppies. And wouldn't you know it, that slick-assed beanpole of an egomaniac figured out how he could stand down those missiles in half the time the brass was thinkin' it would take, and with half the manpower. Problem is, braggart that he was, Thurmond shared his plan with one of his superiors. Some kiss-ass light colonel who ended up implementin' the deal and takin' all the credit. Thurmond was bitter for the rest of the time I knew him over the fact that some up-buckin' officer stole his idea and his glory."

"When's the last time you talked to Giles?"

"Six months or so back, or thereabouts. He was livin' in Canada, workin' for some medical equipment company. Seemed to be doin' okay, as far as I could tell. We talked about the old days, and about some of the twists and turns life always seems to take. And we spent a little time talkin' about my kid, who'd been a college basketball bust. I remember tellin' Thurmond that the boy seemed to have finally found himself and that he'd started his own business. Never talked to him again after that. Guess I should have, given the way things have worked out."

"Did he have any enemies that you know of?"

"Besides the husband of that lieutenant who killed herself, you mean?"

"Yes."

"None that I recall."

"One last question, and I think we're through. Was Giles in any way linked to the antinuclear movement that took place out here in the Rockies back in the late '70s and early '80s, and is there any chance that he was friendly with any of the movement's leaders?"

"That's two questions, and the answer's no on both counts. Thurmond didn't have much use for dipshits, fainthearted patriots, commies, or whiners. He was red, white, and blue through and through. We done?"

"Yes," Bernadette said, surprised by Breen's directness. "Let me give you my cell-phone number in case you remember something important you may have forgotten. You can get me on it anytime." She recited the number.

"Got it," said Breen. "But I can tell you right now, I've told you pretty much everything I know about the man. By the way, do you know anything about funeral arrangements?"

"I'm afraid not."

"Terrible for Thurmond not to have anyone there for him at the end. But I guess there's probably nobody out there who cares, really, except maybe me. It probably goes all the way back to our basketball connection and the sharin' and carin' we did there. Sort of a been-through-the-wars-together, squadron-leader-to-wingman kind of thing. Something that you bein' OSI and not a pilot wouldn't understand."

"Perhaps not," Bernadette said, glancing down at her pilot wings. Polishing the wings with the cuff of her shirtsleeve, she hung up, wondering how Cozy's meeting with Wilson Jackson had gone.

Most of what Cozy had so far been able to get out of his visit with Wilson Jackson as he and the reverend sat in Jackson's dingy, musty parsonage office were complaints. That and a 1960s-newsreel-type rehash of how blacks had been getting the shaft in America for more than 235 years.

Each time Cozy tried to get Jackson to talk about Thurmond Giles, the sad-eyed, balding, ebony-skinned man with oversized teeth and the barest hint of a mustache segued into another tirade about America's lengthy mistreatment of the black man, emphasizing with each new assault that the Giles killing had to have been a hate crime.

When Jackson, scrutinizing Cozy from his massive, throne-like wingback chair, asked indignantly, "How much black blood have you got in you, Mr. Coseia? If I had to guess, I'd say you're easily half."

"As much as any Dominican transplant," Cozy said, checking his temper and thinking back to what his grandmother, the proud firstborn of a French mother and Nigerian father and an outspoken critic of onetime Haitian president Papa Doc Duvalier, would have certainly said about a zealot like Jackson: *Papa Doc likes to boast about being French, and about not having but a pinprick of African blood, but Lord knows the only thing French about that lying African is the toast he eats in the morning.*

"Well, you need to find out how much for certain," Jackson scolded.

Having had his fill of the bombastic, opinionated little preacher, Cozy sat forward in his chair and locked eyes with Jackson. "I'll do that, asshole. Now, can you tell me anything useful about Thurmond Giles?"

Surprised and insulted, Jackson said, "I can tell you this. He was the kind of man who'd sell you out in a heartbeat."

"And you know that because?" Cozy said, with the authority of someone who'd just unmasked a fraud.

"Because he spent two years as a member of my congregation, and I knew him. Black man or not, he was a loser and a user."

Sensing that Jackson's dislike for Giles was somehow personal, Cozy asked, "Nothing more specific?"

"Nothing. We can sit here all day, and I'll say the same thing. So let's not," Jackson said, rising from his chair to indicate that their mostly one-sided discussion had reached an end. "All I can say is that I hope the authorities find his killer."

"Makes two of us," said Cozy, standing and making a point of not shaking Jackson's hand. He was halfway across the room when he stopped and turned back to face the irritating little preacher. "One last question. Why so vocal about the Giles killing being a hate crime? Nothing at all has surfaced that I'm aware of to suggest that it was."

"Because, as I've been telling you for the past twenty minutes, Mr. Coseia, I know America. It's my job, and it should be yours, to keep a spotlight on our racist oppressors."

"Guess I've got it wrong, then. I thought my job was to deliver the news, and yours was saving souls." Leaving Jackson looking dismayed, Cozy continued toward the door. "You've got my number. Call me if something you think might be important surfaces."

Thinking as he walked across the parsonage grounds to his truck that Jackson was the kind of man his grandmother would've called *a nobody looking to be somebody,* Cozy paused briefly and shook his head, certain that the good Reverend Jackson hadn't told him everything he knew about Thurmond Giles.

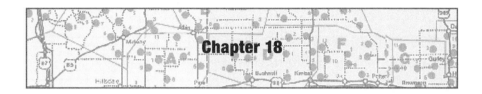

Chapter 18

The FBI agent who stopped by Freddy Dames's office unannounced a little after nine forty-five a.m. sounded far more homespun than the half-dozen or so spit-and-polish agents Freddy had run across during his journalistic career. To top it off, the man looked foppish and out of FBI character, dressed as he was in a Panama hat, black-and-white wingtip British walkers, and a barely wrinkled seersucker suit.

After announcing who he was in a slow West Texas drawl, removing his hat, handing Freddy his business card, and shaking Freddy's hand, Thaddeus Richter, a twenty-two-year veteran of the FBI, took a seat across from Freddy in one of the room's three eight-thousand-dollar overstuffed, imported Italian leather chairs and went straight to work. "I've been following your stories on the internet, Mr. Dames. You're quite the persistent reporter. Three groundbreaking stories in the space of two days. Made me want to drop by and see if you wouldn't mind sharing any information about the Thurmond Giles murder that you haven't yet sent into cyberspace. And while you're at it, perhaps you can tell me more about Sergeant Giles's link to the possible sale of American nuclear secrets—which you've so intriguingly hinted at in your stories. To tell you the truth, sir, our agency hasn't been able to establish such a connection."

"That's probably because there's not a straightforward link," Freddy said, watching Richter slip a trifolded sheet of paper out of a suit-coat pocket, unfold the paper, and lay it on the coffee table in front of him.

"But it says right here in a story you posted this morning that 'Thurmond Giles was a man with virtually unlimited access to our nation's most sophisticated nuclear weaponry, a man with the skill and authority to have worked for twenty years on the air force's arsenal of nuclear-missile warheads. He was a man who knew not only what made America's Minuteman missiles tick and where they were located but who moved them around the High Plains West with impunity until his sexual misconduct caused him to be shipped off to an American Siberia. It's entirely possible that Giles, long smarting from a series of perceived slights, career-ending reprimands, reductions in rank, and transfer of duties, may have decided that his nuclear knowledge was worth selling. That decision may have gotten him killed.' Have I quoted you correctly, Mr. Dames?"

"To the letter," Freddy said, smiling. "But my story clearly states that Giles *may* have decided to sell what he knew and that it *may* have gotten him killed, not that it actually did."

"There's a fine line between fiction and fact, Mr. Dames."

"I'm simply reporting what I've been able to gather, Agent Richter. And in case you missed it, the heading above my story clearly labels it as an opinion piece."

"I know news business jargon very well, Mr. Dames, but it seems to me that you just might be editorializing your way toward a wrong conclusion, maybe even a lawsuit."

"Maybe, maybe not, but either way it's my business and my reputation that are on the line."

"'Web-based journalism,' I believe they call it these days," Richter said, smiling. "Truthfully, I didn't realize until now that you web-based folks have as much influence as it appears you do."

"Sorry you didn't, and I'm sorry you don't care for the way I choose to report the news. But like they say, it's a free country."

"What I don't care for, Mr. Dames, is irresponsibility. Hypothesizing, hyperbolizing, and hiding behind the shield of the fourth estate in order to sell some product that pops up next to your story on a computer screen."

"Then I suggest you get your news elsewhere."

Richter's cordial tone was gone. "And I suggest you listen, sir. I had an agent from our Albuquerque office talk to Howard Colbain this morning. Figured it was prudent to do so since you tossed Colbain's name around so liberally in your last story. Mr. Colbain, it turns out, was quite cooperative and very forthcoming. He told our agent that he was quoted out of context in your piece. That you made him sound like a man bent on revenge when he clearly isn't."

"Then I guess Mr. Colbain and I are seeing things through very different lenses."

"I guess so," said Richter. "And I have this gnawing feeling that Mr. Colbain's not the only person out there who'll have a different view than yours. No problem, though. Someone from one of our offices will speak with those people, too. Rest assured that you and I will be talking to one another quite frequently from this point on." Richter broke into a self-satisfied smile. "Oh, and I'd appreciate it if you'd pass on the gist of this conversation to your associate,

Elgin Coseia. I understand the two of you played baseball together at Southeastern Oklahoma State. And on a national championship team, no less. Too bad about Coseia's leg injury costing him a chance at the majors. Hope to God he doesn't blame you."

"Yeah, too bad," said Freddy, smiling and thinking of the fun he would have describing the seersucker suit–wearing, two-tone shoed FBI dandy to Cozy. Suspecting that Agent Richter probably had a three-inch-thick dossier on the both of them, he said, "Glad to know that the FBI takes such a keen interest in the lives of former collegiate baseball players."

"We're interested in anyone and everyone who might be able to assist us in the solution to a murder, Mr. Dames." Stern-faced, Richter rose to leave. As he adjusted his suit coat, Freddy understood clearly that the salt-and-pepper-haired, solidly built FBI agent was far less homespun than he'd initially appeared. Thinking that before Richter left, he might as well try to coax an official FBI take on the reason for the Giles killing out of him, Freddy asked, "So, since your agency doesn't believe that Sergeant Giles might have been trying to peddle U.S. nuclear secrets, what do you think got him killed?"

"We don't discuss ongoing cases with the press, Mr. Dames, or for that matter take unfounded positions. It would be much the same, I'm afraid, as editorializing. The job of the FBI is to act as an investigative arm of the Department of Justice and to gather facts. My advice to you is that in the future you try to do the same. Gather facts, that is."

"I'll do that," said Freddy, watching Richter take a half-dozen long strides across the room and disappear through the doorway.

As the door closed behind him, Freddy frowned and said, "And hopefully I'll gather those facts before you do, dickhead."

The diner on the outskirts of Casper, Wyoming, where Grant Rivers and Sarah Goldbeck were meeting for breakfast was two hours south of Rivers's ranch and three hours north of Sarah's Hawk Springs home, enough distance that it had seemed to both of them to be the perfect place to meet and be assured that no law enforcement person or reporter might drop in. When Rivers had suggested the previous evening that they meet for breakfast there at ten a.m. to hash over their ongoing Thurmond Giles problem, he was certain they'd be able to do so in private.

He'd just ordered a waffle and a double order of hot link sausages, and Sarah, a bit road-weary from the drive up from Hawk Springs, was in the midst of taking her first sip of coffee when, after surveying the longtime ranchers' hangout for the fourth time, looking for anyone who didn't seem to belong, Rivers said, "First that reporter, Coseia, shows up on my doorstep, then the Platte County sheriff, and yesterday evening the FBI. Like I said to you last night, this Giles killin's turnin' into a nightmare."

"Would you calm down?" Sarah said, patting Grant reassuringly on the back of his hand and setting down her coffee cup.

"Calm down, hell! Don't you realize that this whole Tango-11 murder mess may very well end up in our laps? How'd I ever let myself get tied up with you and your mother's gang of left-leanin', antinuclear flake-offs all those years back, anyway?"

"Just lucky, I guess," Sarah said, smiling at the man who'd once been her lover. "I've talked to the same people you have, Grant, and to an air force OSI officer as well. A black lady who's a take-no-prisoners sort. So I'm one up on you."

Rivers frowned. "So you're tellin' me to sit back and wait for the same woman to show up on my doorstep? No way. You know as well as I do that sooner or later the air force is going to dig up a bunch of thirty-year-old protest photos and Lord knows what else that'll link the two of us to Giles. And if they dig deep enough, they'll figure out that I was the one feedin' your mother and Kimiko Takata information about which air force silo sites they should protest at or vandalize. In the end, they'll figure out that I was gettin' my information from an inside source, Thurmond Giles. And for a goddamn pretty penny, I might add."

"No need to curse, Grant."

"Damn it, Sarah! You were just a kid back then. There's no way they could possibly hold you responsible for your actions. It's not the same for me. And you seem to be forgettin' that there's a dead man involved. Besides, I've been tellin' the cops, reporters, and FBI that I didn't know Giles. They'll catch me in a lie. Then what? Why the hell did I ever start down this road?"

"Because," Sarah said seductively, "you liked tender young meat, and you let your little head do your thinking for you back then instead of your big one. Besides, you wanted to get even with the government."

"A government that snookered me out of an important chunk of my land and then tried its damnedest to steal my water. The sons of bitches! You're damn right I wanted to get even."

"And you sued them and won."

"Yeah, and what did I get for it other than them comin' back later and tryin' to destroy my son?"

"You can't prove that, Grant. You should have forgotten about trying to get even a long time ago. Maybe if you had, we wouldn't be in this mess."

"Hey, at least I didn't jump ship for some gangster biker."

"Let's not go there, Grant. Okay?"

"Fine, we won't." Rivers picked up his fork and toyed with it nervously. "So what's our strategy now?"

"We sit tight and keep our mouths shut."

"And what do we do when they find out about the Takatas?"

"They already know about Rikia and Kimiko. I told that air force OSI major and the Platte County sheriff about them both."

"Why on earth would you give them a heads-up like that?"

"So they'd go sniffing up someone else's shorts instead of mine."

"Have you told Kimiko and Rikia to keep their guard up?"

"Of course. I've talked to Kimiko twice. And do you know what her response was? She headed off for Heart Mountain. Stupid, but she's been tiptoeing toward senility for years."

"What a fuckin' Achilles' heel those two could turn out to be," said Rivers as a waitress arrived with their food.

"Anything else for you?" the waitress asked, placing their meals on the table and refilling Sarah's cup with decaf.

"No," Sarah said. She watched the waitress walk away until she was certain she was out of hearing range. "I'm afraid I have to agree with you about the Heart Mountain thing, Grant. Mother always said that place would be Kimiko's undoing."

"For once I'm in agreement with your mother." Rivers stabbed a sausage link with his fork and ate the link whole.

"Then why not let that place be Kimiko's Waterloo? I think we should worry less about her and more about that reporter I mentioned on the phone, Elgin Coseia. Worry about him, that OSI major—Cameron's her last name; I don't remember her first—and the Platte County sheriff."

"Agreed," said Rivers. He took a long, thoughtful sip of coffee before asking, "What's Buford's take on all this?"

"The same as always. Shoot and ask questions later."

"Could be he's right for a change."

"If so, it would be the first time in a long time." Sarah found herself staring wistfully at her former lover.

"Hey, you're the one who chose him."

"That I did." She scooped up a forkful of scrambled eggs, frowned, and said, "Cold."

"The same way I'm hopin' this Tango-11 thing gets—cold and forgotten real fast. Like my granddad used to say, old crimes may not be bold crimes, but they can get you hung just the same."

"I don't think we've done anything to warrant anything as barbaric as a hanging, Grant." She leaned from their booth and waved for their waitress.

"Something wrong?" the waitress asked, quickly returning.

"My eggs. They're cold."

"Sorry, I'll have them scramble you up a new order."

"Thank you. And while you're at it, maybe you can warm up the disposition of the man sitting across from me."

The two women smiled at one another before the waitress walked away, but their smiles were lost on Grant Rivers. Stroking his chin, he asked, "What if Rikia and Kimiko end up tellin' the sheriff, that lady OSI major, or Coseia somethin' different from what you and I have been tellin' them?"

"They won't."

"You're sure of that?"

"As sure as I can be. But if they do, I'll make certain to have Buford nudge them a little."

"Your knight in shinin' armor to the rescue once again," Grant said sarcastically.

"I've already told you: don't go there, Grant." Sarah slammed her right hand down on the tabletop, causing the couple at the next table to look up.

"Sorry," Rivers said, aware that no matter how wistfully she may have looked at him earlier, when Sarah Goldbeck said she was finished with an issue, she meant finished.

After driving Colorado and Wyoming for two straight days, Cozy was happy to be back home even though he hadn't slept well the previous night. Just past two in the morning, the dream that had haunted him for years had kicked in full bore, and he'd once again found himself riding a motorcycle into a misty haze. He'd finally drifted back to sleep around four, awakened late for work at nine, showered leisurely, and headed for the office, just missing Freddy and Thaddeus Richter.

Red-eyed and yawning, he now stood in the sparsely furnished Digital Registry News front office, leaning his butt against the front edge of Lillian Griffith's desk. Lillian had stepped out for her mid-morning vanilla latte, and as he absentmindedly sorted through his mail, looking for Colorado Rockies tickets he'd ordered, he found himself wondering why, despite all the disappointment he'd had in association with the game, he still loved baseball.

Had he been standing at anyone else's desk, he would've let the voice messaging system that Freddy constantly complained about do its job when the phone started ringing. But knowing how much the compulsive, multitasking Lillian disliked having to return phone calls, he lifted the receiver and said, "Digital Registry News."

The no-nonsense-sounding man on the other end of the line said, "I'd like to speak to Mr. Dames."

"He's not here. Can I take a message?"

"Yeah. Tell him Otis Breen called from Kansas City and that I've got the name of that company Thurmond Giles went to work for after leavin' Seattle. He called here last night at close to midnight askin' for the name. And as strange as this may sound, first thing this morning, some air force OSI officer called here to ask me the same thing. You Dames's secretary?"

"No, just one of the reporters who works here."

"Guess it's okay for me to give you the information, then. Anyway, the company Thurmond went to work for was Applied Nuclear Theratronics of Canada Ltd. Took me a while to find the business card Thurmond sent to me. Finally found it in one of my sock drawers this mornin'."

"Do you know what Giles did for the company?"

"Nope. Just give Mr. Dames my message, okay?"

"I certainly will, and thanks. Here's my cell-phone number if anything else comes up." He recited the number, hung up, and headed for his workstation. For a change, his computer was up and running and he quickly Googled Applied Nuclear Theratronics of Canada Ltd. What filled the screen turned out to be the computer equivalent of a television infomercial, a lavishly produced, three-minute, praise-filled piece detailing the lengthy history and landmark achievements of the first company in North America to successfully develop and manufacture radiation therapy equipment for treating cancer. The testimonial credited the work of a Canadian medical physicist, Harold Johns, for his invention of the cobalt-60 teletherapy machine in the early 1950s and stated that although the machine had run its course in Western medicine, having been replaced by the more efficient, less tissue-damaging linear accelerator, the cobalt-60 machine had nonetheless remained a low-cost workhorse in Third World markets.

As he scrolled through the references at the end of the piece, Cozy found himself wondering whether Thurmond Giles's nuclear-missile savvy might not have earned him a shot at peddling an outdated product to an unregulated Third World market. Although he didn't know one thing about the rules regarding the sale and transport of radiation therapy equipment, he did know that anything nuclear and American had to be regulated by the U.S. Nuclear Regulatory Commission and that he was going to put a call in to Applied Nuclear Theratronics immediately. He also understood that black-market sales of Western goods to Third World countries was big business, whether those goods were two-hundred-dollars-a-pair sneakers or outmoded radiation therapy machines. What mattered in the end, no matter the product, was profit, and he'd learned enough about Thurmond Giles to know that making money was one of the things that had made the man tick.

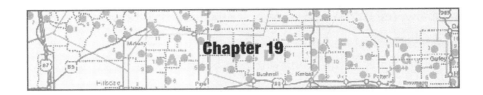

Chapter 19

The human resources department at Applied Nuclear Theratronics of Canada Ltd. didn't provide Cozy with any more information about Thurmond Giles than he'd gotten from Otis Breen, and aside from affirming that Giles had once worked there, in response to Cozy's concocted story about running a background check because his company was considering hiring Giles, the person fielding the call wasn't of much help.

Cozy disappointedly hung up and walked from his living room, where he'd been stretched out on the couch while talking on the phone, into his kitchen to retrieve the ham and cheese on rye he'd made for his lunch before calling Canada.

Plucking the larger of two Golden Delicious apples from an antique fruit bowl on the kitchen counter, he polished the apple with a shirtsleeve, took a bite, and thought about where to head next with his Thurmond Giles murder investigation.

At least he knew more about the murdered man than he'd known three days earlier. Knew for sure that Giles hadn't been any old nuclear-warhead maintenance man but a military-brass-connected, ego-charged, down-home, slick warhead expert and an athlete. Giles had also womanized his way from base to base over his twenty-year military career. The question that needed to be answered, it seemed to him, was which of all those attributes had triggered Giles's murder.

Deciding that his next course of action would be to powwow with Freddy, he took another bite of apple, sat down at his kitchen table, and stared down at the burnished nicks and bruises in the hundred-year-old table's patina. He suddenly felt alone. It had been two years since his grandmother's death, and for much of that time he'd been spinning his wheels. He was pretty much the same small-market, web-based reporter he'd been a couple of years earlier, and although he had a decent job and had inherited a house that was paid off and filled with valuable antiques, he felt somehow bogged down. He had no real reason to gripe. He enjoyed what he did, his boss was his best friend, and he even had a little money in the bank. What he didn't have was a life that had real meaning or existed outside the sphere of Freddy Dames. Everything he did revolved around Freddy. His friends, even most of his acquaintances, were also Freddy's. The women he went out with, made love to, and occasionally argued with always seemed in one way or another to be connected to Freddy. He had the sinking feeling that if he weren't there already, he was rapidly becoming anything but his own man.

He'd lost a shot at his lifelong dream because of hotheaded, competitive stupidity—linked to whom else but Freddy—and although investigative journalism seemed to be a good fit for him, in spite of its increasing reliance on computers, cell phones, BlackBerries, modems, and other assorted technocrap, he wasn't sure that Digital Registry News was where he wanted to be in five years.

Finishing his apple and thinking that if his career as a journalist ever began to crumble, he'd best have an exit strategy, he decided that after the Tango-11 investigation was finished, he'd spend some time putting together just that. For the moment, however, he planned to finish his lunch, then head back to the office and call Bernadette, tell her about the stonewalling he'd gotten from the people at Theratronics, and see what she had that was new. He had to admit that the exotic-looking major had rubbed against the edges of his lonely circle of one, and although Bernadette Cameron seemed to be the kind of thoughtful, feminine, self-assured person that Freddy typically labeled *Too good to be true,* Freddy wouldn't be the final judge on the matter for a change—he would.

The vein that ran along Colonel Joel DeWitt's properly trimmed, regulation-length right sideburn bulged in anger. Bernadette, who'd seen the odd-looking phenomenon before, tried not to stare.

Slapping a hand down on his desktop, DeWitt shook his head in disgust. "I never would've ever expected that I couldn't trust you, Major."

Standing at attention in front of DeWitt's desk, eyes locked straight ahead, Bernadette said, "I'm not certain I've done anything to lose your trust, sir."

"Major, please. You talked to the very people I ordered you to stay away from. Are you aware that by speaking with Dames and Coseia you may very well have compromised the integrity of our Tango-11 investigation and, even worse, cast a shadow on my command?"

"Sir, all I was trying to do was determine whether Coseia and Dames had information that might be helpful to us."

"By meeting with them for a clandestine midnight huddle in a private corporate jet? Come on, Major. I certainly wouldn't want to have to defend your actions to my superiors."

"Our meeting wasn't clandestine, sir, and as it turns out Coseia and Dames provided me with information about several individuals who may have been involved in the Tango-11 security breach and perhaps even Sergeant Giles's murder," Bernadette said, relaxing and widening her stance.

"And while they were at it, did either of them outline a plan for you that might prevent break-ins and future security breaches at other decommissioned silo sites? Did Dames promise to polish up our image here at Warren after raking OSI over the coals in that last internet story of his? Have you found out, like I have, that Reverend Wilson Jackson's wife once had an affair with Sergeant Giles? And just by chance, did Dames or Coseia tell you who murdered Sergeant Giles?"

"No, sir," Bernadette said, caught off guard by the information about Jackson's wife.

"Then as far as I'm concerned, your meeting was worthless." DeWitt cleared his throat as if that might bring extra clarity to what he had to say next. "Two men, one of whom happens to be exceedingly wealthy and somewhat of a playboy, I'm told, and a female air force officer hunkered down under the cover of darkness at an airport in some corporate jet. Now, I'd say that's an image that sends out terribly bad vibes, Major."

Incensed, Bernadette said, "I beg your pardon, sir."

"Your actions wouldn't look at all prudent to middle America, Major Cameron. That meeting of yours has put us all in a compromising position."

Struggling to maintain her composure, Bernadette said, "I find your insinuation offensive, Colonel."

"What you find offensive is immaterial to me, Major Cameron. Besides, I have it on good authority that you topped off that whole unsavory airport situation by leaving in the company of Mr. Coseia."

Her face flushed with anger, Bernadette asked, "Did Captain Alvarez happen to supply you with any other juicy tidbits?"

"I'll ignore your attempt to defame Captain Alvarez and pretend I never heard it. The issue here is your behavior, not Captain Alvarez's. You disobeyed my orders, Major."

Her teeth clenched, Bernadette said nothing.

"Fortunately, your missteps haven't inflicted any major damage on our investigation of the Tango-11 matter. While you've been out there, quite possibly exposing this office to additional ridicule from the press, I've been able to clarify several important issues. For starters, I've gathered more than a dozen photographs of Kimiko Takata and a young Sarah Goldbeck talking with Sergeant Giles at several antinuclear protests at missile sites during the late '70s and early '80s. Most of the photos were taken at a single silo site in Nebraska. A site that was constructed on land formerly owned by a rancher named Grant Rivers. Were you aware of that information, Major?"

"I'm aware of Kimiko Takata and Sarah Goldbeck's involvement in the antinuclear movement, of course," Bernadette said, feeling the bottom drop out of her stomach.

"And Rivers?"

"I've been gathering information on him."

"With the help of your reporter friends, I suppose. Did you know that thirty years ago Mr. Rivers made a vow to get even with the air force and the federal government for supposedly stealing his land?"

"Yes."

"And you haven't said a word about that to me!"

"I haven't had the opportunity, sir."

"And you won't, Major. I've decided to temporarily assign another OSI officer to the Tango-11 investigation."

"Captain Alvarez?" Bernadette asked, disappointed.

"Another officer, Major. That's all you need to know. In addition to the problems you've caused me by playing patty-cakes with the press, I've had Reverend Wilson Jackson in my office twice today complaining that the air force doesn't appear to want to look into the possibility of the Giles murder being a racially motivated hate crime. To say nothing of the fact that Professor Rikia Takata called to complain about your unprofessional conduct and abrasiveness during a visit you made to his office. And to top things off, Sarah Goldbeck is threatening to lodge a complaint against this office, claiming that you and your reporter friend, Mr. Coseia, assaulted her husband the other night."

All but speechless, Bernadette said, "I wasn't abrasive to Dr. Takata, and I certainly wasn't unprofessional. And I can assure you that no one assaulted Buford Kane. The man leveled a shotgun on me, for God's sake."

"It's your word against each of theirs, Major, and since your friends at Digital Registry News seem intent on continuing to show the air force, and this office in particular, in such a negative light, I've stepped in to manage damage control."

"I think you might be overreacting, sir."

"No, Major. What I'm doing is *reacting*. Reacting to your mishandling of this entire investigation, and to the fact that General Preston summoned me to his office this morning to rap my knuckles. My knuckles instead of yours, Major, and that's a very serious problem for us both. So here's a suggestion that I'm thinking will help," DeWitt said, smiling. "Take a week of leave—maybe even two. Put a little distance between yourself and the Tango-11 investigation while I right the ship and handle the damage. Head down to Denver or over to Salt Lake, relax, enjoy a spa treatment, do some shopping."

"What!"

"It's only a suggestion," said DeWitt, watching a look of absolute anger spread across Bernadette's face. "I can order you off the investigation altogether, and we both know that wouldn't look good on your record. Take the leave, Bernadette. It'll turn out to be a win-win for both of us. Ten days from now, things will have settled down. I'll have our Tango-11 security-breach problems resolved, and the Giles murder investigation will be fully in the hands of civilian authorities, where it belongs. Think of it as a cooling-off period. By then no one will be looking to scapegoat anyone."

"And if I don't take leave?"

"Then your temporary absence from the investigation will turn into a permanent assignment off it. And then, who's to say? You could conceivably end up at a new duty station."

"I see. And how long do I have to mull over your suggestion?"

"Until this conversation ends."

Bernadette suddenly found herself thinking about every single bad and improbable thing that had happened to her in just two short years. She'd lost her ability to fly; she'd been reassigned to a job she tolerated rather than enjoyed; she'd had to fend off the unwanted advances of more than just Captain Alvarez; and she'd been forced to carry out her duties under the watchful, what's-in-it-for-me eye of a colonel who had but one objective: earning a general's star. Instead of shouting, "Take this job and shove it," she thought about something her father had always told her to remember when things weren't going her way. Something that had served her well over the years: *Inhale before you yell, baby, and always exhale before you scream.* Inhaling deeply, she said, "I'll take the leave," then slowly exhaled.

"Good. You'll be happy you did, and when you come back to work, I can pretty much assure you, our Tango-11 problem will be water under the bridge."

"Anything else, sir?" she asked, taking another long, deep breath and holding it.

"No. I'll have Sergeant Milliken get your papers ready for my signature. And Bernadette, don't take it too hard; we all run into obstacles now and again."

Bernadette smiled without responding and pivoted to leave. She made it to the first-floor fire-door exit before exhaling, and she'd slipped behind the wheel of her Austin-Healey and cranked the engine before she finally screamed.

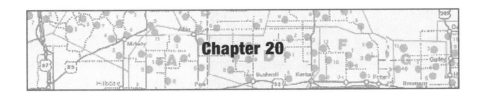
Jimmy "Jackknife" Cameron was dripping sweat in Scottsdale, Arizona's 102-degree heat and sizing up the nine-foot putt that he had a thousand dollars riding on when his cell phone began ringing. Shouting, "Damn it!" and shaking his head, he slipped the phone out of his shirt pocket. Recognizing the number on the screen as Bernadette's, he dropped his putter and took the call.

"Who the hell's calling you now, Jackknife?" the sandy-haired retired three-star general standing beside him groaned.

Jackknife grinned and pressed the phone to his ear. "Nobody but Bernadette or the president. And as you know, I haven't been taking calls from the White House for years."

Laughing at a remark that only Jackknife would make in earnest, his three companions simply shook their heads.

"Cut the man in the White House some slack," the three-star shot back. "Who knows, he could be calling to tell you that your confirmation as a Vietnam combat ace has finally come through."

"Fat chance." Jackknife moved the phone to his good ear and finally said, "Hello."

"Dad, it's me."

"Well, hi, sugar." Jackknife smiled, mouthed, "Bernadette," to his buddies, and then said to Bernadette, "What's up?"

"I've got a problem I need to run by you."

"How big a problem, honey?" The three men at his side, men whom he'd gone to war with and who'd all known Bernadette since she was a baby, suddenly looked concerned.

"Pretty big. Have you got time to talk?"

"I'm in the middle of a round of golf, but—"

"Oh. Sorry for interrupting. Go ahead and finish," Bernadette said, aware that any golf game her father was engaged in more than likely involved a hefty wager.

"The game can wait." Jackknife glanced at his friends and saw each man nod his approval.

"No. Finish your game. This will probably take some time."

"Bernadette, it's—"

"Daddy, my problem is about inhaling and exhaling."

The man who should long before have been recognized as the second of only two U.S. Air Force combat aces during the Vietnam War but never had because the envious lieutenant colonel who could have verified his fifth enemy kill wouldn't do it, turned stone-faced. The intense look was one his golfing buddies knew well. They'd all seen that expression on Jackknife's face during many of the 151 combat missions he'd flown in Vietnam.

Relaxing his stance and picking up his putter, Jackknife said, "I'll call you back in thirty minutes, Bernadette." Turning to his golfing buddies, he said authoritatively, "We need to get done here quick."

"No problem," the three-star said.

Jackknife flashed him a look that was the clear equivalent of a salute, then said to Bernadette, "Half an hour, baby. Okay?"

"Yes."

Jackknife closed his cell phone, slipped it into his shirt pocket, and calmly stepped up to his golf ball. Briefly sizing up the putt and without another word, he calmly stroked the ball in.

Before the ball had rattled its way to the bottom of the cup, he glanced up at his friends and asked, "Got my thousand, boys?"

Realizing from the seriousness of Jackknife Cameron's face that he wouldn't be joining them for any friendly postround banter in the clubhouse that day, his air force buddies nodded in unison.

Jackknife returned Bernadette's call twenty-five minutes later as he sat in the clubhouse, sipping a twenty-four-ounce frosted mug of lemonade, his longtime substitute for the alcohol that had largely ended his twenty-two-year air force career.

A midlife surprise, Bernadette had arrived in his and his college sweetheart's life in 1982, halfway into his career and nearly eleven years after his return home from Vietnam. For a man for whom drinking, fighter-pilot bravado, and camaraderie had long been key to his inner being, Bernadette's birth had been a blessing. That blessing, however, couldn't put a damper on his drinking, and only after his wife died of a heart attack on a frigid North Dakota New Year's Eve, three days before Bernadette's seventh birthday, did Jackknife Cameron turn off the spigot on his habit. By then it was too late for the African American war hero—a man whom many had once pegged as a future member of the Joint Chiefs of Staff—to salvage his career.

Although he would ultimately earn a general's star before retiring from the air force, a star that some in the know claimed was a backhanded consolation prize for his never officially having been named a Vietnam combat ace, his daughter was the only thing that seemed to matter to him after the unexpected loss of the love of his life.

When Bernadette, with a freshly minted UCLA architectural degree in hand, announced at her college graduation that she wasn't going to take a job with an architectural firm in San Francisco but instead planned to join the air force and become a fighter pilot like her father and grandfather before her, Jackknife, instead of being surprised, had beamed. Eighteen months later, he'd pinned Bernadette's pilot wings on her, and six months after that, he'd taken what she still jokingly claimed were at least a thousand photographs of her standing beside her A-10, the day she'd been assigned a Warthog. He'd been there to console and comfort her when she'd been grounded, and he'd encouraged her to take the assignment with OSI.

Now he could only hope that the problem Bernadette had called about earlier wasn't the kind that had stolen her mother from him.

Setting his lemonade aside, adjusting his cell phone to his good ear, and trying his best not to sound overly concerned, he said, "So what's up, Major C.?"

"First off, did you skin 'em, Dad?"

"Like cats, sweetie, like cats," said the man who'd earned his nickname not because of his aerial exploits but because he'd once been an Olympic-caliber springboard diver at San Diego State.

"Who were you playing with?"

"Bernie Watson, Happy LeGrange, and Bob Sowata."

Bernadette whistled. "Enough military star power there to light up a boardwalk."

"And me, the lowly one-star," Jackknife said with a chuckle.

"And the only ace," Bernadette said to the man who'd taught her to race sprint cars, ride a motorcycle, and ultimately fly a four-engine plane by the time she was sixteen.

"Yeah," Jackknife said, looking deeply reflective. "So what's the problem, baby?"

"That Tango-11 investigation I talked to you about a couple of days back has reared an ugly new head."

"Which means you've got yourself one of three problems: a brass problem, a civilian problem, or a political problem."

"A little bit of all three, I'm afraid."

"Any chance that bonehead DeWitt is leading the parade? If so, I've still got a little juice I can send your way—maybe make that numskull back off a bit."

"Daddy, please. It'll only make matters worse. But yes, he's the problem."

"So what's he done now?"

"I'm not sure that he's done anything. It's what I've done that's the problem. I've made a few wrong turns with my investigation."

"Like what?"

"For one, I've talked too often and too much to the media. Especially to a web-based outfit out of Denver, Digital Registry News. Bottom line is, DeWitt's pulled me off the investigation and put me on what in the civilian world would amount to administrative leave."

"So what the heck did you say to the press?"

"Not much, really. But I made the mistake of having a meeting with the Digital Registry News publisher and one of his reporters last night to talk about the investigation. Turns out DeWitt had one of his lapdogs, a captain named Alvarez, following me."

"So if you didn't say anything to either defame the air force or breach security or intelligence, what's DeWitt's beef?"

"It's got more to do with appearance than substance, Dad. That publisher I ran off at the mouth to has taken some serious shots at the air force, and at OSI in particular, for its handling of the Tango-11 break-in. He's written a couple of pretty unflattering stories that took DeWitt to task."

"He's probably not far wrong. I served with the man back when he was a boot-licking first lieutenant, remember? Sometimes you just have to call a spade a spade. Anyway, you're positive you haven't had any slips of the tongue that would compromise air force security or national intelligence?"

"Yes."

"Then my advice for now would be to ride things out. Let DeWitt hang himself with his incompetence. Hell, on most days the man couldn't find a paper clip in an ashtray if his life depended on it. How long does he want you to stay on leave, anyway?"

"A week, for sure. Maybe two."

"And what's he plan to do with the Tango-11 investigation while you're gone?"

"I'm not sure. All I know is that he's personally taking over the investigation and claims that by the time I come back, our Tango-11 problem will be solved."

"Fat chance."

"Maybe not. That captain I mentioned, the one who fed DeWitt the information about me meeting with the Digital Registry News people, is pretty sharp. Lecherous but sharp. He might actually end up doing a decent job with the investigation, and of course DeWitt will take the credit."

Jackknife took a slow, thoughtful sip of lemonade. "Now, that's a problem. Since you really can't trust DeWitt or his lackey, what about those two reporters? Can you trust them?"

"I think so. The wingman, Coseia, for sure. His boss is a little squirrelly, but I think he's been on the up-and-up with me so far. And if worse comes to worst, there's our base commander, General Preston. I know he'll play it by the book."

"I forgot about old Hammerhead being in charge there at Warren. Hell, Happy LeGrange and I pretty much raised him from a pup."

"I know what you're thinking, Dad, but no. I need to handle this on my own."

"Okay, sugar. It's your call. But if you need me to intervene with Preston, let me know. As for your two media types, what do you think they're after?"

"Breaking the Tango-11 story wide open—what else?"

"You're sure they aren't out to simply grind an ax against the air force?"

"Nope. What they're after, I'm pretty sure, is to be the first outfit to break the news on who killed Sergeant Giles."

Recognizing a degree of uncertainty in his daughter's voice, Jackknife asked, "And just what are you after, Bernadette?"

"I'm after proving that I know what I'm doing, and finding out who killed Sergeant Giles, I guess."

"Proving that you know what you're doing's fine. But figuring out who killed that sergeant isn't. You've told me all along that your assignment is to determine what led to the security breach at Tango-11 and to help prevent any future ones. Stick with that."

"I know, but there could be national security issues at stake, Dad. Giles was a former nuclear-warhead maintenance expert, and until six months ago he was working for a Canadian company that manufactures radiation therapy equipment. I don't know exactly what he did there, but I'm thinking his job might have involved patching up outmoded radiation therapy equipment, which he may have then pilfered and peddled to a Third World market."

"So what's the connection to Tango-11?"

"Nuclear, Dad. Nuclear. Applied Nuclear Theratronics of Canada Ltd., the company he worked for, is the largest manufacturer of radiation therapy equipment in the world. Maybe while Giles was globe-hopping and peddling his stolen equipment, he was also supplying somebody out there with technical information about America's nuclear-missile arsenal."

Jackknife took another sip of lemonade. "I hope your imagination's not running wild, Bernadette. Right now, if I were you, I'd find out exactly what Sergeant Giles was doing at that Canadian company. He may have simply been screwing nuts on bolts. Just remember, don't do anything that might end up costing you your career."

"I won't," said Bernadette, aware of the hidden meaning behind the warning. Her father had let alcohol put an early end to his career, and she knew that it still ate at him every day. The air force, however, with all its camaraderie and macho trappings had never had the same attraction for her that it had had for him. She'd simply always wanted to fly, and although Jackknife might have passed on his tenacity to her, encouraged her daredevil spirit, and taught her in many ways how to fly by the seat of her pants, she had an equal part of her mother's athletic and artistic spirit. Those qualities had made her a two-time NCAA tennis champion at UCLA; turned her into an accomplished childhood ballerina until, at the age of fourteen, her five-foot-ten-inch height had ended that pursuit; and led her to become an architect.

Convinced that there had to be a way to unravel the mystery of the Tango-11 security breach and the Thurmond Giles murder without scorching the landscape as her father might have done, she concluded that she would have to tread more lightly in the future. Confrontations with Colonel DeWitt would have to end. She couldn't blindside him again. There could be no more kicking over-the-hill bikers in the jewels and no stumbling into ill-timed, poorly thought-out meetings with eccentric mathematicians or former antinuclear activists.

"You still there, Bernadette?" Jackknife asked after a lengthy silence.

"Yes."

"Good. Now, take my advice and don't overreach on this Tango-11 thing. Like I've always told you, this too shall pass."

"I expect it will," said Bernadette, wondering how her career and perhaps her life would be affected when it did.

"So, where are you headed on leave?"

"To Denver for a couple of days. Then to La Jolla to spend some time walking the beaches and inhaling the ocean breeze."

"Sounds like a plan," said Jackknife, recalling the hand-in-hand sunset strolls he and Bernadette's mother had taken along the same beaches. "Now, if I can drag my tired old bones out of this chair my butt's just about molded to, I'll go see if I can't find those loser friends of mine."

"Tell them all I said hello," Bernadette said, knowing that the men Jackknife had jokingly called losers could no doubt still hold their own behind the controls of a fighter jet. "Love you," she said, hanging up. Moments later she found herself thinking about what had caused her mother, an Iowa farm girl, the third of five children from the only black farming family in a lily-white county, and Jackknife Cameron, a kid straight off the South Central streets of LA, to click. The answer came quickly—after all, she'd heard her father repeat it often enough over the years: *Your mother didn't need me to be somebody, sugar. She was already somebody when I met her. Turns out for some reason she just decided to pick up a stray who needed one hell of a lot of couthing.* Whispering to herself, "This too shall pass," Bernadette rose from the stool she'd been sitting on in her kitchen, snapped open the locket that swung from the chain around her neck, opened it, and glanced at her mother's picture. Thinking, *Already somebody,* she headed for her bedroom to pack enough clothes for a ten-day absence from Cheyenne.

Rikia Takata's flight from Laramie to Denver had been smooth and uneventful, and his four thirty connecting flight from Denver to El Paso had started out the same way. But an hour into the trip, the ride had become a choppy, knee-knocking dance around boiling thunderstorms at an altitude of thirty thousand feet.

His seven-hour drive from Heart Mountain that morning and back home to Laramie had been tedious and nerve-racking enough.

The bumpy plane ride was only adding to what had become nearly a daylong stomach upset.

For half the car ride home to Laramie, he'd had to listen to Kimiko read from his grandfather's diary. He'd left behind some papers he'd intended to bring to his El Paso meeting—papers that would now have to be faxed to him—and after rushing to make his one o'clock Laramie to Denver flight, because of weather he was going to arrive in El Paso an hour and a half late. Trying his best to keep the half-full cup of soda he held from spilling, he thought about the paper his underachieving but articulate graduate student was going to give for him. He'd worried for weeks that he might be rushing along science that needed a little longer gestation period, but he couldn't take the chance of being scooped. His paper, therefore, had to hit perfect pitch.

When the pilot ordered the flight attendants to take their seats for the remainder of the flight, Rikia gulped down the rest of his soda. As he leaned forward to place the empty cup in the seat pocket in front of him he realized that he'd sweated through the armpits of his new suit.

Although he'd long been fascinated by World War II–era airplanes and the men who'd flown them, he was, in truth, terrified of flying, in part due to his claustrophobia. The fear had surfaced during his childhood when Kimiko had so often locked him for hours at a time in either the pantry or a linen closet as punishment for some real or imagined transgression.

He felt a sense of relief when, twenty minutes later, after bumping through choppy air for what seemed like hours, the pilot announced that they'd be landing in about thirty minutes. But his relief disappeared when the plane hit an air pocket and plummeted almost a thousand feet. With most of the passengers screaming and the woman next to him sobbing, he found himself recalling Kimiko's authoritative parting instructions before he'd left Laramie: *We've still got this Tango-11 thing hanging over our heads, Rikia. Let me know as soon as you land. Do you hear me?*

When he landed thirty-six minutes later, he did just that.

They were laughing at him. He knew they were. Four men whispering to one another at a table in a dimly lit bar as he walked in. He didn't need to hear their words nor suffer the indignity of their criticism to know that he was the butt of their jokes.

Rikia had never been a drinker or a glad-hander, so he was hard pressed to come up with a good reason for stepping inside the math conference hotel's stale beer–smelling bar other than, unable to find the hotel's restaurant, he'd wandered in, in search of a soft drink. Glancing across the room and toward the men at the table, he frowned and turned to leave.

He'd barely made a half turn when one of the men, a white-haired, 250-pound jowly behemoth with muttonchop sideburns, 1920s-vintage wire-rimmed glasses, and a deep, gravelly voice that had always irritated Rikia, rose from his chair and, waving like a cop directing traffic, called out, "Rikia! Rikia! Come join us over here."

Rikia had just spent fifteen minutes on the phone listening to an excited and worried-sounding Kimiko complain that in his absence, she'd not only had to field a slew of questions from an FBI agent earlier that afternoon, she'd also had to speak with and schedule face-to-face meetings with the Platte County sheriff and an impatient-sounding Warren Air Force Base OSI colonel to discuss the Thurmond Giles murder. Still unsettled by the call, Rikia was in no mood to spend time with a gaggle of jealous white men who were among his biggest detractors. "Can't right now," he said, waving the burly man off. "I'm just looking for a soda."

Ambrose Weir, a Cal Tech distinguished professor and a man who'd long been as critical of Rikia's research as he was of Rikia's MacArthur Genius status, persisted. "Never hurts to talk with friends," he said, smiling. "As it happens, we've actually been sitting here chatting about your work."

Chatting about who would be the one to put the dagger in my back, Rikia thought to himself. "I really don't drink," he said. The word *drink* came out an infantile, tongue-tied-sounding *dink.*

"Okay," said Ambrose. "I won't twist your arm. But let me ask you this, if I may. It relates to your equivalence studies. Since equivalence relations are as ubiquitous in mathematics as order relations are, can you please tell me why you're so convinced that the algebraic structure of equivalence might play any significant role in combating terrorism." Nodding toward his three friends, he said, "It seems to me, no, to us, that your assumptions draw primarily on group theory rather than on much more established and reliable aggregates like lattices or even simple categories." Ambrose smiled. It was a smile that seemed to Rikia to scream, *Wanta answer that for me, Jap?*

Sweating, Rikia struggled to get his words out. "Listen to my paper tomorrow and you'll have your answer."

"I'll be there." Ambrose Weir said, grinning. "And we can

expect as usual that your senior postdoc, Patricia Recard, will be giving the paper?"

"Yes," Rikia said, struggling to control his temper.

"Why, yes, of course," Ambrose said, loudly, directing his response toward his table of friends. "I'll say this for you, Rikia. You seem to always pick grad students who are as talented as they are pretty. We'll be interviewing Dr. Recard for a faculty position at Cal Tech during this meeting, by the way. She's top drawer." He winked and added, "And you can bet that if she's lucky enough to join our group, we'll set her straight on equivalence relations and math logic."

"Do that for me," said Rikia, barely able to enunciate through what was now clenched-jaw anger.

"Hope you find your soda," Ambrose Weir said, pivoting to return to his colleagues.

Rikia glanced briefly over his shoulder and back at the table full of insipid-looking Americans as he left. They were busy talking and laughing again. No doubt they'd soon again be whispering about him. He recalled something that he'd once read: *It's paranoia to think that someone's after you when they're not; it's simply common sense, however, to guard against such a possibility; and it's pure logic to remove the risk in whatever manner necessary when called for.* Smiling to himself as he reflected on the premise, Rikia left the room in search of a nerve-calming soda.

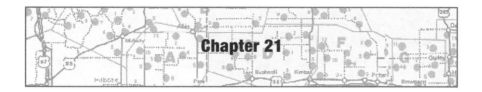

Chapter 21

Bernadette's suite on the seventh floor of Denver's JW Marriott Hotel overlooked a cobblestone street filled with quaint shops, and save for the slightly annoying swishing sound of the suite's air conditioning, the tastefully appointed space was otherwise quiet and relaxing. A set of turquoise earrings and a silk scarf that she'd bought at the nearby Cherry Creek mall sat on the chair next to her. After returning from shopping a few minutes earlier, she'd changed into an oversized T-shirt and a pair of old running shorts with the barely recognizable washed-out letters "UCLA" stenciled just above the hem of the right leg, and she was barefoot, as was her custom.

She'd brought along a half-dozen books to read, only to realize when she'd strolled through a bookstore in the mall that the books she'd packed were entirely too much of the same: military histories, mysteries, and biographies, the whole lot. Deciding that she needed more variety in her reading, and perhaps in her life, she'd bought a couple of romances in the bookstore before scooping up famed UCLA basketball coach John Wooden's gem, *Wooden: A Lifetime of Observations and Reflections On and Off the Court.* Surprisingly, even though she'd been an elite UCLA athlete, she'd never read the book nor met Wooden. However, she knew enough about the quiet, introspective man they called "the Wizard of

Westwood," who'd brought UCLA ten NCAA basketball championships, to be open to absorbing some of his wisdom.

She'd just picked the book up, relaxed back in her chair, and started reading the blurbs on the back cover when a call from Cozy Coseia interrupted her. "What's up, Major?" he asked casually, sounding as if he were right there in the suite.

For a moment she thought about lying to him and saying she was busy or tied up at the base. Instead, she blurted out, "I'm in Denver."

Cozy's response was surprised silence.

"Are you still there?"

"Yeah. Why didn't you tell me you were headed this way?"

The way Cozy asked the question, sounding as if he had some reason to be hurt, surprised her. "I didn't know I was coming until this afternoon. Colonel DeWitt pulled me off the Tango-11 investigation, so I decided to head this way and lick my wounds."

"Did he pull you off because of Freddy and me?"

"Yes, and no. He thinks I've been a little too friendly with the press, but he had other reasons."

"I'm sorry."

"Don't be. Actions always have consequences, and mine have put me here in Denver on leave."

"How long are you here for?"

"A couple of days."

"Two days of being something other than an air force major? That'll be different."

"I know how to play at being a civilian, Cozy."

"Hey, no offense intended, and I believe you. So what's on your agenda for the evening, Ms. Cameron?"

"I thought I'd do some reading."

"Pretty confining. How about I take you to dinner instead?"

"I don't think it would be—"

"Appropriate? You're on leave, Bernadette, remember?"

"Hard to forget." After a long, thoughtful pause, she said, "Okay. Dinner it is. But no shoptalk. Nothing about Tango-11, Colonel DeWitt, or Thurmond Giles?"

"Promise. Where are you staying?"

"At the JW Marriott in Cherry Creek."

"Why don't I pick you up around seven thirty? How's Asian food sound?"

"Great. As long as I can get something that's deep fried and loaded with calories. Might as well break a few rules while I'm on leave. I'll see you in forty-five minutes," Bernadette said, glancing at her watch.

"Good."

"And no Tango-11 talk, remember?"

"Got it memorized." The smile on Cozy's face broadened into a Cheshire cat grin as he hung up, rose from his chair, and headed for his bedroom closet, hoping to find something freshly laundered to wear.

Little Ollie's restaurant, which billed itself as a "purveyor of New Asian cuisine," was packed with a Friday-night mix of yuppies, Gen Xers, Me-Mes, wannabe hipsters, aging boomers, and businessmen. Nearly everyone in the tantalizingly fragrant, sweet-and-sour-smelling place looked happy to have made it through the week, especially the tired-looking man with graying hair and a stick-on *Hello, I'm Ralph* name tag peeling from his lapel who sat alone at the table across from Cozy and Bernadette, drinking from a tumbler filled with something amber-colored and potent-looking.

As Cozy enjoyed a generous swallow of beer, Bernadette toyed with the glass of cabernet she'd barely touched, wondering whether she looked as Friday-night worn out as the rest of the customers. Dressed casually from head to toe in black, Cozy didn't look tired or at all like the stereotypical rumpled newspaperman. With his unruly mop of wind-tossed-looking, curly black hair and nut-brown skin, he reminded her instead of a somewhat overdressed surfer.

Watching her finally take a second sip of wine, Cozy said, "Thought for a minute you'd made a bad choice."

"No. The wine's perfect. I've just been people-watching and thinking about the future."

"Gotta do them both from time to time."

"Guess my time's now, to look toward the future, I mean. You, on the other hand, seem to be set. Good job, best friend for a boss, and you get to nose around in a world that never lacks for a story."

Cozy found himself staring at Bernadette and thinking about a favorite Freddy Dames mantra: that beautiful, successful women always have a fatal flaw. A flaw that, according to Freddy, was somehow always rooted in insecurity. Although Bernadette had more of a wholesome, outdoorsy, athletic look than the silicone-breasted, fatally flawed, Hollywood-starlet types Freddy preferred, she was successful and striking enough to have Cozy all of a sudden wondering.

"I'm enjoying what I do," Cozy said, looking up as their waitress set a steaming bowl of rice and his order of puffy, deep-fried shrimp down in front of him.

"Hot," the waitress warned, wagging an index finger and placing two sets of chopsticks on the table before setting an overflowing plate of General Tso's chicken in front of Bernadette. "Anything else?" she asked politely.

Eyeing the food-cluttered tabletop, Cozy said, "No."

"Looks fantastic," said Bernadette.

"Just like the lady sitting across from me," Cozy said, raising his beer mug and tipping it at Bernadette. When she didn't respond, he lowered the mug, looking embarrassed.

Recognizing his embarrassment, Bernadette reached for her chopsticks, smiled, and said, "Well, thank you, Cozy. I needed the lift."

The waitress had cleared their table and Bernadette had finished a second glass of wine by the time their now comfortable dinner conversation turned to the issue of Cozy's injured leg.

"I didn't mean to pry," Bernadette said, toying with the stem of her wineglass and looking far more embarrassed by the question she'd just asked than Cozy had looked when he'd toasted her earlier. "I just wondered about your motorcycle accident. Sometimes my inquisitiveness bubbles up when it shouldn't." She suddenly felt convinced that she'd offended the man she'd just told more about herself over two glasses of wine than she'd told any man in years. "Guess we've reached the obligatory bumpy spot in the evening's road."

"Not really," Cozy said, staring into his empty beer mug. "In fact, as fate would have it, the whole issue with my leg started out with a road. Almost twelve years ago now, out in eastern Colorado." He glanced toward the ceiling and stared at it, looking as though he needed to be tethered to something above him before he could continue. "Back then Freddy and I were on top of the world. We'd both been picked in the first round of the major league baseball draft a few months earlier, and we were due to report to our respective Double-A clubs the next week. I'd been riding Freddy for days about him being Mr. Golden Boy, as always, heading off to play for a Yankees farm team, and he'd responded in kind, saying it was only my dumb Dominican luck that had landed me a spot with the hometown Colorado Rockies Double-A affiliate in Tulsa.

"The day I got hurt, we'd driven out to Julesburg, Colorado, to look at six hundred acres of farmland Freddy was thinking about buying so we'd have a place to go pheasant and quail hunting in the fall after baseball season was over. Freddy had decided to bring along his newest toy, a 1999 Ducati motorcycle."

"Not that bike in the Gulfstream?"

"No. The bike in the plane's much smaller and a whole lot slower. The Ducati's ancient history. Anyway, Freddy insisted on towing along the Ducati, announcing on the way to Julesburg that he planned to find somewhere that he could top-end the thing. The bike was a rocket, touted by the manufacturer to top out at a hundred and sixty-one," Cozy said, his voice trailing off. He paused, then went on.

"We'd gotten a late start out of Denver, so we didn't get to Julesburg until about two. The real estate agent who had the property listed met us in town, then drove us out to the farm. We checked the place out for over an hour, looking for bird cover and water habitat and getting a general feel for the lay of the land.

"By the time we finished walking the property, it was close to five. We drove back into Julesburg, grabbed something to eat, and then took off to look for a stretch of I-76 frontage road the real estate broker had assured Freddy would be the perfect place to test the Ducati without having to worry about cops.

"We spent a good half hour trying to find the road, and by the time we did it was almost dusk. By then the South Platte River, which ran just east of the frontage road, was misting up, and a temperature inversion fog had begun to blanket not just the road but the woods around it and the interstate."

Sensing what was coming, Bernadette grimaced.

"We parked on the road's shoulder, which was pretty much pure sand, and Freddy unloaded the bike and fired it up. When I warned him to be careful because of the fog, he shouted, 'Careful's for condoms, Elgin!' hopped on the Ducati, and took off.

"He made three half-mile runs down that frontage road, each one a little faster than his last. He came back from the third run yelling, 'Topped her out!' stepped off the bike, and said, 'Your turn.'

"To this day, I don't know why I got on that motorcycle. But I did. I wasn't as skilled a rider as Freddy, but I could ride pretty well, and since the two of us had always thrived on competition, I told myself, *What the hell, I'll top-end the thing, too.* I couldn't see more than fifteen yards ahead of me when I jumped on the Ducati and took off."

Bernadette all but gasped.

"I was doing just over ninety when the Ducati's front tire nicked the shoulder. I barely went off the pavement, really, but the tire sank in the sand, the bike catapulted forward, and I went sailing."

Looking as if the crash were somehow recurring right then, Cozy said, "If there'd just been a little wider strip of sand to that shoulder, no more sand than you'd find in a playground sandbox, I probably would have ended up landing in it and suffered nothing more than a bunch of bad bruises and a couple of broken ribs. But there wasn't, and I landed on a collection of boulders."

Bernadette nodded sympathetically.

"Freddy was there screaming, 'No, no, no!' in what seemed like nothing flat, and although I've always claimed that I never lost consciousness, he still says that when paramedics pulled my leg from where it was locked between two boulders, my eyes rolled back in my head and I went out like a light.

"I don't remember the ambulance ride back to Sterling, the Flight for Life helicopter ride to Denver, anything about the six-hour surgery, or even waking up afterward. All I remember is post-op in the recovery room, Freddy standing beside me crying and blaming himself, and my grandmother standing at the foot of the bed crossing herself and praying. And, of course, I remember the fog," Cozy said, more to himself than to Bernadette, before placing both hands palms up on the table as though the gesture might provide him absolution for a transgression.

"Did you try to play baseball again?" Bernadette asked, her voice a near whisper.

"Yes," Cozy said, his eyes glazed over. "After I rehabbed until I was purple in the face. But what I had was gone—my mobility, my speed, my timing. Some sportswriters claimed that even my will had disappeared. But no matter how hard I tried, I couldn't get what had been there back. I had a couple more surgeries, minor ones compared to the first, but all they did was finish me off."

"Athletically, you mean," Bernadette said sternly.

"Yeah, athletically," Cozy said, trying his best to force a smile.

"Glad to see you appreciate my point," said Bernadette.

When the waitress appeared seconds later and asked if either of them would like another drink, Bernadette reached out, cupped Cozy's left hand in hers, squeezed it reassuringly, and said, "No, just the check."

Chapter 22

Bernadette wanted Cozy to do anything but to drop her off at the Marriott. Drive around town, have an after-dinner drink, go for a walk—any of them would have worked. She wanted to confide in him, talk to him longer, tell him her story, but by the time they reached the hotel, she could tell from the emotionally drained look on Cozy's face that the evening needed to end.

"It's been a wonderful evening," she said as he nosed the dually into a spot for guests in front of the hotel.

Waving off an eager-looking parking attendant, Cozy jumped out of the truck, limped quickly to the other side, and opened the door for Bernadette. "Emily Post says to always see the lady inside."

"She a friend of yours?"

"My second cousin."

They laughed, walked down a short cobblestone sidewalk, and entered the hotel. "You up for something tomorrow?" Cozy asked as they stood staring at one another in the middle of a hallway that led to the lobby.

"I haven't thought that far ahead, truthfully. I can call you, though."

Cozy looked disappointed. "We can always put our heads together on your Tango-11 problem."

"I'd rather not."

"Then we could drive up to the mountains." There was a dogged insistence in Cozy's tone.

"Sounds better. I'll call you when I'm up."

"Fine."

"And thanks again for the great evening."

"Turned out a little one-sided, I'm afraid," Cozy said.

"No, it turned out perfect." Bernadette smiled, briefly clasped Cozy's right hand tightly in hers, and headed for the elevator.

The openmouthed stare of someone who'd seen something he couldn't quite believe remained plastered on Cozy's face as he watched Bernadette disappear inside the elevator. He was back outside and behind the wheel of the dually when he said loudly, "Yeah, perfect!"

Sarah Goldbeck cleared her throat, announced, "I'm as nervous as hell, Grant," into the mouthpiece of the '50s-style rotary-dial telephone that hung on the front wall of her potter's shed, and began fidgeting with a tattered edge of her potter's apron.

Buford had built the seven-hundred-square-foot pottery shop, which Sarah called the Barn, pretty much by himself, and except for the shop's one glaring error, a concrete floor that caused Sarah to have leg cramps and, like some predator, sat waiting for any errant stumble or loose grip on her pottery, the shop was the treehouse she'd never had as a child, a kind of fantasy place her mother had taught her never to believe in. Her own special place to escape the world. Above all, it was somewhere to get out of the shadow of her late mother's antinuclear, Greenpeace, civil rights, and animal rights causes, which, as the standard-bearer of her mother's legacy, she'd never been able to champion effectively.

"Nervous as hell, Grant," she repeated, staring out one of the shed's two slightly off-kilter front windows and up the hill toward her darkened house. She drummed her fingers on her thigh, wondering when Buford would be home.

Fed up with her whining, Grant Rivers, who'd spent most of the afternoon and evening in Cheyenne buying fencing materials and looking for a new brush chopper, said, "Everything will be all right, Sarah. Just calm down, for God's sake, and stop complainin'." His cell phone erupted with staticky interference.

"Where are you, anyway? The reception's terrible. Between the static and that asthmatic voice of yours, I can barely understand you."

"In Cheyenne at Menards. I drove down to pick up a piece of equipment and a load of metal fence posts."

Not at all surprised that her penny-pinching former lover had driven 175 miles from Casper down to Cheyenne and to within an hour of her doorstep in order to save ten bucks, Sarah shook her head and said, "I talked to Kimiko a little bit ago. She sounded scared and a little angry. Claimed she might even drive over here to talk."

"Now, that's hard to believe. I always thought the only thing that old bird was afraid of was that she might not live long enough to mete out punishment to the sons and daughters of the people she holds responsible for her time at Heart Mountain. I've talked to her, too, by the way. Did she tell you that she came home from a trip to Heart Mountain just this morning, or that she had an FBI agent camped on her doorstep this afternoon? She said he peppered her with questions for close to forty-five minutes. Asked her about her protest days and about her connection, and of course ours, to Thurmond Giles. She said he even had photographs of all of us from back then. Your mother included."

"Oh, my God! Was Rikia with her?" Sarah asked, hoping Rikia had been present to keep the increasingly forgetful Kimiko from saying the wrong thing.

"No. She said as soon as they got home from Heart Mountain, Rikia left for El Paso to present a research paper to a bunch of math eggheads at a conference."

"Not good. Not good at all. You know how badly Kimiko needs a buffer."

"Well, she sure doesn't need Rikia. He's as off-the-wall as her, as far as I'm concerned. Forever mutterin' about how he and his contributions to science have been disrespected. What frickin' science? The man counts credit-card receipts and totals up people's phone calls, for God's sake."

"So, what do we do?"

"What we do is sit tight. Bide our time and let the cops, the air force, and now the FBI do their thing. We aren't the ones on the front line with this Thurmond Giles killin', anyway."

"What my mother saw in a letch like Giles, I'll never know," Sarah said, her voice brimming with disgust.

"The same thing you saw in me a few years later, my dear—sex! What does it matter, anyway? What kind of connection can the FBI possibly make between you and Giles from back then? You were just sixteen."

"The kind that would let them know I hated the man for destroying my mother."

"She made her own bed, Sarah."

"She was an out-of-touch college physics professor with no grasp whatsoever of the real world, Grant. A homely semirecluse, and she was taken advantage of by that womanizing Elmer Gantry of a black pervert. He stole her money, her dignity, and her soul."

"I've heard it all before, Sarah. Let's move on, okay? The operative word from here on out is *chill*. Don't talk to the FBI, that Platte County sheriff, any air force OSI type, or even Kimiko without talkin' to me first. Got it?"

"I'll try. But if they dig deep enough—"

"They'll find China." There was simmering anger in Grant Rivers's gravel-throated reply. "Lean on Buford if you have to," he said sarcastically.

"He's not here."

"Then go read a book, make some damn pots, go to bed. Do whatever in the shit you have to to focus on something other than Thurmond Giles. Do like I did after our meetin' in Casper this morning. I decided to concentrate on a fencin' project at the ranch, and it did wonders for me."

"Your analogy's idiotic, Grant. Are you sure all those steroids you take to keep your airways open aren't affecting your brain? Besides, I'm not you. I can't turn things on and off like a water spigot, in case you've forgotten. Are you headed back to Buffalo?"

"As soon as I'm off the phone with you."

Sounding calmer, Sarah said, "Drive carefully. You know how bad the deer are this time of year along I-25."

"Yeah, I know. But after all these years, I've learned how to dodge 'em," Rivers said, laughing. "You need to think about doin' the same thing when it comes to Tango-11. Nobody says you have to be at home when the authorities show up wantin' to chat."

"I'll consider the possibility."

"Good. I'll talk to you later," Grant said, snapping his cell phone closed to leave Sarah staring at a half-dozen pots that needed to be fired and wondering why she'd called someone for moral support whom she'd seen shoot elk out of season and leave wounded deer lying in the field to rot.

An hour later she remained as disgusted as, and no less nervous than, when she'd been talking to Grant. Buford still hadn't come home, and two calls to Kimiko Takata had gone unanswered. No matter how hard she tried, she couldn't shake the feeling that the blame for the Thurmond Giles killing would soon be headed her way. Upset with herself for hanging on to tired old friendships and long-extinguished love, she decided to put away her pottery tools, head up the hill to the house, and go to bed.

The crunch of tires on the gravel driveway outside the shed filled her with a momentary sense of relief. Telling herself that Buford was finally home, she rushed to the front door and swung it open, only to realize that the vehicle idling just feet from the door wasn't Buford's. Unable to recognize the driver in the darkness, she barely had time to yell, "What?" when two blasts from a sawed-off shotgun took away most of her face. Moaning, with her hands clutched to her face, she fell face forward onto the gravel. She rolled around on the driveway screaming as the driver reloaded, stepped from the car, and pumped a third blast into the back of her head before slipping back into the vehicle to drive away.

Buford Kane found his common-law wife's body, her head in a pool of blood, thirty minutes later. For half those minutes he'd nosed around the house absentmindedly looking for snacks and sorting through a stash of porno tapes. When he finally decided to look for Sarah in the potter's shed, his stomach was growling from the five cans of beer and the nearly dozen chicken wings he'd consumed earlier at a bar in Chugwater. When he found Sarah lying facedown in the dark as the shed's open front door swung lazily in the night breeze, a projectile of sour beer and partially digested chicken parts shot from his mouth. It was only the lengthy scream that ensued that stopped the flow.

Wiping vomit from his face, he ran into the shed, called 911, and then checked Sarah's dead body for signs of life before racing up the hill to the house. Barely able to breathe and with tears streaming down his cheeks, he located Bernadette Cameron's card in a kitchen drawer. Certain that Sarah's death was connected to the Tango-11 murder, he dialed Bernadette's cell-phone number and waited.

When Bernadette, who'd stayed up to read for a bit after coming home from dinner, answered, Buford said breathlessly, "I need your help, Major. Sarah's been murdered. Right here at our house. I found her lying outside her potter's shed a few minutes ago. Half her face is missing," he said, shivering uncontrollably, barely able to get his words out. "It's all connected to that murder at Tango-11, goddamn it! Help me, Major, please! Help me!"

"Have you called 911?"

"Yes. Can you come, too, right now, Major Cameron, please?"

Feeling helpless, Bernadette said, "I'm afraid I'm not involved with the Tango-11 investigation any longer, Mr. Kane. You'll need to contact Colonel DeWitt."

With sirens wailing in the background, the still sobbing Buford said, "I don't want to start with somebody new."

Bernadette swallowed hard, fighting to maintain her composure. "All I can do, I'm afraid, is give you Colonel DeWitt's number."

"Then give it to me, damn it!"

Bernadette gave him the number and added, "That's his direct line."

"Wait a minute. I've gotta find something to write with. Okay. Let me have it again," he said, fumbling with a ballpoint pen.

Bernadette repeated the number. "I'm so sorry."

"The paramedics are here! Oh, my God, I came home too late! Too fucking late." Buford slammed down the receiver to leave a wide-eyed and visibly shaken Bernadette listening to a dial tone.

Seconds later, as she dialed Cozy's cell-phone number and her throat went dry, she whispered, "Answer, Cozy, please."

The Southeastern Oklahoma State baseball T-shirt and jeans Cozy had hastily thrown on after Bernadette's midnight phone call were wrinkled and in need of washing, and as he sat in her hotel suite, hair barely combed, feeling slightly self-conscious, drinking a Coke, and watching the normally unflappable major pace the floor, he found himself thinking that his unkempt look might be adding to her upset.

Bernadette, who was dressed in loose-fitting khaki shorts and one of her father's oversized air force–blue dress shirts, was typically barefoot. Cozy locked eyes with her and, in response to her description of the disjointed conversation she'd had with Buford Kane, asked, "And Kane really sounded that bad?"

"He was crying like a baby, Cozy. It was terrible."

Cozy nodded understandingly and said, "But you're off the case, Bernadette."

"I know."

"What could you do, anyway?"

"Help him, I guess. And maybe solve what are now two murders."

"How many times do you need to be reminded? You're not a cop, Bernadette."

"Yeah, I know. But somebody needs to pick up the pace on the Tango-11 investigation. Colonel DeWitt sure won't."

"There's still Sheriff Bosack."

"Come on, Cozy. The man's probably more interested in grooming his horse."

"Well, you certainly can't take it on yourself to find out what really happened there. You'll buy yourself more trouble."

"Yes, I can," Bernadette said, surprising Cozy with the swiftness of her response. "But I'll need your help."

"Are you serious?" Cozy asked, shaking his head.

"Absolutely. As for trouble, I've been there before."

"Okay, Ms. Trouble's My Middle Name. Where do you plan to start?"

"I think that *we,* Mr. Coseia, should start from the rear of the bus. Begin with Sarah Goldbeck's murder and work our way up to the front from there."

"Fair enough," Cozy said, uncertain whether he was out to simply placate Bernadette or truly help her.

"So, here's the first question. Why kill Sarah Goldbeck if you're Sergeant Giles's murderer, and how are the two murders connected?" Bernadette stopped pacing, sat down on the floor, stretched both legs out in front of her, and leaned back against a leather ottoman, deep in thought. As her partially buttoned shirt separated to reveal her navel, she said, "Might as well get comfortable," to Cozy before leaning forward to tug the uncooperative shirttail back into place. "We're going to be here a while. I'll call room service and order some coffee. What time is it, anyway?"

"A little past midnight."

"Late," she said, sighing. "Anything you'd like besides coffee?"

"Yeah. Ask if they have any French raisin rolls. My grandmother used to bake them by the dozen and send them vacuum-sealed to me in Oklahoma. Freddy and I lived on those things."

"You're on, *mon ami,*" Bernadette said, smiling. "I'm partial to them myself. Got semiaddicted to the things while I was touring with the U.S. tennis team in France the summer after I finished college. They're right up there on my list of favorite pastries, right behind sticky buns."

"Too gooey for me," Cozy said, frowning and shaking his head.

"You're badly in need of expanding your horizons, Mr. Coseia," Bernadette said, smiling and again leaning back against the ottoman. This time she made no attempt to tuck the navel-revealing shirttail back into place.

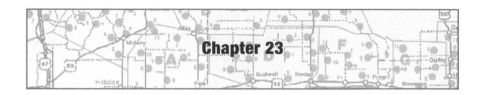

Chapter 23

After diagonally crossing Missouri and half of Oklahoma, Silas Breen had reached the outskirts of Oklahoma City. It was twelve thirty a.m., and as he rolled past billboard after billboard beckoning him to bed down at this or that motel for the night, he planned to stay where he always stayed when he was on the road: Motel 6. He'd have easy access to I-40 in the morning, and the coffee and doughnuts were free. Thinking that even if he slept in until eight, he'd be able to make Lubbock by two, he slowed down to fifty and relaxed.

Despite the trip's rough spots, which now included an Oklahoma Port of Entry citation and a three-hundred-dollar fine for running on illegally recapped tires, he was still making progress. He'd been delayed for nearly an hour at the port of entry while some overzealous POE officer had called God knew where to verify the origin of his load. But things were now pretty much back on keel. By this time the next day, he planned to have a wad of cash in hand and a big-chested girl on each arm to help him spend some of it.

The bizarre trip had one other downside, however. His delivery deadline had forced him to bypass Kansas City, so he'd missed hooking up with his father. He and Otis had had their differences, especially after he'd lost his basketball scholarship and dropped out of college. But now that he'd successfully started his own business, those differences appeared less magnified, and OT, the initials Otis Breen preferred to be addressed by, seemed to be less the snap-to-attention, drill-sergeant personality he'd been raised by.

Cruising beneath an overhead sign announcing that his exit was two miles ahead, he patted his belly. It was his late-night way of telling himself that his day would soon be done. His only lingering worry was that he hadn't heard from F. Mantew all day, and although he'd vowed not to obsess over that fact, he was worried, especially since Mantew had indicated that he'd be in touch one way or another every day of the trip.

He rubbed the underside of his jaw thoughtfully, slowed to take his exit, and once again found himself wondering what on earth F. Mantew actually had him hauling. The issue had begun to bother him so much that before going to bed, he planned to call OT to discuss the issue. Then he might uncrate one of the boxes he was hauling and have a look inside.

The Motel 6 he pulled up to looked like any of the dozens of cookie-cutter sleep boxes he'd stayed at since starting his trucking business. The woman at the front desk, tired-looking but friendly, gave him a first-floor room that was clean, had towels aplenty, and had a bed that, although a bit too rubbery for his taste, at least didn't sag.

By the time he'd finished a soda, brushed his teeth, and changed into the Notre Dame running shorts he'd bought in South Bend, it was a quarter past one. Exhausted, he sat down on the edge of the bed, checked his cell phone to make sure it had a healthy charge, and punched in his father's number, knowing that even though the friction between them had lessened, OT would be unhappy to hear from him or anyone else at one fifteen a.m.

Otis Breen's response to the call was a groggy "What?"

"OT, it's Silas. I'm in Oklahoma City."

"What the hell time is it, boy?"

"A quarter past one."

"And you couldn't've called me earlier?"

"I was on the road trying to make up time."

"Well, did you?"

"Yep."

Offering his usual critical counsel, Otis said, "Then I guess you're finally learnin' what responsibility means. Where you headed for, anyway?"

"Lubbock."

"Hell, if you're in Oklahoma City, you're almost there."

"Six and a half more hours of driving at the most. But I'm dog tired, so I decided to bed down for the night. Need to ask you something important first."

"Get to askin'."

"It's about the load I'm hauling and the person who hired me to haul it. I'm worried about them both."

"What are you transportin'?"

"Used hospital equipment—at least that's what the manifest says."

"Sounds safe enough. So, what's got you spooked about your employer?"

"Just the fact that the son of a bitch is weird. I don't really know if I'm working for a man, a woman, a midget in tights, a seven-foot giant, or a drug runner and thief. All I know is that whoever it is goes by the name F. Mantew and that we communicate generally by fax. Even stranger, I've had my destination changed midstream. Started out on my way to Amarillo."

"Does sound a little odd." Otis flipped on the lamp on his nightstand and sat up in bed. "How'd you get the job, anyway?"

"The easy-money way, OT. The same way white folks get jobs—contacts. In fact, this one came by way of an old friend of yours, Thurmond Giles. He called me about seven weeks back and hooked the whole thing up."

"What!" Otis leaped out of bed.

"What's the problem, OT?"

"You mean you ain't heard about Thurmond?"

"No."

"He's dead, Silas. Murdered. They found him hangin' inside an abandoned Minuteman missile personnel-access tube a few days back."

"Shit!"

"You got that. And right now, I'd say you're swimmin' in it. Have you taken a look at what the hell you're haulin'?"

"I've checked it out a couple of times, but everything's crated up."

"Then you need to uncrate somethin', see what the shit you're transportin', and be prepared to call the cops. Hell, with Thurmond buyin' it the way he did, and with him at one time bein' a hotshot missile-warhead mechanic, you could be haulin' around a damn nuke."

Silas shook his head. "I picked up my load from a hospital. Come on, OT."

"Who in the hell says you're really haulin' hospital equipment? Where'd you start your trip from, anyway?"

"Ottawa."

"Canada. Well, hell. The last time I talked to Thurmond, he told me he was workin' for some company up north of the border. Damn it, Silas, I'm thinkin' you've got yourself caught up in somethin' that's hell-bent serious here."

Silas stood and started pacing the room. "Think maybe I should go pop one of those crates I'm hauling right now?"

"I sure do, and I think you should call the cops. I've already had some air force OSI major and a reporter from a news outfit outta Denver called Digital Registry News talk to me about Thurmond."

"Have the cops called?"

"No, thank goodness. But now I'm thinkin' they probably will. Never figured you'd ever be tied in to any of Thurmond Giles's messes. Damn."

"I'm not sure that I am tied to one of his messes, OT. As far as I know, I'm still just hauling a load of used hospital equipment."

"Well, make damn sure you are. Get your ass in gear and go open up one of them crates this instant."

OT's commanding tone, the same authoritative tone Silas had been forced to live with for most of his life, triggered a rush of resentment. "I'll handle this, OT, okay?"

"You better, boy, or I'll be callin' the cops myself."

On the verge of yelling, *I'm in charge here, Sergeant; butt the hell out!* Silas instead said, "I'm headed to have a look at my cargo right now."

"Fine. Call me back and let me know what you find. You hear me?"

"Will do," Silas said, biting his tongue and hanging up.

A carton containing a single half-eaten raisin roll sat on the coffee table in front of Cozy. His sweet tooth satisfied, he was sitting on the floor of Bernadette's hotel suite, legs outstretched like hers, eyeing the raisin roll. The suite smelled strongly of sweet rolls and coffee past its prime.

Bernadette was busy jotting notes on a yellow tablet and glancing back and forth between the dozen maps of deactivated air force missile-silo sites in Colorado, Wyoming, Nebraska, Missouri, Montana, and North and South Dakota that she'd spread out on the floor. She'd been studying the maps for the past half hour as she and Cozy ate raisin rolls, drank coffee, and tried to come up with a connection between the events at Tango-11 and some eight hundred deactivated missile sites in seven states. With their thighs touching in a leisurely, unromantic way and their shirts untucked, they looked more like a couple of college students cramming for an exam than two people trying to solve a murder.

Amazed by Bernadette's dogged persistence as she continued to check off missile site after missile site, jotting each one's code name, number, size, activation date, and decommissioning date down on her tablet, Cozy leaned forward and asked, "Think maybe we should move past the silo sites and on to something else? How about Sarah Goldbeck? What do you think about the idea that Buford might have killed her?"

"No way. The man was devastated when he called me to say he'd found her body."

"Maybe he was faking it."

"I don't think so."

"Then who killed her?"

Bernadette flipped several pages of her tablet back and stared at a note she'd written a few minutes earlier. "Somebody who didn't want Sarah spilling her guts to the authorities would be my guess. I've got a feeling she knew who killed Sergeant Giles."

"Maybe the killing involved a love triangle—between Sarah, Thurmond Giles, and Grant Rivers, perhaps. Didn't you say earlier that Rivers and Sarah were once an item?"

Bernadette shook her head. "No, I said that's what newspapers hinted at back in the late '70s when Sarah's neurotic mother was busy dragging the poor girl around the countryside to missile-site protests. I hate to admit it, but thanks to Colonel DeWitt, I located a bunch of official air force photos of Sergeant Giles, Sarah, and her mother in a couple of old OSI files at Warren just before I left. Sarah couldn't have been more than fifteen or so."

"So maybe Rivers liked robbing the cradle, and maybe for some reason after all these years he ended up being as mad at Sarah as he is at the government. He has a landing strip on his ranch, and that means he has access to rapid transit, you might say. He could've killed Sarah and been back home to Buffalo pretty quick."

"Okay, Mr. Love Triangle," Bernadette said, nudging Cozy's hip with hers. "I'll make a note of your *As the World Turns* concerns. And just so you know, that preacher Wilson Jackson's wife had an affair with Giles, too. Colonel DeWitt told me so himself. Wanna move on to Howard Colbain and the Takatas?"

"Might as well," said Cozy, briefly considering the new Wilson Jackson wrinkle. "First off, Colbain's too far away to have dashed up here from New Mexico to kill Sarah. As for the Takatas, I'd need a motive."

"Too far away? I don't think so," Bernadette said with a sly smile. "Grant Rivers owns a plane; why not Colbain?"

Eye to eye with Bernadette and with his face inches from hers, Cozy said, "No reason, and I've been told that like angels, they have wings."

"Yes, but angels—" The sound of Bernadette's cell phone ringing cut her response short.

Without looking at the caller ID, she flipped the phone open and said to Cozy, "Probably my dad."

"Is this Major Cameron?" came the uncertain response.

Shaking her head to let Cozy know that the caller wasn't her father, Bernadette said, "Yes."

"It's Otis Breen, calling from Kansas City, and I've got sort of a problem on my hands."

"Which is?" Bernadette grabbed her pen and tablet and printed "Otis Breen" in bold letters at the top of the tablet's first page.

"I think my son, Silas, has gotten himself mixed up in that murder case you called me about."

"Why's that?"

"Because it turns out Thurmond Giles set Silas up with a job to haul somethin' across country."

Unable to stand the suspense, Cozy leaned into Bernadette and turned the cell phone partially toward him to listen in.

"Any idea when Giles hired him, and has Silas told you what he's haulin'?" Bernadette asked.

"I know Giles set up the deal about seven weeks back, and Silas is supposedly haulin' old hospital equipment. He started out headed for Amarillo. Now his destination's Lubbock. He's scheduled to make his delivery tomorrow."

"To whom?"

"To someone named F. Mantew. I told him just a little bit ago to go take a look at what he's haulin' and if need be, call the cops."

"You mean he hasn't seen what he's hauling?"

"Nope. He told me his shipment's all crated up. I'm callin' you because I figured you might have some inkling of what's inside those crates."

"I'm afraid I don't," Bernadette said, feeling the warmth of Cozy's breath on her neck. When he tapped her on the shoulder, mouthing, "Let me talk to him," Bernadette shook her head and said to Otis, "So how long had Silas and Thurmond Giles known one another?"

"Since Thurmond and I were in the service. Silas was just a kid when they first met. It was at one of our basketball games. I'm the one who told Thurmond when I talked to him last Thanksgiving that Silas had started his own truckin' business. Shoulda kept my damn mouth shut."

"There's nothing to suggest that Silas was involved in Sergeant Giles's murder, Mr. Breen."

"I wasn't thinkin' he was. But knowin' Silas like I do, I'm worried about the boy's safety. He tends to run up against trouble a whole lot more than most."

"Why didn't he tell you Giles had set him up with the job when he first got the offer?"

"'Cause Silas just ain't the kind that would've done that. The two of us ain't always seen eye to eye, you see. Especially when it comes to dealin' with where a person's headed in life, if you know what I mean. For Silas, callin' me and tellin' me that Thurmond had set him up with a job would've been the same as tellin' me that he couldn't stand upright and get a job on his own."

"So when's he going to call you back with word on what's in those crates?"

"As soon as he pops one open."

"After he calls, would you call me back?"

"If I'm not busy makin' a phone call to the cops first."

"Why would you call them?"

Otis let out a long, deliberate sigh. "Because unfortunately, Major Cameron, that boy of mine don't always do what he says."

"Meaning?"

"Meanin' that since long-haul truckin' money's involved in this deal, he may very well head on to Lubbock, make his delivery, collect his cash, and never call the cops."

"I sure hope not. Any idea where his final destination is in Lubbock?"

"No."

"What about a phone number for him?"

Otis gave her the number. Hastily jotting it down, Bernadette asked, "What's his truck look like?"

"It's a twenty-six-footer, one of those big U-Haul types. It's painted shamrock green with 'Breen's Moving & Storage Company' painted white in Old English script on the sides. Helped Silas pick the typeface out myself. Oh, and there's one other thing about that truck. The number 18—that's the number Silas wore when he played ball—is stenciled in thirty-six-inch-high screamin' red on the cargo roof. I had him put the number there for what in the army we called 'spy-in-the-sky' ID purposes."

"Good thing to know if things get funky."

"Yeah." Sounding disconsolate, Otis said, "Seems like no matter what, I'm gonna forever be lookin' out for that boy."

"Anything else I should know about Silas or his truck?"

"Nothin' I can think of at the moment. Afraid I've gotta go. I don't wanna miss a phone call about that cargo of his, and I sure as hell don't wanna miss no phone call from the cops."

"Call me back when you hear something either way, okay?"

"I'll do that," Otis said, hanging up.

Bernadette snapped her cell phone shut, looked at Cozy, and said, "Damn!"

"Yep!" said Cozy. "Think I'd better call Freddy, since we're in the news business here." He turned to face Bernadette and kissed her softly on the lips. The bitter taste of coffee mixed with raisin-roll sweetness filled his mouth as he penetrated the curvature of her lips with his tongue. Offering no resistance, Bernadette opened her mouth to enjoy a probing bittersweetness of her own.

"Damn it, Cozy. I'm in bed, and for the record, I'm not alone." Freddy Dames patted the woman in bed next to him on the rear, rolled over, and propped himself up on one elbow.

"Hey, man, I wouldn't be calling you at this time of night if it weren't important," Cozy said, enjoying the impromptu back rub Bernadette was giving him, which ended suddenly when Cozy said, "Bernadette and I need an airlift down to Amarillo. One that'll have us there tomorrow morning without any airport hassle."

"Can't do. Afraid I'm busy seven up to seven down tomorrow."

"Oil business?"

"The very best kind," Freddy said, grinning.

"Damn it, Freddy. We just got a new lead on the Giles killing. Can't you juggle your plans?"

"We? I take it by 'we,' you mean you and Major Cameron. Thought you told me she was off the Tango-11 case."

"She is and she isn't. I'll explain it to you later. We need that lift, Freddy."

Freddy shook his head in protest as the woman lying beside him slowly ran her hand up his inner thigh. "So, what's the new lead?" he asked, gently grasping the woman's hand.

"We just got word that before he bought it, Thurmond Giles set up a deal that involved trucking a load of hospital equipment from Ottawa to Lubbock."

"So what's the connection to Tango-11?"

"Bernadette and I think a man named Silas Breen might be delivering a load of radiation therapy equipment that's bound for a Third World market to somebody named F. Mantew."

"Nothing illegal about that."

"There is if the equipment's either stolen or has been deemed unsafe. I've checked. We know that Giles had the kind of contacts you'd need to access and move that kind of merchandise. Remember, Bernadette talked to a woman at a Seattle company a couple of days back who confirmed it."

"How big a news story are we talking about here?"

"Big. Especially if the guy delivering the goods to Amarillo can lead us to Giles's killer."

Freddy sat up in bed, thought for a moment, and said, "Put Bernadette on. Assuming she's there, of course," he added with a sly chuckle.

"Freddy wants to talk to you." Cozy handed Bernadette the phone.

"Hello."

"Late hours you're keeping there, Major. Got a question for you. Think you can handle my *Sugar*?"

"I'm certified to fly anything up to four-engine jet bombers, if that's what you're asking."

"No offense intended. I'm just protective of my baby."

"Understood."

"Put Cozy back on, okay?"

"Yeah?" Cozy said, taking the phone.

"What time do you need to leave Denver in the morning?"

"By ten at the latest, and that's assuming we know the final destination for that truck, the truck's ETA, and that the cops haven't gotten to this guy Breen first."

"You mean the law could be in on this? Hell, that means our exclusive on the story could go up in smoke. Those blabbermouths are likely to tell the world."

"It's news either way, Freddy."

"Guess so," Freddy said, smiling as his impatient bedmate cupped his testicles in her hand. "I'll have *Sugar* fueled and a flight plan filed by nine. Let's hope you still have first dibs on the news story by then. And Cozy, when you get back from Texas, you can fill me in on a local story I seemed to have missed. The one about you having Major Cameron there to tuck you in at night. Talk to you tomorrow, and be sure Bernadette treats *Sugar* like a princess. 'Bye.'"

Shaking his head, Cozy snapped his cell phone closed. "We've got ourselves a plane."

"Sort of figured we did," Bernadette said, wrapping her arms loosely around Cozy's neck.

"And for what it's worth, Freddy said you should tuck me in."

"But we're sitting on the floor," Bernadette said, snickering.

"That makes it all the more newsworthy." Cozy slipped Bernadette's arms from around his neck and kissed her passionately as he lowered her to the floor.

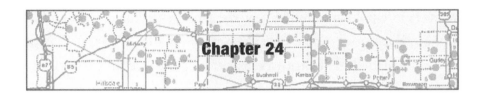

Chapter 24

The crowbar Silas Breen was using to open one of the crates he was hauling had belonged to his grandfather, a blacksmith and cobbler from Joplin, Missouri. The ten-pound, four-foot-long, eighty-year-old, hand-forged, crooked-cane-style piece of iron lacked any hint of rust. After three minutes of effort, Silas had the front of the crate open. Light from the three highway safety lanterns he'd hung from the truck's ceiling flooded the inside.

Taking a nervous step backward, he dropped his crowbar, stooped, slipped a flashlight out of the tool kit near the door, and aimed the beam at the crate's contents, an oddly shaped object that reminded him of a giant shower arm and nozzle. A metal strut the size of an old-fashioned barber's pole rose from a shiny metal floor base to support the arm and "showerhead." The support strut and the cream-colored arm and head were attached to one another by a metal arm with an elbow. When he reached out to touch the arm, it flexed at the elbow, and the head rose to the top of the crate, slamming into it with a loud bang.

Startled, Silas grabbed the arm and pulled the head back down into position, thinking as he scanned the crate with his flashlight, *What in the hell?*

He examined the odd-looking apparatus for another couple of minutes looking for markings, serial numbers, or a manufacturer's name before poking around inside the musty-smelling crate for additional pieces of equipment or even maintenance records. Except for a burnished spot on the support strut where he suspected a hospital inventory label had once been, he found nothing. When he stooped and popped open a housing cover near the bottom of the support strut, he found a highway of wires and a stack of six-gun-gray metal boxes inside. The boxes were each about half the size of a laptop computer. He tried to pry the top one open with his pocketknife but couldn't.

Bewildered, he moved to flex the arm once again, but it failed to budge. He was certain that whatever he was looking at had been used for treating patients, but he wasn't at all sure whether he was dealing with a piece of operating-room equipment, a portion of an X-ray unit, or something designed to look inside an expectant mother's womb.

What he did know was that he was indeed hauling hospital equipment and that at least one of his twenty crates was free of drugs, weapons, stolen goods, and jail-time-inducing contraband.

He suspected, nonetheless, that there was a connection between what he was hauling and Sergeant Giles's murder. Enough of a connection for him to drop everything and call F. Mantew, or whoever in the hell Mantew really was, pretty damn quick.

Nudging aside the crowbar with the toe of his work boot, he stepped back to the tool kit near the door, retrieved a battery-powered screwdriver, stepped back to the open crate, shouldered its plywood face back into place, and started screwing it back down. As each screw sank into place, he thought about the possibility of his payday flying out the window. He sure as hell hadn't killed anyone, but the man who'd gotten him the current job was dead, and he needed F. Mantew to clear the air. Deciding to send Mantew a fax from a twenty-four-hour FedEx Office, he put his tools away, retrieved his crowbar, and moved to get out of the truck. As he closed the cargo-bay door, he thought about what the fax to Mantew should say. Brief and to the point would work, he decided. Something like, *Hey, asshole, what the hell am I hauling? You can tell me or tell the cops,* seemed just about right.

Awakened at two thirty a.m. from a sound sleep, Howard Colbain grumbled, "What the fuck!"

The person on the other end of the line spoke softly and slowly, informing Colbain that a chiming, sleep-disturbing cell-phone message he'd just received via a computer-linked fax from Silas Breen had informed him that there was a problem that required their immediate attention.

Colbain spent the next ten minutes arguing unsuccessfully that there had to be a better way of dealing with a man who was simply delivering a load of outdated hospital equipment to Lubbock, Texas, than to hijack his truck. That argument lost, Colbain now stood wide-awake in his kitchen, drinking black coffee and trying to figure out how to extract himself from something that had turned into one hell of a god-awful mess.

Kimiko Takata was having a hard time sleeping, so she'd decided to take a three thirty a.m. bath. The hot water, though soothing enough, wasn't helping her psyche. Thirty minutes earlier she'd been awakened by a call from the Goshen County sheriff informing her that Sarah Goldbeck had been murdered; that Sarah's husband, Buford, had insisted that he call Kimiko immediately; and that the sheriff would come by to interview her concerning the murder the next morning at nine. She'd already had a disturbing late-evening call from an FBI agent named Richter who'd asked for a time he could speak with her as well.

Adjusting the water flow, she told herself that things had started to go downhill from the very moment Rikia had called early in the evening to say he'd be coming home from his conference in El Paso a day later than he'd planned. When she'd told him that Sarah Goldbeck had called her three times in the space of two hours and that she'd sounded scared to death, Rikia's response, "I'll deal with her when I get back," had been anything but reassuring. She'd called Sarah back to let her know about Rikia's delay, only to be forced to listen to fifteen additional minutes of Sarah's fearful whining. The whining had finally caused her to scream, "Sarah, shut the hell up!"

Deciding that no hot bath would be able to erase her problems, she leaned forward, flipped up the drain lever, and sat immobile in the water as it slowly swirled away.

Even though he was exhausted, Silas Breen understood exactly why he'd agreed at four in the morning to drive 250 miles from Oklahoma City to Amarillo, rather than to Lubbock. Five thousand dollars! A five grand bonus that F. Mantew, in response to Silas's fax, had promised, in a surprise call to Silas's cell phone, to pay if he had his delivery to Amarillo by first thing the next morning. Silas didn't like the idea of racing to Amarillo and risking another citation, but with a packet of No-Doz, a thermos of coffee, and his grandfather's crowbar lying on the seat beside him, he was back on the road, thinking of how he'd spend his extra five grand.

The bonus money had been incentive enough for him to call OT back and let him know he'd checked out his cargo and determined that he wasn't carrying anything illegal and to assure him that there'd be no need for either of them to call the cops. After agreeing to meet Mantew outside Amarillo at nine a.m., just off I-40 at exit 74, he'd felt euphoric. Knowing that an unexpected bonus was in the offing and that he might also actually finally find out what he'd been hauling, he'd decided that *hear no evil, see no evil, speak no evil* seemed the most prudent tactic.

Thaddeus Richter was sitting in a wingback chair across from the front desk in the lobby of the JW Marriott at seven a.m., reading the *Denver Post,* when Cozy came down to get a morning newspaper and breezed past him. As Cozy turned to head back upstairs, newspaper in hand, he spotted the spit-shined, black-and-white wingtips and the Panama hat that Freddy had joked about when he'd described Richter to him. Before Richter could stick his head out from behind the newspaper, Cozy asked, "How's the weather outside, Agent Richter?"

"Just beautiful. Sunny, 72, no wind," Richter said, unfazed.

"Can't beat that. So, why the visit? You are looking for me, aren't you?" Cozy asked, sounding equally nonchalant.

"Afraid not. I'm here to talk to Major Cameron. She's here, isn't she?"

"Yes."

"Maybe you should call her, give her a heads-up, and let her know I'm here before we head up?" Richter said, rising from his chair. "Wouldn't want to put a damper on what the two of you do in private."

"Chivalrous of you, but there's no need," said Cozy.

"Your call," Richter said, smiling.

Cozy folded his newspaper in half, tucked it under an arm, and, with Richter leading the way, headed for the elevator.

Bernadette, barefoot and dressed in loose-fitting running shorts and a lime-green T-shirt, seemed less surprised to see someone at the door with Cozy than by the fact that Cozy had returned without refreshments. "What, no raisin rolls?" she asked.

"I got intercepted," Cozy said, rolling his eyes. "Meet FBI Agent Thaddeus Richter."

"My pleasure," said Richter, shaking Bernadette's hand. "Sorry about your raisin rolls. I'll order some up. On me."

"That's okay," Bernadette said, trying to sound unflustered and leading the two men into the suite's sun-washed anteroom.

"So, how'd you run us down?" Cozy asked, taking a seat on the couch next to Bernadette.

"I'm FBI, remember?" Richter said with a wink as he took a chair facing them.

"Yeah, almost forgot," said Cozy.

Adjusting himself in the chair and looking briefly at his shoes, Richter said, "I understand that you're no longer assigned to the Tango-11 investigation, Major." He glanced down at the maps that Bernadette had spread out on the floor next to the couch, seeming to take a lingering interest in the red dots that pinpointed the hundreds of onetime active missile sites in each state.

"No, I'm not." Bernadette leaned down and gathered the maps and the yellow tablet she'd been writing on into a neat stack, making certain that she placed the tablet facedown on top of the maps.

Richter smiled, leaned forward in his chair, and pushed the tablet aside, partially exposing the map of Colorado. He adjusted his designer reading glasses backward on his nose. "Lots of nuclear payload holes still out there in the Colorado ground, wouldn't you say, Major?"

"Two hundred or so."

"And all of them arranged so neatly into such nice little quadrants," Richter said, continuing to stare down on the red-dotted Colorado map.

"Air force magic," said Bernadette. "And we prefer to call them 'flights' rather than 'quadrants.'"

"I see. So what's your continued interest in them? I mean, since you're off the Tango-11 investigation."

"Just fascinated by maps, I guess." Bernadette shot a nervous glance at Cozy. A glance that as much as shouted, *I'm winging it here.*

"I think *fascinating* might be the better word choice here, Major Cameron. Fascinating enough, it seems, that you were the first person Buford Kane called after he found his wife murdered last night. Now, that's a good healthy amount of fascination, wouldn't you say?" Richter eased out of his chair, knelt, wrinkling the knees of his perfectly creased pants, and slipped the Colorado silo-site map aside to reveal a map of Wyoming. "More flights and more red dots," he said smiling and retaking his seat. "But I think I'll just cut to the chase. We're dealing with two murders now, in case you missed it, Major. Murders that might very well be related to national security. So, as the old TV ads from the 1980s used to say, which I expect the two of you are far too young to remember, 'It's not your father's Oldsmobile.' Now, do either of you have any information about those murders that I should know about?"

Glancing at one another, Bernadette and Cozy remained silent.

"It's your career, Major."

"You can ease up on the threats, Richter," Cozy said. "I'm the nosy investigative reporter here, not Bernadette. Since I'm not in the air force and I don't have some windbag career-conscious colonel peering over my shoulder telling me what I can and cannot do, maybe you should direct your questions my way."

"Okay. Why not?" Richter said, relaxing back in his seat, awaiting Cozy's response.

By the time Cozy finished bringing Richter up to speed on everything he and Bernadette had learned during their Tango-11 investigation, starting with Cozy's visit to the Tango-11 site shortly after Giles's body had been found and ending with Silas Breen's mysterious destination-changing trucking assignment, it was a little past nine. Looking satisfied and as if he'd just finished a delightful meal, Richter, who'd taken two and a half pages of notes, ran an index finger slowly down his first page and said to Bernadette, "And the name of that woman again at Gromere Electronics and Engineering?"

"Elaine Richardson."

"And you're thinking she and Sergeant Giles may have been more than just friends?"

"Yes."

Richter flipped the page. "And you haven't been in touch with Silas Breen himself, just his father, correct?"

"That's right," said Cozy, miffed that Richter seemed intent on either repeating or questioning everything he'd just been told.

Noticing Cozy's frustration, Richter said, "I'll call the father."

"Do you plan to do anything about intercepting whatever it is that Silas Breen's hauling?" asked Bernadette.

Skirting the question and glancing down at his shoes as if to make certain there were no new scuff marks, Richter said, "It's a beautiful day here in Denver. I'd recommend enjoying it."

"Meaning we should stay put here and butt out?" Cozy said sharply.

Richter smiled, buffed his wingtips on the backs of his pant legs, and rose to leave. "I meant exactly what I said, Mr. Coseia." He walked quickly across the anteroom toward the suite's door, with Bernadette trailing him. "Enjoy the rest of your day. I'll be in touch." He smiled back at her as he let himself out.

Bernadette stood at the door for a few seconds, looking bewildered, before walking back into the anteroom to find Cozy down on one knee, flipping through her maps.

"Lots of holes in the ground," Cozy said, mimicking Richter as he stared intently at the red-dotted map of Wyoming.

"Right at two hundred in Wyoming," Bernadette said, playing along.

"Colorado, Wyoming, the Dakotas, Montana, Nebraska, Missouri. Why the heck not Ohio or Tennessee or New York?"

"Because they lack a certain Western essence," Bernadette said smugly.

"Which really means that the holier-than-thous back East would have had a cow if the government had tried to punch a bunch of holes for nukes in their backyards."

"Probably," Bernadette said, shrugging. "So should we enjoy the day, like Agent Richter suggested?"

"Absolutely. And you know what? I think we should start by flying south to warmer weather." Cozy flipped his way slowly through the rest of the maps.

"Lubbock?"

"No," said Cozy. "Albuquerque."

"What? I thought we were taking *Sugar* down to Lubbock."

"Nope. Your maps got me thinking otherwise. New Mexico, after all, is, as it says on their license plate, the 'Land of Enchantment.' Besides, it's where Howard Colbain lives."

"I thought we were out to track down Silas Breen."

"We are, and we will, but those maps of yours got me to thinking about, of all things, baseball diamonds, the shortest routes to fly balls, defensive infield positioning, and Texas."

"You're talking in riddles, Cozy. Want to translate for me?"

"Okay. I'll give you part of the translation. I haven't quite figured out the rest. Your maps and Silas Breen's ever-changing delivery destination got me to thinking about baseball and Texas. Freddy and I bumped around the Lone Star State working for Freddy's dad, oil-rigging our butts off, for three college summers.

We both know the place pretty well, in fact. Turns out, if you think about the location of the cities Silas Breen's been headed for, Amarillo and Lubbock, they're pretty much two points of a triangle. Wanna guess what the final city is in that triangle?"

"It wouldn't be Albuquerque, would it?" Bernadette said, feigning surprise.

"You've got it, beautiful. Ready to fly?"

"Absolutely," Bernadette said excitedly. "Absolutely."

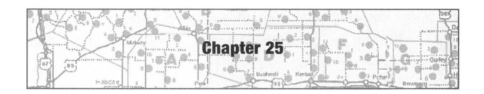

Chapter 25

The dry, static-electricity-filled Texas Panhandle day broke blustery and cold, and the weather forecast called for high winds and record-breaking below-normal temperatures for the rest of the week. Parked at an I-40 truck stop two miles east of where he was supposed to meet F. Mantew, Silas Breen had just rummaged through his foul-weather gear and dug out his watch cap and gloves after seeing that the thermometers mounted on his sideview mirrors were reading 38 degrees. He wasn't as tired as he'd thought he'd be after his four-hour, fifteen-minute mostly predawn highball from Oklahoma City—in fact, he was riding a wave of payday exhilaration, and since he wasn't scheduled to meet Mantew until nine, he had almost an hour to take a last look at his load.

Shivering and with his watch cap pulled down over his ears, he'd gotten out of the cab, sprinted to the rear of his truck, and unlocked the cargo door when a boy who looked to be in his teens strolled by and asked, "Cold enough for you, mister?"

Silas shrugged without answering.

Looking disappointed, the boy continued across the motel parking lot, never looking back.

A half hour later, after opening three crates, searching through them from top to bottom, and finding the very same thing he'd found inside the crate he'd broken into a few hours earlier, Silas felt a lot more comfortable about his decision to deliver his cargo early, collect his money and bonus from Mantew, and head back home without calling the cops.

He was back behind the wheel with the engine idling and the heater on high when the boy he'd encountered earlier walked back across the parking lot. "Feels a little warmer now," he called out to the boy after rolling down his window. Looking detached, the boy kept walking without offering a response.

Dressed in an ankle-length duster, F. Mantew walked the half mile from the parking lot of the Big Texan Steak Ranch and Motel just off I-40, where he'd been dropped off by a cab an hour earlier, and into a wooded area a quarter mile south of the off-ramp Silas Breen would be taking. The off-ramp merged into a country road that then paralleled the northern boundary of a two-mile-square stretch of woods. Pleased that the entire Texas Panhandle was shrouded in clouds, and with his sinuses tingling from the cold, Mantew thought about a quotation he'd always loved. Though he couldn't remember its source, he'd long remembered its message: *The dimmer the day, the more errant man's focus; the colder the day, the less man's quickness.*

He didn't expect that he'd have any difficulty spotting Breen or his shamrock-green truck, especially since Breen's website featured a photo of him standing next to the vehicle, grinning proudly.

The treeless spot he was standing in wasn't new to him. He'd been there before—four times, in fact, over the past six months. Each of those times, he'd checked out the wooded area's boundaries, its fences, and the general lay of the land in order to determine if any of the acreage could be seen from the interstate. Dozens of times he'd walked the length of a grassy strip between the leading edge of the woods and the frontage road that Breen would have to cross. He'd even brought a stopwatch during each of his earlier visits so he could determine how frequently and at what times of day vehicles favored taking exit 74, ultimately determining that on average, between the hours of seven a.m. and six p.m., the off-ramp saw a vehicle about once every seventeen minutes.

He'd never planned to have Breen drive all the way into Amarillo to make his delivery, and he would have told him that himself that morning if Breen hadn't faxed him in the wee hours of the night, causing him to accelerate everything by eight hours and throwing a monkey wrench into his meticulous planning.

Checking one of his coat pockets to make certain that his gloves were inside, he stood rocking back and forth in the clearing at the end of a four-by-four trail. The clearing was blocked from any highway view by a clump of forty-foot-tall ponderosa pines. He was ready to do business with Silas Breen. Smiling and thinking that his long-planned mission was now in its final stages, he rubbed his hands together to warm them and waited.

Silas Breen eased his truck off the interstate and down the exit ramp's slight grade to the sound of the Eagles singing his favorite song, "Desperado." He'd been nervous about making his delivery to Mantew ever since the original delivery destination had been changed from Amarillo to Lubbock, and he was no less so now that his destination had been changed back to Amarillo. That was why his grandfather's crowbar sat next to him on the seat along with a .32

Smith & Wesson. He didn't know whether Mantew had arranged for the necessary equipment to off-load and transfer his cargo or if they'd end up driving into Amarillo to make the exchange. What he did know was that all of a sudden he'd begun to sweat.

When he saw someone dressed in an olive-green range duster, a coat that seemed to swallow the person in it whole, waving at him, arms above his head, Silas wiped a trickle of sweat from his brow and thought, *Almost home.*

As the person in the duster waved him off the roadway and toward what looked like a Jeep trail, the muscles in Silas's stomach tightened, and when his truck momentarily sank in the soft road shoulder, he had the urge to jam it into reverse, back up, and leave. Instead he inched his hand across the seat, patted his grandfather's crowbar and then the butt of the .32, and continued moving slowly toward what he could now see was a man wearing a watch cap nearly identical to his.

Rolling down his window, Silas stuck his head out of the cab and yelled, "I'm not moving this rig any further till I know if you're Mantew."

Nodding, the man said, "I am," jogged up to the cab, and handed Silas an envelope.

Silas tore the envelope open and took his time counting the five thousand dollars in one-hundred-dollar bills inside. "You got equipment to off-load your shipment?" he asked, stuffing the envelope into a jacket pocket.

"A Bobcat."

Puzzled by Mantew's clipped, two-word responses, Silas shrugged and looked around for the Bobcat.

When Mantew said, "This way," pointing toward the Jeep trail, Silas gripped the steering wheel with one hand, patted the crowbar with the other, and inched the truck forward. Thinking as he moved deeper into the woods that he should have seen the Bobcat by now, Silas watched Mantew suddenly sprint for the rear of his truck. Grabbing the crowbar and the .32, Silas swung his door open and jumped out of the cab. He'd barely reached the rear bumper when Mantew, now just feet from him, pulled a World War II–era Japanese sword from beneath his duster, whirled in a half circle to gain momentum, and buried the razor-sharp edge in Silas's neck.

His right carotid artery severed, Silas dropped to one knee. The look on his face begged for explanation as blood streamed down his neck.

Aware that he'd delivered a fatal blow, Mantew walked away, blind to Silas's struggle to breathe. Flopping in the dirt like a pithed frog, Silas tried for the better part of a minute to stand as Rikia Takata, no longer in need of an alias, stood, oblivious to him, looking back in the direction of the exit ramp. Silas curled into the fetal position and gurgled a final breath.

Moving 290 pounds of dead weight into the cargo bay of a truck turned out to be more of a struggle than Rikia had expected. But in just under twelve minutes he'd wedged Silas Breen's body between two wooden crates and tied it down. He'd washed away most of the blood that he'd gotten on himself with water from the two sixty-four-ounce bottles he'd earlier stuffed in his range duster, changed clothes, and slipped into a shirt and the jeans he'd brought along.

There was still blood splatter on his shoes, and as he sat behind the wheel of Breen's truck, inspecting his face for blood in the rear-view mirror, he could see that tiny blood droplets still peppered his forehead and cheeks. Wiping away the droplets with a shirtsleeve and feeling a sense of relief, he sighed. He'd executed a critical part of his plan, and even though Breen's two thirty a.m. fax had forced him to resort to what had always been an alternate piece of the plan, he now had the most important piece of what he needed to complete his task. The twenty dollars he'd nervously paid a cab driver for his eight a.m. cab ride to the motel outside Amarillo was a fading memory now, as was his red-eye bus ride from El Paso to Amarillo late the previous evening.

He glanced in the sideview mirror before backing slowly toward the highway. Thirty yards from the frontage road, he saw a lone car come off the interstate and move slowly down the exit ramp. He stopped so as to not risk being seen by the driver, then smiled as the vehicle turned left onto the frontage road and quickly disappeared. Laughing now, he found himself thinking about the imperfectness of science. His experiments to determine how frequently he could expect a vehicle to access the critical I-40 exit ramp had proven to be wrong, off by more than half. The vehicle he'd just seen was the first one to take the exit ramp during the entire forty-five minutes he'd been there.

Easing Breen's truck onto the pavement and telling himself as the truck jiggled from front to back that all too often the most intricately designed experiments simply didn't pan out, he headed down the frontage road for an I-40 on-ramp, aware more than most that those kinds of variations happened when it came to math and science.

The bushy-headed, overweight FBI agent searching Silas Breen's Oklahoma City motel room hadn't found anything out of the ordinary in the fifteen minutes he'd been there except a half-smoked joint and a six-month-old crumpled page from an over-the-road trucker's time-and-distance log that had obviously been doctored.

Shaking his head and feeling a little put out, the agent slipped his cell phone out of a shirt pocket and dialed his longtime colleague, Thaddeus Richter. When the veteran FBI agent answered, "Richter here," his friend said disappointedly, "Thad, it's Ken, and I've got nada. A motel room full of nothing. No Breen, and nothing that looks suspicious for foul play. Are you sure the info that reporter and the OSI major gave you on Breen is correct?"

"Yes. Now what about Breen's truck?"

"Couldn't locate it, and the desk clerk on duty doesn't remember seeing one. I can ask the employees who are here now if they saw a truck that matches the description of Breen's, but I'm thinking I'll need to talk to someone from the previous shift to cover all my bases."

"Do that for me, Ken, okay?"

"You got it. So, what's up next?"

"I'll get Breen's father on the horn and see if I can't squeeze some answers out of him. After that I just might head down your way."

"Sort of ugly and gray here right now. Think I should call in the locals?"

"No. They'd just get in the way. But you can do one thing for me. Call the bureau office in Lubbock and see if they have anything on either Breen or his truck."

"Will do. And Thad, if you do head this way, how about bringing me a box of Rocky Mountain oysters from the Buckhorn Exchange there in Denver? The ones they sell down here always turn out as hard as rocks when you fry 'em up."

"Damn it, Ken. You're the only person I know in the world who actually likes the taste of bull nuts. What's with the obsession anyway?"

"Guess I like my food chewy, that's all."

Richter shook his head. "I'll round you up some of the little nuggets if I head your way."

"You're the man, Thad."

"Yeah," Richter said, snapping his cell phone shut and wondering how on earth a man and a twenty-six-foot-long, shamrock-green truck could so easily have vanished into thin air.

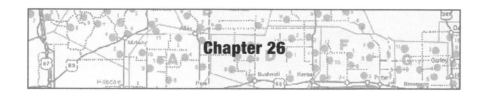

Chapter 26

Barefoot, as usual, listening to the second of the Gulfstream's engines power up, and staring at a cockpit computer screen, Bernadette flipped a toggle switch to her right and said to Cozy, "I still don't fully understand why we're flying to Albuquerque instead of Amarillo."

"Like I've been trying to explain since before we left the hotel, because of your maps."

Concentrating on the task at hand, Bernadette said, "I'm afraid you'll have to explain your reasoning a little better once we're in the air, and this time, no baseball analogies, okay?" Staring at the plane's instrument panel and looking for all the world like a kid in a candy store, she reached up, flipped several additional overhead toggle switches, adjusted her seat, and smiled.

"If I didn't know better, Major Cameron, I'd think you were more interested in playing with this here aeroplane of Freddy's than in what I'm saying," said Cozy.

"Sorry."

Staring at the serious-faced woman next to him and thinking that she seemed nothing like the playful, perhaps even a little vulnerable, woman he'd made love to and held in his arms the previous night, Cozy smiled. When Bernadette slipped on her headphones and motioned for him to follow suit, he had the sense that he was looking at someone whose birthright had somehow been taken away.

Feeling Cozy's stare, Bernadette said, "Can't talk until this bird's in the air, okay?"

"You're the captain," he said, flashing her a thumbs-up as she turned the plane in a broad half arc toward a taxiway. The contagiousness of the back-in-the-saddle look on her face had him smiling and suddenly thinking about fastballs, pickoffs, and headfirst slides into home.

They'd cleared the cloud layer and leveled off at eighteen thousand feet when Bernadette, who'd barely said a word during their climb, adjusted her headset and, staring out at the azure sky, said, "Feels good."

"Looks like you're back on your bicycle," Cozy said, squeezing her thigh affectionately before placing several of her silo-site maps on the console between them.

"Don't get fresh, Mr. Coseia," Bernadette said, trying to keep a straight face and playfully slapping his hand. "I can have you escorted off this ship, in handcuffs if necessary, when we land." Turning to face him, she gave Cozy a sensual, openmouthed kiss. The second their lips parted, she was all business again. "We've got a fifty-knot tailwind. That'll put us into Albuquerque a good fifteen minutes ahead of schedule. Let me take this bird on up to our final cruising altitude, and then I'll let the computers Freddy overpaid for do the flying for a while."

Four minutes later, after leveling off again, she turned to Cozy and said, "Now, would you like to explain, so it makes some kind of sense to me, why on earth we're headed for New Mexico instead of Texas, Mr. Baseball Hotshot?"

"Do I have to?" Cozy asked, toying with her earlobe.

"Yes, Cozy, you do. I Googled you and Freddy last night, after we had dinner, by the way. Division II college baseball championship co-MVPs, career batting averages of .338 and .333, five Gold Glove awards between the two of you. Gadzooks, Batman, you two were bigger than big."

Looking reflective, Cozy said, "All things pass," eased forward in his seat, and pointed to the top map in his stack. "So here's the deal on Albuquerque." He eyed Bernadette's maps. "Nothing clicked with your maps here until I started thinking in baseball-diamond, shortest-distance-between-two-points terms. When I realized that if I drew lines connecting Amarillo, Lubbock, and Albuquerque, I had myself that triangle we talked about, I knew I had something. My imperfect triangle was squeezed down and flattened out a bit, but it was a triangle nonetheless. One with I-25 as a side, U.S. 60 and U.S. 84 as another, and I-40 as an almost perfect straight line from Amarillo to Albuquerque as the base."

"Makes baseball-diamond sense, I guess, but what's the take-home message?"

"The message, my sexy major, is time, distance, and Howard Colbain. Lubbock and Amarillo are each four-, maybe five-hour drives from Albuquerque. Which means you could drive from any one of the points of the triangle to the next in a hurry if you had to. Especially if you needed to pick up an important shipment of something. And since Albuquerque's the only city of the three with a known Tango-11 connection, we're back to Howard Colbain."

Nodding, Bernadette said, "So, if you're having some trucker deliver goods to a location you don't really want anyone else to know about, changing the destination from Amarillo to Lubbock would keep anyone intent on any kind of intervention guessing. And you'd still be within striking distance of your real target: Albuquerque." Winking at Cozy, she smiled and said, "By the way, air force fighter pilots and the army field artillery boys prefer to call your baseball-diamond analogy 'target triangulation.' So, what on earth would Silas Breen be delivering to Colbain?"

Feigning upset, Cozy said, "What's in a name? As for what Breen's delivering, I don't know. What I am certain of is that Colbain's absolutely in the Tango-11 mix and that Breen's more than likely delivering something related to the Giles murder to Colbain."

Looking puzzled, Bernadette slipped her headset off and down around her neck. "Wait a minute, Cozy. I think we could be moving too quickly to a conclusion here. We just might be asking ourselves the wrong question."

"How's that?"

"First off, I've spent way too much time looking for a possible connection between Tango-11 and the 999 other missile sites out there when what I probably should've been looking for is not any kind of connection but what on earth made Tango-11 the odd man out. Maybe it's related to your time-and-distance thing. Suppose that while Silas Breen may indeed have been hired to deliver something to Amarillo or Lubbock, or perhaps even Albuquerque—let's consider them geographic equivalents of my 999 silo sites—someone was planning all along to intercept him along the way, providing us with a nice little outlier just like Tango-11."

"Damn. You know, you might be right. I knew you were more than just another pretty face," Cozy said, smiling.

"And I fly jets, too," Bernadette added coyly. "So given that possibility, what's our game plan?"

"We get *Sugar* to Albuquerque as fast as we can, and then we head for Colbain's place. In the meantime, I'll think a little more about your odd-man-out theory. There's something about it that's mighty appealing."

Wrapping a bare foot around Cozy's spindly ankle, Bernadette said, "Sort of like you, Mr. Coseia." They didn't say anything to one another until Bernadette announced several minutes later, "I'm about to begin our initial approach into Albuquerque."

Feeling relaxed and content and convinced that for the first time in years, the nearly constant tingling in his leg had at least temporarily all but disappeared, Cozy looked at her and said, "Aye, aye, Captain."

Rikia Takata was on schedule and feeling confident that he'd left nothing behind that could derail his mission or that could be specifically traced to him. He'd paid cash for his bus ticket from El Paso to Amarillo and for his taxi ride from the bus station to a motel just off I-40 that had been within walking distance of the woods where he'd killed Silas Breen. There'd been cash payments for the World War II–era Japanese sword and the two dozen untraceable cans of spray paint he'd spent months purchasing from various stores across Wyoming, Colorado, and New Mexico. He'd mailed the sword and the spray paint to himself at his hotel in El Paso. The paint had been exhausted when he'd spray painted the sides of

Silas Breen's truck ruby red forty-five minutes earlier. There were no credit-card paper trails whatsoever, and although it was possible that the cab driver or bus ticket agent might remember him, it was unlikely. His one concern was that Howard Colbain had refused to help him deal with Breen or Breen's truck when he'd called to ask for assistance. His amateurish paint job was therefore going to have to suffice.

He'd made a fifteen-minute stop just outside the town of Santa Rosa at a junkyard ninety-five miles east of Albuquerque to pick up the final two things he needed to complete the mission. The rough-looking, Vandyke-bearded man he'd met there, whom he'd talked to three weeks earlier on a phone he'd stolen from a student, had supplied him with those things, but not without scrutinizing the truck and its poorly done paint job with obvious suspicion. However, since the man, a Mexican illegal and a longtime supplier of stolen heavy-equipment parts to Howard Colbain, spoke English that was barely understandable, dealt only in cash, and had a Quonset hut filled with everything from stolen AK-47s to Mexican porn, Rikia knew he would keep his mouth shut.

He'd loaded the three microwave-sized cardboard boxes the man had packed for him onto the truck's front seat, hitched a rusted-out beater of a '72 Volkswagen beetle that the man had sold him to the rear bumper, thanked the man in Spanish, handed him five thousand dollars in cash, and driven off.

Now, as he sat parked on an abandoned stretch of cracking asphalt that had once been old U.S. Highway 40, twenty miles west of where he'd picked up the boxes and the VW, he had the sense that destiny was truly on his side. Stepping from the cab, he walked to the rear of the truck, peered into the more than 115-degree heat of the truck's cargo hold, and wrinkled his nose. The rank smell of feces and urine emanating from Silas Breen's body caused him to take a step back. Not having anticipated how overpowering the smell of death could be, he took a deep breath, pinched his nostrils together, and stepped up into the cargo bay. Everything inside was just as it had been in Amarillo. Breen's body hadn't moved. When he heard what sounded like a twig snapping outside the truck, he pulled the cargo-bay door closed. Spotting a jackrabbit running through the sage, he let out a sigh.

Satisfied that everything he needed and had been promised by Thurmond Giles was in the truck, he stepped back from the rear bumper and, gagging from the smell, threw up the bananas and cereal he'd had for breakfast. Five minutes later, he was back on I-40 headed west for Albuquerque and the U.S. 285 bypass that would skirt him around the city.

The SUV that Cozy rented at the Albuquerque airport had that fresh-off-the-assembly-line new-car smell and less than two hundred miles on the odometer. Cozy was busy adjusting an uncooperative side mirror when Bernadette, who'd been rummaging around in the vehicle's trunk, got in next to him and casually slipped the lug wrench beneath the front seat. "Just for good measure," she said, smiling.

Cozy's response was an understanding nod.

As they sped east on I-40 toward Howard Colbain's office, Bernadette looked up from the silo-site map of Colorado she'd been studying and glanced at the SUV's speedometer to realize that they were doing ninety-five. "Would you please slow this thing down, Cozy?"

Cozy eased his foot off the accelerator. "Thought you liked speed."

"I do. But only when I'm at the controls." She juggled the order of the maps in her lap and began scrutinizing the silo-site map of Wyoming. Looking both exasperated and puzzled, as if she'd reached the end of the road with her maps, she said, "Remember that wad of paper they found jammed in Sergeant Giles's mouth along with the head of his penis?"

"Yes," Cozy said, thinking, *Where the heck did that come from?*

"Well, it's a peculiar combination that's never made a lot of sense to me."

"It's a combination that screams revenge, Bernadette."

"The amputated penis head, yes, but what about the paper?"

"The killer used it to shut Giles up."

Bernadette teased a tracing of a map from the middle of her stack. "Somehow, I don't think so. I was there when the coroner found the wad. It was too small to have shut Sergeant Giles up. Bosack faxed me a flattened-out copy of it the day after we found Giles's body. I made this tracing of it. Want to see?"

"Sure." Cozy glanced briefly at the five-by-six-inch tracing. "Looks like a piece that's been torn from one of your silo maps to me, and it's got one of those missile-silo dots on it. So, what's the point?"

"I don't really know," Bernadette said, overlaying the tracing with its single dot and two barely visible lines that clearly represented borders of some state onto the Wyoming map in her lap. "Except that the one dot on my tracing doesn't match up with the dot that should be Tango-11 when I overlay it on the Wyoming silo-site map. Not by a long shot. The dot ends up being too far north and way too far west of where Tango-11 and the town of Wheatland should be. I've overlaid the tracing on silo-site maps of the Dakotas, Montana, Nebraska, Missouri, and Colorado—dozens of times, in fact—and no matter how I turn or adjust the tracing, it doesn't match up with a single silo site in any of those states."

"Have you tried New Mexico?"

Bernadette shook her head. "There weren't ever any missile silos in New Mexico," she said, still adjusting her tracing. Seconds later, her eyes widened, and she screamed, "Damn! No—make that double damn!"

"Something click?"

"Yes, something loud and clear—and strangely horrific." Sounding desperate, she said, "Cozy, I need a map of New Mexico right now."

"There's one in the glove compartment with the rental agreement. Mind telling me what's got you so spooked?"

"In a second." She slipped the New Mexico map out of the glove compartment, unfolded it, and then folded the edges in to get rid of the advertisements and state history summary running along the sides until she had a map of the state that showed its border with Colorado. "Not quite as square as either Colorado or Wyoming, as Western states go, but square enough." There was a look of trepidation on her face as she overlaid the tracing of the map fragment that had been found in Giles's mouth onto the map of New Mexico. "How could I have missed it?" she said, adjusting the tracing into place. "How on earth! I should have seen it long before now."

"Would you please clue me in, Bernadette?" Cozy said, his voice rising.

"Okay, okay," she said, staring down at the tracing overlay. "The distance from the lone dot on that wadded paper fragment the coroner found in Sergeant Giles's mouth to the barely visible line that would clearly have to represent some state's border— Colorado's, for instance—is pretty much the same as the distance from the southern border of Colorado to the north-central part of New Mexico on the map beneath it. Have a look and remember where the dot is, okay?" Bernadette held the map and tracing up for Cozy to see.

Cozy glanced at the tracing with its underlying map of New Mexico and said, "It looks like the dot on your tracing is pretty much sitting on top of a good-sized New Mexico city. The city name's too small for me to read. It's too far north to be Albuquerque, so I'd say it's probably Santa Fe."

"Close but no cigar," Bernadette said, shaking her head. "If you look real close you can see that the dot on the tracing is farther north and a little west of where Santa Fe should be. Look, right near the end of my fingernail."

"I can't read the map and drive, Bernadette."

"Then let me spell it out for you. The edge of my fingernail's sitting directly on Los Alamos."

Cozy frowned. "Los Alamos? The place where they built the first atomic bomb?"

Bernadette nodded.

"What the heck would anybody involved in this whole crazy-assed Tango-11 fiasco want to do there?"

"Make another bomb, perhaps?"

"That's nuts, Bernadette. There has to be a better explanation than that."

Bernadette swallowed hard and set her maps aside. Her cinnamon-colored skin now had an adrenaline-charged pink cast. Staring across the median into the oncoming traffic, as if hypnotized, she said, "Okay, instead of making a bomb, maybe somebody plans to set one off there instead."

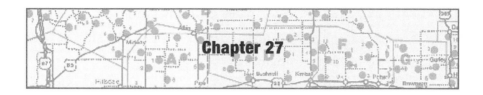

Chapter 27

A sudden windstorm had just sent trash and tumbleweeds spiraling into the fence that separated Howard Colbain's property
from a 160-acre parcel of Bureau of Land Management ground
to the east.

The microburst proved powerful enough to sail a stray truck
tire through the fence, knocking a gaping, four-foot-wide hole in
it and ripping out a half-dozen steel support posts. Colbain and
Jerico Mimms, his six-foot-seven-inch lot man, were inspecting
the damage when Cozy pulled off the highway and stopped a few
feet from them.

Mimms, accustomed to travelers stopping to ask for directions,
watched the SUV's front windows roll down before walking over
to Bernadette's side, stooping, and asking, "Help you?"

"We're looking for Howard Colbain," Bernadette said, eye to
eye with the lot man.

Mimms glanced in his boss's direction before straightening
up to lean two massive forearms against the SUV's rain gutter.
The SUV shook when he took a half step back. "That's him over
there," he said, pointing toward a man standing about twenty
yards away.

Thinking that the blockheaded Mimms reminded her of someone, Bernadette said, "Thanks," and moved to get out of the SUV.

She'd barely opened her door when Mimms jammed a knee into it. "This is private property, miss. Why don't you just stay in your vehicle. I'll go get Mr. Colbain."

As Mimms walked away, Bernadette said to Cozy, "Sort of protective, don't you think? And you know what? He reminds me a little of Frankenstein's monster."

"Does at that," Cozy said. "Could be we're both imagining things, though."

"Could be," Bernadette said, feeling beneath her seat for the lug wrench.

Watching her, Cozy said, "Come on, Bernadette. You don't really think he'd cause us any trouble."

"I don't really know, but like my dad always says, 'Better prepared than not.'" She placed the lug wrench on the console between them and watched as Mimms chatted with Colbain and both men walked casually to Bernadette's side of the SUV. "Looking for me?" Colbain asked, leaning down and blowing stale beer breath into Bernadette's face.

"Yes," said Bernadette, uncertain whether or not she should announce who she was in any sort of official capacity.

"The two of you got names?"

"Elgin Coseia," Cozy said, surprising Bernadette with the swiftness of his reply.

"And your name, miss?"

Deciding to leave off "Major," Bernadette said, "Bernadette Cameron. Mr. Coseia and I are looking into a murder that took place recently up in Wyoming. The victim was a former air force sergeant."

Colbain flashed an insightful smile. "And I bet the two of you are hooked up with a guy named Freddy Dames."

"We know him," said Cozy, watching Mimms, who'd been rocking back and forth on his heels, start toward the rear of the SUV.

"Then you probably know he's already been down here to Albuquerque and tarred and feathered me with questions. I'll tell you the same thing I told him. I don't know a damn thing about your murder. So why don't the two of you skedaddle on outta here and head back where you came from."

"We'd be happy to," said Bernadette. "But since you talked to Mr. Dames, there's been another murder. A woman named Sarah Goldbeck has been killed. Did you know her?"

"No."

"Odd," Bernadette said, realizing that Mimms was now on Cozy's side of the vehicle and closing in on the driver's door. "But if you don't, you don't. Strange, though, you not knowing the dead woman, because believe it or not, I've seen a couple of old photos that show the two of you together, standing outside the gates of an air force missile-silo site." Going for the jugular, she said, "I've also seen photos of that dead sergeant I mentioned hugged up real close and tight with your late wife."

"You fuckin'. . . ." Colbain's face turned crimson. Reaching inside the vehicle, he grabbed the throat of Bernadette's blouse and ripped it, buttons popping, down the middle.

Without a word, Bernadette grabbed the lug wrench and jammed the sharp end into the soft flesh just above Colbain's Adam's apple as hard as she could until Colbain stumbled backward, clutching his throat and coughing up mucus and blood.

Cozy, who'd been watching Mimms close in on his door, swung the door open, catching the giant lot man's testicles with the edge. Mimms yelled, "Shit!" and dropped to his knees, gasping. Cozy recocked the door and slammed it into the lot man's head several times until Mimms rolled to the ground, semiconscious.

"Cozy, toss me your belt," Bernadette said, her voice barely rising as she stepped from the SUV. With Colbain still clutching his throat and the lug wrench now in the waistband of her jeans, Bernadette kicked Colbain's feet out from under him, grabbed him by his wrists, yanked his hands behind his back, and knotted them together with Cozy's belt. "Don't you think about moving," she said, again jabbing Colbain in his neck with the lug wrench.

"What about this guy?" Cozy yelled, staring down on a rapidly recovering Mimms.

"We tie him up, too." Bernadette ripped her blouse the rest of the way down the front, slipped out of it, and tore it down the back. Handing Cozy half the blouse and kneeling beside Mimms, she said, "It's not a belt, but it'll work. I'll do his hands, you do his feet. We need to get them to that fence over there and tied to it while they're both still out of it," she said, glancing toward the damaged fence.

"What'll we use to secure them to it?"

"We'll have to use some of those pieces of smooth wire dangling from the steel support posts. Let's move it."

Bernadette grabbed Colbain, who was gasping and calling for a doctor, by one arm and started walking him toward the fence. When he yanked out of her grasp, she slammed the lug-nut end of the wrench into his belly. "You can do this willingly or unwillingly, Colbain. Makes no real difference to me."

Gasping for air, bleeding from his mouth and nose, and with his head hanging, Colbain staggered toward the fence. Moments later Bernadette had him, hands behind his back, seated, and secured to a wooden fence brace with wire. Less than a minute later, she and Cozy had the semiconscious Mimms wired to the fence as well.

With their arms behind their backs and fencing wire looped around their chests, the two men reminded Cozy of a couple of subdued silver-screen desperadoes from some grade-B 1950s cowboy movie. Dripping sweat, Cozy slipped out of his shirt and draped it over Bernadette's shoulders. As she slipped the shirt on and pondered whether to call the FBI, the cops, or no one at all, she realized that Cozy had been wearing a faded Southeastern Oklahoma State baseball T-shirt beneath his shirt. Smiling, she ran an index finger across the faded lettering. "Looks like pitchers and catchers reported today."

"Think we did, Coach," Cozy said, returning her smile and thinking that, dressed in his partially unbuttoned shirt and glistening with sweat, Bernadette looked flat-out Hollywood sensual.

During his army days, Otis Breen had always considered FBI agents pompous asses. The five minutes he'd just spent on the phone with Thaddeus Richter hadn't changed his mind. The arrogant-sounding Richter was clearly more concerned about whether Silas might be involved in some kind of scheme to sell nuclear secrets than with whether Silas was in harm's way. Otis found himself wishing Richter were standing in front of him so he could shove a fist down the agent's throat.

He'd told Richter everything he knew about Silas's cross-country hauling job, including the fact that Thurmond Giles had been the one to set the job up. And he'd tried, unsuccessfully, it seemed, to explain that his son was a decent, law-abiding person, not some felon on the run.

When he finally asked Richter whether he thought Silas might have unwittingly gotten involved in some scheme that could end up getting him killed, Richter, sounding puffed-up and self-important, launched into a lecture on the overarching importance of national security. Otis listened for about thirty seconds before slamming down the phone and promptly calling Bernadette Cameron.

Bernadette's cell phone started to ring as she re-buttoned her shirt and she and Cozy turned their backs to a biting thirty-mile-per-hour wind. For the past five minutes, they'd been trying unsuccessfully to get something other than silence and hate-filled stares out of Howard Colbain and Jerico Mimms.

"See if you can't get something besides evil looks out of them while I take this call," Bernadette, looking frustrated, said to Cozy. Cupping the phone to her right ear to fight off the wind howl, she said out of habit, "Major Cameron." Surprised to hear the voice on the other end of the line, she tapped Cozy on the shoulder and whispered, "It's Otis Breen."

Cozy nodded, then knelt in front of Colbain and Mimms. "Pick your poison, boys. You can talk to us, the cops, or the FBI."

Neither man said a word as Bernadette, squatting with her back to the wind in hopes of better reception, listened to Breen.

Looking at Bernadette, then Colbain, then Mimms, Cozy said, "That could be the FBI that Major Cameron's talking to right now, gentlemen. Telling them about the two of you killing that air force sergeant up in Wyoming." He locked eyes with Colbain. "It's bad form to rip a lady's blouse off, friend, but who's to judge? Maybe your late wife liked it rough."

Colbain cleared his sinuses with a snort and spat a mouthful of bloody mucus past Cozy's shoulder. "Fuck you."

"That's bad form, too, asshole." Cozy rose, kicked the sole of Colbain's boot, and took a step back as Bernadette, having explained the situation she and Cozy were in to Otis Breen, said, "Just stay on the line, Mr. Breen, okay?"

Turning to Colbain and bending the truth in hopes of getting something out of him, she said, "I've got someone on the phone who wants to know if you're the person who's got his son hauling a truckload of stolen military hardware across country."

"What?"

"You heard me."

"Tell him to—"

Mimms cut Colbain off. "Hell, boss! No way I'm gettin' hung up in no mess that involves stolen military shit."

"Be quiet, Jerico."

"Be quiet, my ass!" Mimms stared pleadingly at Bernadette. "Listen here, Major. I ain't no killer, and I sure ain't no terrorist or traitor."

"If you've got something to say, now's the time, Jerico."

"Okay, okay. I think I know somethin' about that shipment you just mentioned." He hesitated, watching a scowl spread across Colbain's face.

"In for a penny, in for a pound, Jerico. Go ahead and finish." Bernadette flashed Cozy a look that said, *Think the pot's about to boil over.*

"Yeah, think I will. A few hours back some guy called here, a real nervous-soundin' guy, mind you, and asked me to put Mr. Colbain on the phone. I went into the boss's office, told him he had a call, and transferred it to him. A couple of minutes later he rushes out to the yard where I'm workin', lookin' pale as a ghost, and asks if I could help some guy paint a truck. I said sure. He hustled back to his office, spent another couple of minutes or so there, then came back out and told me the paintin' deal was off. Sounded sort of relieved, to tell you the truth."

"So why'd you change your mind about painting that truck?" Bernadette asked Colbain.

When he didn't answer, she said to Cozy, "Paint or no paint, I'm thinking that truck of Silas Breen's is headed this way."

Cozy shook his head. "Maybe not. Why stop in Albuquerque when your real destination is Los Alamos and you've just been told that you're not getting any help with painting your truck?"

"Good point," Bernadette said, turning her attention back to Colbain. "Any other requests that Silas Breen might've had besides wanting help with that paint job on his truck, Mr. Colbain?"

Colbain said nothing, but the surprised look on his face told Bernadette that she'd obviously said something that had clicked with him. Recalling something her father had once told her about the kinds of mental intimidation he'd had to endure as a POW in Vietnam, and remembering the rise she had gotten out of Colbain when she'd mentioned his late wife, she kicked a scattering of sand into Colbain's face. "Can't hold out forever, Colbain. Your wife sure didn't."

A look of pure anger spread across Colbain's face, but he remained silent. Looking disappointed, she said to Mimms, "Did the man who called about that paint job sound young, old, scared, impatient?"

"Couldn't tell you how old or young he was, but he damn sure sounded impatient. And there was one other strange thing about him. He sounded kinda mush-mouthed. You know, like he couldn't quite get the whole part of his words out. Like he was tongue-tied, maybe."

"Well, I'll be damned."

"Breen?" asked Cozy.

"I don't think so. Don't think so at all," she said, smiling. "But I've got a good idea of who called." Kneeling until she was again eye to eye with Colbain, she said, "The worm just turned, Colbain. Now, why on earth, sir, would a tongue-tied mathematics professor be calling you for help with a paint job on a truck?" When no answer came, she said, "If I were you, I'd start talking fast and furious, because trust me, you're in way over your head here, friend. I don't know what the heck Rikia Takata has on you or how on earth the two of you are tied to the Giles murder, but here's something for you to chew on. Mr. Coseia and I think Rikia Takata and perhaps a man named Silas Breen are headed for Los

Alamos in that truck Takata wanted painted, and they may be hauling a nuclear device."

"No way!" Colbain screamed.

"My, my. Funny how that word *nuclear* starts tongues a-waggin'. I'm surprised at your naïveté, Mr. Colbain. I figured that of all people, you'd be one who understood the poison we call revenge. And you know what? I think revenge is what's been driving the whole Tango-11 breach from the start."

Colbain's head slumped as he stared at the ground, silent once again.

Looking at Mimms, Bernadette asked, "How long ago did the tongue-tied man call? I need you to be as precise as you can."

Mimms stared skyward, deep in thought. "I'd say it was about three hours ago, or pretty darn close."

Running a quick timetable in his head, Cozy said, "Assuming that Rikia was somewhere between Amarillo and Albuquerque or Lubbock and Albuquerque when he called, that would put him pretty close to Albuquerque by now. That's if he's not still fooling around trying to paint that truck."

Surprising everyone, Howard Colbain looked up and said, "He's long past Albuquerque by now. He was an hour east of the U.S. 285 bypass around the city when he called. As for painting a truck, you can spray paint one the size he's driving with a couple of dozen cans of paint from a hardware store in less than forty-five minutes."

Amazed at the sudden outpouring from Colbain, Bernadette looked at her watch. "So if he's traveling at sixty or so, and he did actually paint the truck in that short a time, where would that put him now, Mr. Colbain?"

"North of the 285 bypass for sure," said Colbain. "There's no way you'll ever catch up with him now."

"Oh, there's a way," Bernadette said. "How long did it take us to get from the airport to here?" she asked Cozy.

"Ten minutes, and that's with you complaining about my speed, remember?"

"Think you can cut that to five?"

"I can try," Cozy said as a swirl of wind and sand blasted everyone.

Spitting out sand and wiping it from her eyes, Bernadette squatted and duck-walked her way around Colbain, then Mimms, making certain they were still securely tied to the fence braces. Looking at Colbain, she said, "On our way to the airport, I'll call and have someone with a badge come out here and pick the two of you up. I'm sure they'll be real interested in your ties to Rikia Takata. In the meantime, you can both sit here and enjoy the sun, the sand, and the surf." Eyeing Colbain pensively, she asked, "Why'd you decide to finally give Takata up?"

Colbain hesitated briefly before answering. "Simple," he said, spitting out granules of sand mixed with blood and mucus as he talked. "If you're right about Rikia wanting to set off some kind of nuclear bomb up there in Los Alamos, and believe me, I don't know a damn thing about that, I'd end up having myself a real health and safety problem down here in Albuquerque. As you can see, the wind blows pretty hard and steady off the mountains around here, and if he did set off a bomb, I'd end up sucking down nuclear fallout 24-7."

Shaking her head and thinking that most of the time self-preservation tends to win out over revenge, Bernadette looked at Cozy and said, "I'm thinking it's time we see if we can't cut that ten minutes of driving time in half."

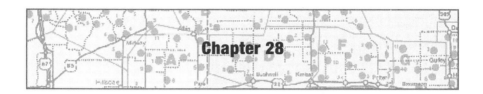
Just south of the town of White Lakes, New Mexico, and some sixteen miles north of where he'd turned off I-40 onto the U.S. 285 Albuquerque bypass, Rikia Takata pulled off the highway and drove into a clump of box-elder trees in order to take a final look at several maps of Los Alamos. He'd never been to the place where men had assembled the first atomic bomb, making it a point to never show his face in the remote mountaintop town during the planning phases of his mission. That way there could be no finger-pointing and no premission recognition of him as the triggerman, the Shigeo Fukumoto of his day.

He'd planned from the start to wait until just after the workday wound fully down in order to detonate his bomb during the quiet time when people in the town of twelve thousand would feel safe and secure in their homes.

It had taken him more than three years to move his plan to its current point. There'd been months of false starts, wrong turns, and dead ends. Endless hours of strategizing, digesting informa-tion, and reading. He'd talked with con men, doctors, scientists, other mathematicians, engineers, and entrepreneurs, and not only had he determined how to gather the necessary components to construct a crude nuclear weapon, he'd also found someone to unwittingly load those components into the cargo bay of a

U-Haul truck and transport them two-thirds of the way across a continent.

The most difficult part of his plan had been obtaining cobalt-60, the artificially produced radioactive isotope of cobalt that would serve as the lethal energy and ionizing, radiation-producing source material for his bomb.

He'd initially tried to secure the cobalt-60 from a food processing plant in Michigan, one of several around the United States that used radiation to kill harmful bacteria and other organisms in meat, poultry, and fish and to extend the shelf life of vegetables. The cobalt used in those plants, in rods no bigger than an inch in diameter and a foot long, known in the industry simply as "pencils," would certainly have served his purpose, but he'd had to scrap that plan when his industry contact, a Michigan State University food sciences professor, had started asking too many questions about why, as a mathematician, he'd suddenly become so interested in food preservation technology. The subsequent cooling-off period had cost him a year.

There'd been another four months of downtime after that year, time he'd spent looking at other possible nuclear sources. He'd been close to giving up when he'd stumbled across an article in a New Delhi newspaper reporting that five people in India had recently been injured by radiation that had been traced to a scrap-metals yard in West Delhi. Two of the injured persons had had their hands turn black; lost patches of hair; and developed ulcerative, saucer-sized red blotches on their arms and legs after supposedly coming in contact with the radioactive material.

The Indian government ultimately traced the source of that

radiation to a megavoltage radiation therapy machine that had been discarded by an Indian hospital with the cobalt-60 source still inside the machine's cancer treatment head. It was then that he knew he'd found a new cobalt-60 source.

It took him another nine months to insinuate himself into the cancer treatment and therapeutic radiation resources and recovery community. Using his university credentials and reputation as a mathematician, after months of painstaking research he was able to determine exactly how the U.S. government's inefficient and highly bureaucratic salvage and scrapping protocol for old, out-of-service, hospital-based cobalt-60 units worked. It took a while to determine precisely how the government's salvage process was flawed, but ultimately he solved the puzzle, concluding that the biggest flaw in the protocol was linked to the fact that U.S.-based cobalt-60 machines, which were to be scrapped or shipped to the developing world, 90 percent of the time were shipped to a single Canadian company for either salvage and/or refurbishment. It was there that the machines underwent a final inspection before being deactivated, scrapped, or recirculated to the underserved world, and there that the cobalt-60 source material was ultimately cataloged and either recovered, reclaimed, or disposed of.

Grueling hours of legwork and a random phone call had ultimately put him in touch not with some high-ranking government official in charge of overseeing such a critical nuclear risk but instead with a man who was in charge of the North American Cobalt Recovery, Radiation Mitigation, and Storage Program. A program administered by a Canadian company, Applied Nuclear

Theratronics of Canada Ltd., and run by a man named Thurmond Giles.

He'd first called Giles nine months earlier with the pretense of asking the man he'd learned had once been an air force sergeant and a nuclear-missile maintenance expert if he had any suggestions about how a nuclear resource recovery company that he was interested in starting and locating on the desolate plains of Wyoming might get running and certified.

The journey from that first phone call to Giles to where Rikia now sat had been one of highs and lows. A bumpy, tumultuous road that he had never strayed from in spite of Giles's constant threat to tell the world about Rikia's plan if the money he was receiving didn't keep flowing in. He'd spent most of the $1.2 million of his MacArthur Genius Grant money on Giles, but now that he was within hours of his goal, the difficulties of the past seemed minuscule.

The twenty 35-mm-film-case-sized, lead-shielded containers, or "capsules," as was their preferred scientific name, with their five thousand curies of cobalt-60 that he'd earlier spent a half hour removing from the treatment heads of the twenty teletherapy machines Silas Breen had been hauling, were now safely stored in two pickup-bed tool caddies in the cargo bay of Breen's truck. It had seemed preposterous to him that all he'd needed to access the cobalt-60 in those treatment heads had been a screwdriver, a three-quarter-inch wrench, and a pair of pliers. Giles, who'd greased the skids for him by doing most of the disassembly months earlier, had made but one error during the entire project. He'd insisted that the final two-hundred-thousand-dollar cash payment for his services take place in a face-to-face meeting with Rikia in Wyoming. That demand had cost him his life.

The three boxes and sixty pounds of TNT that Rikia had picked up when he'd bought the Volkswagen that would whisk him out of harm's way represented more than enough explosives to turn the cobalt-60, the truck, and its contents into a dirty nuclear bomb. A bomb that would by his calculations ultimately contaminate a geographic area the size of Texas and, more importantly, make Los Alamos, birthplace of the world's first atomic weapon, and much of New Mexico, the state that had been the bomb's womb, quickly uninhabitable. Los Alamos's twelve thousand inhabitants would be exposed to radiation amounts that would give them a 50 percent chance of dying from fallout within three to four months and a 30 percent chance of dying from a radiation-associated cancer over the next forty years. Los Alamos would become America's Hiroshima.

The rest of New Mexico, although affected, would be less contaminated, but it would be years before most of the state would once again be habitable. The psychological impact and the economic and personal damage, although significant, couldn't begin to equate to the damage unleashed on Hiroshima and Nagasaki, only because he couldn't produce a fissionable bomb with power equivalent to the world's first two nuclear devices used as weapons, Fat Man and Little Boy. And the psychological damage and suffering he'd inflict wouldn't equal the suffering of his grandfather, who'd died twenty years after Hiroshima from bladder cancer, or his grandmother, who'd died ten years before her husband from thyroid cancer. Nor could it equal the suffering of his own mother, who'd endured years of depression after losing both of her parents to Fat Man–induced cancer. Filled with enough oxycodone to kill three people, she'd died in the decadent San Francisco belly of the American beast while at the wheel of a speeding BMW, with his father as her passenger.

More hurtful than all those things, however, was the fact that his father, a man whom he'd always considered weak and capitulating, had brought him to the shores of the very nation that had delivered the Takata family and Japan such destruction, defeat, and humiliation. Rikia had always been secretly delighted that the car crash that had killed his mother had removed his spineless, dishonorable father from the world as well.

He'd once asked Kimiko why she hadn't felt equally dishonored, soiled, and insulted when the U.S. government in 1988 began doling out twenty-thousand-dollar reparation checks to internment camp survivors. When she'd told him that the money was the ultimate act of appeasement on the part of the U.S. government and thus worth accepting, he'd decided sadly that Kimiko had far too much of his father in her.

In the end, however, it wasn't Kimiko or his father but the pompous, omniscient, overbearing, insatiably power-hungry monster known as America that had forced him to act. America, a place where he'd been shunned, passed over, and made fun of for most of his life. America, a place so perfectly suited for his very special kind of retribution.

He'd calculated the odds of his mission succeeding and determined that he had at least a 95 percent chance of success, and now, with Silas Breen out of the way, those odds had risen. The years he'd spent working out equations and devising algorithms that could be used to combat terrorism would assure him of success because he understood better than anyone that the biggest stumbling block didn't rest with law enforcement, the military, or the intelligence community. After all, all three dysfunctional components of the American justice and security systems were still spinning their wheels, trying to determine why a former air force sergeant had been murdered at some abandoned missile-silo site instead of recognizing and pursuing the real threat. No, the biggest stumbling block to success, he'd long understood, was bringing in someone else to help with his mission. He'd unfortunately been forced to do just that in order to get his mission off the ground, and he could only hope that it wouldn't come back to haunt him. It appeared that he'd sidestepped that problem when Breen had been killed, but he realized now that he never should have called Howard Colbain to ask for help with painting Silas Breen's truck, never should have given Colbain the chance to say no to him. But he had, and what was done was done. All he could do now was play out his hand and hope that Colbain, a man he'd been able to manipulate easily, would keep his mouth shut—or, even better, suffer the consequences of radiation fallout and die a slow, painful death.

He felt a special sense of accomplishment as he glanced across the truck's front seat at the cell phone that he would use to detonate his bomb. A simple call to the cell phone would send an electrical current from the phone's battery through a thin wire filament, not much different from the filament in a lightbulb, ignite a combustible liquid in a syringe nestled inside his sixty pounds of TNT, set off the TNT, destroy the truck, and send a shower of radioactive cobalt-60, truck parts, and metal spiraling into the air to leave behind a long-lived blanket of contamination.

Thinking that he was not the madman he'd be labeled if caught but merely a thoughtful man who dealt with things in terms of mathematical equivalencies, he found himself wondering why anyone would question what he was doing. He was, after all, only doing what any person of honor, under similar circumstances, would be expected to do.

Suddenly he found himself laughing at the fact that most of his inside-the-box, narrow-thinking mathematician and physicist colleagues had always argued that a so-called world-ending doomsday bomb would necessarily be fraught with failure because of the huge amounts of cobalt-60 that would be needed to make a bomb capable of destroying the world. All his colleagues were impractical fools, as far as he was concerned. Fools who hinged their argument on the premise that the earth's massive surface alone would prevent anyone from making such a doomsday weapon.

The problem with their assumption, he told himself, as he set aside the maps he'd been studying and restarted the truck, was that, like the worldwide antiterrorism community itself, the community's arrogant intellectual leaders too often thought only in global terms, never in terms of simple formulaic mathematical equivalence, which states that the union of all the blocks in a set must always equal the original set. He had no global desires, no goal of contaminating the world, and he certainly wasn't out to trigger doomsday. His desire had always been to simply mete out justice. To carve a hole in the American heart and psyche equal to the one that had been carved out of Japan's in 1945. To, in effect, establish a simple mathematical equivalence.

As he retook the highway and the truck gained speed, Rikia found himself smiling at the fact that Silas Breen had never had the slightest inkling of why he had chosen to call himself F. Mantew. But then again, there was no need to laugh at such a simple man's ignorance. How could Breen have possibly known that F. Mantew was a bastardization of "Fat Man," the code name given to America's second atomic bomb used as a weapon, detonated over Nagasaki. And there was no way on earth that Breen could have figured out that the pseudonym Rikia had chosen for himself stood for a third bomb, Fat Man II—a bomb that this time around would be detonated on American soil.

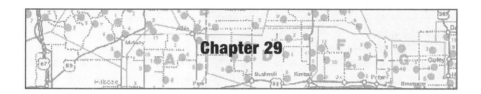

Chapter 29

Sugar's landing gear retracted with a thump loud enough to cause Cozy to turn to Bernadette and ask, "Something wrong with this chariot?"

"It's the crosswinds. We barely missed being grounded back there because of wind shear." Bernadette glanced at the altimeter. "We're on top of the winds now but will be bucking sixty-knot headwinds all the way to Los Alamos."

"Think you'll be able to fly low and slow enough to spot that truck?"

"Slow enough for sure. Low enough, maybe not. It's pretty tough to buzz a major U.S. highway in a private jet and have it go unnoticed. Fifty-fifty we'll end up explaining ourselves to the cops, the FAA, the FBI, and homeland security, or if we're lucky maybe even rate a couple of F-18 interceptors on our tail. But if we spot Rikia, who cares?" Bernadette glanced at an aerial map of the area on her computer screen. "We'll probably only get one good chance to spot that truck before Rikia spots us. Once he starts up the hill to Los Alamos, the terrain gets pretty rugged. Mesas, canyons, and national forest everywhere. Tough to fly low and in and out of that kind of terrain. Now, if I had my A-10, I could give it a better run. A lot more power and maneuverability with that bird than with *Sugar* here."

"Suppose Rikia makes it all the way up the hill without us ever spotting him?"

"Then we land at Los Alamos and look for him on the ground. By that time we'll probably have enough FBI agents, cops, and media types glommed on to us to scare Sasquatch out of hiding. But I don't think he's that far ahead of us. We're in a jet and he's in a truck, remember?" Bernadette leveled *Sugar* off at 2,500 feet. Looking worried, she said, "We're cruising low enough now that somebody's bound to spot us soon."

"Let 'em. Just keep looking for a U-Haul truck with the number 18 painted on the top of the cargo box."

"Rikia or Breen could've painted over the number."

Shaking his head, Cozy said, "I don't think they would have had the time. Besides, I'm betting Rikia doesn't know there's a spy in the sky tracking him." Straining to see out his window, he asked, "See anything?"

"Blue sky," Bernadette said, wondering how something that had started out as a simple break-in at an abandoned missile-silo site had reached its current level.

Noticing the thoughtful, almost brooding look on her face, Cozy said, "You're looking awfully serious there, Major."

"Nuclear gadgets tend to do that to me," she said with a wink.

"Then I say we go down for a closer look."

"Closer it is," she said, nosing the Gulfstream lower. "At least as close as we dare."

The dispatch call to the Pojoaque Indian Reservation cop, telling him that several locals were claiming to have spotted a jet buzzing

Highway 285 just before State Road 502 turned west and headed up the hill to Los Alamos, normally wouldn't have gotten much attention. But the fact that the jet had reportedly flown up and down a twelve-mile stretch of 285 between Santa Fe and Pojoaque, cruising along at no more than a couple of thousand feet, not once or twice but three times, as if the pilot were searching for something on the highway, had gotten the res cop's attention.

When the res cop mentioned the dispatch call to a New Mexico state trooper friend he was having a cup of coffee with at a Pojoaque diner, the trooper's eyes lit up.

"Damn, Redbird, the feds are looking for a truck that's reportedly headed north up 285 from Albuquerque," the wide-eyed trooper said, setting his coffee cup aside. "We've had two FBI bulletins on it this afternoon. Could be that plane your folks spotted was looking for the same truck. Word on the street is that the truck's hauling either stolen Indian artifacts or drugs. Maybe your plane was a government jet? FBI, even?"

"Nobody mentioned seeing any government markings."

"Strange," said the trooper. "I'll call your info in to the number listed on those FBI bulletins when we're done. It's an Albuquerque exchange. That's strange, too, since there's a bureau office right up the road in Santa Fe."

"Think it's real urgent?" the res cop asked.

"Everything's supposedly urgent that comes in with 'FBI' stamped on it." The trooper took a sip of coffee and waved for their waitress. "But right now what's urgent is me getting myself a slice of cherry cobbler."

After two unproductive midmorning conversations with Otis Breen about his missing son, Thaddeus Richter sat down at his desk just before noon to stare blankly out his office window and contemplate the suddenly overcast Denver skies. When his administrative assistant buzzed him at twelve thirty to let him know that he had someone from the U.S. Nuclear Regulatory Commission on the phone, he shrugged and took the call. A couple of minutes later he knew what Silas Breen had been hauling, although it hadn't been easy for him to get a straight story out of the bureaucrat. In fact, it had taken something akin to diplomatic maneuvering on his part to get the man to admit to knowing anything about Silas Breen's connection to Applied Nuclear Theratronics of Canada Ltd., or to that company's former employee Thurmond Giles. It turned out the connection had come to light and been passed on to an Oklahoma Nuclear Regulatory Commission office after an inquisitive Oklahoma Port of Entry officer on I-44 had reported that a truck that had begun a trip in Ottawa was running on illegally recapped tires and that the driver, Silas Breen, had been cited and fined three hundred dollars. The suspicious port of entry officer had called Ottawa to find out exactly what Breen was hauling, then called the Nuclear Regulatory Commission after learning that Breen's load included twenty out-of-service radiation-therapy-unit cobalt-60 heads. A Nuclear Regulatory Commission bureaucrat had ultimately called Richter in response to seeing the same FBI bulletins that the New Mexico state trooper at Pojoaque had seen.

Just before two p.m. an FBI agent in Albuquerque called Richter to tell him that an Albuquerque police officer, in response to an anonymous tip, had found a man named Howard Colbain and an associate, Jerico Mimms, wired to a couple of fence braces on the Colbain property and that Mimms claimed that the incident was linked to a mysterious U-Haul truck. A truck that the Albuquerque PD had received an FBI bulletin about, with Richter listed as the agency contact person.

Fifty minutes later Richter was on a plane bound for New Mexico. By five p.m. he was in Albuquerque interrogating Colbain and Mimms.

As the three men sat in a dimly lit police substation room that reeked of Lysol and recently painted drywall, Richter, looking far less haggard than either Mimms or Colbain, slipped his reading glasses up on his nose, stared across the table directly at Colbain, and said, "We can string this out as long as you'd like, Colbain. Your claim that Major Cameron and Mr. Coseia assaulted you is only part of a bigger story. I want to know about Silas Breen."

Looking weary, Colbain said, "I've told you, just like I've told half-a-dozen other cops around here, I don't know anything about any Silas Breen."

"What about you, Mimms?"

Mimms shrugged. "Nope, don't know him."

"And you're positive you didn't know what Breen was hauling?" Richter asked Colbain.

"I don't know him. I don't know what the hell he was hauling, where he was headed, or for that matter the exact distance from here to the moon, okay?"

"Suppose I told you he was hauling hospital equipment."

"No news there," Colbain said. "Before you waltzed in, another cop told me the same damn thing."

"And if I told you Breen was hauling a bunch of treatment heads salvaged from old radiation therapy machines? Heads that may contain cobalt-60? Would that mean anything to you?"

"Afraid I don't know what the hell cobalt-60 is."

"It is a radioisotope of cobalt. A nuclear source material."

"Then I'd say that maybe he was just hauling those treatment heads of yours from one useful place to another."

Mimms nodded as if to say, *Makes sense to me.*

Shifting his focus, Richter said, "You knew Thurmond Giles, of course."

"From a distance."

"And your late wife knew him as well?"

Colbain forced out a reluctant "Yes."

"Did you know that it was Giles who arranged for the shipment of those treatment heads?"

"Of course not," Colbain said, looking and sounding totally surprised.

"You sound a bit snookered, Mr. Colbain."

"Are we close to being done here?" Colbain shot back.

"Nowhere near, I'm afraid."

Colbain sighed and, looking like a man who couldn't quite decide what direction to take next, stared past Richter. When Richter repeated, "Nowhere near," Colbain rested his elbows on the tabletop, dropped his bloody chin and lacerated neck into his hands, and continued staring blankly at the wall.

In November 1942, the Manhattan Engineer District, the government agency responsible for the development of the world's first nuclear weapon, authorized the Albuquerque Engineer District to conduct a site investigation into the possibility that a location near the Los Alamos Ranch School in Otowi, New Mexico, might satisfactorily serve as the site for the final development, processing, assembly, and testing of a nuclear weapon known then as the atomic bomb. The project was code-named "Project Y."

The site had to meet several requirements, the foremost of which was the requisite isolation. In addition, the location had to encompass an area large enough to provide an adequate testing ground for the bomb, the climate had to be mild enough to allow for work on the project to take place during winter, access to roads and rail needed to be adequate, the population within a hundred-mile radius had to be sparse, utilities and housing had to already be present or easily developable, and the location had to be far enough from any American seacoast to eliminate the potential of an enemy attack.

In March 1943 the forty-seven-thousand-acre Otowi location, isolated on a New Mexico mesa on the eastern slope of the Jemez Mountains, was chosen as the site for Project Y. Sixteen miles away from the nearest town, the site ultimately became known as Los Alamos. Local residents simply called it "the Hill."

Primary access to the Hill in 1943, just as now, was via what is now known as State Road 502, and the site, crisscrossed by mountain streams and canyons, including at least a dozen box canyons, with no access to the mesa on either side, had remained just as remote as it had been during World War II.

Cozy was busy studying a computer-generated topo map of Los Alamos and the surrounding Jemez Mountains when *Sugar* hit air choppy enough to send him a half foot out of his seat. Grabbing the seat cushion, he muttered, "Damn."

Concentrating on State Road 502 below as it snaked its way up the hill from Pojoaque for Los Alamos and totally unperturbed by the unstable air, Bernadette maneuvered *Sugar* between two canyon walls and to within 1,500 feet of the highway below. "We're gonna have fighter jets on our tail sooner or later," she said.

Increasing the size of the image on the computer screen, Cozy said, "You pays your dime, you takes your chances."

"Where'd that come from?"

"My grandmother. It was a favorite saying of hers whenever times got rough."

"That's one way of looking at things, but I've always preferred having the odds in my favor. That's one reason I called my dad before we took off from Albuquerque. I just hope he still has enough contacts to keep me from being court-martialed and you from doing five to ten if this whole thing goes south."

"Makes two of us." Cozy's stomach headed for his knees as Bernadette dropped the jet lower and followed a forest service road into a canyon.

As Bernadette dipped the plane's left wing, Cozy said, "I'm still not sure why you think Rikia would head for one of these canyons and not straight for Los Alamos."

"Just a hunch. A hunch of my dad's, really. Something left over from his days in Vietnam."

"Mind sharing it with me?" Cozy asked, adjusting his headset as they swooped down the canyon at almost 300 knots.

"One word—isolation. The same reason the government chose Los Alamos as its bomb-making site in the first place. It's the kind of place the Vietcong would have chosen to assemble their troops before an assault during the early years of the Vietnam War, according to my dad. A place where from the air you literally can't see the forest floor for the trees. And that's something that pretty much makes recon impossible. The Vietcong would assemble in a place like that, map out their assault strategy, disperse, pull off a hit-and-run attack, and then go their separate ways. It worked quite well for them until a nosy U.S. jet jockey, disobeying orders and cruising along slow and low on a return from a bombing mission, figured out what they were doing."

"Your dad?"

"No other than. And you know what it got him? A reprimand. But it also got the Vietcong a little present in the long run. A chemical weapon known as napalm," Bernadette said, smiling.

"Looks to me like you're determined to follow your dad's lead."

"Always have," Bernadette said proudly.

Thinking, *The apple doesn't fall far from the tree,* Cozy continued studying the topo map on the screen as they shot up out of the canyon. "Guess this is what happens when you pays your dime," he said, his stomach doing somersaults as gravity slammed him into the seat back.

Rikia had initially planned to detonate his bomb in front of the Irradiation of Chips and Electronics ICE House Memorial in Los

Alamos, the site where the nuclear components of the original prototype nuclear-charged Trinity device were assembled. Several months earlier he'd changed his mind, however, deciding that the contamination he was aiming for didn't require detonation of his bomb in what now amounted to the town square.

As he sat sweating inside the cab of the U-Haul in a heavily for-ested canyon six miles outside Los Alamos, he thought through the final bits and pieces of his plan. He'd be miles away when he trig-gered his device—outfitted in protective radiation gear and headed for Colorado. He hadn't had a chance to test-drive the Volkswagen he'd purchased, but he'd started it several times, so he knew that it ran. He expected that the car would easily and swiftly get him back home to Wyoming and out of harm's way.

He felt a sense of relief as he got out of the cab to go check on his protective gear, the Volkswagen, and the cobalt-60 source material one final time. When he thought he heard a plane over-head, he glanced up toward a canopy of evergreen limbs and the unmistakable sound of jet engines. Obscured by the tree cover, the plane couldn't be seen, but it was there, flying low enough above the treetops to cause him concern. There perhaps was some kind of last-minute obstacle to his plan. As suddenly as he'd heard the plane, however, it was gone.

He knew better than to chase on foot after what amounted to nothing more than a noise, and he wouldn't chase after it in the Volkswagen or the truck. There was too much at stake for him to do so, too many unforeseen things that could happen if he did. There was nothing to suggest that the plane had been trying to spot him and nothing to indicate that the person flying it had seen

Breen's truck. Even so, he now had something to worry about besides simply setting off his device, donning his protective gear, and speeding down the hill.

He wasn't concerned about being caught. The two cyanide capsules in his shirt pocket were there to guard against that. His worries now were simply two. First there was the off chance that his plan, which he'd spent years piecing together, wouldn't work and that the bomb wouldn't go off. Glancing skyward toward the muted light, he again listened for the sound of a plane. When he heard nothing, he smiled. There was, however, a nugget of insecurity behind the smile. Insecurity born of his second, more serious worry. He couldn't be at all certain that he or his truck hadn't been seen by the plane.

Cozy pressed both hands against his headset and nodded excitedly. "I'm telling you, I saw the 8 plastered on the roof of that truck as plain as day, Bernadette. I didn't see a 1, but I sure as heck spotted an 8."

Bernadette, who'd rolled the Gulfstream belly up and over a mesa before uprighting the plane and dropping down into a canyon next to the one in which Cozy claimed he'd seen Silas Breen's truck, said nothing. Judging from his queasiness and the ringing in his ears that they were flying either sideways or upside down, Cozy grunted, "Are we upside down?"

"We were for a little bit," Bernadette said, leveling *Sugar* off. "When you spotted that truck, I knew I needed to reduce our engine noise pronto or have whoever was down there on the ground spot us. No better way to make sure they didn't than to hop over a mesa and duck down inside a canyon. That's the problem with these Gulfstream 150s—they tend to let you know they're coming and whine like little babies."

With every organ below his diaphragm floating in a sea of jelly, Cozy asked, "What do you think Rikia, or Breen if he's with him, will do now?"

Watching Cozy's face turn parchment-paper pale, Bernadette said, "Take long, slow, deep breaths, and whatever you do, Cozy, don't dare throw up. Good," she said, watching Cozy comply. "Now, in answer to your question, I'm hoping that whoever's down there in that truck stays put because in exactly eight minutes, I'm going to set *Sugar* down and we're going to find either him or them."

"How on earth will we know what canyon the truck's in?"

"It's a mile off 502 to the south and a half mile or so from the blind end of a canyon. And it's sitting on a forest service road with a little pond to the west."

"Are you certain?"

"Sure am. The air force used to pay me to be certain of things like that." She nosed the Gulfstream due west. "What I need for you to do, starting right now, is to count every road that intersects 502 to the south as we make our descent. Every road, Cozy, until we land. It's important."

"Okay," he said, loudly calling off, "One," and looking for the next road. "By the way, does Los Alamos have a runway long enough to put this baby down?"

"Absolutely. And from quite a long way back. We built an atomic bomb here, remember."

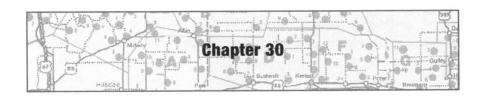

Chapter 30

Bernadette set the Gulfstream down in Los Alamos at four minutes after six p.m. on a 5,500-foot runway that had been built in 1947 by the Atomic Energy Commission. As they taxied toward the terminal, she said to Cozy, "Remember, that's twelve right-hand access roads down the hill from the airport's southern boundary fence."

Cozy shook his head. "How on earth did you spot that fence from the air?"

"Practice," Bernadette said, looking smug and staring out the cockpit window at a man approaching the plane. "Somebody's here to ask about our unexpected arrival. Let me do the talking, okay?"

"Your deal, Major." Cozy snapped off a crisp salute. "While you're dealing with them, I'll get Freddy's toys from the back."

"Make it quick," Bernadette said, wondering what additional toys besides Freddy's motorcycle Cozy could be referring to.

Cozy nodded as the plane rolled to a stop. He'd opened the forward entry door and let down the stairway when a man with a bulging belly in a gray suit rushed up the stairs. Stopping Cozy as he headed for the rear of the plane, the man said, "I need to speak to you about your unauthorized use of airspace and your unscheduled landing, sir."

"Talk to the pilot," Cozy said, brushing past the indignant-looking man, who then stepped to the open door of the cockpit, looked at Bernadette, and asked sternly, "This plane yours?"

"Nope," Bernadette deadpanned, slipping her shoes on. "Mine's an A-10."

All Cozy could think about as Bernadette continued to be counseled by the man in the gray suit and as he stared at Freddy's BMW HP2, which he'd struggled to get out of the Gulfstream and down onto the tarmac, was how many times he'd watched Freddy off-load the motorcycle so effortlessly. Suddenly he was thinking about fog. Fog rising from a river bottom that ran alongside a deserted eastern Colorado road. He stood, momentarily transfixed. When he glanced down at his left leg and then back up, Bernadette was racing toward him.

"Did you finesse him?" Cozy asked.

"Yeah. Enough that he'll be spending the next hour and a half tangled up in paperwork. He impounded *Sugar*, though. So I gave him Freddy's number."

"Oh, shit."

"Hey, she's Freddy's plane. So I figured he should handle it. Let's get the heck out of here before Gray Suit starts asking questions about this motorcycle."

Cozy slipped the oil-stained strap of a soft-sided, tennis-racket-sized case he'd taken from the plane over his right shoulder as Bernadette eased onto the back of the motorcycle. "Awfully small for the two of us," she said, wrapping her arms around Cozy.

"Beggars can't be choosers." He reached back and double-checked the bike's sissy bar.

"What's in the case?" Bernadette asked, shouting above the bike's throaty roar as they took off.

"Freddy's pistol-grip shotgun," Cozy yelled back. "What else?"

Setting up the bomb's trigger proved to be more time-consuming than Rikia had expected, and as he began checking the ten syringes that he'd pilfered from a university chemistry lab to make certain that they each contained exactly 20 cc of combustible liquid, the clock in his head started to tick louder. Moving from syringe to syringe, he found himself sweating. The muted daylight and forest canopy that had once been his protective shields and friends were rapidly becoming his enemies. Even with one of Silas's highway safety lanterns in hand, the crates in the cargo bay seemed to suck up all the light. Thinking that perhaps he should've done at least one practice run, he quickly ticked off the reasons he hadn't. Practice runs established a track record, leaving behind traceable shards of information, and he understood the significance of never leaving footprints in the sand.

With New Mexico State Police Colonel Andy Gutierrez impatiently rocking from side to side next to him, Thaddeus Richter stood talking to the portly man who'd minutes earlier chastised and then lectured Bernadette about her unscheduled landing at Los Alamos. An hour earlier, Richter had finally put most of the pieces of the Thurmond Giles murder puzzle together, convincing himself that Silas Breen's truck more than likely contained the makings of a dirty nuclear bomb intended to be set off at the birthplace of the first atomic weapon. Uncertain how he could possibly get from Albuquerque to Los Alamos fast enough to make what he'd figured out matter, Richter had about given up any hope of doing so. He'd reluctantly called the bureau office in Santa Fe to tell agents there to take over and race up the hill to Los Alamos. As he'd fueled his vehicle for what he expected to be a run to Los Alamos that would turn out to be too little, too late, word about a New Mexico state trooper's investigation of the buzzing of Highway 285 at Pojoaque by a jet had crackled across his two-way.

He'd rushed inside the bureau's office complex, called that trooper, verified that the information he'd just heard was correct, and, after assuring the confused-sounding trooper that the plane doing the buzzing wasn't an FBI aircraft, sprinted from the building prepared to run, lights flashing, to Los Alamos.

As he'd slipped into his vehicle, an Albuquerque bureau agent had raced up to let him know that the aircraft that had been buzzing U.S. 285 at Pojoaque had just landed at Los Alamos and that a ranking New Mexico State Police officer was headed by chopper from Albuquerque to Los Alamos to check the situation out. Following an eight-minute race to the Albuquerque airport and lots of pleading on his part, Richter had hitched what turned out to be a thirty-three-minute helicopter ride to Los Alamos with Colonel Gutierrez.

Now, as he wrapped up his conversation with the rattled-looking airport official, Richter looked up to realize that five New Mexico State Police cars, a half-dozen Los Alamos patrol cars, and two homeland security vehicles had joined them on the tarmac. Surveying the scene and turning to Colonel Gutierrez, Richter said,

"As I mentioned on the way up, this whole Tango-11 incident isn't about delivering drugs, stolen artifacts, or even moving second-hand radiation therapy equipment to Third World black markets, Colonel. Not by a long shot. Somebody's planning to set off a nuclear device here. Trust me."

"You could be wrong, you know," Gutierrez said skeptically.

"I don't think I am. Until yesterday, that pilot Mr. Fordyce here described so precisely was the U.S. Air Force officer in charge of investigating the break-in at Tango-11. Her name's Major Bernadette Cameron, and the guy operating that motorcycle they blasted out of here on is a reporter named Elgin Coseia. They know what we know, Colonel, and likely a whole lot more. There's a truck with cobalt-60 nuclear source material bumping around this mesa somewhere." Turning to Fordyce, Richter asked, "Which way did you say that motorcycle headed?"

"Beelined straight for the airport exit and made a left turn. Didn't slow down for a second."

"Sounds to me like they knew where they were going," said Gutierrez.

"Yeah. Like maybe they'd spotted that U-Haul truck from the air," said Richter.

Looking frustrated, Gutierrez said, "I've got three state troopers who were already up here on the hill searching buildings inside the National Laboratory compound, and Los Alamos PD has every available officer on this. I'll APB that motorcycle and call for backup, but it's a winding thirty-minute drive up the hill from Pojoaque, and this can be one hell of a big mesa when you have to comb it foot by foot. Anywhere specific you think we should look?"

Richter stared toward the airport exit. "Down the hill. I'm thinking we need to be on the ground right now. Not upstairs in a chopper."

"Your show. I'll have a car here in less than a minute."

"Good," said Richter, his eyes now locked on the airport exit as he considered not how to locate a U-Haul truck but rather how to spot a motorcycle.

Everything was in place—secured, jelled, glued, and ready. Rikia Takata's protective radiation gear sat on the front seat of the Volkswagen along with Silas Breen's .32 and the all-important cell-phone bomb trigger. As a final precaution, he'd let the air out of the tires of the U-Haul to make certain that if things got dicey, the truck bomb casing, as it were, couldn't easily be moved.

With his hands wet with perspiration, he recalled something a high school Latin teacher had once crammed into his head: *Thrice is better than twice*. Heeding that teacher's singsong advice, he decided to check the leads to the cobalt-60 capsules a final time.

The twenty lead-encased capsules didn't look very ominous. In fact, lined up as they were, ten each on the top of a couple of pickup-bed toolboxes in the U-Haul's cargo bay, they reminded him of spice-rack bottles. Remnants of the gel that would become the current that would trigger his nuclear blast clung to his fingers. Tacky and slightly rubbery, the gel had a cleansing, post-thunderstorm, fractured-ozone smell. A smell that was overwhelmed by the putrid smell of Silas Breen's already decaying body.

As he surveyed the cargo bay and its contents one last time, he thought briefly about Hiroshima, his photographer grandfather, and the incinerated man on a pink horse. "Done," he whispered as if speaking to someone. Glancing over his shoulder at the capsules for a final time, he stepped down from the cargo bay onto the truck's bumper and jumped to the ground.

Bernadette spotted the turnoff to the forest service road seconds before Cozy. "That's it just ahead," she yelled above the rumble of the motorcycle. "Twelfth road from the airport's southern boundary fence."

"See it." Cozy slowed down and turned onto a narrow, badly rutted dirt road. "It sure looked smoother from the air," he said as the motorcycle bumped through ruts, and over tree stumps and rocks.

"Everything does."

"Think he's still here?"

"Yep."

Cozy eased the motorcycle to a stop, slipped the shotgun, a lightweight pistol-grip double-barrel that Freddy had purchased in Colombia after once nearly being kidnapped there, out of its case, rotated the case aside, and handed the gun to Bernadette. "Think you can handle it?"

"I've handled heavier."

"What about pulling the trigger if it comes to that?" Cozy asked, nosing the bike farther into the forest.

"I'm a fighter pilot, Cozy. They train us to kill," Bernadette said, tightening her now one-handed grip around Cozy's waist.

They'd bumped another quarter of a mile down the kidney-jarring road when Cozy saw a flash of something that looked silver or gray moving in the trees. It took him a second or two to realize that whatever it was was moving fast and headed their way.

By the time Bernadette shouted, "Something's headed for us!" Rikia Takata, tightly gripping the steering wheel of the Volkswagen he was driving with both hands as he sped away from the U-Haul truck, spotted them. Recognizing Bernadette, he muttered, "Shit," and floored the accelerator.

As car and motorcycle closed the gap between them in some bizarre, deep-pine-forest game of chicken, Cozy saw only fog. "Cozy!" Bernadette screamed as Cozy continued to accelerate. They were within sixty feet of each other when Cozy yelled, "Shoot, Bernadette! Shoot!"

Taking aim at the VW's windshield, Bernadette squeezed the shotgun's trigger once. Seconds before the motorcycle's front tire hit a rock, the bike fishtailed out of control and left the trail. The VW's windshield shattered, and the bike danced along a line of boulders lining the muddy floor of a bar ditch. They were twenty yards past the Volkswagen before Cozy could get the bike back under control and stopped. Gunning the engine, he jumped the bike out of the ditch, spun it around in a glade of ferns, and with a blown shock and bent front tire rim headed back for the Volkswagen, which had broadsided the trunk of a fifty-foot-tall lodgepole pine.

The force of the impact had snapped Rikia's left ankle and slammed his head into the dashboard. Bleeding from his nose, he was slumped over the steering wheel. Dazed and with blood curling around one corner of his mouth, he raised his head and swiped at the blood with his right hand. He tried to concentrate, tried his best to refocus on his mission, but his mind was too cloudy, too inexplicably foggy. He tried to force the VW's door open, but the frame was bent, and the door barely budged. Patting the car seat for his cell phone and then his shirt pocket for his cyanide capsules, he grabbed the phone and Silas Breen's .32 in one hand. Powered by a rush of adrenaline, he shouldered the car door open, jumped out, and, with his broken ankle throbbing, hobbled toward a clump of piñons.

Grimacing in pain, he aimed the .32 at two undulating, ghostly human shapes that were crouched low to the ground and seemed to be moving toward him. He squeezed off a right-handed shot, then used his left hand to punch in the first of six cell-phone numbers that would trigger his bomb. He'd punched in the second, third, and fourth numbers and, with a bloody index finger, was prepared to punch in a fifth when a shotgun blast slammed into his neck.

Screaming, he dropped the cell phone and clutched his neck with both hands. Suddenly the front of his shirt was covered in blood, and he felt as if he were falling. As he struggled to breathe, he could hear the crunch of footfalls on the pine-needle-covered forest floor. The crunching sound moved closer and got louder until he passed out.

Bernadette kicked the .32 out of Rikia's hand to send it skittering across a bed of pine needles and soft dirt before kneeling over him to check for a carotid pulse. Looking up at Cozy, she said, "He's alive. Better call 911."

Cozy slipped his cell phone out of his pocket, punched in 911, and in response to the operator's robust "Nine-one-one, what's your emergency?" said, "We've got a badly injured man and a possible nuclear device on a forest service road just outside Los Alamos. Better send someone who can handle the situation."

"Can you give me any more information and a better location, sir?" the operator asked, her voice barely rising.

"No, I can't!" Cozy yelled over a surge of static.

"Are you still there, sir?"

Sensing Cozy's frustration, Bernadette snatched the cell phone out of Cozy's hand and yelled into it: "This is Major Bernadette Cameron, United States Air Force. We're one right turn off New Mexico State Road 502 and exactly twelve forest access roads from the southern boundary fence of the Los Alamos Airport. Get someone the hell out here on the double, damn it!" She snapped the cell phone closed and checked to see if Rikia was still breathing.

"Is he still alive?" Cozy asked.

"Looks like it."

Cozy walked over to Rikia's cell phone and turned it off. "Wonder who he was trying to call when you popped him?"

"No way of telling now," said Bernadette. "Let's leave that problem to the folks who show up."

"Fine by me," Cozy said as the faint wail of sirens erupted in the distance.

"Freddy's not going to be happy about his toy," Bernadette said, sounding apologetic as she stared at the damaged motorcycle.

"Better than if we'd crashed *Sugar*."

Surprised at how intently Cozy was also suddenly staring at the motorcycle, Bernadette asked, "What's got you so mesmerized?"

"I don't know, really," Cozy said as an odd, enlightened look slowly spread across his face. The look seemed to announce as it broadened into a smile that a long-lingering fog had finally lifted.

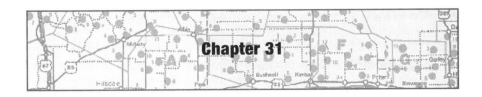

Chapter 31

The oak-paneled room in the Bradbury Science Museum, where Cozy and Bernadette had been sitting for almost three hours, was a small room smelling of floor wax inside a government facility that had been constructed in 1963. Designed to highlight Los Alamos National Laboratory's role in technology and science, including the Manhattan Project, the building, normally open to the public, had four hours earlier become off-limits to anyone without the highest government security clearance. A half-dozen Styrofoam cups containing remnants of stale coffee sat on the large, oval boardroom table that Cozy and Bernadette shared with FBI Agent Thaddeus Richter and a red-haired, beady-eyed man with a buzz cut and closely cropped, military-regulation-length sideburns.

The red-haired man, who'd introduced himself as Melvin Stoops, had remained in the room with Agent Richter after nearly a dozen people from the FBI, homeland security, and the New Mexico State Police had taken turns interviewing Bernadette and Cozy. Everyone had been silent for over a minute when Bernadette, who'd been thinking about Rikia Takata's cell phone, asked Stoops, "Is Takata still alive, and do you know if his cell phone was the bomb trigger?"

"I'm not at liberty to discuss those issues, Major," Stoops said dismissively. "Now, how about we get back to your and

Mr. Coseia's roles in the current matter? My job is to determine whether, in association with Mr. Coseia, your actions represent a court-martialable offense, Major Cameron."

Cozy leaned forward in his chair, dropped his elbows down hard on the table, and stared angrily at Stoops. "Are you going to court-martial me, too, jackass?"

"Cozy, please," Bernadette said, grabbing Cozy's arm.

"Please, my ass, Bernadette. You just stopped some wacko from setting off a nuclear weapon, and you've got this nitwit talking about court-martialing you. Can't you do something about this, Richter?"

Richter shrugged. "No."

"I can have you removed from the room," Stoops said calmly to Cozy.

The look Bernadette flashed Cozy, a look that said, *Please shut up,* served to calm him down, at least momentarily.

Looking slightly less sure of himself, Stoops asked, "Why is it that you decided to strike out on your own with the Tango-11 investigation, Major? And why didn't you inform your superiors of your actions? Especially Colonel DeWitt."

"There wasn't time," Bernadette said, suspecting that Stoops was more than likely an air force OSI internal affairs colonel who had been hurriedly sent to Los Alamos with orders to quickly put a damper on anything that had the potential to embarrass the air force. "Besides, I'd already informed the FBI."

Stoops looked at Richter for confirmation.

"We'd talked," said Richter.

Staring down at the top page of his more than four pages of

notes, Stoops said, "We're almost done for the night, Major. Here's my last question. Why did you stray so far from your original assignment, which was simply to investigate the security breach at Tango-11?"

"I was just hoping to help solve a murder, I guess."

"But you're not a police officer or a sheriff or anyone with such authority, Major."

Unable to bite his tongue any longer, Cozy said, "And the air force says she's not a pilot anymore, either. But in light of the day's events, I beg to differ."

Stoops eyed Cozy impassively and began collecting his papers. "I'll be talking with you tomorrow, Major—in the absence of Mr. Coseia or Agent Richter, you might like to know."

"Fine," said Bernadette, watching Richter, who looked even less pleased than she was by Stoops's announcement, rise and head toward the door.

"You and Mr. Coseia are staying here in Los Alamos, of course," Stoops said, getting up out of his chair.

"Yes," Bernadette said, feeling as if she were somehow a criminal suspect.

"Of course you are." Stoops smiled and headed for the door.

As the door closed behind Richter and then Stoops, Cozy asked, "How the heck did that apple-polishing idiot get from wherever he was to Los Alamos so fast?"

Smiling and tweaking Cozy's cheek, Bernadette said, "He's probably out of Travis Air Force Base in California, and that's not so far when the company you work for has a nice little stash of supersonic jets."

An hour and a half later Cozy sat on the edge of the sagging king-sized bed in his room, banging out a story on his laptop. Freddy Dames had called him a half-dozen times about the story, and finally, at twelve thirty in the morning, bone-weary both mentally and physically, Cozy was close to having it done. He and Bernadette had settled into adjoining rooms in a two-story limestone building that they'd been escorted to by an FBI agent. Not at all surprised that their rooms were adjoining, Bernadette stood in the doorway that connected them and watched Cozy type.

She wasn't certain whether the FBI agent who'd walked them to their rooms was still outside in the hall. She hadn't looked. But she was positive that someone from some faceless government agency was stationed there. Especially since, after being released by Stoops, they'd had a ten-minute hallway interview with an official from the Office of National Intelligence, followed by a twenty-minute hallway talk with a droopy-eyed man from homeland security and finally a fifteen-minute eyeball-to-eyeball chat with the government's regional weapons of mass destruction coordinator, a perky-looking woman named Loretta Vines who'd flown in from Denver. And as they'd headed through the darkened building toward their rooms with their FBI escort at their side, a man from the National Nuclear Security Administration's Office of Emergency Operations had swooped down on them and flashed his credentials at the FBI agent. But the agent, frustrated after forty-five minutes of interruption, had said to the man, "You can talk to them tomorrow."

There'd been media people around, of course, digging and snooping and probing like stud dogs trailing bitches in heat, but not a single journalist had been permitted to talk to them.

Neither she nor Cozy had any idea what happened to Silas Breen's truck, the bomb components Agent Richter had admitted they'd found inside, Silas Breen, or Rikia Takata, and when Cozy had asked both Loretta Vines and the man from the National Nuclear Security Administration's office for information, he'd gotten only silence and blank stares.

Bernadette didn't know how many days they'd have to spend talking with authorities, but with a new round of debriefings scheduled to start at eight the next morning, she knew they both needed to get some sleep.

She had been able to talk to her father, who'd called a couple of longtime friends and high-ranking national security types in Washington to plead her case, but as far as she knew, nothing helpful had materialized.

Freddy had assured them that he'd do whatever was necessary to get them out of the government's clutches, including marshaling whatever help he could get from politically connected friends of his father. But they both understood that Freddy's first and foremost concern was a story.

Surprised that someone from a government agency hadn't confiscated Cozy's laptop, Bernadette continued to watch Cozy pound away at the keys. Walking over to him and flashing him a road-weary smile, she asked, "Why do you think they let you hang on to your computer?"

"Who knows? My fourth estate rights, I guess. Since I've had every cavity and potential cavity in my body including the space beneath my fingernails searched, I'm guessing some politico out there looked at the potential fallout his side might get by clamping down on me and said, 'What's the harm in a laptop?'" Checking the last sentence he'd typed for spelling errors, Cozy said, "Who knows why on earth they allowed us to have adjoining rooms, either?"

"That answer's easy. It's what you do with POWs when they're first captured. You split them up later. For right now they want us in one place. Works for me," she said, smiling, taking a seat on the bed beside Cozy, and kissing him softly on the cheek. "So, what's the gist of your story?"

"You really want to know?"

"Sure do, Mr. Pulitzer."

"Okay. It's the only thing I could write about that could possibly trump the hundreds, if not thousands, of other stories that are out there by now."

"Which is?"

Cozy scrolled to the top of his screen. "Take a look at my working title: *Defusing Fat Man II: An Insider's Look at the Magic*."

"Sounds sort of egotistical to me."

Cozy smiled. "First lesson of the new journalism, Major: it's less about journalism and more about show. Second lesson: there's nothing more interesting or personally fulfilling for a reader than to hitch their wagon to someone who's been on the inside of an ordeal. Freddy wants me to milk it, pound the story out in four parts, make it episodic and *Star Wars*–like. Part I, the piece I'm writing now, starts with Giles found hanging by his ankles at Tango-11. Part IV will take the reader to the brink of the bomb going off. Each piece will end with a cliff-hanger and have to stand on its own."

Bernadette shook her head. "Sounds more like a screenplay than news."

"Good description. But sadly, it's what I do for a living, Bernadette. Hate to burst your bubble, but Edward R. Murrow's been dead for a good long time."

Looking disillusioned, Bernadette said, "If it's what you have to do. But what about all the loose ends? Was Rikia acting on his own? How did he set things up? And is he even still alive?"

"Those things will all be addressed in the series. But you and I both know there's no way in hell that Rikia set things up all by himself. I'm thinking Dr. Takata was a one-trick pony, and his trick was the bomb. He was more than likely in on the Giles killing, but I'm betting he was just along for the ride."

"So if he didn't kill Giles, who did?"

"I don't know yet, but whoever did had help. There's no way any one person could have dragged a one-hundred-seventy-pound man and fifty pounds of block, chain, and tackle halfway across an abandoned missile-silo site, raised a 2,500-pound hatch cover, and dropped a body down the hatch on their own. To say nothing of the Sarah Goldbeck killing. How on earth could Rikia have killed her when he was either at a meeting for math eggheads in El Paso or already down here in New Mexico or Texas, and why?"

"The why's easy," said Bernadette. "If she was in on it, to keep her from spilling the beans about the Giles murder. And more importantly, to keep her from telling the world what Rikia was doing. Could be that when she found out what Rikia was really up to, which wasn't simply a little revenge on Giles, for whatever reason she got cold feet and decided to come clean to someone."

"Turns out a lot of people got used up by Sergeant Giles," said Cozy. "Maybe they all had a hand in killing him. Rikia, Colbain, Rivers, maybe even Buford Kane."

"Kane? Considering how hysterical he was when he called to say his wife was dead, that would surprise me."

"Maybe he was faking it."

"I don't think so. It's hard to fake that kind of emotion."

"Pretty much leaves us with Kimiko as the straggler, then."

"She's a tough one," said Bernadette. "It's hard to figure out why she would've been involved in the Giles killing. Then again, she could have had an inkling of what Rikia was up to and figured that by going along with the Giles killing, she could stop him."

"Reasonable speculation," said Cozy.

"That's the kind of response I'd expect from some highbrow attorney," said Bernadette.

Looking exhausted, Cozy smiled and said, "And you, Major Cameron, are sounding like someone I'd like to go to bed with."

"Only if your intentions are to sleep."

"Trust me. They are," Cozy said, lying back on the bed.

Five minutes later, naked and snuggled tightly against one another like fetal twins, they were both dead to the world.

"Defusing Fat Man II" hit the internet the next day. Within forty-eight hours of the story's debut, it had been picked up by every major newspaper, TV station, and media outlet in the country. The most intriguing part of the story, seasoned media types agreed, wasn't Elgin Coseia's account of how he and Major Bernadette Cameron had thwarted a madman's plan to trigger a nuclear weapon at Los Alamos but Coseia's speculation about how that plan, set in motion by the murder of a retired air force sergeant at a desolate place called Tango-11, must of necessity have included yet unnamed persons.

His detailed discussion of the exact placement and depth of the five stab wounds in Giles's back, gleaned from correspondence between Bernadette and Sheriff Bosack and secured in earnest by the two thousand dollars Freddy Dames had secretly paid Deputy Sykes, along with his account of the former sergeant's penis mutilation, had the phones at Digital Registry News singing and Freddy announcing to anyone within earshot that the bell had tolled for print journalism. Cozy's discussion of the not-yet-released autopsy findings, in which he asserted that two of the five stab wounds were so superficial that they couldn't possibly have killed Giles, was followed by a probing and problematic question: Who had actually delivered the fatal, deep-plunging stab wound that had severed two vital arteries in Giles's lung?

Assuring readers that he would ultimately name names and define the role that each person had played in the murder and the attempted bombing, Cozy had ended the story with a single and powerful "stay tuned" assertion: Rikia Takata couldn't have possibly engineered the murder of Thurmond Giles or orchestrated his plan to trigger a nuclear device on his own.

Cozy's story had America's media types scurrying to find out who the unnamed people might be. Two days after the story appeared, names began to surface, but two weeks after the leaking of Howard Colbain's, Grant Rivers's, and Kimiko Takata's names, their lawyers and the U.S. government had built an impenetrable protective wall around the three. To further heighten public outrage, no one would verify whether Rikia Takata was dead or alive.

Relishing his pot-stirring role during the three weeks following the unsuccessful Los Alamos bombing, Freddy Dames posted a dozen stories about Digital Registry News's role in the thwarted bombing, hammering home in most of them how easy it had been for Silas Breen, an unlucky pawn in the process, to transport radioactive cobalt-60 source material more than halfway across a continent.

The second story in Cozy's proposed four-part series never saw the light of day, largely because Freddy, under threats of legal action against him and Digital Registry News on behalf of Howard Colbain, the Takatas, and Grant Rivers, was forced to pull the plug on the piece.

Kimiko Takata, Grant Rivers, Howard Colbain, and Buford Kane, who'd been dragged into the morass by no more than inference and circumstance, were denying through their lawyers any involvement whatsoever in the Giles or Sarah Goldbeck murders. Rikia Takata, presumed to be alive and the centerpiece in the government's weapons of mass destruction investigation, wasn't admitting to anything.

Threats of lawsuits eventually disappeared, and a month after those threats had first surfaced, with Rikia Takata incarcerated and very much alive and the government amassing its case against him, Cozy had settled back into a regular work routine. Bernadette had given the air force her resignation notice while still fending off court-martial proceedings, and Freddy, continuing to milk the "story of the century," had turned Digital Registry News into a household name.

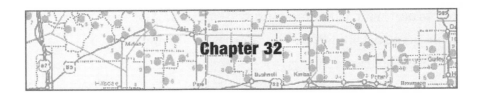
It was Buford Kane who ultimately brought final closure to the events triggered by Tango-11 when, seven weeks after the discovery of Thurmond Giles's body, he walked into the offices of Digital Registry News, looking put-upon because of the government's failed but lengthy attempts to link him to the Giles murder and the bombing at Los Alamos. He asked a surprised Lillian Griffith if he could speak with Elgin Coseia about who had killed his wife, Sarah Goldbeck.

When Cozy rounded a corner in search of a clean coffee cup and saw Kane standing in front of Lillian's desk, looking haunted, Buford blurted out, "Kimiko Takata killed my Sarah, Mr. Coseia, and I'm pretty sure where she hid the murder weapon."

Kane, who looked to have lost a good fifteen pounds since Cozy had last seen him, reeked of dried sweat and motor oil.

Looking Buford up and down, then glancing at Lillian, who was on the verge of holding her nose, Cozy said, "Why don't we step into my office, Mr. Kane."

Limping noticeably, Kane followed Cozy to his newly furnished office.

"What happened to your leg?" Cozy asked as they both took seats.

"Hurt it workin' on an irrigation ditch at my place. But I ain't here to talk about that. I'm hopin' you can help me put the loony old broad who killed my wife behind bars. Ain't you gonna ask me where Kimiko is?"

"Well, where is she?"

"At Heart Mountain, most likely. Where else? There to amp up her craziness. I've been followin' her for weeks, doin' some investigatin' of my own. I owe it to Sarah to nail her killer. And when I do, I'll need somebody to tell Sarah's story. Somebody who'll set the record straight and do her right." He stared pleadingly at Cozy.

"So tell me what you've got," Cozy said a bit reluctantly.

Looking invigorated, Buford rubbed his hands together. "Like I said, I've been followin' the old half-wit around for weeks. Been glued to her like the stink on shit. Three days ago I finally got my break when I saw her buyin' somethin' at a UPS store in Laramie. She came walkin' outta the store with a cardboard box like the kind you'd send long-stemmed roses in to your honey, except it was sturdier-lookin' and a tad bit wider and longer. Heavy-gauge cardboard, if you know what I mean. When I checked the internet later that day to see if I could find the same kinda box, I found that very one at several outlets—UPS, U-Haul, Penske. Took me the longest while, but in the end I figured out what might fit into a box like that. A sawed-off shotgun like the one that killed my Sarah."

"Why didn't you confront her when you saw her leaving the UPS store?" Cozy asked, deciding not to offer much of a challenge to Buford's purely circumstantial tale.

"Because I didn't know what the hell the box was gonna be used for then. Besides, I was nervous. I didn't want her knowin' I was tailin' her and maybe give her the chance to be lookin' for me in the future. Besides, as far as I knew, she was plannin' on makin' that shotgun disappear that very day."

"Do you think that maybe your grief has you imagining things, Mr. Kane?"

"I don't, and I ain't! But what if I am? Won't hurt to check the old bag out. Since you and Major Cameron stopped that crazy cousin of hers from nukin' us and contaminatin' the whole damn Front Range of the Rockies, I figured I might as well start my search for help with the two of you."

Cozy couldn't help but smile. He'd had scores of insincere, butt-kissing newshounds from the *New York Times, Washington Post,* CNN, and Fox groveling to sit at his feet for over a month, and now he actually had someone in need of his knowledge and skills who might actually appreciate them.

"And it was the two of you who figured out that more than one person most likely stabbed that Sergeant Giles to death," said Buford. "So naturally I figured you and the major could also help me pin Sarah's murder on Kimiko."

"I'm flattered, Mr. Kane, but as of yet no one has proven who or how many people killed Sergeant Giles."

Kane looked surprised. "Well, hell. You pretty much said who it was in that article you wrote a few weeks back."

"I'm afraid the article you're referring to was pretty much a speculative piece, which means that, although I believe the facts in the article to be true, I can't prove them to be. And they certainly wouldn't carry any weight in a court of law."

"Call it what you will, straight-out fact or just plain guessin'. I see it this way. Colbain, Rivers, and Kimiko might be out there free as the breeze right now because they've got themselves a bunch of publicity-seekin' slick-assed, big-city lawyers who are good at milkin' the shit outta the system. But in the end, the chickens are gonna roost my way. Trust me."

"Let's hope so. Just remember, justice doesn't always play out the way you expect it to, Mr. Kane. Someone will have to convince a jury that Colbain; Rivers; the Takatas; and maybe even your own wife, Sarah, killed Sergeant Giles."

"Yeah, I know all that. And to tell you the truth, I don't really give a shit about who killed Giles. I'm interested in bringin' the person who killed my Sarah to justice. And I'm sittin' here tellin' you it was Kimiko Takata. I warned Sarah to stay away from her for years, but they had some kind of spiritual 'save the planet' connection I couldn't sever. Connection or not, though, sooner or later Kimiko's gonna head back to Heart Mountain and do whatever she's been doin' in that godforsaken place for the past fifty years. Sarah used to tell me about how when she was just a little girl followin' her crazy-ass mother around from pillar to post, Kimiko would wig out after comin' back from Heart Mountain. And about how Kimiko would cry on that Sergeant Giles's shoulder and sometimes Sarah's mother's shoulder after a trip there. I should have told Major Cameron that the first time she interrogated me at Warren. But I didn't, and you see what it ended up gettin' my Sarah? A spot in the graveyard."

Buford paused and cleared his throat, as if to make certain that what he had to say next came through loud and clear. "I ain't proud or religious, Mr. Coseia, so I'll tell you up front, what I'm after is my pound of flesh. And I'm only askin' for you and Major

Cameron to help me out a little bit. I'll keep an eye on Kimiko. Even stay in a motel in Laramie and watch her every move till she strikes out for Heart Mountain again. But you might as well know that with or without your help, I'm gonna see that old witch either dead or behind bars."

"Okay. Suppose you're lucky enough to be there in Laramie when she strikes out for Heart Mountain again. Takes off all bold and unintimidated, carrying that shotgun you're so certain she murdered your wife with. How do you expect me to get from Denver to either Laramie or Heart Mountain to help out on a moment's notice?"

"That's where Major Cameron comes in," Buford said, grinning. "She flies you there in that plane you tracked Rikia down in. Should be easy."

"Not quite. The plane you're talking about doesn't belong to either one of us. Major Cameron's busy trying to wrap up her military career, and I'm up to my eyeballs with work."

"Well, drop what the shit you're doin' and get with me on this, man. Look at it this way. You'll help send Kimiko to prison, and you'll have yourself one of them prizewinnin' stories you folks in the news business like to brag about so much."

Deciding it would be fruitless to offer Buford another civics lesson on the workings of the judicial system, Cozy nonetheless found himself intrigued. Sarah Goldbeck's murder and her actual role in the events at Tango-11 were two things he hadn't fully addressed. Eyeing Buford thoughtfully, he said, "Suppose you're wrong about Kimiko and about the murder weapon. Suppose a plane trip to Heart Mountain turns out to be a huge waste of money and time."

"I'm not wrong," Buford said, slamming a fist into his palm.

Impressed by Buford's persistence, Cozy said, "Why don't you sit right where you are while I go run your suggestion by my boss."

Buford looked surprised. "You mean you need somebody else's approval on this?"

"Sure do. The man who owns that plane we're talking about. Just sit tight, okay?" Cozy said, quickly leaving his office.

Buford remained seated, staring around the room and wondering how someone who'd been labeled a hero could have been assigned such unimpressive and cluttered digs. Although the furniture looked new, there was barely a picture on the wall, the laptop computer on Cozy's desk wasn't even open, and stacks of paper were piled four inches high and pretty much helter-skelter everywhere. To top it all off, the man the world was calling a hero didn't even have his own secretary, much less an airplane.

Thinking that he might have made a bad decision by coming to Denver to ask for Cozy's help, he was considering just getting up and leaving when Cozy returned with Freddy Dames.

Offering Buford a quick handshake and introducing himself, Freddy said, "How soon do you expect Kimiko Takata to head for Heart Mountain, Mr. Kane?"

"Can't predict."

"But you'd be able to let Cozy know the instant she takes off for the place? You're certain of that?"

"I sure would."

Freddy looked briefly at Cozy, then back at Buford. "Then you've got yourself a reporter, Mr. Kane."

Looking surprised, Cozy said, "But I haven't talked to Bernadette yet, Freddy."

"She'll be okay with it." A sly, knowing smile inched across Freddy's face. "She's in love with you, Elgin. Besides, I talked to her first thing this morning. My dad's been busy bending ears and having arms twisted in Washington. She'll be done with the air force, and with a sterling record as her legacy, by week's end. I'm sure she'll be happy to help out Mr. Kane."

Freddy smiled and glanced over at Buford. "There'll be a plane at your disposal whenever you call for one, Mr. Kane. Just let Mr. Coseia here know when you're ready for him to roll. He'll make certain Major Cameron gets him where you need him, and in a hurry. Right, Cozy?"

"Yeah," said Cozy. He'd always understood that there was a universe of difference between the world he lived in and that of his best friend, and he'd just gotten another lesson.

"Good. I've got some TV execs from LA I need to teleconference with in a few minutes. Gotta go." He shot Buford a parting glance. "Stay on Kimiko's tail," he said authoritatively. Looking at Cozy and grinning, he said, "Looks like we've got ourselves a fifth and final part for that series of yours when it runs, my man."

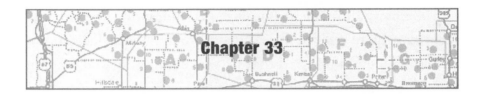

Chapter 33

Kimiko Takata, who hadn't slept well in weeks, rose a little before seven a.m. to face another disjointed day. She spent most of her waking hours now talking to FBI agents, people from half-a-dozen national security agencies, or Rikia's lawyers, and she was tired. She knew she wasn't thinking clearly, knew she was losing her sense of balance in a world that had turned especially angry and ugly for her since Los Alamos. She'd received enough hate mail to fill a Dumpster and so many venomous phone calls that she'd been forced to disconnect her phone, and she rarely now came out of her house. She wasn't so tired or intimidated, however, that she intended to either put off or cancel her trip to Heart Mountain the next day. She'd planned the trip for two weeks, and the timing fit. Rikia was safe and on the mend, both physically and mentally, it seemed, even though he was locked away by himself in a federal supermax facility outside Florence, Colorado. Since Los Alamos he'd remained heavily guarded and very uncommunicative. "Name, rank, and serial number, that's all they get from me," Rikia would say to her whenever they spoke. And when she pressed him about when he was going to talk at length to his lawyers so they could begin building a defense, he said, as if it really didn't matter to him, "I'll get around to it."

She knew, although she'd only seen him twice, that he was recovering quite well from his shotgun wounds, facial lacerations, and broken left ankle and that he was eating well and reading magazines and books. His lawyers, who saw him more frequently, had confirmed as much. She also knew that he was exercising in the chilly, damp, unpainted cinder-block-walled room he was being housed in. She'd seen pictures.

He'd told her more than once that instead of collapsing under the constant pressure and scrutiny of authorities, he planned to outread, outexercise, and outthink them all. What he wasn't going to do was talk.

Besides offering authorities his name, rank (professor), and serial number (his birth date), Rikia had spoken to almost no one besides his lawyers and her. He'd talked to an odd-looking man with a pencil-thin mustache and elephant ears whom they now knew to be FBI Agent Thaddeus Richter. Newspapers and TV stations had carried what he'd supposedly said to Richter while he'd lain injured in the woods, half out of his mind after his car crash in the forest outside Los Alamos. Supposedly he had uttered the now infamous words, "Don't shoot. I'm hurt," while Richter stood over him with an automatic weapon aimed squarely at his head.

Unlike Kimiko, Rikia had been sleeping well. He was safe, sequestered in his cinder-block-walled room. And he knew the government wouldn't dare torture him. After all, he was an American citizen, and, oppressive nobodies that they were, American government officials didn't have the guts to do something like that.

Although his mission had failed, the time for psychological warfare was just beginning.

Walking over to one of two chairs in his twelve-by-twelve-foot room, he retrieved one of the two model planes that Kimiko had brought him a few days earlier from the metal seat. Seconds later he was in the midst of a dogfight, clutching an American Corsair in one hand and his A-6M in the other. The aerial fight had been waged for less than a minute when the door to his windowless room creaked open.

"Your attorney's here, Dr. Takata," he heard someone outside the room say. Ignoring his attorney and the guard standing next to him, Rikia groaned and squealed and snorted the Corsair toward the ceiling, where it tried in vain to outmaneuver the A-6M. With the rat-a-tat-tat of machine-gun fire reverberating off his tongue, Rikia smiled and whispered, "Justice."

Laramie had turned chilly and blustery, and by late afternoon, Kimiko had temporarily pushed aside thoughts of Rikia to concentrate on what she would pack and take with her on her trip to Heart Mountain the next morning. She'd take her father's diary, of course, and assorted flavors of tea, and perhaps one of Rikia's model planes. By six p.m. she had everything packed, and at eight she headed slowly toward her bedroom to read for a while before battling another night of restless sleep. As she entered the room, she thought briefly about Hiroshima and the man on his pink horse. The thought quickly passed, and for the first time in a month, after briefly reading from her father's diary, she slept soundly.

At nine the next morning, Rikia Takata, who had been formally charged by the U.S. attorney weeks earlier with two counts of murder; a single count of attempting to set off a weapon of mass destruction; and eleven lesser counts, including two counts of transporting radioisotopes across state lines without a permit, was found hanged in his room at the government's supermax facility in Colorado. Within minutes of hearing the news, Cozy got a call at home from Buford Kane telling him that Kimiko Takata was headed for Heart Mountain. His voice spiked with nervousness, Buford said, "I watched her pack up her station wagon, and I've been followin' her for the past half hour. I need you and Major Cameron to get up to Heart Mountain lickety-split."

Barefoot and dressed in an undersized air force academy T-shirt and running shorts, Bernadette was busy making coffee and listening to the news on a small television in Cozy's kitchen, paying little attention to Cozy's phone conversation.

Three days earlier, with the threat of a court-martial behind her and her resignation from the air force official, she'd begun ten days of terminal leave. Leave she was spending in Denver with Cozy before taking the next step in her life.

When Cozy spun the kitchen stool he was sitting on to face her and said, "We're on the move, Bernadette. That was Buford Kane on the horn. He's trailing Kimiko Takata to Heart Mountain right this minute," Bernadette was less surprised than exasperated. She'd had enough of Tango-11, and it showed on her face.

"How long's the flight from here to Cody?" Cozy asked, turning off the TV.

"Wheels up to wheels down, a little under two hours. I've told you that before. Add in time for getting from here to the airport, fueling *Sugar,* and filing a flight plan and we're there in three and a half hours, tops."

With the clock in his head ticking, Cozy said, "Then it's another thirty minutes from Cody to Heart Mountain, plug in twenty minutes for renting a car, and four and a half hours door to door about does it. That should put us there a little ahead of Kimiko."

"And where do we go from that point?"

"I'm not sure. Buford said to make certain to rent a red SUV so he'd be able to see it parked off of the U.S. 14 alternate road. He said it's the first road north of Corbett Dam, that he'd pick us up there and take us to Heart Mountain, and that he'd make certain that Kimiko wouldn't spot him."

"Guess we'd better hope the rental car agency has lots of SUVs in red, then." Shaking her head and slipping into her tennis shoes, Bernadette said, "This whole Tango-11 thing just keeps playing out stranger and stranger. We still don't know who actually killed Sergeant Giles, and it's cost me a career. I hope this is the end of it."

"And it's put you on the path to a new one."

Bernadette frowned. "Chief corporate pilot for Digital Registry News? Cozy, come on. Freddy manufactured the title and slapped me on the payroll because money's no object to him. Besides, with me on board as the 'Black Amazon' who stopped the mad bomber, Freddy's got himself a way to add permanent sizzle to our stories."

"See, you said 'our.' You should have left the air force years ago. I've edited all four of the stories you've written, remember. You know how to string words together, Bernadette. It's as if you've been doing it all your life. In baseball terms, you're a natural."

"I didn't know there was such a thing in the world of investigative journalism. I've always envisioned those kind of reporters as people who hid under rocks and only came out at night."

"Come on, Bernadette. Play the game. If only for a little bit. You might end up liking it. You've got a boss who believes in you, a jet plane at your disposal, a healthy paycheck, and a gimpy former baseball player who loves your dirty drawers. At least give it a try."

"But it's so different. I'm not sure I'm cut out to be a reporter, Cozy."

"No more arguing with me, please." Cozy rose from the stool. "If we plan to hook up with Buford in time, we need to get out of here now. Just remember to keep an eye peeled for a couple of rocks we can crawl out from under once we get to Heart Mountain," he said, laughing.

"I'll remember that. Guess we'd better get going."

"There you go again with the 'we.'"

"Can't help myself. I'm smitten," Bernadette said, linking an arm in his and walking him out of the room.

Kimiko couldn't remember the last time she'd come to Heart Mountain without Rikia, but she guessed it had been at least fifteen years. After the seven-hour drive from Laramie, she realized what a blessing it had been all those years to have had Rikia do most of the driving.

As the Volvo bumped down a rutted road toward her destination, she tried to come to grips with the fact that Rikia was dead, and by his own hand. She found herself thinking about all the times she'd forced him to travel to a place that had meant so much to her and so little to him. She couldn't help but think that perhaps that was one of the things that had finally pushed him over the edge. One of the things that had made him cobble together a crude nuclear weapon and ultimately, as she'd heard on her car radio on the way to Heart Mountain, kill himself.

She'd always known deep down that Rikia would one day devise a way to get even with America and the people who had for so long wronged him and dishonored his family. She also understood very well that no native-born American could possibly understand Rikia's sense of traditional Japanese honor and justice. She'd never imagined, however, that Rikia would ultimately attempt to set off a nuclear weapon in retribution. She had cared about Rikia, understood his demons, and she knew he'd simply been a gifted math savant, adrift in an ugly, uncaring world that he'd never truly fully understood. A tongue-tied genius who, although he'd never suffered the psychological or physical pain of a Heart Mountain or a Hiroshima, had nonetheless internalized and swallowed the indignity of both places whole.

Perhaps if she'd given a little more of herself, shown Rikia more trust, offered him more affection, things might have turned out differently. But Rikia was gone, and she had to deal with her own emotional burdens alone.

She was used to drinking in Heart Mountain at either daybreak or nightfall, and it felt somehow out of sync to be paying homage to her internment camp experience in the cold, windy brightness of late afternoon. Ignoring the feeling, she parked the station wagon less than thirty yards from where she'd parked it the last time she and Rikia had been there, got out, carefully retrieved a four-foot-long cardboard box from the backseat, and started walking toward a concrete abutment that rose a foot or so above the gumbo plain.

She'd come to a place she knew very well. The dark gray piece of pitted concrete she was looking at, which resembled a grave marker, had once housed a pump and a spigot from which she'd had to drink iron-tasting water. The three-foot-by-two-foot crumbling concrete slab was, in some twisted sense, a landmark that let her know she'd returned home.

Clutching the cardboard box tightly under her left arm, she turned to face a stiff twenty-miles-per-hour breeze. Staring up at the sun and listening to the wind whistle, she thought about all that had happened in her life since her days at Heart Mountain. Looking somehow relieved, she laid the box on the ground, opened the lid, took out one of seven of Rikia's model airplanes that she'd brought along, cocked her arm, and tossed the plane into the wind. She grabbed another toy plane from the box and tossed it into the wind as well, then another plane, and still another until, as she reached into the box to retrieve the fifth plane, she heard the rustle of something behind her. Until then the wind noise and her single-minded purpose had caused her to ignore anything but the box at her feet, the glorious brightness of the sun, and Rikia's toys.

As she looked around to determine the source of the noise, she saw three people approaching. They were only a few yards beyond the bumper of Buford's truck, walking toward her in a single line. Buford Kane she recognized immediately. It took her a bit longer to realize that the woman and the man with him were the much-photographed and much-written-about air force major and news-paperman who'd stopped Rikia from setting off his bomb.

As they came toward her across the stunted sagebrush, she looked down at her box to realize that only two of Rikia's toy airplanes remained. Buford asked, "What are you doing, Kimiko?"

"I'm tossing away the past," she said, now face to face with Buford.

"That can be a difficult thing to do," Bernadette said, staring down at the box.

"One can only try, Major." Kimiko forced a smile. "Your newspaper photos don't really capture you, Major. Nor you, Mr. Coseia. You're both so much taller and younger-looking than I would've expected."

Bernadette stepped closer to the box and knelt beside it. Kimiko made no effort to stop her as Bernadette reached inside the box. "Just two planes left." Bernadette handed both model airplanes to Kimiko before lifting a sawed-off shotgun from the box.

"The planes were Rikia's," Kimiko said, tossing an American Corsair into the wind.

"And the shotgun?" Bernadette asked.

"It once belonged to Thurmond Giles. He gave it to me a long time ago. For protection, he said. I should've used it on him back then."

"You killed my Sarah!" Buford yelled as Cozy restrained him by wrapping his arms around the other man's waist. "Killed her in cold blood with that shotgun. Why?"

Kimiko hesitated briefly before responding. "It was the only solution to a theft," she said, sounding and looking finally absolved.

"The absolute and only one. Thurmond Giles stole something from me. The same thing he stole from Sarah and Howard Colbain's wife and Sarah's mother. It was time he paid."

"So you, Howard Colbain, Grant Rivers, Rikia, and Sarah stabbed him to death and dropped him down a hole in the earth at Tango-11," said Bernadette. "And you killed Sarah because her guilt had gotten the best of her and she was going to tell the world what the five of you had done."

Kimiko didn't answer. Instead she turned away from Bernadette, cocked her left arm, and tossed the last Japanese Zero into the wind. The plane floated on a ribbon of air, briefly gaining altitude before stalling and plummeting nose-first to the ground.

Epilogue

The government's case against Rikia Takata ended with his death, and although there was muted sympathy for what had been America's plight, some in the world continued to whisper, *You almost got what you deserved.* Only Japanese and British responses to the events at Los Alamos remained overwhelmingly supportive, and while most Americans polled had wanted to see Rikia Takata swiftly executed, 15 percent, when asked whether a deranged person with a perceived and perhaps justified lifelong vendetta against America deserved to have his life spared, said yes.

The results of that polling had so infuriated Freddy Dames that, red-faced and with arms flailing, he'd just knocked over the can of Coke he'd been drinking to flood the top of the 150-year-old, walnut-inlaid French partner's desk that had belonged to his Union Army captain and Indian-fighting great-grandfather.

"Idiots!" he screamed so loudly that the word seemed to echo off every shelf in the library of his Cherry Hills, Colorado, home. Grabbing a handful of tissues from a box on the desktop, he looked across the room at Cozy and Bernadette and began mopping up the spill. "Full-fledged cuckoos," he muttered, tossing the sopping-wet tissues into a nearby trash can and nudging a linen-covered piece of artwork lying on the desktop out of harm's way.

"You can't control people's thinking, Freddy," Cozy said, shaking his head.

"I know that. But you'd think that our own goddamn citizens would've wanted to see the crazy-assed bastard shot at sunrise.

Especially with Howard Colbain out there now yapping like a scalded dog about how he and four other lunatics, including a loose cannon bent on detonating a dirty nuclear weapon, plotted to each have their own special kind of revenge on poor old Thurmond Giles. Hell, I'm willing to bet the four of them knew what Rikia was up to from the start."

"Maybe not," said Bernadette. "Things aren't always what they seem."

"Yeah. Maybe you should go reread *Alice in Wonderland,* Freddy," said Cozy.

"And discover that the Mad Hatter wasn't crazy after all? No way. It might make me start to believe Colbain, Rivers, and Kimiko when they say they didn't know what Rikia was up to."

"They may be telling the truth," said Cozy. "I've spent the last two and a half months tracking Silas Breen's every move from the time he left Ottawa until Rikia killed him in Amarillo, and I haven't found anything that ties Colbain, Kimiko, or Rivers to Rikia's bomb plot. I'm thinking they each wanted a different kind of revenge from the kind Rikia was looking for, and that along with Sarah Goldbeck, when Rikia conveniently served them up the lecherous former sergeant in the flesh, they each simply got in their licks."

"Rikia *purportedly* killed Breen," Bernadette interjected.

"Okay, purportedly," said Cozy.

"Purportedly, allegedly, supposedly. What the shit are we having here, a fool's debate for frickin' lawyers? Rikia killed Silas Breen. No ifs, ands, or buts. Just turns out we've got two levels of revenge at work here. We've got Kimiko's, Colbain's, Rivers's, and Sarah's, revenge aimed at a single person, and then we've got Rikia's retribution—which, it turns out, was simply aimed a little higher."

"No question there," said Cozy.

"It's still hard for me to believe that Kimiko wouldn't have known what the hell Rikia was up to, though," said Freddy.

"I'm with Cozy," said Bernadette. "I don't think she did. I think she was simply looking to get back at Giles."

"For soiling her? Bernadette, come on. That's so old-school Victorian—straight out of the 1890s."

"Like I said, things aren't necessarily always what they seem, and soiling her would certainly help to explain Giles's genital mutilation."

"You could make the same case for Sarah Goldbeck or for the cuckolded Howard Colbain," said Freddy.

"I could," said Bernadette. "But I still believe that the essence of Kimiko's revenge is that of a woman scorned. And I've done some homework to back it up."

"Uh-oh," Freddy said, looking at Cozy. "I think we may have created ourselves an investigative-reporter monster here."

Ignoring him, Bernadette said, "I've dug up dozens of photos from thirty to thirty-five years ago that show Kimiko and Sergeant Giles holding hands and playing kissy-face with one another at antinuclear protests at missile-silo sites in four different states, including one of them arm in arm at Tango-11. Kimiko's even quoted in a Yankton, South Dakota, newspaper article from 1979 as saying that her NukeWatch organization had people on the inside, air force people she was terribly fond of, who were helping her in her efforts to get nuclear missiles removed from the heartland."

"So! Giles was stringing her along and feeding her inside information for sex. Hell, politicians and Hollywood directors do the same damn thing every day without ever getting murdered, and never thirty years after the fact. So whatta you think, Cozy?" Freddy asked, rising from his chair and walking over to the window to look out on the season's first snowfall.

"I think Bernadette's right."

"Okay. Let's say she's right. Kimiko still may have simply been along for the ride when it came to actually murdering Giles. Maybe all she did was whack off his johnson after he was dead. What I want to know is which one of the five of them delivered the fatal stab wound."

"Can't answer that," said Cozy.

"Bernadette?"

"Me, either," Bernadette said with a shrug. "But at least, according to Colbain, we do know one thing after all these months. All five of them stabbed Giles, including Kimiko, the demented spiritualist, and Sarah Goldbeck, the self-avowed pacifist. Which means the three who are still standing are pretty much equally guilty in the eyes of the law."

"Colbain—what a joke," Freddy said, shaking his head. "I wouldn't put a dime's worth of faith in what he says. Singing like a canary in order to save his own butt. That's what he's doing. Hell, his comments are worthless."

"Doesn't really matter," said Cozy. "Like Bernadette said, it won't make much difference in the end. Colbain, Kimiko, and Rivers are going to end up rowing the same life-sentence boat downstream. Who knows, since any three of Giles's five stab wounds could have killed him, maybe they all got in a fatal lick."

"Not if it were up to me," said Freddy. "I'd fry every one of their asses."

"Yeah, we know," said Cozy, "and that's why you're not the one meting out the justice here, my man."

Freddy flashed his best friend a confident, all-knowing smile. It was the smile of someone who knew that, all else aside, and in most ways that mattered, he would always have the upper hand. "But I am still at the helm of Digital Registry News, and I'll be the one in charge at *High Plains Insight* three weeks from now when it debuts. That is, if a couple of employees of mine whom I care about and respect dearly ever deliver the magazine's centerpiece story to me."

"We'll have the story to you," Bernadette said, smiling at Freddy reassuringly.

"Yeah," said Cozy. "Get off your worry stick, would you? I'm just hoping this new venture of yours keeps us all in a job. Regional news and entertainment magazines have been tried before, and believe it or not, Freddy, they've always folded. Remember what they say about millionaire cattle barons."

Freddy laughed. "Yeah, that they all started off as billionaire cattle barons. But then again, that's pretty much what folks said when Dick Durrell and Matthew Maynard launched *People* magazine back in 1974. And no matter what anyone thinks, I'm betting there's still room out there for a slick, in-your-face, tell-everything-to-everybody, people-oriented regional magazine. Something specific to the Rocky Mountain West that characterizes the people here who cause the news, defines those who've been caught up in or dragged into it, or shines a spotlight on folks who try their best to tiptoe their way around or away from it."

Offering himself a single, self-congratulatory nod, Freddy said, "So that's what my little regional tabloid's going to do—spotlight those people and their stories. Like my daddy's always said, screw the folks on either coast and give me the good, proud folks in the muddled middle." Grinning, Freddy asked, "Wanna see the first cover?"

"Sure do," Bernadette said, locking hands with Cozy and walking over to Freddy's desk to have a peek at the inaugural cover of *High Plains Insight*.

"Voilà," said Freddy, slipping a linen cloth from over the seventeen-by-twenty-two-inch proof sheet that featured a two-column-wide color photograph of a motorcycle carrying two riders. Their faces could barely be seen, but they were clearly intended to be Cozy and Bernadette, disappearing into a white mushroom-shaped fog as, overhead, the nose of an A-10 Warthog pierced the fog's leading edge. A third column was a horizontal half split. The top panel featured a grainy-looking black-and-white photo of a map of Wyoming peppered with red dots depicting the locations of the state's once active seventy-six nuclear-missile sites. The much more sharply focused bottom panel showed a close-up photo of a cyclone fence surrounding a missile site. A small black-and-white sign reading, "Warning, Tango-11, Restricted Area—Deadly Force Authorized," was attached at eye level to the fence. In the background, the partially raised hatch of a silo personnel-access tube was clearly visible.

After giving Cozy and Bernadette time to study the cover, Freddy expectantly asked, "So, whatta you think?"

After a brief silence, Bernadette said, "There was never an A-10 involved at Los Alamos."

"Creative license, Bernadette. Creative license. You'll learn all about it if you stick around this business long enough."

Realizing that Cozy still hadn't looked up from the cover and that his eyes remained locked on the motorcycle and the fog, Freddy said, "I haven't decided on the cover copy yet, but it'll be easy enough to drop in. Right now I'm thinking 'Doomsday Disarmed.'" Aware of what Cozy must be thinking, Freddy draped an arm over his best friend's shoulders. "But, what the hell, I'm open to suggestions. Que sera, sera."